ABOUT THE AUTHOR

Alison Jesson grew up in Hampshire and wrote her first novel, aged 8. It was four chapters long and had a happy ending. Fifty years later, *The Mind's Garden*, is a more substantial work.

She has had a dozen poems published in leading poetry magazines, and was shortlisted for the Hamish Canham poetry prize in 2006. She currently works as a psychotherapist.

www.alisonjesson.co.uk

THE MIND'S GARDEN

ALISON JESSON

Matador
9 Priory Business Park
Kibworth Beauchamp
Leicestershire LE8 0RX, UK
Tel: (+44) 116 279 2299
Fax: (+44) 116 279 2277
Email: books@troubador.co.uk
Web: www.troubador.co.uk/matador

ISBN 978 1780883 342

British Library Cataloguing in Publication Data.
A catalogue record for this book is available from the British Library.

Typeset by Troubador Publishing Ltd, Leicester, UK

For my family

"He who has a *why* to live for can bear with almost any *how*."

Friedrich Nietzsche

PART I

CHAPTER 1

It had been one of the high-up's birthdays. People out here were always celebrating something. The evening had started with drinks in the Officers' mess, followed by champagne cocktails and dinner at Raffles, the swankiest hotel in Singapore. Although he had been there once before, John Garrett still felt self-conscious, nervous that he would make some social gaffe. He'd sat with his fellow officers at tables laid out in the palm garden, which had felt cool after the heat of the day. They had dined on iced cantaloupe, crab-stuffed mushrooms, beef Wellington and English trifle; each course was served with different wine.

When he could eat no more, he had watched the women; women in rainbow colours who swirled across the dance floor, steered by their partners in khaki or black. He'd even danced with a couple of them, despite the crush, as if he'd been doing this for years. At the end of the evening, after they had all stood for the National Anthem, he'd been persuaded to go on for more drinks and dancing at the Tanghi Club, where he'd propped himself against the wall, too tipsy to join in.

Now as he surfaced, noticing his muzzy head and dry throat, he wondered why he always felt he had to follow the crowd. From somewhere out in the quadrangle, he could hear a Glen Miller tune; trombones and brassy cornets; the woody ripple of clarinets and oboes, and, underneath the melody, the

1

dark pulse of a euphonium which seemed to match the thumping in his head. The regimental bandsmen were having their usual Sunday morning rehearsal; thirty-eight men strong and about half of them, if the war ever arrived in the Far East, would double up as his stretcher bearers. He hoped that they'd perform in battle as well as they played music. Not that a battle was likely. Singapore was a fortress, armed with five 15-inch guns and garrisoned by nearly 20,000 men. Every authority reckoned it could only be taken after a siege of at least 50,000 troops, and besides, even if the Japanese looked like they might be interested, the far superior British Navy would soon sort them out.

He shuffled his pillows behind him, flung back the mosquito net and took a swig of tea from the cup on the bedside table. His boy, Chen, must have crept in with it and thought not to wake him. The tea was cold but he drank it anyway. It was well past ten and he knew he should get up if he wanted any breakfast. Propped up by the clock was a letter from his mother. He skimmed through it again. This letter, like each of its predecessors, made him feel relieved and guilty. At last she had made the move back to Lymington, away from the dangers of London. But in spite of all the difficulties, she managed to write to him on a regular basis, whereas he hadn't written to her for weeks.

He crumpled the letter and tossed it across the room. What on earth could he write to her about? How could he tell her that on Tuesday's sick parade he'd examined nine men with trivial complaints and later had dined with the Simpsons; that on Thursday he'd seen a movie, on Friday he'd gone sailing and on Saturday he got drunk in the mess? Why would it matter that his car was doing so many miles to the gallon or that there had been heavy downpours recently? Every letter from him inevitably said the same; he was far away in a sunny place with very little to do and few worries. She must see how impossible it was to mention these things and therefore write to anybody at all.

He got up and crossed the room to open the French windows onto the veranda. Warm air enveloped him, coupled with a sweet smell of grass and frangipani. Stretching from his room towards the Officers' mess was a sweep of coral pink and purple bougainvillea. He took a deep breath, but he could still hear her quiet voice telling him how lucky he was to be far removed from the horrors of Dunkirk. Retrieving the letter, he smoothed it out and thrust it into the drawer with all the others. He washed and shaved, combed back his dark hair and donned the weekend civvies of white shorts and shirt. Viewing the finished effect in the mirror, he wondered yet again about growing a moustache, and then ambled across to the mess to see if there was any breakfast left.

In the mess he was pleased to see Captain Richard Henderson, his sometimes squash partner. Henderson, at twenty seven, was the same age as him, though he was much taller and had a flop of fair hair that he would brush nervously off his forehead. He was hunched over a newspaper, munching a piece of toast, and grinned at John as he walked in.

'Well, look who it isn't! Bit of a blinder last night, eh?'

'Too right, and I've got the head to prove it,' John smiled, 'I should have left when you did and not been dragged off to the Tanghi. I don't suppose there is any breakfast left?' He slumped into the chair opposite.

'No, the orderly just cleared the last bits away. You'll have to hang on until Tiffin, unless you want the rest of this.' He proffered a half-eaten piece of toast at John, who shook his head. 'I assume you won't be sailing today, will you?'

'Actually, I thought I might see if there is anyone down at the club wanting to make up a crew this afternoon, once my head is less woolly.' He pointed towards the paper, 'Is there any news?'

Henderson pushed the paper across the table. 'It's pretty bad actually. Paris has fallen; Lord knows what'll happen next. I was just reading a piece about the Dunkirk evacuation. It is just unbelievable both how many men were lost and how many managed to get away.'

John nodded, pulled the paper towards him and began to scan the headlines.

'And Private Simmonds,' Henderson continued, 'he's one of mine in B. Company, he's in a dreadful state, lost two brothers; one was shot and the other drowned when the rescue boat he was in capsized.'

'Yes, I heard about Simmonds, I'd better keep an eye on him,' John replied, 'though I imagine everyone out here is going to be affected by it in some way. Don't you find it all so hard to take in? I followed as much as I could about the evacuation as the news came through, but it was as if it was happening on another planet.'

'I know what you mean,' said Henderson, pushing the toast crumbs round his plate, 'all we can do is hope that Hitler loses interest in England and settles for what he's got.'

'Like you, I can read the paper from cover to cover about the events of Europe,' John interrupted, 'but I can't get any sense of what it's really like for people back home.'

'Major King was bending my ear about it all last night. He's furious that he's stuck out here and not where all the proper fighting is.'

'I know somebody has got to be out here, of course,' John continued, as if Henderson had not spoken, 'but that doesn't reduce the essential futility of it all. I mean, the doctoring I'm doing may be the routine work of the RAMC, but it seems rather pathetic when so many others have a real job to do. I didn't join the army for this.' John flipped over a few pages of the paper, conscious that Henderson was staring at him. 'It's all the red tape and petty bothering that goes on. I loathe it; there is no medicine about it. I just have to be stern to the men on sick parade and then I have to poke around their barracks and grounds for bugs and mosquitoes or I have to write silly letters in reply to tom-fool questions from higher places.'

Henderson looked at him in surprise. 'Oh come on, it isn't that bad, surely!'

'I know you'll say it's all very pleasant – the social life, the hot climate – and that I shouldn't complain, but it's nothing like medicine or a decent job of work by my standards. It's a well-meant routine of boring fussiness that I would give up tomorrow without a qualm. You can't even lose your temper without needing a change of shirt!' John knew how loud he was talking but he didn't care.

'Crikey, John, what's got into you? You really did get out of bed on the wrong side!'

John flushed and turned a few more pages in silence. 'Sorry' he mumbled, 'you didn't deserve to hear all that.'

'Listen, if you like, that is if you don't find anyone to sail with, why don't we have a game of squash later? That would clear both your head and your temper.'

'Thanks, I'll let you know.'

Henderson glanced at his watch. 'Christ is that the time?'

5

Standing up, he stretched and, lightly punching John's shoulder, said, 'Maybe you'll actually beat me this time!'

After Henderson left, John regretted his outburst, though he felt somewhat better for it. He flicked through the paper again, willing himself to concentrate on the appalling stories; the numbers of dead and injured, the political commentary, and predictions of what might occur next. After ten minutes, he gave up and wandered back to his room. Re-reading the letter from his mother, he opened a pad of airmail paper and with a sigh began the long-overdue reply. "Dear Min" – it was the pet nickname for her that he'd used since he was little. His grandfather had called her this when she'd been small and somehow it had always stuck. He tried to visualise her back at Ivyholme, the house of his childhood, next to the Boldre River as it widened out into the sea at Lymington. How many contented hours had he spent in the holidays, messing about in a boat, just yards from the front door, or going on walks with Min, who taught him how to distinguish between moorhens and coots? After months of sultry heat, he longed for the coolness of England, with gentle rain, not the downpours of East Asia.

The last time he'd seen her was the evening he'd left for Aldershot to complete his training. She'd been wearing the pale blue woollen dress which she saved for special occasions. He had stood on the doorstep of their flat in Southfields and, feeling rather dramatic, had shone the torch beam into his face to show his smile as he reassured her that "All will be well". That quotation from Sister Julian of Norwich she had so often said to him as she tearfully waved him off on the train to boarding school.

Though what had surprised him, since he'd been away,

was how little he had actually missed her. In some ways, it had been a relief to get away. Although it had made financial sense for her to let Ivyholme and share the small flat with him while he completed his medical training at St Thomas', it had been claustrophobic at times. He didn't doubt her love for him, but at times it felt more like a burden. And when it came to her opinions about his succession of girlfriends, they'd always argued.

He managed to fill one side of paper before he became restless and, looking at his watch, he realised that Tiffin at the yacht club would soon be approaching. Since he'd missed breakfast and wanted to sail, he'd better get a move on. He climbed into his green Austin 7 saloon and set off down Alexandra Road. He'd bought the car from an officer who was returning to England and he loved the thrill of speeding around the island, on both official medical business as well as off-duty.

Today, in Chinatown, he had to drive slowly to avoid the streams of bicycles that wove in different directions around him. The pavements thronged with Malays, Chinese, Indians and Tamils. Wafts of cooking smells from tightly packed stalls made his stomach rumble; fried rice, sizzling giant prawns, skewered meat, apple fritters. On several stalls there were piles of spices; burnt umber, raw sienna, cadmium yellow, and squawking chickens lay in the dust with their feet tied, waiting for the chop. Families were gathered round huge cooking pots set by the roadside, laughing and gesticulating; there was washing slung over bamboo poles which criss-crossed the narrow alleys; red and yellow Chinese lanterns bobbed in the breeze while children chased each other back and forth across the road. And all around, the stifling tropical heat.

CHAPTER 2

June 15ᵗʰ 1940

I think that the only way I can cope with all this is to go back to writing a journal, just as I did when John was a baby and things were so difficult at home. It used to help me to imagine that I was writing to Father, even though he had been dead for a few years. Sometimes I wrote every day and sometimes I could leave it for weeks, but it always helped me to sort out my thoughts. Having left the few friends that I had in London who were determined to stay and brave it out, I feel a little forgotten. I don't think I had realised quite how much I had depended on John's company and now that I have returned I feel as I used to when he was away at boarding school and I was left to face George on my own.

It is very strange being back here at Ivyholme. Having been away in London for six years, the rooms all seem to have changed shape. They smell musty and un-lived in; I suppose because it's been quite a few weeks since the tenants left and no one has been in to air them properly. The garden looks dishevelled as if it has given up bothering to keep itself respectable, and the uncut grass laps like water around my ankles. All the roses are a tangle of bindweed and blackspot; there is groundsel and couch grass everywhere. It is such a mess. I simply don't know where to start.

Though at least the river is as lovely as ever; that same old slap of the tide against the toll bridge and the swans poking about in the reed beds. And somehow, down here, the blackout doesn't seem to make the streets as bleak and lonely as it did in London. How I hated walking back to the flat in the evening, with no street lamps to light up peoples' faces and every window dark, as if there wasn't a chink of friendliness left anywhere.

The news of Paris falling is frightful, though I suppose Churchill's speeches rallying the nation "to defend this island whatever the cost" are quite encouraging. I know it is selfish, but each time I hear of the casualties and all those poor young men dying on the beaches in Dunkirk, I say a prayer of thanks that John is far away, completely untouched by all this awfulness. I do wish he'd write.

June 28th 1940

I am not at all sure how sharing my house with Frank and Cordelia is going to work out. I know they wanted to leave London as badly as I did, but the minute my bossy sister-in-law set foot in the house today, she started tut-tutting. I suppose I must be grateful to Frank for all the financial help he has given me over the years; John would never have been able to go to medical school without his help, and this pooling of resources does seem to be the only way I can be safe away from London and prevent the entire house being requisitioned by the Army.

July 9th 1940

Now that I am more or less settled, I need to pull myself together and find some voluntary work to occupy me. It will fill in the days and stop me from thinking too deeply. The atmosphere is more than a little tense at times. Two women should never have to share a household. I thought this might happen. Cordelia interferes with everything and wants to take charge of all the arrangements. She really is the most dreadful nag. I was quite pleased with myself when I suggested that she and Frank live upstairs while I convert the dining room to be my own little bedroom. She gave me one of those looks when I announced that no one is going to use John's old bedroom until he returns. We still have to share the kitchen of course, but at least I won't have to hear to her endless prattle every evening. All I want is to be left alone and sit undisturbed in the conservatory, looking out on the jungle that is currently the back garden. I have started to listen to the evening concerts on the radio. To hear dear Rachmaninov and Sibelius again is such a comfort. I will write to John tomorrow and give him all the news.

It is good to have got back in touch with Dorothy. When I wrote to her to tell her I was back, I was really delighted when she suggested I cycle over to her once a week for tea. I had quite forgotten about my old bicycle. Apart from being a bit rusty and dusty, it seems to be in good order. It was a bit of a shock to see that all the signposts have been removed, but I think I can manage the route to Dorothy's all right, though the prospect of pedalling after these past years of laziness is a bit daunting. The roads are busy with a constant stream of khaki and green.

CHAPTER 3

Richard felt stung by John Garrett's outburst; after all, it wasn't his fault that Garrett didn't have enough serious doctor's work to do. Although he'd tried to appear unruffled, he had left the mess with that familiar feeling of hurt and disappointment. He had become friendly with Garrett on the ship that had brought them out to Singapore at the end of '39. Both of them had signed up as soon as war had been declared, albeit for very different reasons and, unlike Garrett, Richard had been delighted to be posted out to the Far East. He wanted to be as far away as possible, and this was a chance for a fresh start with people who knew nothing about him.

He was the only son of a long line of Hendersons who all became city bankers. He couldn't recall that his father had ever asked him if this was the future he wanted. The plan was never discussed; he was a Henderson, and he would follow in his father's footsteps, first to Rugby, and then to London for an economics degree. Eventually he would join Henderson and Sons in Chancery Lane. He had been a pale, skinny child who had suffered from frequent colds and asthma attacks. Indeed his first term at Rugby was delayed, much to his father's annoyance, by a bout of tonsillitis. By the time he was well enough to start, everyone else seemed to have made friends. Somehow he never quite managed to fit in. He'd loathed school; the enforced heartiness, the compulsory games, the cold showers, the taunts about his skinny legs and worse.

But somehow he had survived, went as expected to university and achieved a respectable degree.

In the summer after he had completed his finals, his mother organised a coming-out party for his younger sister. Although the party was ostensibly to find Louise an eligible husband, his mother had seemed far more obsessed with finding Richard a suitable wife. He had bitterly regretted that, aged fourteen, he had shyly confided to her that he had a crush on Teddy Collins, the head boy. 'It's quite normal, Darling; it's just a passing phase. Lots of boys have crushes at your age,' his mother said. 'Best not to mention it to your father,' she'd added as an afterthought. For several weeks after this confession, she had found numerous excuses to burst unexpectedly into his bedroom, her eyes fixed on the bed covers over his crotch. After the coming-out party, he had suffered the tedium of having to agree with her that this or that girl who had been there was very nice.

He tried to be seen as a dutiful son. He worked hard at the bank and participated politely in the regular dinner parties his mother held at their town house in St John's Wood. But he also had another life; evenings spent with pretty boys in back street clubs; moonlit walks over Hampstead Heath; flirtatious glances shared through swathes of steam in the Turkish baths at Jermyn Street. It was at the baths that he had met Patrick, who happened to be a junior clerk at the same bank. Richard was amused to discover a forum where men could wander about clad in bath towels or sit naked together in the sauna room, where social class conveniently seemed to disappear; although Patrick insisted on calling himself Richard's "bit of rough".

But when Richard, after a couple of months of fun, tried

to extricate himself from the relationship, Patrick turned nasty. He threatened to expose him at the bank unless Richard paid off some of his debts for him, and of course it hadn't stopped with just one payment. With a sense of panic, Richard realised that Patrick was very experienced at extortion. It felt like an enormous stroke of luck when war was declared and he saw an opportunity to be rid of Patrick and the tedium at the bank once and for all. When he announced to the family that he had joined up, it was the first time he had ever seen his father smile proudly at him.

After six months in Singapore, he felt pretty confident that no one knew anything about his sexual preferences and he made absolutely sure that there were no witnesses to any of his liaisons in the bars he hung around in down town. The young Malayan lads he met had warm, friendly faces; they were playful and teased him for his English stuffiness. It was as if he'd discovered a world quite unlike anything he'd ever encountered before. Whatever happened with this war, he knew for certain that he'd never go back into the suffocating life of the bank. Even being in the army felt just like another sort of boarding school, except that as an officer he was the one giving the orders. Unlike some of his fellows who enjoyed bullying and yelling at the men, so far Richard had tried to win their trust by being good-natured and reasonably polite.

For the remainder of the day after he left the breakfast table in the mess, he mooched around the barracks, hoping that Garrett would decide against sailing and join him instead for a game of squash. He thought about the time they had spent together on the voyage out, and the excitement there had been throughout the ship's company of officers, troops and civilians as they had celebrated Christmas, passing through the Suez Canal. Richard was comfortable socialising with the wives of rubber planters and mining engineers and had played endless games of bridge. He had noticed that although Garrett appeared to be relaxed in their company, there was an underlying nervousness about him. It had made Richard feel protective. But since they'd arrived, apart from his secret life, Richard had only met other army officers, while Garrett seemed to have built up a busy social life which frequently took him away from the barracks.

CHAPTER 4

It looked like an old-fashioned chemist's; the way the sharp sun glinted off the rows of medicine bottles which were lined up on the shelves. Each was labelled with a Latin name, though in reality they were mostly time-honoured, harmless, army prescriptions. Patients always felt better if you could give them some medicine. John had made some additions of his own with several bogus bottles filled with water and coloured inks; deep blue, red, pale yellow. He was rather pleased with the effect. It made his medical inspection room look professional and gave him credibility and authority.

'Can't you give me something for it, Doc?'

John was examining a young man, a private, who had a crop of tiny red spots all over his chest, under his arms, and behind his knees. The man scratched and itched. His skin looked red and sore. He'd seen dozens of men with the exact same symptoms. It was classic miliaria papulosa, otherwise known as prickly heat. Not that he ever called it by the proper medical term in case the patient panicked and thought he'd said they had malaria.

'There isn't an awful lot I can do for it, except recommend that you keep as cool as possible. I'll give you a bottle of calamine to swab on the worst areas.'

'Keep cool? In this heat, Doc? You must be joking'

John called out to the medical orderly, 'Another one for calamine please, and send in the next one.'

He'd now seen four cases of backache (none serious), one

toothache (which he'd referred to the dentist), three lads who were the worse for wear due to a drunken trip down Lavender Road the previous evening, and two with prickly heat (to whom he'd also prescribed calamine). He'd packed them all off back to work. The sick parade was the same most mornings. He got up at 6.30am after Chen brought him tea and would be in the MI room by 7.15am. There he would see an assortment of soldiers, the majority of whom, were trying to break the monotony of barrack life and get out of some training exercise or other. Like him, they were frustrated with the lack of action.

While he scribbled his notes on the last patient, the orderly announced Bandsman Kelly, who walked slowly into the room, his eyes fixed on the floor. John had heard him a couple of times play a clarinet solo in one of the weekly concerts. He was brilliant. He was a big man, in his early twenties, with dark curly hair and an impressive assortment of tattoos covering both his muscular forearms.

'Morning, Kelly. What can I do for you?

'I don't know, Doc. I don't know what's wrong'.

'Do you have a pain anywhere?'

'No'.

'Well what has brought you here, man?'

'It's hard to describe,' Kelly replied, his cheeks coloured. 'I've just been feeling out of sorts for a few weeks now. I can't sleep, I feel weak in my arms and legs and my heart keeps racing. I'm worried it might be something quite serious.'

'Let's have a listen. Lift up your shirt, will you?' As he moved his stethoscope over Kelly's chest, he noticed the man's eyes begin to fill and his mouth working hard to stop the sound of a sob. Clearly he wasn't swinging the lead. He pulled

Kelly's shirt down and sat back in his chair. 'Why don't you tell me what's been going on?' he asked.

Kelly blurted it all out. He was worried about his mum and sister who were stuck in London looking after his gran, who'd refused to move. Things were getting really bad now that the air raids had started and he reckoned he should be there to look after them all. His father had been killed in the First World War, just after he was born, so he'd always felt responsible for his mum who had struggled to bring up him and his sister. Having grown up in Kent, he longed for English oak trees, woods of beech and silver birch, patchwork fields with sheep and cows, banks of wild flowers, and good old English weather. He couldn't stand this relentless heat, the endless miles of rubber plantations and the tedium of having nothing useful to do. As the words tumbled out, he sniffed and blew his nose, and kept apologising.

John knew just how Kelly felt. Neither at medical school nor in his brief RAMC training had anyone ever mentioned the psychological effects that troops suffered when they were posted far from home for indefinite periods. Along with the prickly heat, an increasing number of men were presenting with these same symptoms as Kelly. He recalled an article he'd read in a recent medical journal which stated that cases of homesickness amongst troops, causing as much distress as wounds and diseases, were recorded as far back as the American Civil War. But here in Singapore, with no one in actual danger, distressing as it might be to Kelly, it was not a valid reason to be signed off sick.

'Look here, Kelly, what you're experiencing is very common. Lots of the men feel just like you do. It's nothing to feel ashamed of. It's jolly awful looking at pictures of England

and worrying if it's all going to be ruined before we get home. Come on. Tell me which part of Kent you grew up in. Were there apple orchards and hops?'

He let Kelly chat on for a while, partly because he was the last man on sick parade, and partly because he had been affected by the man's outburst.

'Right now, back to work with you. The best cure for what you've got is to keep busy. Get plenty of exercise and go and polish that clarinet of yours in readiness for the concert this weekend. What I'm going to do is to put your name down for some holiday leave at Port Dickson. It's a camp on the mainland, west coast somewhere. A lot of the chaps come back from there feeling much better.'

Kelly looked relieved, took a deep breath, blew his nose for the last time and shook John's hand.

After sick parade, John went back to the mess for breakfast and then spent the rest of the morning making house calls on some of the officers' families. Unlike the troops, senior officers could take their families with them wherever they were stationed. As he drove towards the outskirts of Singapore town, he recalled his outburst to Richard some weeks ago and thought that perhaps he had begun to settle down to this life. Like others, he probably was stuck out here until the end of the war. Most likely there would be no real army doctor's work, but he might as well make the most of what he could do. After all, he was gaining confidence and beginning to feel more at ease socialising with all the officer ranks, right up to Brigadier. He would view his time out here as valuable preparation for his future life as a GP.

Out in the Far East there was little to occupy the officers' wives, except playing tennis, golf or bridge, and blending in with the endless social round of the civilian wives who were married to mining engineers, rubber planters or government officials. Because John was young, good-looking and a professional, most of the older women took a keen interest in his love life. Gossip and matchmaking was a popular occupation for all and he enjoyed the attention.

Before lunch, he called into the Alexandra Military Hospital, ostensibly to check on Tom Dean, a sergeant, who was a week post-op after an appendicectomy. He had been on the far side of the island on a training exercise when he had become unwell. John had also been involved in the exercise and, having diagnosed potential complications, had got him transported back to the hospital just in time. (Few patients in the military hospital were seriously ill; mostly they suffered from sprained ankles, tropical fevers, and accidents sustained from the effects of too much alcohol.)

But it was Sister LeBrun who John really wanted to see. Since he'd been in Singapore, he had flirted with almost all the nurses and even dated a couple, but as usual he'd quickly lost interest and moved on to someone new. The Sister emerged from behind the screens around Sergeant Dean's bed, and John watched her bustle towards the sluice to dispose of the dressings. She was slim and rather petite. He liked how little tendrils of auburn hair escaped from under her white starched veil and how her small feet pointed outwards when she walked.

Sister LeBrun was a new arrival. They had got chatting briefly one night the previous week, on one of the infrequent occasions when he was on call. Although he was rarely called out, he still had to sleep in the doctor's on-call room at the hospital. That night, she had asked him to deal with a patient who was delirious with a fever and needed sedating.

Unlike women he'd met previously, she made him feel tongue-tied. She seemed so confident and had settled into her new role at the Alexandra with ease, answering his questions about the patient's condition without the slightest hesitation. After they dealt with the patient, she offered to make him a cup of tea and, because he couldn't think of anything intelligent to say, he asked some banal question about where in England she came from. She began to tell him that she had grown up in Dorset; typical Thomas Hardy country, she'd said. He'd been about to try and impress her by reciting a fragment of a Hardy poem, but their conversation had been cut short by another patient calling for her. He hadn't had a chance to speak to her since.

Sister LeBrun returned from the sluice room and removed the screens from Dean's bed. Seeing John standing there, pretending to look at the charts at the foot of the bed, she gave him a quizzical look.

'Good morning, Dr Garrett. What can I do for you?'

'Oh hello Sister, I just thought I'd check on Sergeant Dean. How is he doing?'

'He'll probably be ready to leave here next week, as long as the wound continues to heal.'

'Jolly good.' John smiled at her, looked at her pale green eyes and freckled nose and waited for her to say something else; something to which he could make a witty reply; anything to keep her talking. She also waited, but when he said nothing she gave him a brief smile and said. 'Well, I must get on. Excuse me, Dr Garrett,' and she swept off down the ward.

Damn! he thought to himself as he trudged back to the mess. For Christ's sake, pull yourself together. After chatting with Henderson briefly over lunch about the squash tournament, he set off on a bug hunting expedition near the Pasir Panjang Ridge. Part of his role was in health prevention and since malaria was a constant threat, he was supposed to identify likely breeding areas. He enjoyed getting away on his own, speeding through the coconut groves and rubber plantations that enveloped the island, their monotony relieved occasionally by colourful drifts of orchids and creepers draped with baggy sleeves of moss.

It was very humid; probably a storm brewing. Once he'd collected as many samples as he had time for, he set off back home to Gillman Barracks. Driving through a small kampong set on the brow of a hill, he noticed massive rain clouds on the horizon. Deciding to park up by the side of the road for a while, he gazed down across the vast expanse of green that flowed all the way into Singapore harbour, stopped only by the rabble of customs sheds, go-downs and office buildings that littered the water's edge. The sea was wrinkled pewter and the purple-grey clouds looked like a heavy fold of cloth unfurling towards him.

As he waited for the storm and thought about what Kelly had said about missing England, he felt his own eyes brimming. Back home, his real home, Min was probably all alone in her small room at the back of the house. How would she be coping with the war now being fought right over her head?

There was a flash of lightning, followed by a long rumble of thunder. He felt the hairs on the back of his neck prickle. A few drops of rain splashed onto the windscreen. Within seconds, the rain was falling in sheets. It sounded like someone was hurling gravel onto the car roof. The car seemed to shake with the force of it. In the road, women called to their children as they ran to take cover in their attap-roofed wooden huts.

The children, already soaked, laughed and splashed though the puddles that now flooded the road. The windscreen rippled. Inside it began to mist up. It felt like the palm house at Kew Gardens. He unwound the window a fraction. The air smelt of sweet spices and damp flannel. The leaves of the trees beside him sagged with the weight of water, dripped like a waterfall.

Then, as if the storm had taken the same deep breath that Kelly had taken that morning after he'd expressed all his distress, it began to subside. The rain sounded more like polite applause. A shaft of sunlight spilled across the village. Steam rose from the drying tarmac.

CHAPTER 5

Ivyholme, Lymington

July 11th 1940

Dear John

I continue to hope that you are safe and busy with your work. Things have changed quite a bit since I last wrote. It started yesterday afternoon. The air was rather muggy, with a pale blue sky and those big hammerhead clouds. I was standing on the toll bridge, watching a pair of swans scoop down across the water, when I heard a rumble of distant thunder. I thought how nice it would be to feel the splash of rain on my face, how it would freshen the air, and how you and I always liked the way that trees and plants seem to fizz after a storm. But the rumble continued and turned into a drone, getting louder each second and coming towards me from the south. The sun was in my eyes so all I could see were the silhouettes of masses of large black birds. They flew in perfect symmetry, wave after wave. It was almost beautiful until I realised what they were. Then they passed over and there was an eerie silence, broken only by birdsong.

A short while later, I was surprised to hear the air raid siren. Frank and Cordelia had gone out so I ran back into the house and put up the blackout, even though it wasn't dark, but I thought it was probably the right thing to do. I heard more planes overhead and I thought I could hear gunfire. I hoped it was the anti-aircraft guns. But after a while I felt a bit silly and rather shut in by the darkness, so I slipped out into the garden just in time to see a plane spiralling down like a sycamore seed, with a plume of black smoke curling up behind it.

When the others came back, Cordelia, as you would imagine, was hysterical and crying, "They're bombing us! They're bombing us!" So we all trooped inside and stood around, unsure what to do next. Eventually I went to make some tea and the three of us sat huddled in the kitchen. We must have sat there for hours, but of course we were fine.

July 20th 1940

Apologies, dear John, I started this letter over a week ago and didn't have time to post it with all the rumpus going on. Now it's day and night; the wail of the siren; the constant overhead drone of planes. Shipping off the Isle of Wight is attacked every day and Portsmouth has been hit over and over again. Frank pores over the newspaper each day, trying to tot up who has lost the most planes, and whenever he sees them, he shouts at the British pilots to shoot down the Germans.

Last night I had just got off to sleep when I was woken by the siren. Cordelia had decided that we weren't protected enough and had spent the whole day clearing out the under-stairs cupboard and putting cushions, a torch, and various useful bits in it. I felt I had to go and join her and Frank. It was a ridiculous squeeze. We had to leave the door open and have our legs poking out across the hall. We sat getting stiffer and colder as we listened to the explosions, though nothing seemed too near. Cordelia kept up a steady patter of inconsequential chatter. It was all I could do not to slap her. I kept saying our mantra to myself, "All will be well. All will be well". Next time, I think I'll just sit it out underneath the table in my own room.

I am trying to maintain some charade of daily life; queuing at the butcher's for rations, washing clothes, dusting books, and chatting to neighbours. It isn't quite what I imagined life would be like back here. Apart from Dorothy, many of those I used to know here when you were growing up have moved away. It has been lovely spending time with her, though she has aged quite considerably in the time I have been away. I think she must be in her eighties now. She still chain smokes and she can't walk further than the end of her garden, but her mind is as clear as anything. I have always seen her as a sort of wise woman, someone I was rather in awe of. But it would be good to make some new friends; women more of my age and with the same interests. There are several ladies who help with the voluntary work in the hospital garden, but so far most of the conversations are about the war and rationing and it becomes quite tedious at times. I would love to have someone who lives a bit nearer, with whom I can walk and talk about music or literature, though I would be reluctant to invite anyone here. Cordelia would be bound to interfere. You know what she's like!

I do hope you will have time to write soon. Perhaps the post from abroad is quite disrupted with all this going on.

Your ever loving Min

August 23rd 1940

Still nothing from John, and yet another sleepless night. It just goes on and on. Everyone is on edge. I've given up taking shelter at night time. There seems no point, so I just hide under the blankets and wait for it to be over. If it's my time, then so be it, though I must be careful not to write anything to John that will alarm him. One night last week, they attacked Southampton and hit a cold storage warehouse. Two thousand tons of butter went up in flames. People said the sky glowed orange for miles around. That's going to make even less to go around.

September 8th 1940

I suppose I am getting used to it now. Everyone seems to carry on as if the skies were always buzzing with planes. Sometimes I stand on the pier simply to watch the RAF boys give chase to the Germans. I try not to think about some German mother, just like me, waiting for news of her dear one. The papers report that the Germans have lost a record number of planes. Does that mean we are winning? What does winning mean? Does it mean that he'll come home soon?

Today, because it was quite sunny, I picked a couple of pounds of late blackberries from Boldre Woods. I remembered how we used to see who could pick the most and we would come home exhausted, our mouths and fingers smeared purple. But today, as I trudged home with a basket on each arm, I suddenly felt quite cross with him. Actually, it was a mixture of annoyance and disappointment. I have written a dozen or more letters to him in the last few months and still he doesn't write. Does he have any idea what it is like for us all back home?

CHAPTER 6

Beatrice LeBrun peered round the treatment room door to watch John Garrett's retreating back, half hoping he'd find another lame excuse to come and question her about a patient. When she'd first arrived, she had been told about the attractive Dr Garrett by some of the voluntary aid detachment nurses, better known as the VADs, and since she had noticed his unsubtle attempts at flirting the night she'd had to call him out, she was curious to see what might happen next. He wasn't exactly tall, dark or handsome; in fact, he was rather on the short side. But he did have gorgeous brown eyes and a charming smile, and at least she wouldn't get a crick in her neck when she kissed him.

Stop it, she told herself. Don't you ever learn? You promised yourself you wouldn't get entangled, especially with another doctor!

She had left England on the *Empress of Australia* with fifty-five other QAs bound for Hong Kong and Singapore. She was an experienced casualty nurse and when nothing seemed to happen in London during the phoney war, she had joined the Queen Alexandra's Imperial Nursing Service, hoping to be sent to France, where her brother James was with the British Expeditionary Force. The training was rigorous and the rules and bureaucratic rituals of the army took some getting used to. She wondered if she had made the right choice when she heard that the hospital in London was now overflowing with wounded soldiers from Dunkirk. Perhaps if she had stayed she could have done so much to help, and surely she would have found out what had happened to Jamie.

When she was informed that she was being sent to the Far East, she didn't know how she was going to tell her parents. Initially, they had supported her decision to join the QAs. Her father had been in the military himself and had lost his leg at Passchendaele when Beatrice was just five. James was younger by three years, but she had always been her father's favourite.

Their reaction was worse than she'd expected. Her mother had pleaded with her not to go. "But don't you see," Beatrice argued, "it's because of Jamie that I want to do my bit. I can't just stay here while British soldiers are getting wounded or worse." And so, when at last she was standing on board the ship, she had tried hard to conceal her excitement. Proudly wearing her striking QA uniform – a grey dress with its scarlet-trimmed cape – she waved them goodbye and set off on her own adventure round to the other side of the world.

The new Alexandra Military Hospital couldn't have been less like the ancient hospital in which she had done her training. It was said to be the most up-to-date military hospital outside of Britain. Built beside the Ayer Rajah Road, in a colonial style, each ward had large windows that opened onto a wide veranda. The grounds had sweeping lawns and flowerbeds filled with bougainvillea. It was like a grand hotel. There was none of the pettiness and absurd rules that she'd been used to in London. From the moment she and her colleagues arrived, she had been treated as a mature professional nurse. Since the hospital had only just opened, it was up to the individual sisters to set up their wards, ensure they had the correct equipment and establish routines and rituals of their own, supported by Matron Jones, the matron in chief.

After John Garrett had left without glancing back at her, Beatrice surveyed her patients. None of them was really ill; two lads with badly sprained ankles, a post-op gastric ulcer, a couple of hernia repairs, a colonel with piles and the sergeant with the appendicectomy. How she envied her colleagues who'd stayed on at Tommy's; they'd still be coping with those wounded in France. And Jamie. She tried not to think about him at all. She told herself that he had probably been captured and would have to stick it out as a POW until it was all over. But the same image kept slinking in from the back of her mind, as vivid as any photograph: on a wind-torn beach strewn with bodies, Jamie lay slumped in a heap, his uniform in tatters, sand blowing into the congealed blood that oozed from the bullet holes in his body; through lips cracked and bleeding he mouthed her name.

CHAPTER 7

'Over here, Lester!' Major King, waving a glass at him, beckoned him over. King's ruddy cheeks and rounded tummy betrayed more than a passing acquaintance with the good life. King was a career army man; late thirties, well spoken, presumably public school and straight to Sandhurst. He was sitting at a low coffee table with the doctor, Captain Garrett, and Major Holland, the regimental quartermaster. Holland, who had seen active service in the Great War, was universally known as "Holly". Roger guessed that all three of them had already downed more than a couple of drinks.

'We need someone for the fourth hand of mah-jong. Henderson's gone and left us in the lurch. You do play, don't you?'

'Of course, thank you very much, Sir.' Roger said with a smile and pulled up an empty chair. In fact, Roger had only played the game once before, but it seemed rude to refuse, especially if he was being invited to team up with three senior officers. Roger was a lieutenant and had only arrived in Singapore a month ago; he still felt like one of the new boys. The errant Richard Henderson was his captain in B. Company.

King signalled the barman to bring them each a stengah, and asked for the mah-jong set to be brought to their table. The bar was crowded. Small circles of officers sat in red leather armchairs, leaning towards each other to catch the lost ends of conversations. In the corner near the bar, a noisy group was playing darts. Despite the doors and windows at the far end being pushed open, clouds of cigarette smoke hovered on the muggy night air.

Major Holland was a big man of about fifty with a broad Yorkshire accent, a well tanned face and a pair of bushy eyebrows that wriggled like a hairy caterpillars when he talked. He loved to tell war stories and, having fought at the Somme, he was well respected throughout the Regiment.

John Garrett looked pleasant enough. Roger imagined he and the "Doc" were about the same age. His slicked back hair and smiling eyes reminded him of a taller version of Fred Astaire. He was telling Holly about the sailboat race in which he had been competing at the weekend. Roger listened with interest; he loved sailing, ever since his Uncle Harry had rescued him from grimy south London and taken him to the Norfolk Broads for a holiday when he was thirteen. At the time, he had thought that learning to sail had been the best thing that had ever happened to him.

An orderly placed the mah-jong set on the table between them. From the only time Roger had played before, he had picked up the basic rules quickly. As far as he could tell, it was much the same as gin rummy, which he had played on many occasions with friends at his local pub. The bamboo and ivory tiles were beautiful. Each tile was carved and painted with Chinese symbols denoting the three suits; bamboos, characters, and circles, and the other more valuable images of flowers, winds and dragons. As a novice, he was relieved that they weren't playing for money. He'd been told that the Chinese played with the tiles facing down, and could identify the differences between them by touch alone. Roger liked the idea that one day he might master this skill.

King built the tiles into four walls enclosing a square and

then dealt them each their starting hands. For a while they sat in silence sorting, selecting, and choosing which suit would be best to collect. Around them the hubbub of men talking, drinking and relaxing continued, punctuated at intervals with raucous laughter.

'So, Garrett, what did you make of that night training exercise you joined us on last week?' King took a cigarette and offered his case around to the others. They all lit up. 'You should have seen him, Lester. It was the best sight I've seen in years. The doctor tripping arse over tit into a drainage ditch, then emerging, covered in mud, with a leech clinging to his chin. The men thought it was hilarious.' King laughed loudly. Garrett's laughter sounded hollow.

'I thought it was jolly good fun actually,' he said, 'in spite of you all ragging me. The whole experience made a real change from the usual.'

'I hope you were impressed with the acting skills of those men I detailed to be "wounded" in order to give your stretcher bearers a taste of what they could be doing!'

'I think over-acting would be a more accurate description.' said Garrett with a smile.

Roger sensed the tension between the two men and glanced at Major Holland, but he seemed preoccupied with rearranging his mah-jong tiles.

'Hah! You could be right about the acting,' conceded King, 'but it never pays to lose the initiative. We have to keep the men alert and ready just in case.'

'Yes of course,' Garrett agreed quietly, 'though I can't really imagine it's ever going to come to that.' They played on in silence.

'Cong-mah-jong!' Holly shouted triumphantly, taking them

all by surprise. Having won the first game, it was his turn to buy the next round of stengahs. Three games later, won by Garrett and Holly between them, King left them to rebuild the wall of tiles while he staggered out to make what he muttered was a call of nature. The bar had begun to empty out and their conversation turned to the nightly air raids that London had been suffering since the beginning of September. They talked for a while about areas of the city that had been destroyed. Garrett turned to Roger, offering him a cigarette,

'So, Lester, do you have family in London?'

'Yes, my parents live in south London, quite near Balham. There was a massive bomb blast at the underground station in October. I haven't heard any details but I think their house is all right. It's just terrible what's happening night after night. It makes you feel a bit guilty sitting here, drinking and playing mah-jong doesn't it?'

'You'll get used to it, lad,' said Holly, 'but we'll have our work cut out here if the Japs do decide to have a crack at us.'

Roger imagined his parents sitting in the Anderson shelter his father had erected in the back garden. By day, his father was a foreman in a metal works factory that was now churning out munitions. By night, he was an ARP warden. As a union leader, he had the right temperament to order people to "Put out that light!" His mother used to work in same factory, but now she was involved with the WRVS. Roger had always enjoyed telling people that she had once been a suffragette, who had only stopped going on marches when she fell pregnant with him. "I don't think she ever forgave me for depriving her from a spell in prison for a worthy cause," he would add with a wry smile.

It made an amusing story, but in fact it wasn't that far

from the truth. He always had a feeling that he'd let them both down. It was his mother who had pushed him to try for the scholarship that won him a place at a good grammar school. She wanted him to go to university, but his father seemed to resent his academic abilities and muttered endlessly about his new school friends being stuck-up. Confused, Roger chose not to go to university, but flitted between several tedious jobs, leaving each one abruptly before he was pushed. He never took any of them seriously, frequently bending the rules, turning up late while nursing a hangover and sometimes not even turning up at all. But he was popular and had plenty of friends who drank or partied as wildly as he. He was restless, always looking for something new. His father finally shouted at him that enough was enough and lectured him about the need for hard graft and the dignity of labour. In the end, Roger meekly submitted to taking a post as a supervisor in a small company that made wireless components. His father had put in a word with one of his union mates. Roger felt trapped; he'd been bored rigid and couldn't wait to enlist when war broke out.

King returned unsteadily to their table. 'Met any new lovelies, Garrett?' he said. 'You want to watch this one, Lester. He has a canny charm with the ladies.' John flushed deeply. 'Ah yes, the sure sign of a man in pursuit of a new quarry. Well, don't ask me for any advice, will you?' King winked at Roger, patted Holly on the shoulders and announced, 'Well, chaps, I must get off to my bed, I've got a thirty-mile march in the morning!'

'Christ Almighty, that man tries my patience,' muttered Garrett as King left the mess. Holly glanced at him.

'Oh, don't worry about King,' said Holly, 'he's just envious of you, Doc. Between you and me. I think he's got a bit of wife trouble back home. He spilled the beans to me last week after he'd had a few.'

'I'd no idea he was even married,' said John

'Well apparently it was a marriage of necessity, if you take my meaning, but now it seems she wants a divorce. And of course with him stuck out here and her back in England, I don't know what he'll do. I tell you, lots of lads had those sorts of troubles in the last war. I just thank my lucky stars I don't have to worry about my missus. She's a rock.'

They all left the mess and drifted back to their quarters, but Roger couldn't sleep. Having started to think about his parents and the bombing of London, he couldn't stop. It was awful that they might be suffering but he still felt relieved that he had escaped. Not from the bombing – that would have been quite exciting – rather his relief was that he had finally got away from his father's endless criticism and the look of grim resignation on his mother's face. He couldn't recall the last time he'd seen her laugh. Laughter and frivolity were frowned on by both parents, who never missed an opportunity to remind their three children how lucky they were compared to others who were less fortunate. He missed his two younger sisters, though. Penny, the older of the two, had run away to Cornwall with a travelling salesman when she was just eighteen. The travelling salesman had continued travelling after he'd given her two children and hadn't been seen since. Lizzie, the baby of the family, had seized the opportunity to join her and help out, and now the two of them shared the care of the children and ran a village grocery store together. All three had found a way to leave.

CHAPTER 8

Ivyholme, Lymington

October 25th 1940

Dear John

This morning I woke early after a restless night full of strange dreams, so instead of trying to get back to sleep, I pedalled to the shops and saw that the fishmonger had some rabbits for sale. I bought one for 1/6d. It will make a good stew, with some of the cabbage left over from yesterday. I showed it to Cordelia, who announced that she couldn't possibly eat rabbit. Miss La-dee-dah. I expect she'll climb down from her high horse when she smells it cooking. The sugar ration has been cut again, to 8 ounces a week. I am glad I picked some blackberries and made them into jam in good time.

I'll have to see what Dorothy has to say about my dreams; she has a knack for trawling to the depths of something. Last week, when I cycled over, we first talked about astrology and how much of all this mayhem could have been predicted. Then we spent a while discussing God and what He must think about Hitler. She reminded me of when you were about fifteen and I took you to meet her for the first time. You boldly announced that you were an atheist and one by one she attacked all your arguments against the existence of God; though she says that these days she is leaning more towards the Buddhists. I am not sure what I believe in any more. I feel so fond of her. She is an oasis in the middle of my desert and I feel I can say anything to her. It is strange how certain friendships can stand the test of time and distance. While we were in London, we only corresponded occasionally, but I always knew she was there, and now it is as if the intervening years have been folded away.

The trees have that ragged autumn look these days, with some leaves still clinging bravely to the branches and the rest lying in damp heaps, trodden into the mud by the passage of feet. It gets dark quite early now. I miss the twinkling lights from across the river. Whenever the others go out in the evening, I feel relieved to have the whole house to myself. Though now I recall I did have a really nice dream when I took a nap this afternoon; you and I were sharing a dear little cottage on the Dorset coast. You were a GP and we lived together, just the two of us, like before. Wouldn't it be lovely to have that dream come true?

I will write again soon. Take care.

All the best Min.

November 4ᵗʰ 1940

Happy Birthday to me. I don't think so. It is nothing like the times John and I spent together at the London flat, when we ate those picnics, sitting on the carpet. It was one of my favourite treats – prawns, brown bread and butter and a glass of port. I've had cards from the family, Walter, Charles and Geraldine. Nothing of course from John – too busy having a good time to bother about his old mother. Even his friend Jim remembered. Why couldn't he? It has made me think about the beginnings of friendships; how one makes those first tentative moves, after meeting someone and having some spark of connection, and then how to make the next move without the fear of being rebuffed. Children seem to do it so naturally. They just ask, "Can I play with you?" and off they go. How do friendships move from being superficial to something more nourishing? Is it time or is it trust?

November 15th 1940

It just gets worse and worse. Coventry was bombed to ruins last night. The old cathedral is a smouldering heap of stones. The centre of the city has been burnt to a cinder. No one has ever seen anything like it. I can remember all the times when I was a girl and visited Mother's relatives in Coventry. I don't recall where they lived, but I don't think it was in the centre. I must ask Frank if he knows who might still have been there. Hundreds of people were killed. The news from London is terrible. Every night they have raids and I listen to the wireless reporting the damage and think of who I know who might have been caught up in it.

December 6th 1940

The last week has been absolutely frightful. Overhead it sounded like the end of the world was coming. The planes came over and over in endless waves, chased by the searchlights, and the ack-ack guns fired all night. People say that incendiaries were flaring everywhere, and even Frank rallied himself to help them douse the flames on the pier.

Southampton was bombed for three nights continuously and apparently there is little left of the centre. There is talk of having to abandon the whole town. Refugees have been flooding into the New Forest to any village or hamlet that has any spare room, while the town hall has got rows of exhausted people camped out, with the few meagre possessions that they had managed to salvage. Some say they looked ashen-faced and walk around if they are sleepwalking. Everyone is exhausted. Then last evening there was a massive air fight over the Isle of Wight, but most of the bombers got through, heading once again towards Southampton. I saw a plane that had been hit caught in the searchlights. It looked like a giant bird flying straight towards me. I couldn't move, waiting to see where it would crash, as if this wasn't something real, but something I would read about in a newspaper.

December 31st 1940

Last day of the year. What an awful year it's been. I have been reading in the newspaper about the dreadful firestorm that raged all around St Paul's two nights ago. It is a miracle that it was saved. I had never thought that I would have to live through another war. I feel as if everything is falling apart. Will anything ever be the same again? If there is a God, how can he allow us to systematically destroy the world? Will the new year bring any relief?

CHAPTER 9

He had been in Singapore for nearly a year. By keeping busy, John found that he could stay detached from the news of the chaos and devastation caused by the Blitz; news that was discussed and analysed in the Officers' mess; news he read about in the papers of whole streets being demolished; news described in letters from home of ordinary people being killed or injured.

The routine of daily sick parades, hospital visits, families' surgeries and malaria insect hunts became a welcome distraction. Whenever he was on call overnight at the Alexandra, he hoped that Sister LeBrun would be on night duty again. In spite of finding a number of plausible excuses to be seen around the wards, he had no real reason to be at the hospital during the daytime, since the other RAMC staff took care of all the admitted patients. But she always seemed to be on day duty when he was covering the night and the only other times he saw her, she was with a boisterous group of other QAs.

Just once, he'd seen her on her own, walking briskly back towards the hospital. She had not been in uniform, but in a pale green floral dress and her gorgeous auburn hair, no longer hidden under her veil, bounced off her shoulders as she walked. He'd slowed down the car and called out to her. 'Hello there, you look as if you are in a hurry. Can I offer you a lift?' She looked a little startled,

'No, really, it's only ten minutes from here.'

'But it would be no trouble, and besides, it's awfully hot.'

She looked at him again and, with a slight smile, got into the car, folding herself onto the seat and tucking her legs in afterwards. She was wearing perfume; something flowery, gardenias perhaps. A sheen of perspiration glistened on her brow and her nose looked freckled in the sun. He watched her breasts rising and falling as her breathing slowed now that she was no longer rushing. A small gold crucifix on a chain round her neck sparkled. He was staring at her. It must seem so rude. Fumbling for the gear stick, he stalled the car, jolting them forwards. She said nothing but raised one of her delicately shaped eyebrows. He blushed. 'I'm most dreadfully sorry. I've been having a few problems with this gearbox recently.' He tried again and managed to ease the car smoothly forward. 'So back to the hospital, is it?' he asked unnecessarily.

'Thank you. I have to be on duty at 4.00. I'm on a split shift today.'

'By the way, I've been meaning to ask you, your surname sounds quite unusual, is it French perhaps? Has your family lived in England for a while?'

'Well, I suppose you could say that. Our ancestors are believed to have come over with the Normans and we've lived in Dorset for centuries.' she replied with a grin.

'Of course, I remember now, you told me you came from Thomas Hardy country. I grew up just a little further along the coast, in Lymington. My mother still lives there with my uncle and his wife who have moved in with her to escape the bombing. I haven't lived there since I left to go to med school in London.' He'd prattled on, wondering how slowly he could drive the car without it looking too obvious.

'Oh really, I trained in London as well.'

By now he had pulled up outside the sister's mess and was about to ask her where she'd trained when she opened the car door and slipped out, saying,

'Thank you so much for the lift Dr Garrett, but I simply must dash. I've still got to get changed.' And then she was gone, leaving him to bang his head in frustration on the steering wheel. He couldn't believe he was being so pathetic.

This was the first time in his life that he had been celibate for any length of time, having spent most of his early twenties having fun with a number of women. Throughout his childhood, he had been shy and felt acutely self-conscious. Social circumstances meant that he attended very few children's parties and his father's apparent indifference to him hardly helped with his feelings of inferiority. At boarding school, he alternately craved acceptance while dreading the disapproval he imagined others would show for his second-hand school uniform. As a teenager, he never felt that he looked very manly and, being an only child, he rarely met any girls of his own age. Most school holidays he spent either on his own or in the company of his mother; he'd always felt he had to take care of her and protect her from his father's temper. Once at medical school he became a bit of a poseur, wearing colourful ties and adopting other mildly eccentric mannerisms. He started dating. From then on, it never ceased to amaze him that every time he plucked up the courage to ask out one of the nurses, she would appear to be genuinely flattered by the attention he showered her with and in no time at all seemed to have fallen for him. It was a trick he just had to keep repeating. But his lust, which he confused with ardour, and his need to keeping proving himself faded as soon as he had bedded each girl. Beginning to feel trapped, he would spend the next few weeks of the relationship trying to extract himself with the minimum of damage. Each one begged him to stay, despite him becoming suddenly unavailable or showing indifference. He knew it was a cliché, but all he wanted in a woman was someone who would be gentle and courageous, intelligent and enthusiastic. Each time he met someone new, he convinced himself that at last he had found the perfect lifetime partner. He longed for what he imagined could be the stability and security of marriage, despite the terrible role model he'd had from his parent's disastrous liaison.

Sister LeBrun was different from the other nurses he'd met either here or back home in his student days, whom he'd written off as restless souls, desperately looking for a husband to provide for them. She didn't seem to be taken in by any of his overtures, yet nor was she giving him the cold shoulder. He couldn't understand where he was going wrong.

He wasn't exactly lonely, but there was no one he considered to be a close friend. No one like Jim, from medical school, with whom he had spent so many hours either tramping over Dartmoor or sailing on the Norfolk Broads, when they'd had heated debates about life and all its fascinations taking them late into the night. Jim was someone who knew him better than anyone else; someone who shared his sense of humour. He missed all that. Some of the other officers were quite good company and faithful Henderson was often badgering him for a game of squash. But something was still missing. It all felt superficial. Each week, driven by guilt, he'd begin a letter to his mother; he seldom finished it, and the following week he'd start it all over again.

Reluctant to risk being turned down again by Sister LeBrun, he frittered the weeks away until Christmas. It was his first Christmas out East, since last year he had been on board the ship with Henderson, coming through the Suez Canal. Somehow it didn't feel right without snow or cold winds; there were no fires, candlelight or feelings of cosiness. Everywhere he went, families had made an effort with crackers, decorations and Christmas trees of some sort, but the atmosphere was definitely subdued; their thoughts were inevitably with those back home and with those who had lost loved ones in the bombing.

CHAPTER 10

Beatrice stared out of her window across the swathe of grass and gaudy flowering shrubs that lay between the sister's mess and the rest of the hospital. By half shutting her eyes she tried, unsuccessfully, to imagine that she was looking at the view over the fields and woods from her childhood bedroom. She wished she could feel some enthusiasm for the new year but instead she felt as if all her sparkle had disappeared. She twisted the chain of the gold crucifix she always wore; a present from her mother on her confirmation. From her parent's letters, she could tell how hard they were finding it with her out of reach on the other side of the world and Jamie still missing in France. The awful images she had of him lying wounded had begun to recede as long as she didn't talk about him. She hung on to the old saying that no news meant good news, but her parents seemed to have given up all hope. She imagined that they were still annoyed with her for coming out to Singapore, and now she was beginning to feel like a fraud, since there was no action and no wounded soldiers to care for. Wearily, she pinned up her hair, fixed her white veil on top and went downstairs to make her way on duty.

It had recently rained and as she stepped outside into the bright sun she saw steam rising from the freshly mown lawns. She noticed the pungent smell from the blossoms of plants whose names she still hadn't had time to learn. The hot damp air clung to her skin and she could already feel beads of sweat trickling down into the small of her back, despite now wearing her tropical uniform; white dress, white stockings and white shoes. At least her mother had been right to insist that she'd brought sensible cotton underclothes rather than the lacy silk ones she preferred.

Crossing the gardens, she saw John Garrett talking with a fellow medical officer. She hadn't seen him for a few weeks and recalled that she'd been a bit abrupt with him when he'd given her a lift that day. She slowed her pace, pretending to look as if she might have forgotten something. Seeing her, he immediately excused himself from his colleague and came towards her with a big smile.

'Well hello Doctor Garrett, where have you been all these weeks?'

'Oh, hello Sister LeBrun, I thought you might have heard that I'd been the MO up at Port Dickson since Christmas.'

'Yes of course, I did.' She grinned at him, aware that she was already feeling better. 'It was just my way of saying that we've all missed seeing you around. Welcome back.'

She said "we" rather than "I" deliberately. She couldn't resist stringing him along for a bit longer. His smile drooped but he quickly rallied and said casually,

'Well, it's really good to be back. It was actually more like a little holiday and I was lucky to be able to do a lot of dinghy sailing while I was away. In fact, I er… I wondered if you'd like to come for a sail with me this weekend, if you are free?'

She was so taken aback that he had finally come out with it that she couldn't think how to reply. Should she tease him for a little bit longer or would he simply give up and pursue someone else? Deciding she deserved to be cheered up, she smiled back at him.

'Thank you. That would be lovely. As it happens I'm not

working this Sunday but I will only agree to be your crew if, off-duty, you stop calling me Sister LeBrun and start calling me Bea. It's spelt B.E.A, but it's pronounced like the bumble bee; short for Beatrice, which apparently means "voyager", which might be quite appropriate if we are to go off in a boat together.' She paused, breathlessly. Oh for goodness sake, now she was the one who was prattling on.

He beamed at her, 'Thank you, er... Bea. And of course, you must call me John. I'll pick you up outside the hospital at say, eleven o'clock?'

On Sunday he was there, a good ten minutes early. She had spent at least an hour trying to decide what to wear, trying on several different outfits and finally settling for a pair of olive-green slacks and a cream shirt. As they drove down through the town towards the yacht club, she felt excited and silly; a bit like a school girl being taken out on a day trip. She kept squashing the little voice inside her that warned her to be careful, not to get hurt like the last time.

She hadn't dare tell him that she'd never been in a boat before, but fortunately he seemed to have made that assumption and gave her clear instructions as to where to sit, how to pull the sheet and how to move quickly to the other side to avoid the boom as they went about. Considering it was still the monsoon season, the weather was perfect, with enough breeze to give them some really good runs as they tacked across the straits past the island of Blakang Mati. John looked in his element, leaning far out to get them as close to the wind as possible so that they skimmed across the waves. His normally well-combed hair was tousled with the wind and with some of his shirt buttons undone, she could see his chest was smooth and hairless. She noticed how his arms and legs

47

had caught the sun and wondered how many other girls he'd taken out in this boat before her.

By the time they returned to the yacht club, she was drenched but exhilarated. She could feel the sea salt drying on her cheeks and her hair was a tangled mess since all her hair clips had fallen out.

'So Second Mate, I hope you will do me the honour of having dinner with me tonight.'

'I'd be most charmed, Captain. Perhaps you could drive me home, and I'll get showered and changed. I don't think they'd let me in anywhere looking like this.' She dragged her fingers through her wet hair, and pointed to her soaked shirt. 'Pick me up at seven?'

For the second time that day, she couldn't decide what to wear. It mustn't be too formal, but then again, not knowing what sort of restaurant he had in mind, she couldn't look as casual as she had for the sailing trip. Eventually, she chose a pale turquoise silk dress that she'd recently had made for her by a tailor in Chinatown, recommended by all the other girls. She brushed her long curly hair, twisted it into a chignon, then pulled all the pins out again and left it to flow over her shoulders. It looked good against the turquoise.

They ate at the Mandarin restaurant downtown near the Padang; chicken satay, shredded beef noodles, fried rice and tiger prawns cooked in spicy coconut. She even managed to manipulate the strange chopsticks without spilling anything down her front. Thank goodness she'd chosen the right dress. The restaurant was busy and she hoped they wouldn't bump into anyone either of them knew – not because she didn't want to be seen with him, but because she didn't want anyone to interrupt them. If it was going to work, she would be able to tell from how the next few hours played out. If she was destined to be another one of his conquests, she might as well find out before she got too involved.

Now that he didn't have the distraction of managing the dinghy he had reverted to his previous nervousness and quizzed her with all the standard biographical questions. She was so surprised to discover that this man, whom everyone had said was such a charmer, would turn out to be so tongue-tied. To put him at his ease, she told him about her family; about how she had grown up near Dorchester, gone to a boarding school in Sussex, and how her parents now lived in Lyme Regis. And then, without thinking, she was telling him all about Jamie.

'It's just awful. We are so close. I feel as if a part of me has gone missing. I can't help thinking that if I'd stayed in England I might have been able to find out what happened to him. Maybe I could have tracked down some of his friends from his regiment who did make it back after Dunkirk. It's too dreadful to think that he may have been killed, so I pretend that he's safe, even if he is a prisoner of war.' She became teary and as she scrabbled in her handbag, John passed her his handkerchief.

'I can only begin to imagine what it's like for you. I don't have any brothers or sisters. I've always wanted a brother. The closest I ever had to one is a friend at school. He's called James as well, but I know that if anything ever happened to him I'd be awfully upset.'

Dabbing her eyes, she wished that she hadn't allowed herself to become so vulnerable, but as if John knew that she needed to recover her composure, he began to talk about his school days at the Quaker boarding school he'd been sent to at Reading, adding that he wasn't really religious. He had just begun to tell her about his time as a medical student at St Thomas' when she interrupted,

'You weren't at Tommy's as well, were you? I don't believe it, we must have overlapped. I did my training there. You must have recognised a true Nightingale nurse?'

For the rest of the evening, interrupted by hoots of laughter, they swapped tales about bedpans and battleaxe matrons, student pranks and pompous professors. Much later, he drove her back to the sister's mess. Leaning over, he kissed her lightly on the cheek.

'Can we do this again, sometime soon, Bea? I have had such a good day.'

'I would really enjoy that as well.' She smiled and, briefly touching the end of his nose, as if he were a small child, got slowly out of the car, turning to wave at him as he drove off, relieved that he'd passed her test.

CHAPTER 11

Ivyholme, Lymington

January 24th 1941

Dear John

The snow we had last week has almost cleared. I like it when it first falls and everything is covered in a thick white blanket; there is that lovely muffled silence. Then of course it all gets trodden and either goes straight to slush or it freezes in layers and makes getting about such a nightmare. There have been more air raids on London. Cousin Martin wrote to tell me that a fellow fire warden was crushed to death when a burning building collapsed on top of him. I can't imagine how frightful it all must be up there. I don't think I'll ever want to go back to town and see the places I have loved laid waste.

Today has been one of those bleak overcast days with a biting north east wind; the river looks grey, the sky is grey, and I feel rather grey. I can't bear this weather when I have to button myself into all my winter woollies. Not like you of course with your lovely tropical climate. I have decided that February should be abolished and that we should just skip from the cold days of January to the first buds of spring in March. Yesterday, I gave myself a little treat and went on the bus to the cinema in New Milton to see Charlie Chaplin in *The Great Dictator*. Everyone seems to be talking about it. There was quite a long queue to go in and at the end of the film after the speech, which was so moving, everyone clapped. It seemed

51

rather odd to be applauding a film, but when we all rose as one for the National Anthem at the end, I felt quite buoyed up.

You will be pleased to hear that I am quite busy these days with the WI and up at the hospital where I try and make myself useful. No change here of course but Frank said to send his love.

Your ever loving mother Min.

April 19th 1941

Today I had such a strange conversation with Dorothy. For some reason I began to tell her about Freddy and George; the only two men in my life. We were talking about destiny and why certain couples are drawn to choose each other (assuming that their parents allow them any choice in the matter). She knew all about George but I had never really told her the whole truth about Freddy. Even today I felt embarrassed to admit how naive I was at eighteen, engaged to a promising lawyer who was playing around with some awful girl behind my back all the time. Oh, I was so devastated when he had to admit that the girl had got herself pregnant and brazenly presented him with his child only weeks before our wedding. Of course it had to be called off and hushed up, and he was banished to India until the scandal died down. If it hadn't all gone wrong, I still believe he could have given me a very comfortable life; we always seemed to have so much in common. He was so handsome.

Afterwards I thought I could never love anyone again and for a while I resigned myself to spinsterhood and a rather dull life. All the girls I knew of my age were married and had started having babies. I remember feeling awfully left out. Dorothy gave me one of those raised eyebrow looks when I told her that if he came back into my life now, I think I would fall for him all over again.

So of course, poor little me, within twelve months I had been deserted by my fiancée and lost my mother to cancer. I didn't think my life could get much worse and it was such a surprise when I met George the following year at the Mansfield's. He flattered me and intrigued me with tales of his travels as a mining engineer and all the exotic places he had been to. As I explained to Dorothy, he certainly sounded as if he had the means to support me and, after all, his father had been a medical surgeon in the navy so he did come from a good background. I know I should have listened to my father. Thank goodness he never lived to see what a mess it all turned out to be, but how was I to know at the time that it was all a pack of lies? I knew I didn't love him, but I thought that perhaps over time we would learn to love one another. When John was born in 1913, after just ten months, I felt complete. Perhaps I was so wrapped up in my baby that I ignored George, who became more and more jealous, to the extent that he couldn't bear for me to pay John too much attention. He began to drink heavily and would stay away for weeks at a time; Lord knows where he went or who he was with. And then there was that day he returned out of the blue and said he was going to start a new career as an actor. Well given how he'd fooled me with the mining tales, I thought he might do rather well. What a silly woman I was.

I still shudder to think of all those terrible years after

the Great War when he drifted in and out of work. I tried as hard as I could to shield John from his drunken spitefulness and violence, but I know he saw things that he shouldn't have. I wouldn't have survived if the family hadn't stepped in and helped me buy Ivyholme. I was lucky they agreed to help fund his education (I suppose that's why Cordelia has always disapproved of me).

Poor John he could have done with a good father, someone he could have looked up to. I'd forgotten that I'd never told Dorothy that John had actually disowned his father when he reached twenty-one. Secretly I've always been rather pleased that he adopted my family name instead, but it isn't the kind of thing one wants to talk about. Thank goodness George is dead now and can never trouble us again.

I have never wanted a man's company since then. John is the only man I want in my life. And now, if this war doesn't end soon, I may end up losing the only person who really matters to me.

CHAPTER 12

Richard Henderson and Roger Lester had been driving for a couple of hours. The humidity was overwhelming and both men's brows dripped with perspiration. The road stretched out before them, an unending stripe of charcoal grey. Hemmed in by long green tunnels of tropical jungle, they drove through clumps of bamboo, tall palms, ferns, creepers and swaying banana trees, broken only by interminable miles of rubber plantation. The rubber trees were planted in rigid rows, their canopy shielding any light from reaching the ground and filling the air with a powerful smell of latex. Occasionally, the road curved through swamps and heathland, and all along the route, on either side of the road, they saw a maze of streams and creeks and trails that disappeared into the vast Malayan greenhouse.

They were returning from a week-long training exercise that B. and D. Companies had been involved in the Kluang and Yong Peng area of central Johore. Since the Japanese were now allied with the Axis powers and occupied airfields in northern French Indo-China, only 1000 miles from Singapore, the whole strategic situation had been transformed.

Richard hadn't said much to Lester for most of the journey, lost in own thoughts about how badly the exercise had gone. He was anxious about what to say in his report for Lt Colonel Bill Ellerton. Ellerton had commanded the regiment since the autumn of 1940. He was a decent sort of man and was well respected by everyone. He had a reputation for being fair, but hated ineptitude. It might be easier, Richard thought, if Ellerton was more of a bully, then he would at least know exactly what to expect.

'Christ, I'm bloody knackered,' said Lester, who'd been driving since they'd left the training camp. 'All I can think about is ripping off this filthy uniform, having a long shower, a big plate of meat and potato pie and a large glass of scotch.'

'Oh, I'm sorry. I was miles away, thinking about my report. Do you want me to take over?'

'No, don't worry. We're nearly at the causeway aren't we?'

'Yep, it shouldn't be much longer, but I'll drive if you want.'

'What will you tell the Lt Colonel about the exercise?' asked Lester, 'it didn't go that badly, did it?'

Richard looked across at his lieutenant. Lester's dark curly hair was greasy with sweat and his nose had caught the sun, causing the skin to peel in several places. Even when they had set out on this training exercise with clean uniforms, he had reminded Richard of a rather scruffy mongrel puppy, and his pronounced cockney accent completed the picture. As usual, he had a cigarette balanced between his lips, which he smoked from start to finish without ever removing it. Lester was in fact a couple of years older than he, but from the stories he'd told about his life before the war, much of the time he behaved just like the sort of yob Richard's father would have disapproved of.

'No. I thought it was a bit of a disaster actually. Didn't you notice how ignorant most of the men seem to be about life in the outdoors? I mean, they don't know anything about camping methods, water conservation, or generally how to survive in the jungle. In spite of all the training operations they've undergone in the past year, half of them don't seem to take any of it seriously. They don't really see the point of it all. I'm trying to work out how I can make it sound better than it actually was in my report to Ellerton, but I'm just a bit nervous about how he'll take it. It's probably my fault. I should have drilled them better.'

'I suppose you've got a point. Some of them do seem to think it's all a bit of a picnic. Christ help them if it ever does kick off over here in this godforsaken country.' Lester gestured to yet another tunnel of green they were passing through. 'Look, why don't I organise some exercises locally up at Pasir Panjang? I could take small groups of them out in the wild, with limited equipment or supervision for two or three nights, and see how they cope when they don't have someone else thinking for them,' said Roger.

'Well, I'll have to see what Ellerton has to say first.'

As they reached the mile-long causeway between Johore and Singapore, Richard had once more lapsed back into silence. His thoughts had turned to John Garrett and the fact that he hadn't seen much of him since Christmas. He wondered if he'd done something to annoy him; these days he always said he was too busy for a game of squash, though he still seemed friendly enough when they did come across each other in the mess.

Lester swung the car into the Gilman Barracks and brought it to an abrupt halt. Stretching his long limbs, he jumped out, stuffed his mud-spattered shirt tail back into his trousers and grabbed his kit bag. In spite of the heat and the long drive, he still appeared to be full of energy.

'See you in the bar later?' he asked.

'Yes, thanks very much for doing the driving. I'm sorry I

wasn't very good company. I'll buy you a drink to make up for it.'

When Richard finally made it to the mess bar later, Roger Lester was already sitting there, a large glass of scotch in his hand and a cigarette dangling from his mouth. He'd been collared by Major King, who raised his glass to Richard as he walked in,

'So how did it go? Lose any of the little blighters, did you?'

'No, all present and correct, but some of them need a big kick up the backside.' Richard sank into a chair and signalled the barman to bring him a drink.

'The trouble with you, Henderson, is that you're too soft on them. You've got to keep the upper hand or else they'll think that you're some nancy boy and just take the piss.'

Henderson flushed and stuttered some reply about the need to be firm but fair, causing Major King to launch into one his pet topics about discipline and respect for senior officers.

Roger watched the two men. Seeing Henderson flustered by the comment about nancy boys confirmed something he'd wondered about him for a while. A few weeks back, Roger had seen him wrapped around a young Malay man in one of the seedier bars off the Lavender Road. Henderson hadn't realised he was there, and Roger had been rather preoccupied, making a liaison of his own with a couple Chinese girls. Now it made sense; his soft features, his gentle manner and the nervous gesture he had of pushing his fringe off his forehead. He had always thought that Henderson was just a nice boy from a posh family who was a bit shy. He wondered what it was like being a queer in the army; not that Roger cared – he didn't mind queers – but it wasn't the sort of information you'd want to have flying about; it could even get him court-marshalled. Some might have used it against him; he would be so easy to blackmail. Roger wondered if he should warn him to be a bit more discreet. With all this time away from wives and girlfriends, the establishments that Roger frequented in the Lavender Road were doing a roaring trade. Anyone from a private to a brigadier might see him and decide to spill the beans.

CHAPTER 13

'Something I've always been meaning to ask. How come it took you so long to ask me out?' Beatrice had been lying on her back, her eyes closed, soaking up the sun. Now she flipped onto her side, smoothed out the ruckled edges of her beach towel and, propping her head on one hand, looked at John quizzically.

'Well, for ages I was simply too scared of you.'

'What on earth is there about me to be scared of?'

John sat up and looked away from her towards the waves splashing onto the shore.

'Well, now I know you a lot better, I have no idea. It's just that you seemed so confident and pretty and intelligent and well read. And I suppose if I'm truthful, you weren't fawning over me like some of your colleagues have done in the past and that sort of took away all my confidence.' He surprised himself with his honesty.

'I never saw you as an under-confident man. You could have had the pick of any woman out here, and if the rumours are true you already have.'

He glanced at her and quickly turned away again. 'You don't want to believe everything you hear.' He was about to make some witty comment about his reputation but stopped himself. 'Actually, Bea, much of the time, it's all just a bit of a front. I've been out with a fair number of women and I suppose I can be a bit of a charmer, but somehow it always seems to go wrong. '

Beatrice wriggled onto her front and started raking the fine white sand into little shapes. He lay back down on his side facing her. The skin on her bare shoulders seemed to glow; he felt himself hardening. Slowly he reached across to walk his fingers down each of her vertebra from the top of her neck towards her tail. He paused for a second and then slid his fingers under the edge of her swimming costume, until, frustratingly, she gently removed his hand.

'I think quite a lot of people may feel like you do; soft on the inside, with a hard shell on the outside to prevent attack,' she said quietly. 'I think I developed a shell just like yours when I was at boarding school.'

They were on their private island – or rather, the uninhabited island they had come across by accident on one of the sailing trips they had been making since that first sailing date a couple of months ago. It was the real tropical island of fiction; one hundred yards long and eighty yards wide and at its centre was a small flat hill with a few stubby trees. One side of the island was sandy and the other rocky with coral which was exposed at low tide. All around were palms and small scrubby mangrove trees. This was the third time they had been there, and since they had never seen anyone else, they'd claimed it as their own. They'd identified where they would build a little house and where they would construct hideouts to defend it from any marauders. They bathed, ate picnics, made love, and slept under the shade of a palm tree. They watched sandpipers, blue kingfishers and little green herons that haunted the beaches, and lost count of the lizards and small crabs that swarmed out of the rocky crevices at low tide.

Since they'd started dating, they'd seen each other whenever their duties allowed, often only for an hour or two when she

61

came off shift. Sometimes they went to the cinema or browsed the shops in the busy marketplace. Or they would drive through Chinatown in the early evening, seduced by the smells of spice and roast meat. Whenever he could, he would smuggle her into his quarters where they'd sit together quietly in the cool of evening on the verandah before retreating inside to his bed. She was no virgin, but was unforthcoming about her past and John didn't want to ruin it by being too curious. Getting to know her was like rediscovering a favourite piece of music; some themes felt so familiar, while at the same time he heard chords and variations that he'd never heard before.

Often, while walking or over dinner, they chatted about the English countryside and what they missed most. They discussed films and theatre and what books they liked. They'd even had quite a few heated debates about politics. But more recently, with the arrival of the first Australian troops in Malaya, they had begun to talk about the possibility of the war actually spreading to Singapore itself. It was so refreshing to talk with someone who was intelligent and had views of her own; this felt more like a relationship of equals.

Beatrice twisted round to face him, leaving her sand shapes for a moment.

'So I suppose you're looking for the perfect woman. What do I have to live up to? Don't tell me Freud was right about men and their mothers!' Her eyes twinkled.

He glanced at her crossly, wanting to defend both himself and Min, but seeing she was teasing, he reached over to tickle her until she scrambled to her feet and fled into the sea. Running after her, they both collapsed into the waves, laughing and yelping. Later, once they'd played and swum, they flopped back down on the beach.

'So, if we are going for the truth, what made you decide to risk going out with a terrible womanizer?' he asked, after they had made love once more.

'Simple. I had to see if the rumours were true. And anyway, I was as bored as you, waiting for some action to happen out here, so I thought I'd create some of my own. At least it was possible that with you, I might have some kind of adventure.'

'And have you?'

'Well, yes,' she looked quite serious, 'in some ways it's been really exciting and refreshing, but in other ways being with you feels comfortable, like coming home to a pair of really cosy slippers.'

'Are you seriously telling me that I am like a pair of old slippers?'

'No! Not you, silly. I am talking about the relationship, about the two of us, and how safe and content I feel with you.'

He leant over and kissed her. 'Well, I think I feel the same, though I'd choose a different metaphor. But until I come up with one, this old pair of slippers had better get you back to base before matron's curfew.'

It was the last trip to the island that they were able to make for a while. Over the next few weeks, John became much busier at work, with first aid lectures and inoculations for newly arrived soldiers. Although each day the troops half-heartedly prepared in some way or other for the possibility of a Japanese invasion, no one really believed it would happen. As for the civilians, life in Singapore carried on as if the rest of the world and all its troubles didn't exist. Everyone seemed cocooned in a sort of blissful tropical siesta.

CHAPTER 14

May 16th 1941

Cousin Martin is staying. He needs time to recuperate. He is so changed from the jolly man who used to take John fishing sometimes in the school holidays. He is exhausted; his hands are raw and blistered from the fires and he has a hacking cough. He has been a volunteer firefighter since the start and seen plenty of awful sights, but from the fragments he has told me about last Saturday in London, it was the worst anyone has experienced.

For some reason I want to write it all down, almost as he related it to me; it seems important to keep a record. Perhaps when this is all over I will read some of this journal to John, so that he can understand what has happened over this side of the world while he has been free of it all, living the life of Riley.

Martin told me that on this particular night of bombing, it didn't get dark until late. It was Double Summer Time of course. The streets of London were busy with people enjoying a Saturday night out. I think he said that here had been a football match at Wembley. As the sky turned from rose to velvet, there was a full moon that just seemed to hang there as if it was waiting for something. Everyone dreads a full moon because that's when the bombers come. Just before midnight, the sirens started wailing.

Then there was nothing but noise and din; the stutter

of ack-ack guns aiming at planes that buzzed like wasps against the moon; bombs shrieking and whistling as they fell; panes of glass shattering and raining like confetti; explosions ripping out the very heart of buildings; office blocks toppling and smashing all around. Martin said he felt the earth tremble as he lay face down, waiting for a chance to run for cover. The air was thick with smoke, dust and the smell of burning. It choked in his throat.

He described how the church of St Benedict's had its roof caved in; all the statues were on fire, their paint blistering in the heat, as if the saints were being martyred all over again, and then a flaming pigeon crashed onto the altar like a bizarre sacrifice.

And yet there were rows of ordinary houses which looked untouched, until there would be a gaping hole in the middle, as if several teeth had been knocked out in a brawl, leaving a crater of smouldering rubble.

All night, incendiary bombs fizzed and sparkled on the roofs and he and his fellow firefighters ran back and forth with buckets of sand and stirrup pumps. He remembered looking up at the silver barrage balloons strung up like fat sleepy fish, reflecting the flames that were tearing the buildings apart beneath them. Even the lampposts buckled in the intense heat.

St Pancras station had its tracks ripped up as if a child had had a tantrum with his train set; shattered, derailed trains lay meekly on their sides. The noise, the bombs, the fires, the destruction, went on and on. I don't know how he survived it. He was quite tearful as he told me. I have never seen him like this.

The all-clear didn't sound until about six in the morning.

The dawn was grey and the fires still raged all over the city. The daylight showed everything, despite a feeble sun that struggled to glow through the thick palls of smoke reminiscent, he said, of the old pea-soupers that I recall as child. A black snow storm of charred paper fell all day.

Countless streets that were still criss-crossed with water hoses were roped off, as those returning from a terrifying night huddled in the underground trudged back to see their homes sliced open and exposed like doll's houses. Roads ran with water and blood. There were dead bodies, and parts of bodies strewn across the rubble. I could hardly bear to listen to this part of the story.

And yet, everyone was so brave. As the city crawled back into life, some people started to sweep the shattered glass into piles and some rallied round to search for missing people, while others returned to their skeleton houses to retrieve their possessions before making their way to a rest centre.

And what's more, on Monday morning, clean-suited office workers, clutching their briefcases, thronged the streets as they walked into work, a look of grim determination on their faces.

CHAPTER 15

Heavy rain pounded on the roof. It was still early; grey light seeped in around the blinds. John stretched out, remembering with pleasure that today, May 29th, was his twenty-eighth birthday. He thought about the dinner party he had planned for the evening. He had never had a proper birthday party before. When he was young, his mother had never liked to risk his father's displeasure if she invited anyone over to tea, and later on he'd always been away at boarding school. At medical school, when money was tight, Min expected him to celebrate with her; it had become a habit he couldn't break from. This evening would probably cost him a lot more than he could really afford. It was going to be at Raffles and he wanted it to be perfect. He'd spent ages sketching little caricatures of each guest on cards which he was going to distribute around the table instead of place names. Each person would have to identify themselves before they could take their seats. Bea's was easily recognisable, with her white uniform and flowing veil, and he had drawn a tall skinny Richard with his hair flopped over his face as usual, waving a squash racket.

Chen rapped at the door and entered, bearing his usual morning tea, then disappeared with a brief nod. He sipped the tea slowly, deciding just for once that he wouldn't rush to get up for sick parade and was startled by another loud knock. When Chen did not reappear, he quickly wrapped his sarong around him and opened the door to find Bea standing there, breathless and dripping wet. Clearly she'd been caught in the sudden downpour just as she left her quarters. He pulled her towards him and, closing the door with one hand, grabbed a towel with the other and started to dry her off.

'Bea! You poor thing! My goodness, you're soaked. I think you need warming up.' He led her towards the bed.

'No JG, I can't stay, I am due on duty in fifteen minutes. I just wanted to wish you happy birthday and give you this.' Taking the towel from him to rub her hair, she withdrew a small parcel from under her cape and held it out to him. 'I hope you like it.'

John pulled off the wrapping paper to reveal a small carved wooden box. Inside was a silver propelling pencil. He grinned at her. He had admired it the previous week on a stall in Chinatown. Now he realised why she had told him to carry on down the street, saying she thought she had dropped her scarf and needed to go back to look for it.

'Oh Bea! It's lovely. How clever you are!'

He turned the pencil between his fingers. It was engraved with a pattern of twisted leaves and flowers and it rattled with the spare leads held inside.

'Thank you so much Bea. I really like it.' He drew her towards him and kissed her on each eyelid, on her freckled nose and on her smiling mouth.

By now, the rain had stopped and pale sun crept through the window. Bea's hair was still damp, and he watched, fascinated, as she tweaked and pinned it back into submission.

'I must dash. I am really looking forward to the party. It should be fun.'

After she left, he put the silver pencil back in its box and tucked it away in his drawer. He washed, dressed and strode towards the MI room, humming as he sat down at his desk.

'You're in a good mood, Doc. Anyone would think it's your birthday,' remarked his orderly once the last patient had gone.

'Well, yes, as a matter of fact it is!' With that, he headed to the mess for breakfast, and sat down next to Henderson who was, as usual, munching his way through a large plate of toast. Henderson beamed at him, wiped his fingers of marmalade and reached into his top pocket to pull out a small wrapped gift.

'Happy birthday, Garrett. I thought you might like something to keep your cigarettes dry in the rainfall,' he said, flushing slightly.

'Oh, you really shouldn't have gone to any trouble. I don't normally tell anyone about my birthday. It's only because Beatrice wanted me to throw a party and of course I had to tell people the reason why.' John turned the cigarette case over in his fingers. It wasn't cheap. 'Thanks Henderson. This is very generous of you.'

'Don't be silly, it's nothing. So who's going to be at this party tonight?'

'Well, only about a dozen of us. I didn't want to overdo it. There'll be you and Bea of course, some people from the hospital and then some non-army people you won't know but who have been awfully hospitable to me over the last year or so.'

'Sounds like fun. I'll see you later.'

Richard had spent several hours searching for just the right present for John, nervous of how it would be received. Going to birthday parties and taking an appropriate gift was a part of social etiquette that had been drummed into him all his childhood. He'd timidly shown the cigarette case to Lester the night before, hoping for his approval. Lester had whistled and said, 'Christ! That looks pretty pricey. I didn't realise the two of you were such good friends.'

'Oh yes, we came out together on the same ship and we're regular squash players, though I don't see quite so much of him these days,' Richard had stammered.

'No, I hear he's busy with a certain little lady, isn't he?' Roger gave him a rather knowing look and Richard had blushed.

That evening at the dinner party he found himself placed towards the end of the long table, surrounded by a middle-aged woman and a couple of nurses. They were mildly amusing, rather self-obsessed, and he was hardly required to contribute much, except to nod and make encouraging noises as they gossiped about Singapore society and hospital life. He'd always found it difficult trying to make conversation over a dinner table, in spite of all the practice he'd had at his mother's interminable soirées. He never seemed be sitting in the right place, near enough to the people who sounded the most interesting. John and Beatrice sat at the centre of the table like a king and queen, clearly relishing all the attention. The more they all drank, the more wine John ordered. It was as if all thoughts of the war and the hardships of life back in England had been left tucked inside their uniform pockets, not to be retrieved until the following morning, when they would return to their sensible duties.

Richard was relieved once dinner was finished, and when the dancing started he wandered off outside into the palm garden. He stayed there for the remainder of the evening, gazing up at the night sky, calculating how soon he could decently leave. Nobody joined him.

CHAPTER 16

Ivyholme, Lymington

July 20th 1941

Dear John

It has been such a lovely day; clear blue skies with fluffy white clouds and warm enough to sit in the garden for my breakfast. And then, the biggest treat of all – a letter from you, with lots of news. I read it very slowly, wanting to savour every detail and to make it last. Once I'd finished it, I read it all over again and I had a look at the picture book of Singapore you sent me last year and tried to visualise all the places you describe.

Your birthday party at Raffles Hotel sounds as if it was a very grand affair; I am so glad to hear that you have good friends with whom you could share it. I can't remember when I last ate such a big meal. It is good to hear that your work is a little bit more satisfying. I am sure you do everything quite splendidly but I know how frustrated you have been and how left out of things you feel.

But going back to your letter, there was your other piece of news about your new girlfriend, Beatrice. You tell me I will really like her. Now where have I heard that one before! I was intrigued by the coincidence about the name of her parent's house in Lyme Regis being called Ivy Cottage in Holmes Road. It sounds like a composite of ours. Dorothy will be most amused when I tell her. I do hope you won't rush into anything just because there is a war. Of course I want you to be happy and find a nice girl to settle down with and give me a little flock of grandchildren, but I am sure you see the sense of waiting until this is all over.

You will be pleased to hear that I am keeping myself very busy with my voluntary work at the hospital. I am really beginning to enjoy the whole process of planting vegetables, weeding, watering and then being able to collect the harvest. I also belong to the knitting and sewing group, as well as the WI, so all my days are pretty full up.

Compared to last year, we hardly ever see a plane these days. I think Hitler has been scared off and has turned his attention elsewhere. Of course there is still rationing and young lads being called up, but much of the time it isn't too bad here.

I'd better sign off now and catch the post.

Your ever loving Min.

July 22nd 1941

It was so lovely to have that letter from John, but it did give me very mixed feelings. I can understand why he said he was in two minds as to whether to tell me about his extravagant birthday party; a six-course meal washed down with copious amounts of champagne. I feel very jealous, almost angry. All that meat, delicious pastries and deserts sprinkled liberally with sugar. He really has no idea of what it's like back here. It sounds as if he and his friends will have guzzled, in just one meal, more than a month's worth of rations that would feed a large family over here very nicely. They are all living so comfortably while so many families are homeless and have lost everything.

I rarely mention him to people these days, except to say that he is safe and well. With so many people having lost family members in the bombing, or who have had sons and husbands killed in Europe or North Africa, sometimes I feel a little ashamed of the life he is leading out in Sing. He will hate it if he has to return home with no stories to tell except of a life of decadence and plenty. He was always like this; so worried about what others would think, so needing to be admired. I remember one day when he was quite little, probably about three. Walter and Evie were visiting and we were all watching him building a castle with his bricks, very carefully. When he had finished he turned round to us and said, "Aren't me wonderful". And of course we agreed that indeed he was truly wonderful. In some ways he is still a bit like that little boy, wanting people to be impressed. I don't suppose his father's endless criticism helped him much.

Now he has gone and fallen for some nurse out there. He says I will really like her. It is the same every time; he loses his head and thinks he is in love, then he becomes bored and abandons some poor girl whose heart is broken. And of course I know what that is like. Is this one really going to be any different? I shall be quite cross if he goes and marries someone whom I have never met. I know he will meet someone eventually, but I do want him all to myself first.

August 29ᵗʰ 1941

Today I feel quite irritable and worn out. I overheard Cordelia talking to Hester, who is down here on leave for a week. They were discussing me. Hester was asking "what

Aunt Florence does all day" since I never seem to be in the house. Cordelia, in her most sarcastic voice, said "My dear, your Aunt Florence is heading for sainthood. On Mondays she toils in the hospital garden growing vegetables. Tuesdays, it's the WI. Wednesdays, she's back at the hospital mending sheets or something. Thursdays I think she knits or sews in the sewing circle, which is probably just an excuse for a good gossip, and on Fridays, after she has queued for our food rations, she cycles over to take tea with some eccentric old lady she used to know when John was a boy. Oh, she is so fearfully busy all the time."

I was fit to burst when I heard all that. I just stood there out of sight, hoping that Hester would ask, "And what do you do all day, Mummy?" Then there would have been an awkward silence and Cordelia would have stuttered something about the church women's committee. At least someone around here is pulling their weight for the war.

I keep having to remind myself that as every day and night comes to an end, it must mean that we are much nearer the conclusion of this whole ghastly business.

CHAPTER 17

'I still don't understand, John. Why couldn't you have even asked the Palmers if I could be included in the party?'

John sighed. They were leaning against an old hull on the slipway near the yacht club and they had been over this several times. 'Bea. You're just being ridiculous. When someone of Palmer's standing asks you to join his family for a week's holiday, you can hardly ask if you could bring along some friends of your own.'

'But I'm not "some friends", I am your girlfriend. Doesn't that make a difference?'

'Well I think you are making a bit of mountain over this. It's only for a week, and anyway, it's too late now. We'll be leaving first thing.' John replied, picking up a handful of pebbles and chucking them into the sea, one by one.

Colonel Palmer had invited John to join him, his wife and some friends, for a week's leave in the Cameroon Highlands. In the old days, people had taken their holidays on the islands – Java, Sumatra or Borneo – but with the current situation it was now impossible to leave the country and the only places left to get a change of climate were the hill stations of Malaya. John had been flattered. Although he had attended a few evenings with the Palmers over the past few months, he was quite surprised to be asked to spend a whole week with them. All he had done was to successfully treat a skin condition with which Mrs Palmer had suffered for some time. Although Palmer probably knew that Beatrice was his girlfriend, she had not been invited. John wondered if it had something to do with the perceived difference in status between doctors and nurses, but of course he hadn't shared his thoughts with Bea.

'So who else is going on this little jaunt?' Bea persisted. Her hair was tied back into a ponytail and with the sun in her eyes she was forced to squint at him. She looked like a petulant child.

'Look Bea, I really don't know. Just his wife Diana and some civilian friends of hers. Oh, and I think Palmer's sister may be there too.'

'So you and a lot of nice young women. How cosy.'

'Oh for God's sake, you're not going to get jealous just because I want to do something that doesn't involve you?'

'Don't be ridiculous, I am not getting jealous, as you put it. But after all you do have your reputation to live up to,' she said in a choked voice. 'I hope you have a wonderful time.' She sprung up from where they were sitting by the slipway and strode towards the club house.

'Oh don't be like that, Bea. Come back!' John watched her go, knowing he should run after her but determined not to indulge her pettiness. Christ, why were women so difficult? All he wanted was a break. He'd had no time off since early January up at Port Dickson, and now there was a chance to spend some quality time away from the barracks and, if truth be told, away from Beatrice. The last couple of months since his birthday had been fun, but he'd had no time on his own, no time to take off the mask of the cheerful doctor; someone always wanted something from him. Recently he'd begun to notice things about Bea that irritated him; the way she always wanted to know exactly when their next date would be, the way she felt compelled to keep uttering little family mottos that made no sense to him and how she kept dropping hints about their future together. He was even beginning to wonder if he still fancied her. She no longer seemed to be the confident, independent woman he'd first met. Perhaps she was going to be exactly like all the previous women and become unreasonably possessive whenever he wanted some time to himself.

He continued to hurl pebbles into the sea as his anger churned around inside him. Not realising how long he'd been there, he reluctantly got to his feet and walked in the direction she'd gone, composing a grudging apology in his head. But she was nowhere to be seen. She must have called a taxi from the yacht club and he drove back to Gillman alone. Although they had a stilted conversation on the phone that evening where he had sworn to her that he would be the soul of virtue, he left the following morning with nothing resolved.

The Cameroon Highlands of Malaya were about five hundred miles away. The trip by car would have taken at least two months worth of petrol coupons and so they travelled first class by train. There were eight of them in the party and they stayed in a newly developed holiday resort of luxury bungalows. It was a relief to be away from the atmosphere of the mess and although he felt nervous on the first evening, once he relaxed, he enjoyed himself. He liked how the air felt cool and dry; nothing like the muggy heat of Singapore. It was even chilly enough in the evenings for them all to gather around a log fire. Inevitably, the conversation over dinner was about the war; the real one in Europe, and the threat of one in Malaya.

On the last morning, wanting to have some time away from the other guests, he followed a steep track that wound up into the mountains. After a long climb through trees that clung like moss to the steep slopes, he came to a clearing. To the west lay a flat plain that stretched all the way to the sea and, beyond it, the island of Penang. To the east, miles of endless mountain peaks were wrapped in banks of cumulus cloud; a vast impenetrable land that looked as far as John could tell, totally impassable to any enemy.

Being able to see a long way into the distance always made John feel peaceful and invigorated. It gave him a sense of freedom, a fresh perspective where he no longer felt hemmed in or obedient to anyone but himself. As he stood there, he heard a familiar low cry and two eagles soared past him. His skin prickled and he felt a rush of air into his chest; an exhilaration that he had not experienced for over two years. He watched as they circled and swooped and felt totally content with his solitude. If only he could stay there, drinking it all in.

As he returned to Singapore, he realised how much he had missed Bea. He hoped she was not still cross with him. Perhaps it would be better now that they had a break. For the first time in a while, he thought about Min and how much he missed her too. The sight of the eagles had brought back memories of the first holiday they'd spent in Scotland, after his father had finally left, when they'd both felt as if they'd been released from an interminable prison sentence.

For the remainder of the summer and into autumn of 1941, plans for the defence of Malaya and Singapore constantly shifted. The map looked like a jigsaw puzzle, with each new arrival of troop reinforcements being assigned a different piece of it to defend. Opinion was divided; if the Japs dared to attack Singapore, would it be from the north over the

Johore straits, assuming they had first been able to capture all of Malaya, or would it be by sea from the south, where they would have to face the big guns based at the Johore battery and Blakang Mati? Most of the civilians whom John came across still treated it all as a rather elaborate joke that would never quite reach the punch line. And anyway, now they had General Percival to protect them; he had made it quite clear that the production of rubber and tin was absolutely essential for the general war effort.

One evening, having spent an exhausting day supervising blood donor sessions for both troops and civilians, on top of all his routine work, he dropped in to the mess for a quick Stengah. Major King was sitting alone in his usual spot. He'd put on weight; his tunic strained at its buttons and his neck bulged over his tight collar.

'Drink, Garrett?'

John looked around the empty bar and felt he had little choice but to join him. As soon as they'd both got their drinks and lit cigarettes, King started to quiz him about his love-life. Not satisfied with the short answers John gave, King persisted with questions about where they went and what they did. It felt intrusive, almost voyeuristic. Rather than continue to fob him off, John began to relish telling him about how good the relationship with Bea was; how they often sailed to their magical island where they made love under the palm trees, and how much he had missed her when he'd been on his trip a few months back to the Cameroons, with Colonel Palmer. He made sure that he emphasised what a personal friend he was of the Palmers. King looked uncomfortable and gazed round the bar. When Richard Henderson walked in, King hailed him loudly.

'Ah Henderson, just the person, come and join us.'

'Hello Garrett,' said Henderson as he pulled up a chair, 'How are you? I hardly see anything of you these days. We haven't had a game of squash for months.'

John noticed his suntanned face framed with his flop of fair hair, now bleached fairer, and his sad blue eyes.

'Oh he's much too preoccupied for that, dear boy. He's got his hands full of romance,' King butted in.

Henderson blushed and looked away. 'Of course, Beatrice, how is she?

'She's fine, working as usual. Rotten shifts nurses seem to have. But we must have a game soon. I've been getting fat and lazy. Blame the woman! I was just telling King about my trip up to the Cameroon Highlands. Have you ever been?'

More drinks were called for and John, feeling slightly ashamed of how he'd baited King, attempted to steer the conversation back to the prospect of war. They chatted for a while about the whole situation and as soon as he could John made an excuse to leave. As he strolled across the parade ground, thick velvet air scented with frangipani wrapped itself around him. The tropical night whirred and hummed with a multitude of insects doing whatever insects do, oblivious to the plans of men and politicians.

CHAPTER 18

Bea sat on John's bed and looked around at the room. It was so much larger than her own at the sister's mess. Being only single-storey it had air holes at the top of the walls which kept it cool. Sparrows and occasionally bats flew through from one side to the other, and lizards darted about the cream-painted walls. A verandah ran along one side of it with a view of the bougainvillea-splashed garden, and on the other side a door led towards the Officers' mess.

'JG, why don't we try and do something with this?' Beatrice gestured to the empty walls. 'We could make it much cosier, a sort of home from home.' As soon as she'd posed the question, she regretted it, nervous that he would think she was being too pushy. 'Only if you want to, of course; it's just that the walls and floor look a bit bare and military.'

While John had been away with the Palmers in the Cameroons, she'd felt lonely and despairing. She couldn't understand why his attitude towards her had changed. She remembered something similar had happened with Nigel, her first great love. Of course, it wasn't until afterwards that she realised that the love had been one-way. She'd given Nigel everything; her time, her patience, her love and, worst of all, her virginity. But after a few months, he had apparently lost interest and had never returned any of her telephone calls or letters. She'd had a couple of dates with another man but then had joined the QAs and became too busy. There was something about the last few months with John that had convinced her that at last she had found the right man; that was of course until the frightful row. She had braced herself for an inevitable parting and resolved to spend more time with her friends at the hospital, but on his return there had been an emotional reunion and since then she couldn't fault his attentiveness.

'What a lovely idea Bea,' John replied, with an enthusiasm which Bea hoped wasn't artificial. 'We could go down town and perhaps find some rugs and pictures for the walls. What do you think?'

She made sure that it was he who brought the topic up again, but when he did, decorating his room became their next project. For several weekends in a row, they scoured the shops and markets. One afternoon in Chinatown, she pulled on his elbow and steered them into a small, dark shop where every inch of the floor and walls were covered with oriental rugs; burgundy, claret, indigo and pale cream. In the corner sat an elderly Chinese man, puffing on a cigarette and grinning at them as they gazed around. He shuffled towards them and, with a practiced flick of his arm, flung back the rug on the top of a pile to reveal the one underneath; and the next, and the next.

'Aren't they wonderful?' said Bea, 'I'd love to have a room that had rugs hanging from the walls and flowing across the floor. Just imagine the luxury.'

They bought two; one was russet, which John said matched her hair, and the other one was cream and red. To Bea's surprise, John talked about how he could imagine the rugs in a future house that one day they would live in back in England. She hardly dared hope. He also bought a small burgundy one which he was determined to package up and send to his mother. Since his trip he had mentioned her several times; clearly he was beginning to miss her. Bea wondered how she would ever match up to her.

In October, she persuaded John to take her to the Thimithi Festival of fire walking at the Sri Mariamman Hindu Temple. Her friend Margaret had told her it was a spectacle not to be missed.

'It'll be so interesting, JG,' Bea pleaded, sensing his reluctance. 'It's all about the goddess Draupadi, who was made to walk barefoot on burning coals without showing any pain in order to prove her fidelity to her husband. So now, to respect the courage of the goddess, every year the Hindu priests and other devotees demonstrate their faith and fortitude by walking across a twenty-one foot pit of burning coals without showing any pain.'

'Oh crikey, I'm really not keen on all that sort of stuff, all that unconditional devotion, but I suppose it might be worth a look, so long you don't decide to join in and go hopping across the coals.'

When they reached the temple, the courtyard was already packed with noisy spectators. They climbed up to a balcony set aside for Europeans which provided a wonderful view. Even up there they could feel the heat of the embers. As the ceremony started, devotees of all ages, dressed in yellow robes and carrying boughs of green foliage, processed slowly in, lead by the most important priest. One by one they crossed the pit of embers. Some ran, others hopped and some seemed to stroll across, as if they were just out for a walk. Once over the other side of the ember pit, there was a trough of white liquid, allegedly goat's milk, into which each devotee gratefully dipped his feet before sitting to rub yellow turmeric all over their soles. From where Bea was sitting, she couldn't see any obvious injuries.

'Gosh, wasn't that amazing?' She turned to John, her eyes shining. 'They must have tremendous faith in order to avoid getting burnt.'

'Actually I think it's more about the heat of the coals, walking fast and being clever not to reveal that it's painful.'

Beatrice groaned at him. 'Oh you cynic, don't you believe faith comes into it at all?'

'Well I just don't see how having faith in something can stop the natural laws of physics.'

'So don't you believe in anything, JG? Is everything explained by the laws of physics?' She turned away from him, her sense of excitement crushed.

'I don't think I have a faith in the way you mean it. Come on, let's get out of here and go somewhere quieter.'

He pulled her hand as they dodged through the crowd and, finding a relatively empty side street, they slowed their pace to stroll back towards the hospital.

'Come on JG, I really want to know. What do you believe in? What happened to your Quaker upbringing?'

'I don't think much of it really rubbed off on me. Every Sunday at boarding school we had to attend Quaker meeting, but mostly I used the time to drift off into my own thoughts. When I was about fifteen, my mother took me to see her friend Dorothy Walton; she was the woman my mother used to discuss religion and philosophy with, as a refuge from the civil war that raged at home. The first time I met her, I was a rather arrogant teenager and I told her bluntly that I was an atheist. She smiled and asked me to explain myself, which of course I couldn't do very convincingly. After that, she invited me to visit her regularly to talk through the whole issue and she lent me lots of books. For a while I really got caught up in it all, but once I went to London, I'm ashamed to say I had rather too many other things to distract me.'

'Yes. I can just imagine you as the arrogant teenager. So what did she believe in?' Bea felt less annoyed with him now and began to enjoy the discussion. Although they had explored all sorts of topics, they had never touched on religion.

'Lordy, it's hard to remember all the details. Something about theosophy, and the suggestion that if each person makes their own search for truth through the study and experience of world religions, philosophy, science, the arts and so on, they would be lead towards the Divine.'

'I've never heard of theosophy,' said Bea, 'My parents are C of E and I was brought up to say my prayers and go to church on Sundays. I've never really questioned it, but it still makes sense to me now. But I don't quite understand what this Dorothy person did believe in after all her studying.'

'I used to be quite confused by it all,' replied John, pulling her down beside him one of the wooden benches in the hospital grounds. 'Dorothy talked of concepts I'd barely heard of, such as, universal consciousness, reincarnation and the concept of karma. But it seems that from her own study of Hinduism, Buddhism, Christianity and astrology she sifted out her own interpretations and came to the conclusion that each person has to find their own truth, rather than blindly accepting some kind of religious dogma that they never question.'

'So JG, that takes me back to my original question. What is your truth? Do you believe in any sort of god?' She looked straight at him. He wasn't going to wriggle out of it this time.

'Well, I don't really believe in a personal creator who

expects me to behave in a certain way and will become angry with me if I don't. If there is a God, I have never been quite sure why we have to gather together gratefully, week after week and tell him what a good chap he is.'

Bea felt quite shaken. She had never heard someone talk so disrespectfully about God. Before she could stop herself, she imagined the shock on her parent's faces when they discovered what sort of a man she had married. She didn't know how to respond and was gathering her thoughts when John, sensing her discomfort, added gently,

'But right now Bea, I'm not sure what I believe. I just have a really strong sense of being alive and wanting to stay so.'

CHAPTER 19

November 1st 1941

Dear John

A little while ago at the hospital canteen, I was washing up with Mrs Whittaker's ladies maid – a nice little old-fashioned quiet party – and we were talking about all sorts and I asked her, "What do you most wish for in life?", and she said, "Just freedom and a home of my own to do what I like and not simply serve other people." And then she turned to me and said, "What's your greatest wish?", and without thinking, not meaning to say it, these words came out, "I want to see my son once again before I die". Well there it is, in all its crude simplicity and sincerity; nothing more to be said. I probably shouldn't have said anything, as she looked a bit taken aback.

Mrs Whittaker of course is one of the more fortunate ones as her maid is over the age for call up. I must say though, having managed for so long with just you and I in the flat looking after ourselves, it tickles me rather to hear the reactions of certain other wealthy la-dee-dahs around here who are losing their "help" because now all the young women are being called up for war service. The havoc that has been caused in all those households where previously they rang a bell and "someone" came, but where now, the bell is still there but the "someone" has gone. Life's tragedy summed up in two words – "Cook's gone!" So not for nothing have I been through umpteen cook-less years.

There is an uneasy atmosphere round about. Everyone is keyed up for the expected winter onslaught. I've just got my tin helmet and Fire Guard badge. We are all taking on more and more. Yesterday I was asked to take over the entire management and running of the hospital garden as the head girl is leaving, but it means at least four days a week given up to organising both the workers and the planting of vegetables, apart from all the physical labour. But without a car and the way my joints seem to creak these days, I really don't think I could manage it, though I was flattered to be asked. So you can see how your poor old mother is working hard.

You would have smiled if you'd seen me give my talk about different sorts of religious faith at the WI the other day. First I read out the description of the Hindu fire-walking ceremony that you wrote about which you had attended with Beatrice (I was surprised how quickly your letter arrived this time). Then I rang my little Tibetan bell to show the faith of the Holy Man of Tibet who trusts that food will be brought to him if his belief is strong. Then I finished with my own favourite about the little black boy who is running a race but is clearly losing. His legs are going slower and slower. But then suddenly his little black legs seem to go faster and he mutters something to himself with his eyes half closed. He wins the race and afterwards when they ask him about it he says, "I was talking to de Lord, saying, 'You pick 'em up, I put dem down, you pick 'em up, I put dem down' and my little legs went faster and faster!" It sounds like me when I'm riding my bicycle over to see Dorothy. I am so enjoying our weekly discussions.

Take care. Missing you. Your ever loving mother.

November 5th 1941

Yesterday I gave myself my own little birthday treat. I went out alone to the five o'clock cinema to see a showing of "Lady Hamilton". Then I came home and had a quiet little supper in my back room sanctum and listened to a BBC concert, of John Ireland playing Beethoven's *Emperor Concerto*. It was so moving. I find music stirs up my heart and sometimes it hurts so much but somehow I simply can't live without it. I wonder if I shall ever hear it dry-eyed again.

Nov 13th 1941

Such a lovely soft rainy day; such as John would have enjoyed to the full, even though he might be homesick yet for his hot blue sky. Yesterday, when I was tweaking my curtains for the blackout, quite the loveliest thing I looked on was Venus going down over Lymington, as liquid, lambent, lucid and translucent as the water in between me and her and the darkening sky after sunset. It was cruel to shut it out. Tonight two swans were just below and they stood out like two white woodcuts of great beauty against the background of leaden water. I can hardly describe how striking it was, even though I have seen it a hundred times before. A little colony of dabchicks were dipping and bobbing about and the calls of redshanks, snipe and dunlin echoed all around and across the ebbing tide. There is little or no time for bird-watching really, unlike Frank, who has no engagements or social activities, and just does as he pleases. I often feel that it would be so lovely simply to do nothing, never again, not for anyone, but to sit and think till the sap runs down, and then I would be at peace. But I must keep busy.

December 4th 1941

The papers are full of the reports of the two battleships that have now arrived at the naval base in Singapore. They say that the Prince of Wales is really state-of-the-art. I am not sure that I believe that the mere presence of these two war ships guarding Singapore will be sufficient to show the Japanese that we mean business. I have an awful feeling that things are going to get a lot worse.

I wish I understood about war. As far as I can see, we humans have been at it for as long as we have inhabited the planet. I suppose back in history it was a squabble between two countries about land and resources. But this war, like the last one, feels as if it is careering out of control. How many will have to die this time for the greed of just a few? Traditionally of course it was always the men that fought while the women stayed out of it and suffered the consequences, but of course now women are playing quite an active part, even if they aren't on the front line. I remember feeling quite confused about George's reaction to the Great War. His age meant he wasn't called up near until the end. I think he imagined he would escape without having to do anything. But when the call came, he conveniently remembered that he came from a family of Quakers, claimed to be a conscientious objector and got away with joining the East Surrey's with an office job. He didn't care about war or peace. He only cared about himself.

I wonder how I would react if I was a man and expected

to serve my country. How would I feel about fighting and killing others? I suppose one would have to develop a way of coping, by forgetting that the soldier one is expected to kill is actually a real person, with a family, just like oneself.

CHAPTER 20

He felt Beatrice shift in his arms. On the nights they squeezed into his narrow bed, neither of them slept soundly. For a long time after they had started seeing each other, whenever they spent an evening together she would always slip back to the sister's mess, where a friend would make sure there was a door unlocked for her to creep in undetected. But since his return from the Cameroons, she often stayed with him all night. Their relationship had subtly shifted; Bea seemed more relaxed and spent time with her own friends, and now she was less needy of him, he no longer felt trapped.

He was drifting back to sleep when a loud clap of thunder startled him awake. He waited for the inevitable rain to start pounding the roof, but instead heard what sounded like gunfire. The clock on the bedside table showed 4.15am. He slipped out of bed and peeled back the blind. There was a full moon and searchlights were criss-crossing the sky down towards the harbour. Then more stuttering gunfire.

'Quick Bea! Get over here! Something's happening.'

Bea groaned, but rolled out of bed and joined him at the window.

'What is it? It can't be an air raid. What on earth…' Then they both heard the wail of the siren. 'No, it must just be a practice. Look, all the street lights are still on.'

There was another explosion and a drone of planes, followed by silence.

'Do you know, I think this could be what we've all been

waiting for. It's rather exciting, isn't it?'

'Actually, I suddenly feel a bit scared.' said Bea, 'can't we get back into bed?'

They cuddled together for what was left of the night, talking about what the war would actually mean for them. Bea would have to work extra duty shifts if there were casualties. John knew he'd be busy wherever he was. Inevitably, they would see less of each other.

'So if the Japs do invade, you won't be involved in any of the fighting over in Malaya, will you?'

He felt her shivering and drew her closer.

'Honestly Bea, I don't think we're likely to go over the straits. Our lot are supposed to be defending the naval base here and of course all the civilians.'

'Good. Now we've come this far, I don't want to lose you in some awful jungle battle.' She kissed him and snuggled closer.

'It'll be all right, sweetheart. Even if we are near any battles, I'll always be far behind the front line sorting out the wounded and getting them back to you at Alexandra.'

John half hoped that what he was telling her wasn't true. He wanted to be in the thick of it near the front line. Even with all the preparation and training he had received, he still couldn't visualise what a battle would look like in reality.

'And you,' he said, poking her in the ribs, 'if it comes to it, are going to be the sweet, smiling angel who will nurse all the chaps back to health, whose wounds I will have initially dressed back at the RAP.'

'Oh my, how romantic,' she replied, 'Of course I'm a simple, silly nurse who does the doctor's bidding and I haven't a brain in my head. Perhaps you'll be able to send me little love letters, tucked into some poor wounded soldier's blanket.'

'Well that might be interesting if they fell into the wrong hands now, wouldn't it!'

Just after six, they both got dressed. He wrapped his arms around her. 'All will be well. Just you see.'

'Umm, let's hope.' She kissed him and made a brave smile. 'Now I must dash and get on duty.'

Crossing the quadrangle to the MI room, there was a smell of smoke and as John came through the door, his orderly, Derek, greeted him.

'Well, it's happened then Doc.'

'So it was a real air raid then, not just a practice?'

'Seems so. I don't know what the damage is yet, but it's real enough. There is a briefing at 8.00am.'

It became clear that others also believed it was an air raid. The line of usual suspects turning up for sick parade was surprisingly short. Clearly the excitement of some possible action at last had made most of them realise that they didn't want to be signed off after all.

As soon as he'd finished, he went to the mess for breakfast and sat down next to Roger Lester. They were shortly joined by Major King.

'So have you both heard the news?' he asked.

'Yes, I heard the planes and the anti-aircraft guns,' replied John, 'do we know what was hit?'

'It seems,' replied King, 'that most of the damage was confined to Chinatown and they missed the strategic areas completely, which is astonishing since there was a full moon and the whole bloody city was lit up like a Christmas tree. With all the talk and rumours that have been going on, it seems that no one had thought about imposing a blackout.'

'Sounds like the typical civilian approach to the whole idea of war. Do nothing and carry on as usual,' said Roger.

'Well apparently there is a briefing from Ellerton at 8.00am, so I suppose we'd better get ourselves over there.' said John.

As the morning unrolled, the news got worse. There were frequent bulletins on the wireless and a series of messengers reported to the mess, where most of them were assembled, awaiting further orders. The Japanese had landed at three different sites on the east coast of Malaya. They had also dropped bombs on the Philippines, on Hong Kong, and somewhere called Pearl Harbour. John felt rather stupid, because at first he couldn't quite understand what the significance was of the Japanese bombing an island in Hawaii. What did that have to do with anything?

Henderson, who was sitting next to him when the news came through, looked at him with surprise and said, 'Pearl Harbour is where the Americans have their largest naval base. Most of it has been destroyed. America has now declared war on Japan. Don't you see?'

'Shit! Yes of course. How stupid of me,' John replied, 'Does this mean that at long last we're really part of it all?'

Apart from the briefings about the events that had taken place overnight, on a more local level, orders were given that all car headlamps were to be covered with brown paper to deflect the beam downwards; the blackout, which previously no one had taken seriously, was due to be strictly enforced, so much so that they were warned not even to light up a cigarette in the street in case it could be seen by some eagle-eyed Jap pilot.

As they dispersed to go about their normal duties, John's mind buzzed with thoughts and plans. However, his usual list of house calls didn't change just because the world had suddenly tumbled into war. After a quick lunch and on the way to some of his patients, he took a detour downtown to see what the damage was. The most severely affected areas were cordoned off, but he could see that Robinson's department store in Raffles Place had been hit; broken glass was being swept into piles and firemen were still directing their hoses at the smoking remains. In Chinatown, the narrow streets were strewn with rubble where tenement blocks of houses had simply imploded. Dust-covered Chinese were either running back and forth or sitting on piles of bricks, wailing and rocking. Some scrabbled at the debris while others feebly tried to douse the embers with buckets of water. Screaming ambulances were still ferrying the wounded away to the General Hospital. Later it was announced that sixty-one people had died instantly and over one hundred and thirty had been injured.

The damage was nothing compared to what he had heard of the destruction of London and the major cities of England, but still it gave him a rather shocking insight into what his fellow countrymen had been experiencing for the last eighteen months.

That evening, they learnt that the *Prince of Wales* and the *Repulse* had left the naval base and were headed up the east coast of Malaya where the invading force had first landed. Their mission was to attack any Japanese transports that would be landing more troops. Two days later, when both these massive ships had been sunk with the loss of over eight hundred men, John and his fellow officers began to realise that their lives might actually be in danger.

CHAPTER 21

The young man lay propped up on two pillows. His face, or what was left of it, flinched with pain. Most of the skin had been burnt off. His left leg was swathed in bandages which a nurse was slowly unravelling in order to dress the wounds he had sustained when jumping from the deck of the sinking *Prince of Wales*. He had been rescued eventually, but only after he had been floating, semi-conscious, in the flaming oily water for a couple of hours, strapped by one his mates to a spare life belt. He'd been lucky.

He didn't seem to notice that he was now the focus of John and a small group of his stretcher bearers, whom he had brought to Alexandra Hospital as part of their extra training in dealing with casualties. Up until now, all the first aid lectures he had given them had been purely theoretical, with them taking turns at role playing the victims. Now it was time for them to learn what they might actually see in battle.

The nurse removed the final bandage and the blood-soaked dressing underneath. His purple, bruised thigh had a jagged oozing gash which had been sutured, but was clearly infected. John looked round at their faces. Kelly had gone pale. Barker and Johnson were impassive, nodding as the nurse explained how to clean and re-bandage a wound. Stillman appeared uncomfortable and stared at the floor.

After they'd seen several other casualties from the two ships and listened to some of their stories, they walked back to the medical inspection room to continue with the checking and packing up of equipment, should they need to move their base. Kelly fell into step beside John.

'That poor bloody blighter, Doc, with the burned face. He was only a young lad.'

'You looked a bit shocked back there, Kelly. Is that the first time you have seen wounds that bad?'

'Well it was more the sight of his burnt face that got to me, Doc. It makes you wonder though, don't it? After all this sitting on our arses all these months, we haven't got a clue what's going to happen next.'

'You don't need to worry, honestly, you'll be fine. Look, all you have to do is keep your head and remember what you've been taught.'

Kelly paused. 'It's not so much that, it's just that with the first air raid that killed all those Chinese downtown, and now seeing that lad, I'm not sure I'm quite ready to die.'

John was taken aback by his frankness. Apart from his earlier homesickness wobble, Kelly was someone who had always appeared confident and skilful in the training exercises. It suddenly dawned on him that however well he had trained them to deal with casualties in the field, it hadn't occurred to him that they might be afraid. He muttered some banal response in what Min would describe as her, "best foot forward" voice, and strode on ahead of the group on the pretext of needing to do some paperwork.

That evening was the first time he'd seen Bea for what seemed liked ages, but was in fact just over a week. So much had shifted. They drove slowly down town through the blacked-out streets, with the pouring rain challenging his wipers. It was absolutely dark and with his now muffled headlamps, it was difficult to avoid the pedestrians who darted out in front of the car. It was hard to recognise what had once been so familiar under a blaze of street lamps, shop signs, and coloured lights.

He was relieved to have Bea all to himself. She had been on duty almost continuously since the first air raid and was exhausted. Not noticing anything she ate, she spoke rapidly about everything that had happened. The hospital had filled up quickly with survivors from the two battleships, as well as injured troops that had been brought by train down from northern Malaya. Although there was little in terms of wounds that she had not dealt with during her time as a casualty nurse, it was the sheer numbers of wounded young men that had taken her by surprise. When she finally drew breath, looking a little teary, she dabbed her eyes, and reached for his hand across the table.

'Oh goodness, JG, I really needed that. I don't think I could have gone on much longer without being able to let it out to someone who has actually got the time to listen'.

'I'll always have time to listen to you, little bee.' He smiled and squeezed her hand.

'So, that's enough about me. I heard that you'd been up to the one of the wards today to see some patients with a few of your team.'

He began to tell her about his visit that morning and Kelly's reaction.

'I know it sounds totally arrogant Bea, but you know my mantra phrase, "All will be well"? It's just that I have always had such a strong feeling that whatever happens I will be okay, that I had completely ignored the fact that others don't feel the same. Most of the men and officers I've spoken to are so relieved that at last we can join in, they are bristling with excitement waiting for it all to start. Henderson put it quite well this morning; he said that with the blackout, it's as if the theatre lights have gone down and we are all waiting for the curtain to rise.'

John pushed his plate to one side and fiddled with an unused fork on the table.

'Of course they've been trained to deal with aspects of killing and death, but my stretcher bearers didn't sign up to be fighters. I have been going on and on at them all these months about splints and supplies and the need to check and re-check, that I'd totally forgotten that the equipment provided by the War Office doesn't include a philosophy about how to make sense of it all; they have to work this one out for themselves.'

'So you mean they've only really been trained to deal with the wounded, not with dead bodies or the fact that they might be injured or killed themselves?'

'Well, yes, I suppose so. Now that you've said it, I feel totally stupid. I suppose we've all been pretending there'll be a war for so long, that now we actually have a real one, all these issues have got to be addressed.'

'But JG, isn't that the role of the army chaplain? Couldn't you ask yours to come and give the stretcher bearers a talk about it all?'

'Oh I don't know. I'm not sure that I want some God-bothering, do-gooder interfering.'

'Oh John, now you are being stupid. You can't let your prejudices interfere with what's needed. It's what they're paid to do. That's why they have them in the army. Have you even met the chaplain for your regiment?'

'No. Well of course I know who he is, though in fact he hasn't been in Singapore for very long, but if he is anything like the last one he will be a right royal pain in the arse. So far I've managed to avoid actually speaking to him!'

Two days later, John sought him out. He sprang to his feet as John entered the chaplain's office and held his outstretched hand towards him in greeting. About forty, he was slightly taller, slim, yet muscular, with fair curly hair and amazing blue eyes.

'Hello Captain Garrett, I'm Peter Castle. I've really been looking forward to meeting you. I have heard so much about you; it seems that you are a pretty popular medic.' He shook John's hand firmly and gestured to him to take a seat.

Surprised by his friendliness, having expected someone who would be flimsy, quietly spoken, or perhaps oozing godliness at every pore, John sat down in the vacant chair. Peter Castle sat on the edge of the desk and swung his legs.

'I've been meaning to come and see you.' His accent was Lancashire or Yorkshire. John could never tell the difference. 'I'd really like a chance to spend some time with you, get to know you and your stretcher bearers and the basics of all the equipment you will be using. If this thing really kicks off, the best place for me to be will be working right alongside you and your team in the regimental aid post and I want to be able to help as much as possible, not get in the way.'

'Oh, right, yes, of course,' John stuttered back. He had never even thought about the role of an army chaplain in a battle. Of course that's where he would be. His job was to minister to the wounded and dying. But because the previous chaplain had been a lazy sod who had never been anywhere near them on training exercises, he'd assumed that his replacement would be from the same mould.

John began to relax and told him about his work, about

how long the wait had been for this Far East war to begin and how most of the men were eager for the fighting to start. Many of lads in the regiment were disappointed that they weren't up country in Malaya pushing back the Japs, but were having to wait patiently in Singapore in a defensive position. He told him about Simmonds, whose two brothers had been killed at Dunkirk, and how he was so full of hatred for the enemy, any enemy, that John was worried he could become a liability under pressure.

'I was having a chat with one of the lads the other day, a chap called Kelly, after we'd seen some of the wounds sustained by the sailors from the battleships, and he's having a bit of a wobble about it all, you know, expecting the worst, that sort of thing. Someone suggested you might be the best person to chat to them about all the psychological stuff, and how to cope?'

'Of course, Captain. No problem. Anytime. So would you be free now to give me a guided tour of your MI room?'

'Umm, yes, I've got about half an hour before I need to do house calls.' John stood up and they strolled across the quadrangle. 'By the way, do I call you Reverend, or Padre or what? When I'm on duty, everyone calls me Doc, but informally, I'm John.'

'Thanks John. The same goes for me. Call me Peter, but officially I'm known as the Padre.'

By Christmas, Singapore was packed, as refugees of all races and classes had swarmed into the city to avoid the steadily advancing Japanese, who were by now only four hundred miles away. John had been busier than ever, preparing and packing up medical equipment, as well as all the treasures from his room. Their precious rugs and pictures had to be crated into boxes that could be sealed against the ravages of either the enemy or hungry white ants. Meanwhile, his stretcher bearers were either busy working alongside the troops, digging defences on the south side of the island, or assisting him, ensuring that the troops had daily Alum foot baths, to toughen up their feet against blisters. John loved it; at last he could write to Min about something interesting and worthwhile.

But it was still Christmas and not even a war would stop the British celebrating in their traditional fashion. John ate his first turkey meal with the troops at lunchtime, drank too much beer and dozed away the afternoon while he waited for Bea to come off duty so that they could go out to dinner with Colonel Palmer and his family. There were about ten of them around the table that night, pretty much the same people that John had accompanied to the Cameroon Highlands earlier in the year, but this time, he had made sure Bea had been invited.

With the curtained windows, flickering candlelight, and a festive table, it felt to John as if there was absolutely nothing to worry about. There was more traditional Christmas fare and more to drink, with the usual toasts to King and country. But what was different, he noticed, was the way they talked and what they talked about. No longer were they trading snatches of society gossip. Now there was a level of frankness and honesty which would never have occurred in those carefree pre-war days.

At the end of the meal, Palmer raised his glass, 'I'd like to propose a toast to all our brave soldiers who are out there right now, in the dark, damp jungle fighting for England.' They all stood once more and raised their glasses.

'I completely agree with that, Archie,' said Diana, Palmer's wife, as they resumed their seats. She paused, as if still wondering if she should say what she said next. 'I am sorry to sound so cynical, but what about all the innocent civilians? What about us? What about our need to be brave and courageous if the Japs do succeed? I mean, out here, are we really fighting for good old England? It seems to me as if we are trying to protect, on the one hand a bunch of businessmen whose only real interest is in making as much money as possible, and on the other, the population of Chinese and Malays, who are just as likely to swap sides depending on who pays them the most.' John was surprised by her forthrightness.

'But, Darling,' interrupted Palmer, 'that's the whole point. That is what the Empire is for. For years, the British have provided peace and prosperity to countries all over the world. We have given them stability, trade, education, and freedom. That is what this war is about. The fight is for freedom and we have to stick it out until we win.'

'Well I'm not terribly sure that I want to stick around and see who wins,' Diana replied in a low voice. 'Personally I think I'd much rather be on the first boat out of here.'

Pushing her chair back from the table and, looking around her guests, she asked in a small voice, 'Doesn't anyone else think it's time to leave? Just what exactly do you imagine will happen to us if the Japanese, rather the British win the war for Singapore? Look, I'm sorry, I've probably said too much. Excuse me.' She hurried out of the room.

There was a long silence until Bea said in a quiet voice, 'Actually, you know, I think Mrs Palmer was quite brave to say what she did. At the hospital we have been talking about the huge numbers of people who are now in Singapore. We won't be able to look after everyone. Doesn't it make sense for people to start evacuating just in case things get worse?'

'Let's continue this discussion in the drawing room,' said Archie Palmer, 'but let me first check that Diana is all right.'

Once they were seated and coffee and liquors had been brought, John asked, 'I've got a question for you. We are all talking about bravery and courage. Are they the same thing or is there a subtle difference?'

Palmer's sister suggested, 'Well, soldiers have to be brave, don't they? They have to do things that might put them in danger, even if they're frightened. They can't show it, but it's their duty, it's what they signed up for.'

'Yes, and perhaps courage,' Bea joined in, 'is doing something risky, that you don't have to do purely to help someone else; like saving a person who is drowning, or pulling someone from a burning building.'

'I think you are right, Beatrice,' said Diana, who had now composed herself and rejoined the party. 'But don't you think that courage has a special quality to it? If my memory for languages serves me, the word courage comes from the French word, "coeur" meaning heart. Courage is the ability to carry out a dangerous task to help another, knowing full well that the outcome may put you at risk, but you do it in spite of feeling afraid. Bravery, on the other hand comes from the Spanish word, "bravado", meaning a spontaneous act of valour. It refers to an action which isn't planned, isn't necessarily done for any specific person and the outcome is not always predictable. It may even still cause injury, but any fear is generally suppressed.'

A few days after Christmas, John and Bea were sharply reminded about Diana's profound statement. Bea rushed into his room early one evening looking pale and flustered. She and her colleagues at Alexandra Hospital had been summoned to the matron's office where they had been told about what happened when the Japanese soldiers had captured St Albert's Hospital in Hong Kong on Christmas Day. In spite of the staff doing their utmost to defend themselves, not only had the soldiers massacred nearly all the patients, but they had also systematically raped a dozen or more of the nurses. Some of those nurses were the young QAs that Bea had travelled out with on her way to the Far East.

CHAPTER 22

January 10th 1942

Dear John,

The newspaper reports are not very encouraging just now. In spite of my large map, it is difficult to follow what is going on in the Far East. I have no idea where you are. I haven't heard anything since your Christmas cable which arrived last week. So at least I know you were all right when you sent it. In fact, you sounded quite buoyant.

Everyone around seems to be either down with or getting up with gastric flu, though it's no use being ill here now. Dr Stewart has gone to Aldershot and others are being called up on all sides. We shall soon have only Dr Mowbray to mend everything, and I don't have much faith in him. I shall just have to stay well.

It's been so cold I have been wearing one of your sweaters under my coat when I've been doing my stint in the hospital garden. There are potatoes to dig and leeks to pull up and clean with awful icy water. Soon we will have to start preparing the ground as best we can for planting the spring vegetables and there are plans to dig up the remaining lawn areas to increase the production. By the time I have done a day's work, I really do feel as if I am digging for victory.

I have at last made some new friends there; Joan Lovecock and Millicent White. I know you would like them. They must be about ten years younger than me. They joined the gardening team in the autumn. It has made me really look forward to the days when they are there; they really are such characters and we seem to have these most amazing conversations about life and all its mysteries. It was a treat to be invited to their cottage in Shirley Holmes yesterday. I think they both have some independent means. How I envy their companionship and the space they have, with an acre of their own woodland behind the cottage. I believe that Joan was once married, but it all went horribly wrong and for the last few years she and Millie have teamed up together.

Now that the war has reached your part of the world, I feel as if I can talk about you because you are as involved as anyone. It is a delight to be able to start making new friends and have someone else with whom I can share my burdens. It is rare to meet people who are willing to really listen to what one is saying and who don't need to talk endlessly about themselves. Joan and Millie appear to be genuinely interested. Of course I still see Dorothy every week and she always asks after you. We spent a delightful Christmas together. I told a little white lie to Cordelia and pretended that Dorothy was going to be all alone, but in truth her companion was there and the three of us had a very jolly time.

I will continue posting letters to you though I have no idea if you will ever receive them or if they will get lost en route. I hope and pray for your safety.

Your ever devoted Min

January 23rd 1942

My heart sank when I heard the news of the first air raids

over Singapore back in December. I pray that his medical room has a red cross painted on the roof. Up until now I have followed the war overseas rather haphazardly, trusting that others will tell me of the important events; it seemed easier to concentrate on England and what was happening on our own doorstep. But now I have hung a big world map on the wall so that when I listen to the news bulletins I will have a sense of where all these places are.

As long as I can keep busy I can manage, but as soon as I return home I can feel myself fretting about John's safety. I hope no one can see through the brave face I put on. Sometimes it's as if I share my life with a large green dragon who lumbers along beside me and keeps suggesting a variety of catastrophes which might be waiting to befall me; lost keys or purses, a fall from my bicycle or something much worse concerning John. On good days, I can dismiss his more outlandish suggestions, but once he has me fired up with an idea, he sits back on his scaly haunches with a smile of smug satisfaction and watches me while I agonise my way through a range of possible plans. Some days he doesn't bother to get up at all and just when I think I've got away with it, I see a little flock of worries, pecking away at my newly seeded sense of calm. I could do with a brave Saint George to help me deal with him once and for all.

It has been one of those foggy damp days when it never seems to become light. Sitting in my little back room, the twigs and branches in the garden drip with moisture, even though it isn't actually drizzling. The cold has seeped right into my marrow and I don't seem to be able to keep warm. It seems a thousand ages ago since John set sail from these shores and people seem to think that it will be many more before he sets foot in England again. Surely now that America is involved, things should be over sooner?

January 31st 1942

How I hate these dark mornings and the evenings that seem to arrive in the middle of the afternoon! The sun, if there ever is any, seems to hover over Lymington as if it has no energy for anything else. Today I called in at the Herringham's for tea, but it was pitch dark when I left and halfway home my bicycle lamp battery gave up on me. I thought I could manage, but very soon I was completely lost. I didn't recognise a thing. It wasn't until a kind man came along in a car and stopped to ask if I was all right. Then he drove slowly, a little way ahead of me, to make sure I was able to reach home safely. The darkness was so all-enveloping.

PART 2

CHAPTER 23

'So when do you think it will start?' John asked.

'It's going to be a complete shambles,' scoffed Ellerton. 'In all my years as a soldier, I have never seen such an almighty cock-up as this whole campaign. What with the misinformation and all the dithering about, the whole thing is bloody ridiculous.'

Lt Colonel Ellerton paced to and fro outside the rickety Malay hut that served as Battalion HQ; every few minutes, he consulted his wristwatch. John had never seen him so worked up. He was a tall, clean shaven man, over six foot, with short brown hair and hazel eyes. He had a kind, open face. John guessed he was in his mid forties. In all the dealings John had had with him in the build up to the war, he always seemed to achieve a perfect balance between thoughtful observation and a wicked sense of humour. John had never met anyone quite like him.

'Well, put it this way Garrett, to use your field of expertise,' Ellerton continued, 'it's as if a surgeon has suddenly decided to operate on a patient, but has found that there is no ambulance to bring the patient to the hospital, no time to prepare the theatre for the proposed surgery and no proper equipment. Seriously, the whole plan is ridiculous. Unless we have more time to get all the troops and guns into position, there is absolutely no chance that we can surprise the enemy. I just hope I can persuade the brigadier to postpone the attack until dawn tomorrow, when we will hopefully have everyone in place and proper artillery backup.'

John felt anxious for the first time. With his limited experience, if Ellerton had no confidence, then what hope was there? It was supposed to be their first real battle. The Lancashires had been ordered to attack and seize the high ground on either side of the gorge at Bukit Payang. This area was currently held by the Japanese, who, from their position, could pretty much see anything the British were up to for miles around. On either side, the ridge was surrounded by dense jungle. The aim of the attack was to open a way up for the remaining troops of the 45th Indian Division and two battalions of the Australian Infantry Forces to retreat south and so escape total destruction. As preparations were being made, the excitement that had rippled through the troops was palpable. After more than a week of ignominious retreats, they were desperate to attack.

The first orders the battalion had received to leave Singapore Island and travel by road and train to Segamat had been a surprise to everyone. As a reserve battalion, responsible for internal security, they had been engaged for the past couple of months in monitoring fifth column activities and shoring up the defences on the beaches to the south and the east of the island, where it was always presumed that the Japanese would attempt an invasion. When, in the second week of January the call had come to move north into Malaya, it was like a soldier's dream come true. At last, some action to be proud of.

But so far, the only action had consisted of long marches in pouring rain towards Segamat and Jementah. There, they had set up camp, dug defence ditches and cleared areas of land from dense undergrowth. At Segamat, they had experienced their first close encounter with dive bombing and enemy machine gun fire. Fortunately, no one was wounded. The next week was one of total confusion. Orders came and were then countermanded. They joined up with other units with different commanders and were then sent off in opposite directions. They advanced, they retreated. Despite Major Holland's best efforts as quartermaster, they frequently went all day without food as the supply trucks not only had to move between each of the four companies, but also took second priority over the movement of essential fighting equipment.

To begin with, back in Singapore, John had packed his medical equipment, all carefully checked and labelled, into a large lorry that would serve as the regimental aid post. But on arrival at Labis, he was told that the lorry was needed elsewhere and that it would all have to be unloaded. Furious, he gathered what he could and distributed it in haversacks stowed into the few available cars and two ambulance trucks. Some supplies had to be left with B. Echelon. In theory, if the battalion became separated over miles of swampy, inhospitable country, John would try and keep the RAP as close as possible to battalion headquarters, so that he could keep in touch with the latest orders, and any walking wounded casualties would know where he was. But so far, he'd had little to deal with, except a few cases of trench foot, caused by long marches with cold wet feet and skin rubbed sore by sodden army boots. No wonder the Japs all wore gym shoes.

Fortunately, Ellerton was successful in getting the attack postponed and the following morning, as the sky slowly turned from charcoal to pale pink, they were all as prepared as they ever would be.

John had set up his RAP in an ambulance truck, positioned out of necessity on a long straight road, some way behind the advancing troops. Between the ridge and the causeway at Yong Peng, the jungle had been cleared from the sides of the road, forming a narrow tract of open country. Now, together with Kelly, Stillman, the Barker twins and the Padre, Peter Castle, they waited. There was little point in concealing the vehicle; there was no cover. He just hoped that the red cross painted on the top would be respected. John recalled Major King's night training exercise of over a year ago, where he and his men had tended the "wounded". At the time, some of the lads who were pretending to be shot had larked around, giggling and groaning, while his stretcher bearers, to their credit, had taken the whole thing very seriously. They wouldn't be fooling around this time.

'Well, this is it,' said Kelly. 'It's do or die. Just hope I get to do a bit doing before I have to cope with dying.' He was re-rolling some bandages that had become unravelled.

'Oh don't be so daft! We'll be safe enough back here, where we are. It's them poor buggers up there ahead who should be worried,' replied Stillman, as he lit another cigarette and fished a dog-eared pack of playing cards out of his pocket.

'Come on Kelly,' said the Padre, moving over to sit next to him, 'remember what we talked about back at Gilman.'

'I know, Padre, but back in barracks was one thing; out here, it's a bit more real.'

John looked up from the box of medicines he was checking for the umpteenth time. Kelly and Castle had formed quite a close bond since John had asked the Padre to have a word with his team soon after the war had started. Although

Castle made it appear effortless, John had been impressed with how hard he worked with everyone with whom he came in contact. He used humour and sincerity to raise morale, and didn't resort to hackney phrases such as "It's all in God's hands" when the men asked him tricky questions. He admitted that he didn't have all the answers, and that he couldn't explain why God allowed certain things, but simply said, "This is what I believe, and this is what makes sense to me." John had never much liked any of the parsons he'd come into contact with before, but he had immediately taken to Peter Castle. They had a similar sense of humour and only the previous evening they'd both performed a spontaneous imitation of Stanley Holloway's version of "The Lion and Albert", much to the amusement of their fellow officers at battalion HQ. Peter had just the right northern accent.

'It's not the being dead, that worries me,' continued Kelly, 'I suppose I just don't want the dying-in-pain bit. I mean, I do believe we go to heaven and all that, but it's just the process of getting there that I'm shit scared of.'

'Well, I don't know about Heaven,' Stillman chipped in, 'I don't believe there's anything after death and I've no desire to sit around being an angel or anything. Once you're dead, that's it.' Stillman shuffled the cards, glancing at the Padre to see what effect he was having. 'Though I suppose if I were actually dying, then at least I'd probably know that my number was up and I could sort of prepare myself for it. But if I'm going to get killed by a bomb in the next ten minutes, and I'm actually dead, I'd just quite like there to be someone who would just tell me, "It's over mate, you're dead!" and then I'd know and I could just get on with being dead.'

'Well how do you know that there isn't?' chuckled the

Padre. 'In my version of Heaven, that's exactly what happens. Someone will greet me, and say, "Welcome to Heaven, shall I show you around?"'

John was half listening to the conversation and half concentrating on keeping his binoculars focused on the piece of open ground ahead. The minutes crept by. From what he had gathered, they were waiting for the British artillery bombardment of the lower slopes to begin, at which point the companies would advance and the guns would be trained on the crest of the hill and so on, until the entire hill was secured. It was now getting light. What on earth had happened to the dawn attack and the element of surprise?

At last he saw the first shell fired towards the hill. 'Now!' He nudged Castle who was playing cards with the others. But rather than the expected bombardment, for the next hour the shells were being launched one by one and seemed to burst randomly on the hillside. This was no attack. This was a fiasco!

Then he heard the drone of engines. From behind the crest, nine enemy bombers and four fighters appeared, circled and got to work. The air resounded with the crack and crunch of bombs exploding, the rattle of machine gun fire.

They all threw themselves to the ground, and John kept up a running commentary to the others of what he could see through his binoculars. He immediately regretted that they were stuck so far behind the front line. There was no way anyone wounded could reach the RAP until the bombing stopped and by then it would too late.

'Come on!' he shouted to the others, scrambling to his feet. 'This is useless. We need to get up there now.'

They all clambered into the truck and, with Kelly driving,

they headed up the road. Planes still screamed and wheeled overhead. Instinctively, they each ducked.

'Christ! They're so close, I can see the gunners' little slit-eyes!' yelled Stillman.

The first few bodies weren't far from the road. They looked as if they had received a direct hit. John quickly checked to see if any were alive. All four of them were dead. They parked the ambulance at the rough track leading to a tin mine where they could see troops running for what limited cover there was.

'Over here! Medics needed! Three down!'

Kelly and Stillman grabbed a stretcher and set off running through the tall lalang grass towards the group of casualties, followed swiftly by the Barker twins. John and the Padre began to prepare a space by the ambulance.

A loud explosion close by had them dive to the ground, their faces pressed into the earth, mouths full of soil and grass. There was a lull. John looked up. There was no sign of the stretcher bearers. Then he heard a cry.

'Doc, Doc, over here!' He recognised Stillman's voice, and ran, half crouched, towards him.

Stillman had his field dressing pack open and was trying to tie a tourniquet round Kelly's thigh. Kelly's trouser leg was soaked in bright red arterial blood.

'Oh Christ! Not Kelly!' John knelt down beside him, cut the cloth of his trousers and saw immediately that his right leg had been almost severed very close to his groin. He was losing blood fast. He screamed with pain.

'Just put as much pressure on that as you can while I get the morphine ready.' John's hands shook as he filled the syringe.

'You'll be all right Kelly, just hang on. You've got to hang on.'

After a while, the screams stopped. Somehow Stillman had managed to tie a bandage tightly enough round Kelly's thigh to slow down the blood flow.

Peter appeared beside him. 'I've checked the other wounded, Doc. They can all just about walk. The Barker brothers and I will get them to the RAP.'

'No. Don't go. I need you here!' John shouted at him. 'Quick, Stillman, go and help the others get those walking wounded to the RAP and do what you can with them.'

'But Doc …'

'I'm sorry, Stillman. No buts. Just go'.

As Stillman got reluctantly to his feet, it was plain to see how much blood Kelly had lost. He was still conscious, but seemingly in less pain. He couldn't have long.

He looked at John, and mouthed some words. John bent over him, held his ear to Kelly's lips.

'Don't leave me, please don't leave…'

John eyes watered and he grabbed Kelly's hand.

'It's all right. You are doing just fine.'

But Kelly had turned his face towards the Padre, who was quietly saying the Lord's Prayer. John watched the last moments in a sort of daze, as Kelly, his eyes wide and staring, gasped and then was still.

John sunk back onto his heels and watched Peter Castle gently close Kelly's eyes with his hand. With a sense of panic, John simply couldn't think what he had to do.

'Come on John,' said Castle. 'We have work to do for the living. When it's safe, we'll come back and give them all a decent burial.'

CHAPTER 24

Bill Ellerton had been right. It had been a complete shambles. The attack on Bukit Payang had been aborted and they had all been ordered to retreat to the nearside of a long causeway over the swampland just north of Yong Peng. Although the aerial bombardment had temporarily ceased, Japanese infantry now occupied the hills behind and were slowly filtering towards them through the jungle on either side of the road.

John had no time to think about Kelly. It was easier not to. He put him and the others he'd seen killed into a different compartment of his mind, along with his embarrassment in front of Peter Castle, when he hadn't known what to do. He had not expected to be so affected by a death.

Once the bombardment had ceased, there had been just enough time to bury Kelly and the others in a shell hole, before they had to pack up again and move the RAP back to the causeway. Stillman and the others had unloaded everything they needed and Peter Castle left with the badly wounded in one of the ambulances, heading for the dressing station at Ayer Hitam. For the next few hours, there was a steady stream of walking wounded who struggled back through the jungle and needed patching up; mostly minor flesh wounds and sore blistered feet.

Like everyone else, John was hungry and exhausted and he had just stopped for a smoke, thinking he'd dealt with the last patient, when an Australian transport lorry trundled up and out got Major King. Limping round to the back of the lorry King called out, 'Another one for you, Garrett. I think you'll just about recognise this one, but he's a pretty bad way.' John was shocked to see Richard Henderson struggling to get out of the back of the lorry. His face and arms were a network of scratches and deep cuts; his shirt clung to his chest in tatters and one trouser leg was blood-soaked.

Caught in an explosion, he had been wounded in the leg and had lain unconscious in the lalang grass for several hours, long after the bombing had stopped. Somehow he had been missed in the initial search for casualties. When he eventually came round, he'd been too terrified to cry out in case a sniper stumbled over him. Fortunately the only person who did stumble across him, quite literally, was King who, slightly wounded himself, was doing a final search before the retreat. He had thought Henderson was dead until he heard him groaning. King had heaved him up onto one leg and very slowly they had made their way to the road where they had waited until nightfall. A lorry belonging to the Australians had picked them up and brought them to the causeway.

John grinned at Henderson, 'So what sort of a mess have you got yourself into now mate?'

Henderson tried to smile at his Laurel and Hardy impersonation, but was clearly in shock and John quickly went to support his weight on the other side. Laying him down on an empty stretcher, John cut away the blood-soaked trouser leg. There was a large piece of shrapnel embedded in his lower leg and, judging by the depth and the amount of pain Henderson was in, it was almost certainly lodged in the tibia.

'Look Henderson, you'll be all right but I think you are going to be out of things for a while. I'm going to give you a shot of morphine for the pain and I'll bandage up your leg, but I need to get you to a dressing station and then back on a hospital train to the Alexandra. There's a couple of others injured quite badly and Private Mollon will drive you in the CO's car, as the Padre has already left with the first load of casualties in the only other ambulance.'

'Thanks Garrett. I'm sorry for being such a nuisance.' Richard whispered. 'How are you? Are you coping all right with all this?'

'Oh don't you worry about me, I'm having the time of my life. This is what I've been waiting to do, trained to do, and now I'm bloody well doing it.'

As John cleaned up his face and bandaged his leg, he tried to imagine what sort of journey he would have all the way back to the Alexandra. For the first time in what seemed like days, he thought about Bea and how their parting had been so hasty. Once the order had come to move to Segamat, there had been no time for a proper goodbye, and anyway, she had been frantic with the numbers of casualties arriving from the north. He remembered their conversation of a few months ago when they had talked about him being near the front line and how he'd joked that he would send her love-notes hidden under the blankets of the wounded. John noticed that the morphine had taken effect and Henderson was asleep. He looked in his haversack for a pen and some paper.

After Henderson and the last casualties had been driven away, John sat with King and checked the dressing on his wounded foot. 'Oh it's nothing,' muttered King, 'Just a scratch. Here.' He held out a hip flask to John. Share the last of my whisky ration?' John hesitated and then accepted it gratefully. Feeling all his muscles slacken, he realised how worn out he was.

'What a bloody fiasco,' continued King, 'Bloody ammunition didn't work, no one had taken account of the humidity which meant the artillery had to re-register and by then any possible element of surprise was lost. Of course if we actually had an air-force worth mentioning it might have helped or even a tank or two. But really we're just sitting ducks.'

No one slept much that night. The air resounded with the noisy croaking of thousands of frogs; mosquitoes feasted on any piece of exposed flesh. No one had washed or changed their clothes for weeks; they itched and scratched. In the early hours, from a little way off, John heard a shot and a cry. One of the men had been shot through his buttocks as he'd squatted in the marsh grass. A Jap sniper must have seen the whiteness of his flesh.

The following morning, they were ordered to continue the retreat towards Ayer Hitam while preventing the enemy from taking the causeway for as long as possible. One by one, the companies withdrew and the weary troops began to march.

B. Company was the last to begin their retreat when the Japanese tanks arrived. There were seven tanks accompanied by infantry on foot. The British had no anti-tank obstacles in place and the anti-tank gunners had already withdrawn. Roger Lester and his platoon were among those who tried to fend the Japs off with small arms fire. After several hours, Lester had no choice but to escape with his men into the jungle on either side of the road. No one had seen them since. As the Japanese tanks continued to trundle forwards, despite the fact that a large number of troops would be cut off, the decision was taken to destroy the causeway over the swamp. That evening, what was left of the battalion trudged through the town of Yong Peng.

And then it rained. Not a refreshing monsoon shower, but sheets of rain that reduced visibility to a few yards and drenched everyone to the skin within minutes. Rain. Darkness. Mud. The long column of men walked mechanically, hemmed in on either side by walls of dripping leaves. John, from his vantage point in the ambulance truck, could see how exhausted the men were and understood how demoralised they must feel when orders were received that they were to maintain their position overnight, strung out along the road for about four miles, to provide cover while an Australian convoy passed through. Ellerton told him that perhaps more than two hundred men had been either killed, wounded or were missing. John felt slightly ashamed that he had told Henderson that he was having the time of his life, but in truth, he was. Because he still felt invincible, he didn't feel as if he was in any danger. It was exciting, at times quite fun, and at last he was doing something useful.

For the next four days, the battalion continued the slow withdrawal towards Ayer Hitam, while at the same time attempting to make a stand against the advancing Japanese army. The four companies were stretched out on the seemingly endless road. Every day it rained heavily. Every day, men were wounded by sniper fire as the Japs became more successful in penetrating the jungle and approaching unseen. Whenever the rain stopped and the skies cleared, the aerial bombardment began again, with both bombs and machine gun fire strafing the lines of troops. In the darkness there was total confusion. It seemed as if they were surrounded by the enemy who must have spent most of the daylight hours cutting their way in a wide arc though the jungle. Men who were too badly wounded were left behind, their cries ignored. John didn't dare waste precious morphine on those who were near death and hated himself for lying to them, 'Just hold on lad. There's another ambulance on its way to pick you up really soon.'

There was only one day when Major Holland, as quartermaster, was able to turn his cook lorry into a travelling canteen and drive up and down the road with a hot meal of steak and kidney pie, served with whiskey-laced tea. The following day, the open truck in which Holly's QM sergeant was travelling was riddled with bullets from a low-flying aircraft. One of the bullets went straight through the sergeant's steel helmet. He died instantly. After that, the only food available was tinned bully beef and cold water. Each day the tally of missing and wounded rose.

John cleaned, sutured and bandaged. He tried to maintain his humour while he swore about the lack of equipment and the lack of transport to move casualties back to safety in what seemed increasingly to be a lost cause. In spite of Ellerton berating him for being so careless of sniper fire, whenever there was a lull, he would grab a bicycle and pedal silently along the road from one company to another, checking on the men and doing whatever he could for the stragglers. He relished the breathing space alone as he cycled, already composing the tales he would be able to tell Bea and Min when he finally returned home. Whenever his humour threatened to disappear, it was always Peter Castle who helped him retrieve it. He was a born mimic and could take off the voices of Percival and Churchill, as well as an array of theatrical personalities. There were times when he could reduce anyone who was listening to helpless laughter. He was also a clever scrounger, whether it was fuel from abandoned cars, food from willing Chinese natives or from empty houses. When

John teased him about all his activities, he replied, with a saintly grin, 'Is salvation not my trade?'

It had been another fraught day of constant shelling; John and Peter Castle had spent much of the time face-down with their noses pressed into the mud. There was a pause in the bombardment. Castle rolled onto his back to check the sky for more planes while John craned his neck to peer into the dense foliage in case a sniper was approaching on foot; not that he had any idea what he would do if he came face to face with a Jap soldier and his bayonet.

'I know you're not supposed to, but would you ever kill anyone, if you had to, I mean?' John said to him in a hushed voice.

'Oh Lord, that's a hard one. It's one of the debates we constantly had when I was training for this,' Peter replied softly. 'Like you lot, we're not fighters. We aren't even taught how to fire a gun. Apparently, William the Conqueror had a brother who was a priest; Bishop Odo of Bayeux led a hundred and twenty of his own knights into battle; he wasn't allowed a sword so he used a mace instead. I think I could do quite a bit of damage with one of those.'

There was more gunfire, but it sounded a long way off.

'I think you'll find, Padre, that the supply of maces to troops in the Far East is yet another example of equipment that we're lacking. But seriously, if you were face to face with a Jap soldier and you did have a gun, would you use it?'

Peter sat up cautiously and began to brush the earth off his shirt. 'I don't know. I'd like to think that I wouldn't and that I'd be ready at any moment to meet my maker, but in truth, if I was scared and it was just me and the enemy, I just might. Would you?'

'I've asked myself this over and over, but I know my instinct for self-preservation would take over any moral ideals. Not that I've ever fired a gun, but I'm pretty sure if it came to it, and I could get hold of one, I'd just fire and fire until all the bullets were gone.'

They were so engrossed in their discussion they hadn't noticed that the shelling had stopped. Bill Ellerton crawled over to where they lay. 'Sorry to disturb you both, but you may just have noticed that there's a war on!' he said, grinning at them.

Five days later, on the last day of January, having held the enemy off long enough to complete the withdrawal back to Singapore Island, the mile-long causeway between Malaya and Singapore was blown up by the Royal Engineers. A breach of about seventy-five yards allowed the swirling sea water to surge through. What was left of the causeway on the Singapore side was laid with anti-personnel wires, booby traps and landmines.

CHAPTER 25

Jan 31st 1942

I haven't been able to write anything in this journal for a while, I still feel haunted by Dorothy's last few days after her stroke and what she went through. She must have felt like a soul in torment, trying to escape, unable to express anything. When she was being carried out of her house by the stretcher bearers, I am sure she saw the look of horror and distress on my face. Although, on the day she died she did seem more peaceful. At least I was able to sit with her, hold her hand and offer some words of comfort. I couldn't help thinking back to when Mother died, though unlike Dorothy she was in tremendous pain – the nights were the worst; all those arguments with Laura about who should sit with her – not surprising, I suppose, since we had squabbled all of our childhood. The boys were all at a loss and Father just wrapped himself up in his work. Perhaps it was Mother's death that caused the beginnings of the rift within the family. Somehow, it felt as if none of them ever forgave me for being the only one who was with her when she finally went.

I found myself telling Dorothy, just as I did Mother, that it was all right to let go, that she didn't have to struggle any longer. And after about half an hour, she opened her eyes, looked straight at me and gave me a sort of crooked smile. And then she simply died. I wasn't sure whether to smile or cry and so I did both. It was strangely beautiful, seeing her so serene. As I stayed for a while, looking at her and patting her hand, it was as if I was just looking at an empty body and that her soul had already departed. That was when I suddenly felt the loss of her.

I simply can't imagine how I am going to be able to cope without her. She has been my strength these past years and my little piece of sanity. I hope that perhaps now she is at peace with whichever God made the most sense to her. If I knew where John was, I could write and tell him, but he probably has enough to cope with at the moment, without me bothering him with this awful news.

February 2nd 1942

The newspaper reports say that the causeway has been blown up. Will that be enough to stop the Japanese advancing? Perhaps they will just leave Singapore alone and turn their attention elsewhere, like Hitler seems to have done with England.

Yesterday, it was such a surprise in the midst of all this to receive a letter from John, written back in early December before the onslaught started. He warned me that a lot might have changed by the time I read it. How right he was. I feel as if I have lived through many years since then and sometimes I wonder how many more I can stand at this pace. I feel like a woolly night-sock, shapeless and void.

Feb 4th 1942

Today was her funeral. It was quite unlike anything I have ever witnessed before. Because of her lifelong study of theosophy and the writings of Blavatsky, she had long ago devised exactly what sort of format she wanted her funeral to take. I am glad she was cremated. I hate the idea of burial; of being left in the cold dark earth for all eternity.

I always think it is so sad that the dead cannot hear what is said about them at their funerals and to ensure that their wishes are carried out. But I think Dorothy would have been pleased. It was exactly as she had directed; no dowdy hymns or mumbled prayers, no sanctimonious sermon.

Instead there were poems and some lovely quotations from both the Bible and the teachings of Buddha, which she had been collecting throughout her life. One I particularly liked went something like this: "Our existence is as transient as the clouds. Our lives are like rivers, having a tiny source somewhere in the hills and then gathering strength and momentum, moving through a landscape which shapes us, and which we shape, occasionally seeming to broaden out or become static like a lake, but actually moving on, and eventually flowing into the sea, from whence the cycle begins again." What a lovely way of describing life.

The whole occasion has given me much to think about. Just as I was leaving, the solicitor took me aside and told me that Dorothy has left me all her books. I am not sure where on earth I will put them all, but I do feel honoured.

CHAPTER 26

When Roger first realised that he and half a dozen men of his platoon had been cut off by the advancing Japanese Army and that the causeway at Yong Peng had been blown, he still imagined that it wouldn't be so hard for them to make their way through the jungle in a big loop and rejoin the main road. If they were lucky, they would make it to Ayer Hitam and there, meet up with the rest of the retreating battalion. The tank battle had been horrendous. They hadn't stood a chance with seven tanks, infantry on all sides and no backup.

Up to this point, the campaign had all still been one big adventure, but the trek back was far harder than anything he'd come across before. For much of the time, they were up to their thighs in black swamp water. The vegetation above was so dense they couldn't even see the sky. They had no tools to cut through the undergrowth except their bayonets. Swing, chop, swing, chop! By day, when it wasn't raining, they only managed to travel about half a mile an hour and they had to stop frequently, rest and burn the leeches off their legs and arms with cigarettes.

Roger was determined to remain positive and to encourage his men forward. It was the first time he'd been the most senior officer.

'Right lads! Let's take a short break. You're doing really well. Now what have we got between us in the way of food rations?'

To his horror, only Private Gray, Sergeant Stewart and

himself were carrying any emergency rations. So Henderson had been right about how ill-prepared the troops were for surviving in the jungle.

'You bloody useless bunch of gits. What have you done with them? Lost them? Ditched them? Didn't you think they might just come in handy? You'd better be bloody grateful that Gray and Stewart have something and that I've got a few water sterilising tabs,' he shouted. He began to feel the enormity of what they were trying to achieve.

They struggled on, aiming to get closer to the road, hoping that under the cover of darkness they could make swifter progress. As the light began to fade, they came within fifty yards of the road and Roger could hear noisy voices. He could just make out a number of Japanese dragging an infantry gun along and after a few more shouts they halted. Roger and the others crouched in the swamp and waited for them to move on. They didn't. What's more, they seemed to be setting up a roadside camp for the night and were placing sentry pickets at intervals up and down the road.

The night was endless. Each time they tried to wade through the swamp towards the drier ground nearer the road, their squelching feet seemed to arouse the suspicions of the sentries. They couldn't even smoke in case the glowing tip would be seen. All they could do was wait; each balanced on a little hummock which, after about an hour, would slowly subside into the water, whereupon they'd had to try and struggle to clamber onto another.

The next morning, exhausted, eaten by mosquitoes and leeches, they scrambled towards the road as soon as the Japanese had moved on. Using some greenery, they tried to camouflage themselves in a deep ditch beside the road out of sight and slept fitfully until midday. Roger woke first, managed to light a soggy cigarette and timed the intervals between the vehicles that rumbled up and down the road. Clearly the road was not going to be safe. Poking his head up in a quiet period, he noticed there was a rubber plantation on the other side of the road. If they could just get across, the going would be much easier, though there would be a greater risk of being seen. He woke the others, shared out three tins of bully beef between them all and explained the plan.

Once across the road and into the plantation they made much faster progress, and in the late afternoon reached a small kampong. From the outskirts, it was hard to tell if it was Malay or Chinese. The Malays seemed to hate the British as much as the Japanese and were notoriously unhelpful. The Chinese, on the other hand, would do anything to get back at their invaders. The few natives Roger could see wandering around between the huts could possibly be Japs, who often disguised themselves as coolies. If he got this one wrong, the next thing he'd hear would be sniper fire from behind the trees.

Sergeant Stewart volunteered to creep ahead on his own to investigate and after a few minutes signalled to Roger that it was safe; they were Chinese. That night, they had the first proper hot food in days and set off at dawn the next day, armed with chocolate, oatmeal biscuits and clean water bottles, as well as two rifles and some rounds of ammunition.

Roger was relieved to see how much more cheerful the men were now that they'd had some reasonable sleep and their bellies were full of food. However, he reckoned that if they all stayed together they would make a much more visible target, especially when they approached the next small town, which he calculated was only about six miles away. At the edge of the town, there was a choice to be made about the best route to Ayer Hitam. They could either follow the railway line or continue to follow the road, dodging in and out of the jungle depending on the amount of Jap activity. He split the group into two. He would take the railway line with Corporal Gray and Private Courtney, while Sergeant Stewart would lead the others and follow the road.

The three of them had only trudged along the tracks for about an hour when they came across what was left of a burnt-out Red Cross train. It had been bombed. Inside were the charred and blackened bodies of perhaps a hundred wounded soldiers who had been on their way back to Singapore and safety. The air was thick with flies. Roger gagged on the stench of decomposing flesh. They plodded on, each silent, sickened by what they had witnessed.

Towards nightfall, they arrived at an enemy military transport dump beside the railway which appeared to be deserted. Roger decided it would provide reasonably good cover for the night. From nowhere, there was gunfire. They each dived in different directions. Courtney looked like he'd been hit. Roger hid behind a burnt-out tank and pulled a stinking piece of tarpaulin over him. He heard shouts and sounds of scuffling. An engine started up and a Jeep drove off at speed up the road. He waited, trying to identify every sound. The darkness was absolute. He crawled from his hiding place back to the spot he'd seen Courtney fall. With the thin torch beam, he could see that he'd been shot through the head. Gray was nowhere to be seen.

Roger felt all his energy draining from him; here he was alone in the middle of a war zone, his companions killed or captured and he with no idea how he was going to make it back to safety. He reached for his pack of cigarettes; there were only two left. Stuffing the pack back into his haversack, he crawled back under the tarpaulin sheet, curled himself into a tight ball, and rocked himself just as he used to when he was little and frightened of thunder. What would his parents say if they could see him now? Would his dad be proud of him or would he say, as usual, "For Christ's sake lad, don't be so bloody stupid, that's not the way to do it." He looked at his watch. Just get through the next minute, he told himself; now another minute, and another.

He must have slept, for the next thing he knew the sky was lightening and the trees were full of the whistles and calls of the dawn chorus. There was nothing for it but to press on. Walking the rail tracks was hypnotic; if he stared too hard at his boots, he stumbled, if he stared at the sleepers or rails, he felt dizzy; as long as he gazed straight ahead, he could make reasonable progress.

So much for his map-reading skills. Three weary days later, he was surprised to find himself in the outskirts of Johore Baru. With a rush of elation, he knew that very soon he would reach the causeway and be back on Singapore Island. He strode through the apparently deserted streets, promising himself that once he reached the causeway he would allow himself to smoke the very last cigarette.

But there was no causeway. He could see that about halfway across it had been blasted to pieces. On either side it was bedecked with barbed wire. This must have been done by our lot, he thought, but why on earth isn't it swarming with Japs? He wasn't going to hang around to find out. He trudged along the tarmac until he reached the gaping breach and looked down at the tide swirling around the jagged edges. He was a strong swimmer, but knew he could easily be swept away by the current. Discarding his rifle, his remaining rations and his boots, he took a deep breath and threw himself into the rushing water, swimming as fast as he could towards the break on the other side. The current pulled and clawed at him. He took in mouthfuls of water as he sank and surfaced, gasping for air. Then his knee gashed against some boulders and he was amazed to find that he could stand up. He clambered towards the shattered road. In front of him lay four lines of uncovered landmines and beyond them, several rows of coiled barbed wire. The British troops had done a good job.

Three hours later, after lifting and pulling, crouching and crawling to negotiate the wire, he shuffled the last fifty yards towards the sentry, gasping, 'I'm British. Don't shoot! I really am British, please don't shoot!'

CHAPTER 27

Whenever Bea thought about what had happened to the nurses in Hong Kong, rather than feeling scared, it made her fiercely determined to fight back, however bad things might become. All will be well, she told herself, feeling the comfort of John's mantra. Despite large red crosses painted on the roofs of hospitals both in Malaya and in Singapore, many had been bombed to rubble. So far the Alexandra had escaped damage and it now overflowed with evacuated patients and staff. Everyone was exhausted. Bea and her colleagues snatched food or rest whenever they could but worked on hour after hour. Patients who could walk had to sleep on the floor or sit huddled in corners; those who were too badly wounded were assigned beds.

In the first week of February, when the Japanese finally crossed the straits where the causeway had been severed, Percival immediately ordered the mass evacuation of both civilians and nursing staff. Matron Jones regretfully told her QAs that they should leave. However, she felt it was her duty to stay on until the end. 'No Jap soldier is going to assault an old crab like me,' she joked. About a dozen other nurses volunteered to remain with her, including Bea and her best friend Margaret, even though they knew that Singapore was destined to fall.

Bea had only seen John a handful of times since his regiment had retreated back to Singapore. While he'd been over in Malaya, she'd heard no news whatsoever, apart from the hastily scribbled love-note that Richard Henderson had brought with him, after John had patched up his leg wound and shipped him back to the Alexandra. After the causeway had been blown, John had dashed in a couple of times to check on patients and spend a few minutes with her and they'd met once outside. He had looked really well, clearly thriving on the excitement and possible danger. In spite of the endless retreats, he still remained positive about the outcome. Because he was now so close by, back at Gillman Barracks, she somehow felt safer and even more determined to stay. Whatever happened, at least they could be together.

But on Friday 13th of February, she had no choice. All the remaining nursing staff were ordered to leave. The Japanese were closing in fast; they had set fire to the oil storage tanks in Ayer Raja Road and the hospital was now shrouded in thick smoke and oil fumes. The humid air combined with the heat of burning oil was unbearable. The nurses were told that the troops would try and hold the Japanese back for as long as they could so that the last few ships in Keppel Harbour would have a chance to take as many evacuees as possible.

Bea initially said she would refuse. How could she possibly leave all these young, wounded men? How could she leave John? She stood, as if unable to move, at the door of her ward and looked round at them all. Richard Henderson limped towards her on his crutches.

'Bea, for Christ's sake. Go! Get out now. Remember what happened in Hong Kong.' For the first time in days, Bea allowed herself to feel frightened. Hugging him awkwardly, she said, 'Look Richard, you can hobble a bit, please try and escape now, while you still have a chance.'

'Don't worry, Bea, I've got plans. Now go on! Scoot!'

'If you see John, tell him goodbye from me. Tell him I love him.'

It was eight miles from the Alexandra to the harbour. The roads were crammed with people, cars, trucks and bicycles. Each time the enemy planes swooped down over them, those that could threw themselves into the open sewers that lined either side of the road and emerged staggering, filthy and stinking. It took them four hours.

By now it was dark. All along the waterfront, buildings were on fire. The water at the mouth of the river blazed as a giant oil slick drifted upstream, setting fire to small boats and sampans in its path. The sky glowed red behind the choking clouds of burning oil. At the harbour, it was chaos. Some attempt had been made to assign civilians and evacuating troops with passes for the ships on which they were booked to sail. But all Beatrice could see was a heaving crowd trying to squeeze through the few entrances to the quayside that weren't already alight.

Somehow, Margaret, Matron Jones, Matron Weston and herself managed to scramble aboard the *SS Kuala*. She took one last look at what was left of Singapore and where she'd found happiness with her work and with John, until she was jostled forwards onto the deck. Women and children were still struggling up the gangplank as another wave of enemy airplanes attacked. The air filled with screams. As soon as the planes flew, off Bea and her colleagues set to work, with the few supplies they had brought with them, bandaging wounds and soothing terrified mothers.

At last the *SS Kuala* slipped her moorings and chugged out into the darkness. A small sense of calm began to filter through the four hundred and fifty passengers who had managed to get on board.

'Come on Bea,' Margaret pulled at her sleeve. 'You must stop and get some rest. Come down below, I've found a cabin which the four of us can share.'

Bea finished fixing the last bandage in place and gratefully followed her below deck, where they joined the two matrons who had already fallen into an exhausted sleep.

The next morning the sky was an innocent blue; the engines were silent and most of the passengers still asleep. The captain had dropped anchor off Pom Pom Island, about seventy miles south west of Singapore, deciding it would be safer to hide by day and sail by night. Bea had only slept fitfully and she went up on deck to breathe some fresh air. Volunteers had been asked to go ashore to cut branches and foliage to camouflage the ship from enemy planes and she watched a small boatload of men scramble ashore over the sharp volcanic rocks. Twisting her gold neck chain round her fingers, she wondered what John might be doing now. Was he safe? Would she ever see him again? What about all those helpless patients she had abandoned? How could they survive? Overwhelmed, she began to cry.

Out of nowhere there was a roar. Six bombers, almost wing to wing, were flying straight towards her. She instinctively ducked for cover as the first massive explosion rocked the ship. A fountain of water soaked her as she clung to the railings.

'No!' she screamed, 'Not yet. I'm not bloody well going to go yet!' She struggled to her feet. 'You bastards!' she shook her fist at the retreating planes, saw them turn as one and head back again towards her for a second run. All around, people who'd been sleeping on the deck were hurling themselves into the water. The next blast demolished the bridge and sent huge splinters of wood hurling through the air in all directions. The ship began to list. Bea grabbed some life belts and rushed below to the cabin, yelling to the other nurses that the ship was going to sink. Back on deck, anything that could float was being thrown into the sea. 'Jump! Jump!' was the only command to be obeyed.

'Come on Marge! Let's go together!' Bundled into their life belts, they held hands and jumped. She felt a sharp pain in her shoulder as she hit a floating wooden chair. The water was freezing. Thrashing her arms and legs, she looked around desperately to locate the shore. The current was strong; bodies, wreckage and drowning people, their arms flailing, swept past her. She saw Margaret swimming strongly, not towards the shore, but towards one of the few lifeboats that had been lowered successfully. She struck out after her. Strong arms pulled them on board. Machine gun fire splattered around them.

Throughout the morning, survivors crawled to the safety of Pom Pom Island. Bea and Margaret searched in vain for the two matrons. Not knowing what else to do, they began to tend to the wounded. From the dresses and shirts of washed-up bodies, they tore strips of cloth to use as bandages. All day they went from one group of huddled victims to another. The sun blazed down and dried their clothes. Someone found a small fresh water spring and filled a barrel which had been washed ashore. There was only enough for a few sips each. Their lips cracked; their mouths felt claggy. There was nothing to eat. When night fell, they clung to each other under a jacket given to them by one of the sailors. As Bea lay looking up at the stars, she thought about the island that she and John had discovered; their little island paradise. It seemed like years ago.

The following day, three Malay fisherman from a neighbouring island, who had seen *SS Kuala* sink, landed on the island. They brought a supply of coconuts and some fresh fish but they also brought the terrible news of Singapore's surrender. The Japanese now commanded the land as well as the sea. They had no information about what had happened to the British troops and left, promising to try and get word to the Dutch authorities about the island survivors.

It took two more days for the *Tanjong Pinang*, a small Dutch cargo ship, to arrive and rescue some of the women, children, nurses and the more seriously injured men. The captain had already picked up some survivors from other shipwrecks. He only had room for about a hundred more; the rest would have to be left stranded on the island to wait for another boat. Bea wasn't sure who had taken charge of deciding who should stay and who should be packed into the crowded and stifling hold, but was relieved to be chosen. As soon as they set sail, she and Margaret did what they could, checking wounds and handing out rations of food and water. The sea was calm and there were clear skies all day. It was such a huge comfort to be back on a boat and heading towards safety and home. Still feeling rather hungry, slightly light-headed and a bit giggly, that night, savouring the luxury of a blanket each, they snuggled down on the deck and whispered to each other about their families, food and what they would do when they finally made it back to England.

Bea had barely dropped off to sleep when she was aware of dazzling searchlights followed by a deafening crash. Then, absolute darkness. The deck tilted steeply.

Staggering to their feet, holding hands once more, Beatrice and Margaret stepped into the sea.

CHAPTER 28

'Don't worry Bea, I've got plans.' It sounded good, but in reality, Richard had no idea what he was going to do. As soon as he had managed to push Bea away and had seen her scurrying towards the main staircase, he limped back to his sleeping spot in the corner of the ward and eased himself down to the floor, thrusting his plastered leg out in front of him. He coughed as the stench from the burning oil tanks caught in his throat; water had been rationed for days. There was no electricity. Some of the bed-bound wounded were still calling in vain for a nurse. The only remaining staff were RAMC doctors, assisted by Malay or Chinese male orderlies.

After he'd been wounded and regained consciousness, too frightened to move, he'd spent countless hours lying in the grass. All sorts of images had flashed through his mind. He tried to imagine how his parents would react when they heard that he'd died without having fired a single shot at the enemy. He wondered how Patrick's nasty little blackmail trade had fared during the Blitz. As he worked his way back through his life, he recalled his school days and Teddy Collins, the head boy who he'd been in love with for at least two terms and how he'd been too ashamed to tell Teddy about the relentless bullying he'd endured in the dorm at night time. "Who's got a little dick, Dick? Show us your little dick, Dick." It had gone on and on.

He'd been thirsty lying there and as the pain got worse he'd tried to move his leg. Not realising he'd made any sound, he'd been startled to see Charles King peering down at him. Then the slow stagger with King to the roadside; the long wait for a lorry to appear, the throbbing pain in his leg, but at least he was no longer alone. And then there had been John, grinning at him, cheerful as ever. At last he'd felt safe.

Once his leg had been bandaged and the morphine had kicked in, he'd slept for a while. He hadn't seen John again until he'd just been helped into the CO's car, when John had reappeared by the car door and said,

"Look Henderson, I know it's a bit of a cheek, but would you mind taking a message to Bea, just to let her know that I'm okay? It's a little joke we had, before all this started about me sending her messages via the wounded. Would you mind?"

Bea was the last person Richard had wanted to think about. He didn't want to have to be their go-between, but he felt he owed it to John.

"Of course, I'd be delighted," he'd muttered.

Now sitting on the floor, imagining the Japs about to rampage through the building, he wondered where John was. He'd seen him a couple of times when he'd been to visit patients, and of course Bea, but now it looked as if the end for all of them was fast approaching.

In all the weeks and months preparing for war, he had thought at times, about what it would be like to die. He'd imagined that, faced with the inevitability of it, he would be very calm; that somehow he would compose himself and achieve a higher level of consciousness. He'd even written a couple of poems about it. Now, having nearly lost his life a few weeks ago in the bombing, the thought of dying a violent death on the end of a bayonet was enough to force him to his feet. He spent the rest of the day hobbling on his crutches, exploring every possible broom cupboard, storeroom or bathroom where he might be able to hide.

That night the noise of shelling alternated with the groans of the wounded. The following morning, someone ran wildly though the ward, yelling that the hospital was being attacked. From his reconnaissance of the previous day, Richard's first choice of hideout was the store cupboard adjoining one of the operating theatres. Hoisting himself up on his crutches, he hopped as fast as he could and pushed open the theatre door. What he saw was the last thing he expected. Captain Simley, assisted by an orderly, was performing an operation.

'You can't come in here, lad. Sterile area. Well, sort of sterile, if you know what I mean!'

'The Japs. They're here. You've got to get out! They're killing everyone!' Richard shouted as he pushed past into the storeroom. Sliding the door almost shut, he called to them, 'Come in here! Quick,' but to his amazement, Captain Simley shrugged his shoulders and continued to suture the patient's wound.

Minutes later, through the crack in the door, he saw a Japanese soldier burst into the operating theatre, screaming. He lashed out at the orderly slicing his arm, then jabbed his bayonet a few times into the anaesthetised patient lying on the table. With his back to Richard's hiding place, he gestured to the captain and the orderly to line up against the opposite wall. Still yelling in a torrent of Japanese, the soldier lunged first at the corporal and then at Captain Simley's chest and groin, but as he jabbed him for the third time, the captain parried the blow with his hand and shouted, 'Play dead! Play dead!' and collapsed onto the floor. Richard seized his moment and using one of his crutches, wedged the storeroom door shut and held his breath. It was completely dark, except for a thin line of daylight from under the door. There was some more yelling, then silence. He waited, terrified to move. From time to time, he heard shouts and the sound of boots charging down the corridor. He waited again.

Eventually there was a small knock on the door. 'Is there room for two more in your cupboard, lad? I think they've gone for a bit.'

Richard wrenched the crutch out of position and slid the door open. From what he could see in the dimness, Captain Simley had blood all over his hands and a huge patch soaking the front of his trousers. Corporal Bennett had a flesh wound on his arm. They stumbled in, falling over his plastered leg, and Richard wedged the door shut again. He heard a clicking sound and the little storeroom lit up with the flame from a cigarette lighter.

'Thank Christ I didn't give up smoking in the new year. This little beauty has just saved my life.' Simley pointed to his pocket and pulled out a silver cigarette case, similar to the one Richard had given John as a gift on his birthday last year. 'Bloody brilliant. Never thought to ask the chap when I bought it if it was bayonet-proof.'

Between them, with the help of the lighter and dressings from the storeroom, they managed to stop the bleeding. 'Do you think it's safe to try and leave?' whispered Richard after what seemed like hours. Corporal Bennett, clutching his arm, said he'd do a recce, and returned to tell them that he thought it was all clear.

Shellfire still erupted around the building as the three of them crept slowly into the corridor. It was shortly after dawn. There were bodies and blood everywhere. Patients and staff

145

had been beaten and then bayoneted to death. Richard felt sickened. From the groans and whimpers, some were still barely alive. They made their way cautiously to the front hall. Lurching towards them was the grotesque sight of a tall man in a tattered army uniform, which was covered in blood and excrement.

Simley recognised him as Captain Hill, a fellow RAMC doctor. In a wobbling voice, he told them that the Japs had rounded up nearly four hundred patients and staff, roped them together and herded them into a building near to the hospital. There they had been crammed, fifty or more to a room no bigger than a small bedroom, and left without water or food all night. At intervals, he guessed, groups had been taken out and shot. It was only when, shortly after dawn, a shell had hit the roof of the building, that Captain Hill had seized the chance to escape, and just now had stumbled under a hail of shell fire back into Alexandra Hospital.

It was Sunday, February 15th. Since it was clear that outside the hospital they would be no safer than inside, together the four men slowly made their back to the wards and got on with the job of doing whatever they could for their fellow countrymen.

CHAPTER 29

While Richard and Captain Simley were crouched in the darkness of the store cupboard, John was dealing with the increasing number of casualties being brought to him, as the Japanese shelled and machine gunned the Gillman Barracks. He was now back in his own MI room, though his colourful display of medicine bottles had long since been cleared away. He'd been assisted in the last couple of days by George Wallace, a freshly arrived MO who had survived the sinking of the *Empress of Asia* just a few days previously. Together they pulled out pieces of shrapnel, bandaged stumps of arms, legs or fingers, and washed fragments of glass and debris out of cuts and gashes. The noise of the constant shelling and machine gun fire was relentless. The water supply was very limited and the lights flickered with every blast. All around him there were wounded men; their faces were dirty, their uniforms torn and bloodstained. Some were in good humour, probably relieved to be out of direct firing range; others sat slumped on the floor their heads resting against the wall, their eyes vacant.

Since the start of the campaign, half of his stretcher bearers had been either killed or were missing. He could hardly bear to think about all those young chaps who'd played Glen Miller tunes on the parade ground outside his window in those carefree pre-war days. Those that remained ran back and forth under constant enemy fire, retrieving the wounded wherever they could, while two companies attempted to fend

147

off the Jap advance. Everyone was hanging on for the reinforcements that General Wavell had apparently promised would arrive the next day.

In the middle of Saturday afternoon, word came from someone who had narrowly escaped that the Japanese had attacked the Alexandra, killing patients and staff quite randomly. John felt sick. He thought of all the wounded he had sent there over the past few weeks, including Richard Henderson. Now they'd all be dead. What sort of evil bastard could kill defenceless patients? Feeling his legs giving way, he sunk onto a chair and closed his eyes. Since Kelly's death, he'd tried not to be affected each time someone he'd either known or treated had been killed. It was if they had just gone far away, were irrelevant to the current circumstances and therefore did not demand any mental energy. Now as he sat there, all their faces paraded past him and his eyes pricked with tears.

At least Bea had managed to get away with the other QA nurses, even if it had been ominously on Friday the 13th. The matron had got a message through to Ellerton that all the nurses had orders to evacuate and that with much regret they had to obey, even though it meant abandoning their patients. Ellerton had sent a runner to tell John that if there was any let-up he should try and get down to the docks and see Bea before it was too late. John knew that Ellerton had felt terrible not being able to say goodbye to his wife when she had left five days ago on a ship bound for Australia.

Asking the other MO to cover for him, he had leapt into his car. Amazingly, his Austin 7 was still functioning, and now with so many cars being ditched by fleeing civilians, his orderly was quite a dab hand at siphoning petrol. He had weaved his way down as many side streets as he could to avoid the long traffic jam that snaked all the way to the harbour. Over one million civilians had fled from the mainland of Malaya to Singapore since the beginning of December and now it looked as if they were all on the move again.

The city in which he'd spent the last two years was unrecognisable; shattered buildings, whole office blocks on fire or smouldering; bomb craters everywhere and heaps of rubble on either side the road. The air reeked of burning oil and an even worse stench of rotting bodies, which lay strewn and unburied along the roadside. From a distance, it had looked as if the entire harbour was on fire. When it became clear that he could get no closer, John abandoned his car and made the rest of the way on foot. It was dark but the sky was lit by a crimson glow of flame from the burning go-downs and harbour buildings.

He ran, dodging though the crowd, shouting, 'Make way, doctor coming through!' It worked. People let him through and he found himself on the quayside, elbowing his way up and down, desperately searching for the familiar scarlet-trimmed capes of the QA nurses.

Then he saw her. She had just got to the top of the gangplank on a ship that he could make out was called the *SS Kuala*. She was with her friend Margaret and a stout-looking woman who must be Matron Jones. She turned round and looked back briefly at the crowd surging along the quay.

'Bea, Bea, over here!' But she hadn't seen him and she'd disappeared onto the deck just before the planes, which appeared from nowhere, had attacked. He threw himself to the ground, but not before he saw the three women and their children who were still scuttling up the gangplank mown down. When the planes had flown off, he could see no actual damage to the ship and there were still a few evacuees hurrying on board. He knew he was desperately needed back at Gilman, but he simply couldn't leave until he had seen her ship underway.

Now, blowing his nose and looking round the room, he allowed himself to feel a wave of relief as he calculated that Bea must be on her way to the safety of Sumatra or Java. When would he see her again? Wearily, he got to his feet. In the last few days he'd hardly slept and had been almost constantly at work. There had been a brief respite in that first week of February, back in the comparative safety of Singapore Island, after the causeway had been blown and the Japanese temporarily held at bay. Many of the troops had celebrated by getting drunk downtown in the few bars that were still functioning. John had only managed to see Bea a couple of times when he had dashed up to the Alexandra to check on patients. Like him, she just worked and slept. The last time he'd seen her, they'd been caught in an air raid and they'd huddled together behind a low wall until it was over. Their conversation had been rather stilted; nothing memorable or profound or particularly romantic. Neither of them had mentioned the future.

Eventually, some while after dusk on Saturday evening, the din of shells and mortars ceased. He supposed that even the Japanese needed to sleep sometimes. John joined Roger Lester and Ellerton in the crowded sergeant's mess, which now also served as company HQ, sleeping quarters and a storage area. Lester still looked strained since his ordeal. John had spent hours cleaning up his cuts and scratches. Fortunately, there was still an abundant supply of alcohol and they each sat with large tumblers of whiskey.

'I don't know how much longer our lads will be able to hold out,' groaned Ellerton. 'Those yellow-faced midgets just seem to keep going and going, and it's ridiculous because we actually outnumber them.'

'Where are the Americans or the Aussies? Aren't they supposed to be launching a counter-attack?' asked Lester.

'That's assuming there is any actual plan for relief,' replied Ellerton, 'Singapore isn't going to be like Dunkirk. No one is coming to rescue us. According to Churchill's last directive, we all have to fight, and I quote "to the bitter end, with no thought of saving the troops or sparing the civilian population. Commanders and senior officers should die with their troops. The honour of the British Empire and of the British Army is at stake." etc etc. He clearly has no idea what it's like out here.'

John was surprised to hear Ellerton so demoralised. He had put his trust in him and totally believed everything Ellerton had told him about Percival and Churchill. He couldn't believe that this was really going to end badly. 'Do you really think it's so hopeless then?'

'I simply don't know,' Ellerton said wearily, 'but we can't fight on without water, and food, ammo and fuel, and once all those supplies fall into enemy hands we might as well just give up. I'm buggered if I'm going to watch any more young lads getting slaughtered in the name of the Empire, but I'm also buggered if I'm going to let any of my men know how I feel. So, chaps, this is just between ourselves, understood?'

Throughout the following day, the bombardment continued. Some of the wounded were shipped to a hospital on the far side of Singapore town which so far had been respected by the Japs as a no-fire zone. But as the enemy closed, in they were all ordered to withdraw from Gillman

Barracks to the Mount Washington area. About 8.30pm on Sunday, February 15th, there was a welcome silence from the sound of machine gun fire. John, who had stepped outside for a cigarette, noticed the bright headlights of what he assumed must be an army car crawling slowly towards him along the rutted track. Someone was blatantly ignoring the blackout. Others who had seen the approaching lights joined John outside.

The car drew up beside them and out stepped the brigade intelligence officer who said he had brought a message from Lieutenant-General Percival. He handed the note to Bill Ellerton, who in a quiet voice read it out to those who had gathered around him:

"It has been necessary to give up the struggle but I want the reason explained to all ranks. The forward troops continue to hold their ground but the essentials of war have run short. In a few days we shall have neither petrol nor food. Many types of ammunition are short and the water supply upon which the vast civilian population and many of the fighting troops are dependent threatens to fail. This situation has been brought about partly by being driven off our dumps and partly by hostile air and artillery action. Without these sinews of war, we cannot fight on. I thank all ranks for their efforts throughout the campaign."

CHAPTER 30

February 18th 1942

It's over and still there is no news. I am beside myself with worry. I have scoured every paper I can get hold of, but apart from the news of the surrender there is little else. There were a few lines yesterday about some sort of outrage just before the end at the Alexandra Hospital, but I can't believe that unarmed, innocent patients would have been killed. I seem to recall that John sometimes had to see patients at the hospital. I just pray he wasn't there. I can't understand what is going to happen. There must be hundreds of soldiers in Singapore and even more English civilians. What are they going to do with them all? They can't all become prisoners. Where will they put them all? Surely the War Office must know something.

February 23rd 1942

I feel numb, just numb. It is hard to understand what is happening. Everything seems so far away and unreal. This morning I went into his bedroom, and I don't know what made me do it, but I found myself looking at the Cornwall photos – the enlarged tinted photo set – and then I just sat on his bed and wept and wept. He is the only one in the whole wide world who would understand. With Dorothy gone and John perhaps lost, I have never been so alone.

February 28th 1942

Today I have felt heavy all day. I just didn't want to get out of bed. There seemed no point. It was raining or rather sleeting and I was so cold. I had a sense of doom and the only way I could keep it at bay was to try to go back to sleep, but after a while I was nervous that someone would come and find me if they didn't see or hear me up and about. So I made myself get washed and dressed and pulled a smile out of the wardrobe, but I didn't feel any better. I don't remember ever feeling this bad before. I think I could have come to terms with the loss of Dorothy if I knew for certain that I hadn't lost John as well. I went into the garden in spite of the chilly wind, hoping to find a sign, a crocus or daffodil perhaps. I told myself that if I found one little flower, it would mean that good news would come in the post. But there were no flowers and no news.

Of course everyone is being very nice, sympathetic, just a little nod, or a pat or extra affection to show understanding, but in truth sometimes I can hardly stand the kindness. Frank and Cordelia don't know what to say, and so they say nothing. Or perhaps it's me that says nothing. I am sure Cordelia would love me to break down and weep in her arms, but I just won't give her the satisfaction. She keeps trying to make me eat, but I feel sick to my stomach. Dorothy was the only person I could be myself with and I miss her so much. With Joan and Millie away visiting relatives, I feel well and truly abandoned.

PART 3

CHAPTER 31

John spooned the watery rice stew that passed for supper into his mouth. He had tried to pretend to the others that he didn't mind eating it, but in reality he was as fed up with it as everyone else. The lieutenant assigned to take charge of the mess sometimes contrived to disguise it as porridge or rissoles; if he could get hold of dried fish or curry powder, he added that as well. For the last week, the Japs had increased the protein and vitamin content by adding cattle cake, called VitaMeal. The rice now tasted of grit, bugs, weevils, and fish bone manure. They ate it three times a day.

Every day, packs of rumours scurried around the camp. Some quickly collapsed, others were passed round and round, changed subtly with each telling. Germany was apparently finished and Hitler had fled to Sweden; Churchill was negotiating terms for the release of every prisoner of war; they would all definitely be back home by Christmas.

John struggled to ignore them all.

A whole month had passed since the ignominious surrender. The ceasefire had been declared on the evening of Sunday the 15th, but on the following day nothing had happened; everyone had been ordered to stay exactly where they were. John had kept busy, checking the injured and collecting together as many medical supplies as he could. Holly and Peter Castle had spent the day salvaging food, cigarettes, books and anything else they thought might be needed for a period of captivity. Most of their fellow officers and troops had sat slumped in small groups, grateful for an end to the shelling, but shocked and fiercely resentful that the high-ups in their secure burrow at Fort Canning seemed to have abandoned them. Bill Ellerton knew that the Japanese would despise senior-ranked British officers for surrendering; it was against their code of honour. After what had happened at the Alexandra, he was nervous that at any moment they would all be dragged out and shot. John had refused to think about it.

The following morning, a Jap patrol had drawn up outside in a captured British lorry, now bearing the hated Japanese flag. The officer in charge wore a little peaked cap and musty green breeches. Clutching a long .28 rifle that looked ancient, he got out and shouted, 'Numbar one!'

Unsure what he meant, no one moved. John could feel his heart racing; perhaps this was the moment Ellerton had been dreading. A minute or two of silence followed. Then louder and angrier, 'Ingerissoo numbar one, speedo!'

A few weeks later none of them would have failed to get the message which could be interpreted as "Englishman in charge, come here quickly!" Ellerton decided to see what was being demanded and walked slowly outside. At 6 foot 4 inches, he towered over the little man. How humiliating it was to be surrendering to such a small, scruffy individual.

'You Wavellca?' asked the Jap, looking up at the British commanding officer.

'No. I am not General Sir Archibald Wavell. I am Lieutenant Colonel Ellerton.'

The officer conferred for a while with his men, turned around and said firmly, 'You Wavell!' in a voice which brooked no argument. 'You all march Changi, speedo, speedo.'

Changi camp, the barracks for several British regiments before the war, occupied the eastern tip of Singapore Island, about eighteen miles away. Although the wounded and some supplies were given transport, John had marched all day in the hot sun with everyone else. They marched because they had been ordered to and because they had been trained in obedience; passing through the empty, shattered streets which now stank of fire and putrid corpses. Once out of the city, where the damage was less severe, they encountered lines of sullen Chinese workers who walked in the opposite direction. Occasionally, groups of Jap soldiers seized wristwatches and rings from the men as they marched by. John was relieved that he'd had to foresight to conceal his watch and his silver cigarette case in a box of medical equipment. What had started as a trickle became a slow moving river as weary soldiers from every the British regiment joined them. No Japanese sentries guarded them, but then there was nowhere else they could go.

The Changi peninsula was a hilly district and from a distance, exhausted though he was, John thought the camp itself looked alright. Collections of neat white buildings threw back clean sunlight, softened by the green fronds of coconut palms that grew in the hollows between them. The whole camp straggled over several acres which were subdivided into separate prison areas to accommodate the Australian Infantry Force and all the British regiments. It took a few days for the news to reach them that the Governor of Singapore, Sir Shenton Thomas and his wife, as well as all the civilian internees, were lodged in the much less pleasant Changi gaol on the main Singapore road just outside the camp. It was impossible to grasp how a whole population, including women and children, could so suddenly have lost their homes and their freedom. John had no idea who might have escaped before the end and which of his civilian friends might have died in the last few days.

At first, while things got organised, he didn't really feel as if he was a prisoner; he and others were free to come and go as they pleased within the external boundary. Whenever he walked up to Battery Hill, he could see a panoramic view of the Johore straits; sandy beaches fringed with palms and mangrove trees and an intensely blue ocean that sparkled in the sunshine. The troops were even permitted to bathe from the beaches just a few hundred yards away at Fairy Point; a scene, thought John, more reminiscent of a bank holiday at Margate than prisoners of war after the worst defeat in history. Every day, more stragglers arrived at the camp to joyous reunions with their comrades who had assumed they'd been lost.

Gradually, his captive status dawned on him; clocks changed to Tokyo time (1 ½ hours ahead of Singapore time); water was rationed to half a gallon per man for all purposes; he had to salute the Japanese officers or be hit over the head with a rifle butt. Sometimes they would all be summoned to stand for hours in the scorching midday sun to line the roads in the camp, while a procession of high-ranking Japanese officers would be driven around in much-beflagged British cars. When all British officers were ordered to remove the "pips" from their shoulders and replace them with a single pip to be worn on the left breast of their tunics, Major King was beside himself with rage.

'It's outrageous. It's insulting, and above all, it's against the Geneva Convention!' he shouted. 'How can we possibly maintain any discipline in the ranks if they can't tell whether they are being spoken to by a captain or a major or a bloody brigadier?'

King had found the surrender and the loss of his role particularly galling, especially since some of the men had declared that since they were all equal as prisoners, he could no longer order them around. John couldn't help thinking that it might do him some good and make him less pompous.

Ellerton had tried to reassure him. "Look King, I know this is difficult, but I'm going to speak to the troops about discipline and self-respect. But you do realise," he'd continued with a smile, "that the only reason the Japs have ordered us to take the pips off our shoulders is that they aren't tall enough count them!" King had refused to be consoled.

When John thought back to his brief taste of war in Malaya, he realised that for much of the time he'd felt happy and excited; not of course when his first fatality had been Kelly, or when he'd had to leave wounded men behind to die in pain because they couldn't be saved. Apart from a couple of occasions during an aerial bombardment, he had managed to maintain his conceit that he would come to no harm and it was with this defence that he managed to inspire others when they felt downhearted or afraid. His own secret fear before the war began, that he would either prove incompetent as a doctor, or in the face of real danger he might run away, had not materialised. As long as he was occupied, he could cope. What he had really enjoyed was the bond he had forged with Castle and Ellerton and the way they had worked so well together as a team. Afterwards, a couple of times when he had overheard others praising his hard work and optimism, he had glowed with pleasure; he felt as if he had won his spurs in battle.

For him, the first few weeks at Changi camp were not so different the last days at Gilman, just without the noise and disruption of constant shell fire. He was still with same group of people he liked, and with the steady arrival of recovering wounded from Singapore, he still had his usual work. The day Henderson eventually joined them they had celebrated together with a salvaged tin of pineapple. John noticed how gaunt and nervous he looked and how his hand shook as he spooned the fruit into his mouth.

Most evenings, after they had eaten their rice stew, John would sit with his group of friends in the corner of the large barracks building which was now the Lancashires' new home. They swapped rumours, told and retold their battle tales, and endlessly analysed where it had all gone so wrong; they felt that they had been badly let down.

In spite of Roger's protestations, Lt Colonel Ellerton had expressly forbidden any of the Lancashires to attempt to escape, even though army regulations clearly stated that it was every soldier's duty. Roger reckoned it would be easy to slip under the perimeter fence and make his way back into Singapore town; all he'd need was the help of friendly Chinese to find food, supplies and a boat to cross the straits. He didn't believe Ellerton when he was told that all the fishing boats had been destroyed, that the coastline would be heavily patrolled and the chance of surviving in the open sea was nil, let alone the struggle through the jungle if he ever managed to cross the straits. Apparently a few chaps from other regiments had tried it and their headless corpses had been paraded as evidence.

Roger felt frustrated but had contented himself with

flouting the rules, making secret nightly forays to scrounge extra food from locals in the small village quite near the camp. One evening, he was returning with a couple of others from an evening swim. The sky was a gorgeous swathe of flame and crimson that played over the water. As he reached the footbridge over the inlet into Changi village, a Jap soldier appeared, clutching an automatic gun.

'Dammi, dammi!' he shouted, 'Go back camp. Speedo, speedo!'

Obediently, Roger and his companions quickened their pace. They hadn't got very far when two open lorries rattled through the main street, leaving a cloud of yellow dust. Packed into the back were about seventy Chinese, whom Roger reckoned must be members of the Chinese Volunteer Corps. They were all tied together, had clearly been beaten up and were filthy and dishevelled. The lorries turned down the road that led to the beach. There was a screech of brakes and a lot of shouting. Then machine gun fire, followed by a few single shots. Roger looked at the others and felt a sick feeling in his empty stomach. Then the lorries reappeared, driving at speed – empty. Roger realised that the Chinese had just been cold-bloodily mown down on the bathing beach where they had just swum. The following day a double apron of barbed wire was erected around the camp and between each of the different sections. No one was allowed to walk to the hospital or to collect water rations without requesting permission. Sea bathing was now forbidden.

Richard's leg was pretty well healed, though he still limped slightly. He slept badly on the rough matting that served as a mattress; his sleep was filled with nightmares and he woke frequently, soaked in sweat, trying to defend himself from the bayonet that kept thrusting into his stomach. By day, he wanted to hear about every aspect of the campaign that he had missed. No one could convince him that it wasn't his fault that he had been wounded in the battle at Yong Peng. He truly believed that not only had he let his troops down in the battlefield, but that he could have saved more of his fellow patients from the massacre at the Alexandra instead of hiding like a coward. He trailed round after John or Peter Castle, helping where he could, as if to make amends.

But when the first outbreak of dysentery swept throughout the camp, it was he who came up with the idea for the poster. He and John were sitting on a pair of empty oil drums beside an upturned crate that served as a table.

'Hey John, what do you think of this? We could put it up in every barracks.' The poster he'd sketched out read: "Do you like dysentery? No! Does diarrhoea delight you? No! Then make yourselves a swatter and earn 10 real cigs for each 500 flies."

John laughed. 'That's excellent, Richard. We've got to do something. The number of cases is rising all the time. I can't believe how incredibly stupid people can be. It's just down to simple hygiene.'

Charles King walked over to where they were sitting and glanced at the poster.

'Well you won't bloody well catch me running around swatting bloody flies. Dysentery is nothing to do with flies. If people have diarrhoea it's down to the disgusting food we're eating. I swear mine had lumps of mud in it last night.'

John stood up and looked at him squarely. 'It has everything to do with flies,' he snapped. 'The latrines aren't fly-proof and they are too close to the kitchens. Some men are too lazy to walk the twenty yards at night to use them, while others are chucking the rice they think is too disgusting to eat into the drains. Flies eat anything and everything. They eat shit, they eat food, both cooked and uncooked, and they fly very happily from one to the other. It's a fly paradise. Flies and bad hygiene cause dysentery. Do I make myself clear? Two men are dying every day because someone like you thinks it isn't important.'

'All right, Garrett, keep your bloody shirt on! What the bloody hell do you expect me to do about it, come up with a magic cure?'

'Actually, yes, Major King, I do. There are four simple things you can do. Don't let flies near the latrines. Don't throw food waste into the drains. Don't leave any containers lying around to catch rain water for mosquitoes to breed in, and wash your bloody hands. Now all that takes discipline and officers like you should be enforcing the basic rules of hygiene that I've been banging on about since we got here.' John strode out of the room into the blinding sunlight.

'Well if we had the equipment to dig decent boreholes we could sort that all out,' King shouted after him. 'Christ, what a conceited, bloody know-all that man has become!' he said to Richard, as he plonked himself down beside him.

Richard felt acutely embarrassed. He'd always been vaguely aware of the tension between the two men, but had never seen it erupt like this. He felt fiercely loyal to John, but he also knew that if Charles King hadn't found him lying in the grass with his injured leg and helped him to safety, he wouldn't be sitting there now.

'I'm sorry about all that, King. I know Doc Garrett can be

a bit pedantic at times, but he probably does have a point. All the time I was in the hospital, the nurses were always emphasising the need for proper hygiene to prevent the spread of disease and dysentery was one of the ones they feared most. The Doc's only doing what he's been trained to do. Perhaps we've just got to set a good example and make sure the men follow it.'

'Well I'm not running around with a bloody fly swatter. You can keep your cigs.'

John was furious, both with King for being such an arse, and with himself for losing his temper. Gradually he had come to accept that men he had known had been killed in battle or had died subsequently of their wounds. He had learnt to distance himself from it and receive the news of their deaths as dispassionately as if he'd been told that they been transferred to another regiment. But with the chaos of war over, now that they were all POWs, biding their time until their release, no one should be dying – especially from something like dysentery or dengue fever, both of which could be prevented by simple precautions. He stomped off to find Bill Ellerton.

CHAPTER 32

March 3rd 1942

He is missing. The dreaded letter from the War Office came yesterday. I was too frightened to open it in front of the others, so I took it into my room and put the envelope on the table for ages before I could bring myself to read it. Even though it wasn't the very worst news, when I read the words "missing", I felt as if someone had hit me very hard in the chest and shaken all the breath out of me. Afterwards, I lost all track of time and just stared into the garden, where everything looked forlorn and barren. I could feel the chill creeping through me. I'd always imagined that I would have a sort of sixth sense if something had happened to him.

Just for once, Cordelia was actually helpful. She had seen the letter when it first arrived and, sensing that it might be bad news, tactfully left me for a while and then brought me a cup of tea. Then Frank came in and gave me a hug and told me that one of his Rotary Club chums had said that the letter was just routine procedure. It's what they say about anyone when they simply don't know. It doesn't mean he is dead. For the rest of the day, while they came and went, I sat and rocked and told myself over and over, "All will be well. He will come home. He must come home."

March 10th 1942

I couldn't bear the silence any longer. I had to do something. I have put a notice in *The Times* and see if anyone had any information about what might have happened to him. Perhaps someone who got out just before the surrender may have seen him. Perhaps someone may know more than the War Office; after all, they are probably terribly busy. Dorothy always used to say that she simply did not believe that anything terrible would happen to him because it wasn't in the stars. I don't know how much of her astrology stuff I really believe any more, but I find myself clinging on to any bit of hopefulness. I wonder what happened to his girlfriend.

It still feels quite cold. The wind is from the east and the rawness gets through all my layers of clothing. I am wearing that leather jerkin, he sent me which keeps the worst out. I stood on the toll bridge today and watched a lovely little party of dunlins on the mud close beside me. There was a greater black-backed gull sitting on a post and it reminded me so much of the Norfolk Broads and that wonderful boating holiday the three of us had when Jim joined us for the week. The thought of never being able to share that again is too awful. I don't seem to be able to stop crying.

March 21st 1942

Still no news, and nothing from the notice in *The Times*, except a pile of letters from kind friends who read the notice and have written in sympathy; all sorts of people who I haven't heard from in ages. I would never have imagined that he and I could be imbedded in so many people's prayers and thoughts. I simply don't understand why there is no information. There were hundreds of troops out there. They can't have all vanished and they can't possibly all be prisoners. By now, some must have escaped and should have found their way back home, and as far as I can tell, many people were evacuated before the final surrender.

March 31st 1942

Since that first flurry of letters from well-wishers, it has gone quiet again. I don't know how I keep going. I wrote this today. I haven't written a poem for simply years and this one flowed very quickly, straight onto the page. I had forgotten how soothing it is to read poetry, though I am sure my English teacher would not approve of this rhyme-less effort of mine.

MISSING

I am clockwork.
Each day my key is turned my course and tasks are set.
I move like some bright toy, I stand, I sit, drink tea.
"How brave," they say, "how calm; she bears *"no news"*"
so well".

At night when I'm run down, tucked neatly in my box
I sense you everywhere; you are the scratch of leaves
against my windowpane, a glimmer in the dark,
you are the smell of soap on the pillow I clutch,
the taste of salt.

CHAPTER 33

John listened to the noises of sleep around him. For him, the night had been interrupted by the frequent exodus of men trotting out to the latrines. Soon there would be little point trying to go back to sleep. It was nearly sunrise. He wandered outside to have the first of his rationed cigarettes and savour having some time to himself. Propped against the door, smelling the freshness of the air, he ached for Bea. For the thousandth time, he wished he had kept the little silver pencil she had given him last year with him, instead of packing it up safely with their rugs and pictures; now, all lost forever. Once again, he tried to imagine where she must be. If the *SS Kuala* had headed south to Australia or north west to Ceylon and India, surely she would be back in England by now, reunited with her family; perhaps even with her brother, Jamie. Would she have made contact with Min? They still hadn't been allowed to write a letter home and Min must be beside herself with worry. He hoped that she would have received something official from the War Office.

His stomach rumbled and as usual he planned his breakfast. What would it be today? He'd had scrambled eggs and smoked salmon yesterday, followed by toast spread with Min's homemade marmalade. Perhaps he'd comfort himself today, after such a rotten night, with a full English; eggs, bacon, sausage, tomatoes and fried bread. His mouth watered and he felt his belly pinching. The others kept telling him he was mad to indulge in this daily torture, but in fact, they all did it. After rumour and speculation, most of them spent the long lamp-less evenings discussing food; naming their favourite meals, recalling special dinner menus, planning what they'd eat first upon release and reminiscing about the steak and kidney pie that Holly had managed to feed them all with during the retreat towards Ayer Hitam. It was like having an insect bite; you knew that the more you scratched the worse it itched, but you simply couldn't stop yourself. Food and cigarettes were now the main currency, sought after more fervently than dollars, and non-smokers had the advantage of being able to trade cigs for food.

After sick parade, he got permission to take Richard with him, to pay his daily visit to the small hospital on the outskirts of the camp where all the dysentery cases were treated. Richard was much better than when he'd first arrived at Changi, though his nightmares persisted and he only seemed to feel at ease when he was with John. The conditions in the so-called hospital were appalling; too many patients were crammed into wards designed to hold half the number. There was no running water, no proper lighting and not enough bedpans or feeding utensils. It was a wonder that anyone ever came out alive. The hospital was run by what was left of the RAMC staff and orderlies. John offered words of encouragement to all the men from the Lancashires who were there, while Richard slipped them some extra food rations.

With a sense of relief, they left to join Ellerton, Peter Castle and Holly, who were planting pumpkin seeds in the garden plot. It was approaching midday and the sun was blisteringly hot. All three men wore broad-brimmed hats which they had bartered from the Aussie troops and were glad to stop and show off how well their vegetables were progressing.

Ellerton, Peter and a couple of others had started the plot off and had encouraged any of the men who were willing to help them with digging, planting and watering. Everyone could benefit from the extra calories and vitamins to supplement the awful rice, but Ellerton was insistent that those in the hospital, or recovering from dysentery, whose weight loss was greatest, should have the first pick of the harvest.

These days, the troops were kept busy throughout the day, doing tasks directed by the Japs, such as sawing wood, grinding rice into flour, or hauling water and supplies in engineless vehicles from a central depot. When they had any free time, they did very little with it, unless someone organised a football game or persuaded them to attend some of the lectures on all manner of topics that had started up as part of "Changi University". There was even a working model of a six-cylinder engine and a complete motor car which the military transport officer taught groups of them how to assemble and dismantle.

The officers, who were exempt from manual work, fell into two distinct groups; gardeners and non-gardeners. The former were content to spend the daytimes gardening and the evenings talking about gardening. The latter, if they weren't occupied with official duties such as doctor, priest or quartermaster, had very little to do.

'I think we've done a pretty good job there chaps,' remarked Ellerton, as he dusted the earth from his hands and joined the others resting under the shade of a tree. 'I hope you two have had a productive morning, I've just had Charles King bending my ear about how bored he is.'

'Oh lord. It's amazing how someone as intelligent as King can be bored. There's a whole host of things he could do,' replied John.

'I don't think it's got much to do with intelligence. Isn't it more about outlook and control? I think most people have a tendency to be bored in certain situations, especially those beyond our control, but it's how you deal with it that counts,' said Ellerton.

'I reckon it depends on whether you are an optimist or a pessimist. Optimists aren't easily bored, and dear Charles does have rather a gloomy outlook, doesn't he?' said Holly.

'I know what you mean,' ventured Richard, 'but I always thought boredom was about not having enough attention. Whenever I was bored as a child, it was usually when I wanted my mother to pay me some attention or suggest something I could do.'

'You're right, Henderson,' said Peter. 'I think boredom is often about not having enough incentive or variety. It's like the other end of spectrum, where too much pressure causes distress. That's the trouble with so many of the chaps at the moment, both officers and troops. Before the war and even during the battle, they got so used to having their time organised for them and being told what to do, they've forgotten how to think for themselves.'

'If they ever did know,' muttered Holly, pulling the remaining few threads of tobacco from the dog-end he'd stubbed out and stuffing them into his tobacco tin. 'Though, mind you, I was as bored as a bedpost yesterday when we were standing in that sweltering sun, waiting for that bloody parade of generals and whatnots to pass us by. I hope they don't make a habit of it or I'll lose the will to live.'

'I'm with you there Holly,' said Ellerton with a chuckle. 'But I think Peter has a point and that gives us a bit of a problem. We've got to maintain morale here as well as discipline. Then men have to accept that we're still in charge and they must obey orders, but we've also got to help them think up ways of keeping themselves entertained. We have to get the right balance.'

For a while they all lounged under the shade of the palm tree and watched the activities of the camp going on around them. Men wandered between the huts in twos and threes; a small group were kicking around a bundle of rags that had been fashioned into a sort of ball; Charles King could be seen strutting up and down outside the Officers' mess.

'Actually, now I've thought about it a bit more, I think boredom could be about feeling disconnected, either from yourself or from others, and I think for some people it's about not having any meaning or purpose in their life,' said Peter.

'That's where I think you are probably more fortunate, having your faith,' said Ellerton

John lit his second cigarette of the day. He was reminded of earnest talks he used to have with Jim during their student days. Apart from those few conversations he'd had with Peter during a lull in the battle, since the surrender, the only topics for discussion had been rumours and food. Now his mind whirred with ideas.

'As usual, Peter, you have managed to shine a light on this for me. I reckon that for as long as we are banged up in here, we'll all have to learn how to manage the blight of boredom,' he said. 'I suppose finding some sort of meaning for this whole charade will help, but I think for me it's also going to be about developing a familiar routine while making sure that there is enough variety. Look, I haven't really thought this through, but I'm trying to imagine how we spend each day here as a piece of music made up of a theme and variations. It starts with a basic tune, and if it was repeated over and over again, like a simple song or a hymn, it would become tedious and boring. So, as long as the basic theme keeps being varied and new variations are always being created, using different instruments or rhythms, one can remain intrigued and stimulated,' John finished, feeling rather pleased with himself and looked round at the others.

'Blinky blimey. That's all a bit intellectual for me,' said Holly, heaving himself to his feet.

'No. I think that's a pretty good way of putting it, John,' said Ellerton as he stood up. 'There's only one problem. Are you going to explain all that to Major King, or shall I?'

Richard trailed after them to the Officers' mess hut; a small, stone-flagged structure that had been erected near their sleeping quarters within the first few weeks of captivity. Now, thanks to the gardener's efforts, it was adorned with purple bougainvillea and a pale yellow climbing rose; a welcome place to escape from both hot sun and monsoon downpours. Richard regretted mentioning his mother; he thought it probably made him sound rather silly, and wished that instead he had said something as clever as John about music and boredom; though he wasn't quite sure how he could apply it to himself. He was acutely aware of the easygoing relationship John seemed to have forged with the Lt Colonel, the Padre and the quartermaster. It was clearly a result of the long hours they had spent with each other during the fighting; yet another opportunity to make close friends that he'd missed out on. But even now, after the weeks they had spent at Changi, he still felt he wasn't one of the in-crowd.

Not that he could ever admit it after the conversation

they'd all just had, but the truth was, just like King, he also felt bored much of the time. He had no real duties with regards to the troops; he certainly wasn't going to play team games of football or cricket and he knew nothing about engines or plants. Perhaps Castle was right; he was bored because he felt so disconnected from everyone.

It was only when he was with John that he felt he could relax. They'd spent many hours discussing what they each might do after the war. John planned to marry Bea and wanted to buy a house large enough to accommodate his mother, whom he referred to as Min. Richard encouraged him to tell stories about his childhood; he couldn't imagine having such a close relationship with his own mother. When he'd been so frightened during the massacre at the Alexandra, he'd soothed himself by imagining being a small boy again, sitting with his head in his mother's lap while she smoothed his hair. He'd felt so betrayed when he reached the age of ten and she'd told him that he was far too big for that sort of thing. He'd tried to talk to John about his father, but John always changed the subject, saying, "Richard, there is nothing to say about my father, let's drop it." John's voice had had that edge to it, much like his own father's when complaining to his mother that his tea had gone cold. When John had lost his temper, as he had done with King about the flies and hygiene, Richard had felt that same sick feeling in the pit of his stomach as he did when his father yelled at him to account for some misdemeanour or other. The only relief in being a prisoner of war was that he did not have to face his family and admit that during the entire Malayan campaign he'd done nothing worthwhile.

He could see how Charles King irritated everyone so much. He bullied the men whenever he got the chance, complained about the food, the weather, the Japs, the lack of occupation and had now won the title of "Borehole" which was applied to all the rumour-mongers that infected the camp. But Richard still had a soft spot for him and recently more so, when one evening King had confided that his own mother had died just a month before he'd gone to Sandhurst. The first time he had returned home on leave, he discovered that his father had not only destroyed every photograph of her, but he had also given away all his childhood toys; his stamp collection, puzzles and toy soldiers. Everyone, it seemed, had impossible fathers.

Richard knew he could never be this honest in return; King was quite openly opposed to anyone whom he imagined might be homosexual. Although it had been nerve-racking last year when Richard had caught sight of Lester in the bar in Lavender Road, he didn't think Lester had seen him, preoccupied as he was with the two prostitutes, and certainly he'd never mentioned it. No, Richard was fairly confident that no one in the army knew he was a queer.

But he hated having to be ashamed of who he was; he hated the way queers were portrayed as being effeminate, or as perverts to be avoided in the showers; he hated the idea that everyone thought it was all about sex and the concept of one man loving another seemed to be so repugnant.

CHAPTER 34

April 9th 1942

Dear John

I cannot bear the awful silence any longer. Someone suggested I ask at the Post Office if there was any point in posting to Singapore and they said "Oh yes" as if it was all back to a normal service. So I am going to assume that you are alive and I will write to you once a month.

We have now been informed that everyone who has any spare rooms at all must take billets and ours will be with us in the next few days. It seems so unfair that the minute you are missing I have to put up with a total stranger sleeping in your bed. I am really quite cross. I don't know how they found out that we had the extra room. I have spent the morning packing up all your belongings into boxes. It didn't feel right at all. I probably shouldn't have, but I went through all your school reports and the little drawings you used to do when you were at kindergarten. They made me laugh and cry in equal measure. I found that tiny wooden boat you carved when you were only about eight or nine. I remember how pleased you were when you launched it into the stream by Boldre Meadows and it floated. I am sure it had a mast and a sail, though I couldn't find them. It is just small enough to keep in my pocket and I just keep fingering it and sending you messages of my love.

We are all well here. If you ever receive this, I do hope you will be able to reply.

You are ever in my thoughts and prayers. Min

April 28th 1942

Still no word of John, and now the mayhem has started here all over again. They are calling them the Baedecker raids. Because we bombed somewhere called Lübeck, which had masses of wooden buildings which were destroyed, killing thousands of civilians, Hitler seems to have ordered reprisal raids against historic British towns: Exeter, Bath, York and Norwich. They have all been smashed. It is such a waste. Sometimes I want to scream and rage about the ruination of everything.

I suppose the young corporal billeted with us, Duncan, is not such a bad lad really. I am still cross about him taking over John's room, though it isn't his fault. His home is in the north of England and he has such a strong accent that I can't always understand him, but he is very polite and not quite the rough soldier I had been dreading. He is probably much like the soldiers John is dealing with. He goes off each day, though he is not allowed to say what he does in any detail and he returns at night time quite starving hungry. At least we get more rations with him here.

I'll write another letter soon, though it is so hard writing something cheerful when my heart feels like breaking.

May 15th 1942

I have been quite busy all day. I have found this is the only way to stop worrying and crying all the time. I noticed that Duncan had some quite large holes in the elbows of one of the sweaters which he wears when he is off-duty, so while he was at work I sat down and darned them with some wool I unravelled from an old one of mine. He was so surprised when he came home and said I was a much better needlewoman that his mother! I do look forward to the evenings when he comes back. I think he likes to talk about how his day has been; not that he can tell me much, but he tells me all sorts of stories about the other soldiers in his outfit. Of course, just as I had imagined, Cordelia has to interfere and keeps coming into the kitchen to chat to him just when I am about to serve him up his dinner.

May 20th 1942

Duncan was most amusing today. He tells such funny stories and he quite cheers me up. We have taken to spending the evenings in the conservatory just chatting or listening to the wireless. He has quickly got the message about Cordelia and so now when she comes into the kitchen to join us, I simply tell her that we are decamping to my quarters and I bid her goodnight. He doesn't know much about music, except the popular dance tunes, and so last night I insisted he listen to Schubert's *Trout Quintet*. I am not sure what he made of it but it would be lovely if we could make it a regular occurrence. I was watching him while it was playing. I could almost see John in his eyes and he was twiddling with his buttons just like John does. I told him he'd better stop it or I'll have to sew back on all the buttons as well as darn his sweaters! He has probably had enough of me prattling on about my son, the army doctor, and I have shown him all my photograph albums and described the holidays we used to have, but he is very patient.

May 29th 1942

Happy Birthday my dear John! Twenty-nine today! Are you out there? Can you hear me calling? Duncan has been out for the past few evenings. I think he has been cycling into Lym and having a drink with a few of his chums there. He doesn't come back until after I have gone to bed. I feel rather disappointed, I was so enjoying our quiet evenings together. I hope I can tempt him to stay here tonight and help me celebrate John's birthday in his absence.

CHAPTER 35

Alan Rose took his first sip of coffee for over three months and grinned across at Sid Melton, his fellow bombardier from the Field Regiment.

'Well, who would have thought? We've fallen on our feet here mate.'

On the table between them were two cans of pineapple, two cans of condensed milk, three packs of cigs and some carefully wrapped duck eggs; all gifts from the Chinese cafe owner who, refusing any money, had piled them gleefully onto the table. He'd even provided a bag for them to carry their booty away.

Four weeks ago, this would have been inconceivable, but now Alan was part of a working party back in Singapore town, ordered to build a war memorial at Bukit Timah to celebrate the Japanese conquest of Malaya. They were billeted along with soldiers from the Lancashires on the Caldecott Estate which had previously been an area of luxury housing. All the houses were now bomb-damaged and windowless, but some still had flushing lavatories, running water and electric lights. Compared to Changi, it was like staying in a high-class resort. Even the food was slightly improved now that they were doing manual labour for up to twelve hours a day, building the road through virgin jungle near the McRitchie Reservoir; though as the road grew longer, the further they had to walk each day to reach the unmade stretch. When they'd been told they were part of the working party and moving out of Changi, they hadn't minded marching the twenty miles to get to Caldecott; anything for a change of scenery. Once they'd finally reached their new billet, Alan hadn't been sure if he should believe the Japanese guard who threatened that if they strayed outside the area they would be flogged and pegged out in the sun for ten hours, but he wasn't going to risk it.

However, one morning after four weeks of back-breaking work, they woke up to find that there were no guards and no call for work. Surely it couldn't be the Emperor's birthday again; they'd had one day off for that back in April. No one knew what was happening. Everyone had their own theory and was excited at the prospect of a real change. It was Sid's idea to slip into town and try to find out what was going on. Alan was reluctant, but seeing a few other lads disappearing down the street, he'd agreed. They hadn't walked more than half a mile when they saw two Japanese soldiers walking towards them.

'Oh crikey,' said Alan. 'What the hell shall we do now? It's too late to run for it.'

'Let's just smile and salute,' replied Sid.

'Curiouser and curiouser,' said Alan, as the Japs returned their salute and walked on. In every café they passed, friendly Chinese beckoned them to come in for cakes and coffee.

As they sat enjoying their coffee, they were approached by a smart-looking businessman who sat down next to Alan and pointed to his wristwatch.

'Look your watch, Jap time. My watch still Singapore time,' he said proudly. 'You want go India? I can get safe passage for you. We all keep you safe. You want?'

Alan and Sid looked at each other and back at the businessman.

'No thanks mate,' said Sid. 'We think all the Japs have gone away. We reckon we'll be out of here soon. But thanks for the offer.' The man shrugged and left the café.

'Sounded good,' said Alan, 'but I don't think I fancy risking it. Who knows where we'd end up?' Not knowing what else to do, they returned with their bag of food to Caldecott and cooked themselves fried eggs on toast while they waited for someone to enlighten them.

"Freedom Week" as it later became known, came to an abrupt end when the Japanese managed to sort out the administrative difficulties of replacing the old guard with a new one. But even though the old routine was quickly re-established, and they were back on road building, Alan felt more cheerful than he had for weeks and the aching hunger in his guts could now be soothed with the supplies of food they'd managed to collect during their brief gaol-break. Unlike several of his mates, he had not availed himself of the free services being offered by the girls in Lavender Road; in spite of being able to wash daily, he still felt dirty and lice-ridden.

Maybe his new good humour had made him careless, or perhaps it was because he was exhausted at the end of a day of torrential rain, squelching and hacking through the swamp, but the shock of pain as his axe missed its mark and gouged deeply into his leg was like nothing he'd ever experienced. Blood spurted everywhere and he cried out to Sid as he fell. The guards were nowhere to be seen. Sid rushed over to where he lay, shouting for a medic as if they were in the battlefield. He tore off his shirt and tied it tightly around Alan's leg, just as one of the officers ran over to where they both were.

'What's your name, Private?' asked Captain Henderson, who had been on supervision duty that day.

'Lance Bombardier Rose,' muttered Alan between gasps of pain.

'Well, Rose, just hang on and I'll tell the Japs we need some transport to get you back to the camp and get Doc Garrett to sort you out.'

The journey back to one of the less damaged houses at Caldecott that served as a small hospital to deal with the continued presence of dysentery, dengue and malaria seemed to take forever. The pain in his leg was excruciating and, despite the warm evening, Alan shivered with cold and shock. Sid sat with him in the back, telling him to hold on, they'd be there soon.

Doc Garrett gave him a shot of something for the pain almost as soon as he'd hopped on his good leg into the building, supported on either side by Henderson and Sid. An orderly quickly cut his bloodied trousers away from his leg, stripped off the rest of his wet clothes and wrapped him in a couple of blankets.

'Is it bad, Doc?' he asked as John Garrett started to clean the congealed blood from the wound.

'Well it's a deep cut, and it may have just nicked the bone, but it should be fine once I've stitched it up. The problem is, I don't have any more local anaesthetic and it's going to hurt like hell while I put the stitches in. Are you ready?'

'Yes Sir. Just go for it. I feel such a chump. How did I manage to get through the whole war, completely unscathed by the enemy, and now the only wound I've got is self-inflicted?'

'Could have something to do with the fact that you are working long hours on a sod of a job without enough food,' said John Garrett with a smile. 'So, Rose, how did you end up as a bombardier?'

'Well Sir,' Alan winced as the suture needle passed through the skin, 'I used to work in an architect's office as a draughtsman and, being quite handy at drawing and such like, I got signed up as a battery surveyor and came out in '41.'

'What sort of things do you like to draw?'

'Pretty much anything. Give me a pen and paper and I'll draw whatever I see.'

He looked up at the Doc, who was obviously trying to take his mind off the pain. He'd expected him to ask him questions about his war experience, not his drawing skills. As a child, he'd always loved to draw, ever since his parents gave him his first set of coloured crayons. They soon recognised his talent and every birthday he would be given a new medium to try; what he liked best was pen and ink with a watercolour wash. There had been no money to send him to art school, but since he was particularly skilled at drawing houses and street scenes, he became an apprentice to a firm of architects in Surrey. He'd thought it was wonderful to be both trained and paid for what he enjoyed doing.

Like John Garrett, Alan had rather enjoyed the brief war. In the lead-up, he'd been involved surveying the island and selecting possible gun positions and there had been plenty of time for socialising and meeting girls, though he'd been disappointed not to find anyone special. In the final days he'd been holed up with Sid in the law courts taking pot shots with his rifle at low-flying enemy fighters; though nerve-racking at times, mostly he'd felt quite excited.

The Doc had a kind face and pursed his lips together in concentration. Glancing round the room, he noticed that Sid seemed to have slipped out; probably at the sight of the suture needle, but Captain Henderson remained hovering in the background and, despite there being an orderly who was assisting, he kept asking the Doc if he needed any help.

'I've done quite a few portraits of the lads in Changi,' Alan added, 'but now I've run out of paper. Though actually these days there's no time and anyway I'm too knackered at the end of the day.' Just saying the word knackered drained him of all his energy; his leg hurt like crazy, he was cold and shivery and desperately wanted to sleep. As the Doc pierced his skin with the last stitch, he let out a gasp of relief and his thoughts turned to his mum and Betty, his sister. It was at times like these, when he felt the most vulnerable, that he wanted to lose twenty years and go back to being a young boy being comforted by his mum. He saw her standing at the little white gate, a bright autumn sky behind her, as she fought back her tears and waved to him as he strode off to join his unit. He coughed noisily to conceal his own emotion.

At last, he was helped to stagger to a bed and drifted off to sleep to the low murmur of conversation between the Doc and his orderly.

John was quite relieved to have something other than dysentery to deal with. Suturing up Corporal Rose's leg reminded him of being back on the battlefield, with the din going on all around him; Peter keeping up his patter of witticisms, and Holly appearing magically at intervals with mugs of hot tea. The bombardier had barely winced while his pale freckled leg was being sutured and each time John had glanced at him to ask him a question, he'd looked straight back with the bluest of eyes, and answered with a soft West Country accent; John had rather taken to him. Most of the troops who came under his care had little education and limited conversation, so to meet one who knew a thing or two about art was refreshing. John's own watercolour palette that he'd bought when he came out to Singapore was yet another loss, though he'd never had any time to use it. He wondered if there was any chance he could gather more supplies of paper, pens and paint before they all had to return to confines of Changi. Maybe he'd share them with this fellow artist.

Henderson had left John to finish up, saying he had to check on the troops returning from the road building and John, having ensured that Rose was asleep and that the few other patients were comfortable, wandered outside. The torrential rain of the day had stopped and the inky sky was now filled with stars. It was still very warm and later than he'd realised. Pulling out his cigarette case, he lit a dog-end saved from the morning, inhaled deeply and strolled over to the mess, hoping to find Bill Ellerton and join him for their one of their evening chats. Since they'd been at Caldecott, he and Ellerton had taken to spending an hour or so after supper sitting on the balcony, discussing everything from growing up in England to growing vegetables in Changi. Ever since that day in the vegetable garden, he had felt the beginnings of a bond growing between them.

Tucking the cigarette case, which had survived both the battle and the greedy eyes of the Japs, back into his shirt pocket, he tried to recall what day it was. Of course, today was his birthday, and this was the case which Henderson had shyly given him last year. It seemed more like five years. How completely different today had been. He smiled as he remembered how Bea had got caught in the rain shower when she popped in to bring his present of the silver pencil, and how he had enjoyed treating his friends to that extravagant dinner party at Raffles. If only he had kept her gift with him, at least it would have been a little bit of her to hold onto. He tried to imagine Bea back in England, working in London – unless the QAs had sent her somewhere else. He prayed it was nowhere too dangerous. Maybe they'd be allowed to write home soon.

Reaching the room that served as a sort of Officers' mess, he found it unusually deserted, except for Richard who was sitting waiting for him. On the table beside him was a china plate on which were some little iced cakes, a bowl of tinned pineapple, some bread rolls and a small jar of honey. Suddenly the cramped room filled with his officer friends; Ellerton, Holly, King, Lester and the Padre who pushed in after him, shouting greetings and clapping him on the back.

'Happy Birthday John,' Richard said with a big grin. 'I bet you thought we'd forgotten.'

CHAPTER 36

The rain poured through the coconut palms as if someone had tipped out a bucket of water. 'Anyone fancy a shower?' shouted Roger, and without waiting for an answer he dashed outside, stripping off his clothes as he ran. Within minutes, a dozen others had joined him, shouting and laughing as they danced around naked, delighting in the sudden abundance of fresh water. They had been back at Changi for several weeks now and were missing the comforts and freedom they had enjoyed while they'd been billeted at Caldecott.

Initially, Roger had found the return to Changi frustrating. Like Alan Rose, he had also been offered the chance of escape and safe passage through Malaysia. Recklessly he'd accepted the offer and told the man that he'd meet him the following day. He didn't want to simply disappear. He owed that at least to Lt Colonel Ellerton, but he was quite convinced that this time he would agree; after all, this was the perfect opportunity while there was no guard. He was surprised how much he wanted Ellerton's approval.

But without expressly forbidding him, Ellerton had looked annoyed and told him he'd be a complete fool to even contemplate it, especially when hostilities might soon be over and they'd all be on their way back home legitimately.

'Look Lester, for starters don't forget that we Brits are all at least a foot taller than any of the locals and you'd stick out like a sore thumb. Assuming you made it across to the mainland, at best you'll spend months trying to creep through the jungle to Lord knows where, and at worst, not only will you be shot, but so will anyone who knew about the escape or found helping you. You haven't forgotten all those Chinese workers you saw massacred on the beach?'

The excitement that Roger had felt as he'd walked back from the town drained away. It was as if he was thirteen again and his father was scowling at him, berating him for not thinking it through, for being selfish and not considering how his careless behaviour might affect someone else. He felt ashamed and disappointed. How could he have forgotten about the Chinese, who were shot for collaborating with the British, or his gruelling, solitary march back to Johore along the railway line? The only sensible course of action was to stay with the only people he knew he could trust.

But if there was no chance of getting back into the outside world, at least he could try and bring real news back into the camp rather than continue with the daily diet of ridiculous rumours. While others came back with sacks of food, cigarettes, paper and playing cards, he searched for some more unusual supplies. He decided he'd try to make a wireless; after all, he'd had years of practice in the factory before the war. He didn't know how he'd smuggle it back to Changi once this working party was over, but he'd work that one out nearer the time. While the Japs had done a fairly thorough job of ransacking the houses at Caldecott and the Mount Pleasant area, he couldn't believe his luck when in amongst all the debris he discovered that they had overlooked some of the vital equipment he needed. He found a telephone handset under a collapsed sideboard and managed to wrench some piano wire from a smashed baby grand to use for the coil. A few days later he came up with the idea that the tin foil lining of the tea chests in which the Japs supplied the rice rations would probably do for the condenser. His main problem was where to obtain the valves. At this stage, he couldn't risk anyone knowing what he was doing, there might be Jap spies anywhere. It was not until the following week, when the new guard had arrived and they were all back working on the memorial at Bukit Timah, that he came up with the solution. The memorial was not too far away from the Singapore broadcasting station that they passed every day. He took a huge gamble and after several days of waving to one of the Chinese technicians he'd seen entering the building at the same time each day, he beckoned him over and asked for what he wanted. The technician had been a little reluctant, but a few days later hurried towards Roger with a small packet in his hands.

Finally he was ready to test his creation. He'd had to confide in Holly and Lieutenant Mummery, who had seen him ripping out the tin foil, and between them they managed to conceal the strange contraption in an empty water tank in the roof of one of the houses, having wired it up to the electricity supply. Roger was adamant that they did not tell Ellerton about it. He couldn't stand the thought of being disapproved of yet again; first he had to know that it would definitely work. After a lot of trial and error, one evening just before 10.00 pm, in excruciating silence, with a cigarette clamped between his lips, he held the receiver to his ear and heard the muffled sounds of the BBC Delhi News.

Ellerton had been delighted. 'I knew there was a good reason to persuade you not to go off on some ridiculous escapade, Lester. You are far too useful to lose.'

Smuggling the dismantled wireless back into Changi had

been a challenge. Despite Roger's initial urge to rush out and tell everyone, he understood how crucial it was that as few people as possible even knew of its existence. There had been endless discussions about where it could be hidden back in the camp and who should be mainly responsible for it. Holly had come up with the obvious solution; it could be hidden in the supplies room next to the cookhouse, and since Mummery's duties gave him an excuse for being there at night time, Ellerton delegated to him the task of listening in and taking shorthand notes of what he heard. Over the next few weeks, it became known as Mummery's Summary, or if it was bad, Mummery's Glummery. Those who didn't know about the radio assumed that Mummery was getting the news from someone outside the camp.

Roger had felt angry and cheated. After all the risks he'd taken to get the radio assembled, this seemed totally unfair; it was like being told that as the eldest he had to share his special toys with his younger sisters. Ellerton made no mention of the radio, but meanwhile the Padre had been praised for getting a supply of books and Doc Garrett had been congratulated on smuggling back malaria tablets and other vital medical supplies that the Japs wouldn't allow. Back in Changi, he became apathetic and moody. He was bored and took to wandering around with his gaze fixed on the ground, looking for anything that had been dropped or discarded that just might come in useful; bits of wire, butt ends, pieces of string, a button – even scraps of paper. His pockets always bulged.

Dashing out into the rain shower was the first sign that his fury was beginning to wear off. Sod the lot of them, he said to himself. I can't stay cooped up any longer. I think a little foraging further afield is called for. I'll have them grovelling with gratitude for the stuff I'll be bringing back.

He knew how dangerous it was; that was part of the attraction. If the guards caught him, he'd be shot. If the well-established group of Aussie black marketeers caught him, he'd be beaten up and shopped to the authorities. The Aussie group were a nasty bunch who controlled all the illicit supplies that entered the camp. They bribed guards, ignored their senior officers, charged their fellow prisoners exorbitant sums for goods and when they couldn't pay, they lent them money at ridiculous interest rates. They were both envied and feared. Any trips under the wire would have to be solo. For several nights in a row after the others were asleep, he dodged in and out the shadows, searching for the Aussie route through the perimeter fence. He was surprised how quickly he found it.

On his first trip, he came back with nothing more than a supply of cigarettes and some fruit and, apart from a few nervous moments, he had managed to pick his way in the dark, without incident, along the path to and from the village. Above the trees, a half moon had shimmered in the star-filled sky and the night noises of frogs and crickets reminded him of his solitary jungle trek. The next time he crept under the wire, he was luckier. He negotiated with a young Chinese man who sold him a small piece of pork meat wrapped in a cloth. He tied the bundle under his shirt and made it back to the fence just before dawn. He was squeezing back through the twisted stands of cut wire when he heard the sound of footsteps coming rapidly towards him over the gravel path. He rolled as quietly as he could towards the drainage ditch, his arms wrapped around the piece of pork.

'Who the bloody hell is that? You bloody Aussie bastard. I

know what you're up to. You can't wriggle away from me. I've seen you. What have you got there?'

'Shhuush, for Christ's sake, the guard will hear you!' Roger looked up into the face of Major King and crawled quickly out of the ditch.

'Don't you shush me,' said King, lowering his voice. 'Christ, is that you Lester? What the hell do you think you're doing? Give that to me. I know what you've been up to, smuggling stuff in and selling it on the black market instead of sharing it out fairly. Well, not anymore.' He lunged towards him and tried to grab the package. Roger ducked out of the way. King had lost weight since the war, with the meagre diet and absence of whisky, but he was still unfit.

'You've got it all wrong, Major. I was bringing this back to share out. This is only the second time I've been out. I'm trying to set up a regular supply route to outsmart the Aussies.'

'I don't believe you,' said King, taking another lunge. This time he knocked Roger off balance and the two of them ended up tussling on the ground. Roger could have easily overpowered him but he heard footsteps approaching through the thin grey light.

'All right! You can have the sodding meat, but we need to stop this fast – there's a guard coming.' Roger lobbed the bundle of meat into the ditch and, pulling on King's left arm stood up quickly to salute. King saluted as well while dusting himself down with his other hand.

'Thanks Lieutenant, I can't believe I didn't see that tree root. Thanks for helping me up.' The guard looked at them suspiciously. He searched them both, patting their obviously empty pockets. As if he felt cheated, he slapped them both very firmly across the face, a favourite Japanese punishment.

Roger could hear King almost choking with rage.

'Steady,' he hissed.

The guard, now satisfied that he had done his duty, continued on his way.

'Bloody, bloody bastard. That was all because of you,' King spluttered, touching his cheek. 'But right now, you're coming with me and you can explain yourself to the CO.'

'Why on earth? There's no need for him to get involved.' Roger was furious. He pulled out a crumpled cigarette, lit up and reached down into the ditch to retrieve the meat.

'Oh yes there is, you know what Ellerton thinks about trips under the wire. Once one person takes it on himself to smuggle stuff in, others will follow suit and the next thing someone will get shot. We're going to tell him now and that's an order.'

Ellerton hadn't been awake for long but he listened calmly to Major King's version of events and gave Roger a severe bollocking. Roger said nothing; there seemed little point. But then Ellerton asked Major King to step outside while he had a semi-private word with Lester. King left looking decidedly smug.

'Don't worry about Major King. I'd like to thank you for your bravery and ingenuity, but I suggest you don't risk making any more expeditions, because I have news that within a week, us Lancashires, another regiment and some of the Aussies are being shipped out of Changi and up to Japan. I'd hate for you not to be accompanying us.'

CHAPTER 37

June 14ᵗʰ 1942

It is one blow after another. Duncan has been moved on. I had one day's notice and that was it. He didn't seem to mind and even said he was looking forward to a change of scenery; not that he knew where they were being posted. He was sweet and gave me a big hug as he left and thanked me for making him so welcome. I am told that we will have another billet shortly, but I don't want anyone. I feel like a petulant child who has had something she really loves taken away from her. As soon as I feel I am getting to know someone, they are taken from me. I suppose I am just going to have to keep busy and immerse myself in the hospital garden and the Make Do and Mend group which started up at South Baddersley church. At least I still have Joan and Millie to talk to while we are gardening and there is so much work to be done at this time of year, planting, weeding and keeping the slugs away from the lettuces.

Ivyholme, Lymington

June 26ᵗʰ 1942

Dear John

Now we are only allowed to send one sheet of paper, so

my letters to you will have to be carefully thought through so that I don't waste any words. I will try and write very small, though it is hard to know what to write. We are not allowed to say anything that might give the enemy any information, and there is not sufficient space to tell you how I really feel – and of course not knowing if you are even out there makes it all the harder. Some people say these official letters aren't getting through and some say they are, so I feel rather discouraged and don't know whether to send them or not.

However, I am sitting in my small sitting room, listening to a concert on the wireless by the Hallé Orchestra, conducted by Malcolm Sargent. They are playing Brahms' third symphony, one of your great favourites, and it reminds me of being with you in the flat and all those lovely times we had together, talking or visiting art galleries or walking on Wimbledon Common. Not much of that sort of life now. All we have here is summer rain, rations, rumours, and life being one long chase after something to look forward to.

The face of our landscape changes of course for the worse, and I suppose it will continue to do so for some time, but no one can stop the ever lovely ebb and flow of the tide outside my very gate. Yesterday I had such a pleasant walk by the river with Joan and this morning I saw redshanks calling and feeding by the Toll Bridge. I watched through your binoculars with an aching reminiscence.

Take good care. Your ever loving mother Min

July 20th 1942

WRITING TO A GHOST

While my pen plods these pages,
inking the distance between us,
I give you substance,
believe that you breathe.

But once my words are posted,
your face fades to a veiled grey,
your voice to a whisper
in an endless chord of silence.

Out there, somewhere, perhaps
you too are calling,
when you think of me, pacing
round these empty rooms.

August 1st 1942

That awful heavy feeling has returned. I feel weighted down
with a black sadness. I have no energy. Each day is a struggle.
It is as if there are two of me. One somehow still manages
to look cheerful and trots along on her daily round, telling
everyone that she is well, but the other slinks into the
house at the end of the day to avoid speaking to anyone
and scuttles to her room to hide out of their sight. I don't
seem to be able to shake it off. There nothing to look
forward to. How can I keep going, not knowing if he is there
or if he is receiving any of my letters? If after all this I hear

that he has been taken from me, I don't think I will be able to last much longer. I don't know if writing is going to help much at the moment. It is too much of an effort.

September 2nd 1942

Joan is trying to be such a good friend. She telephones to check that I will still be going to the hospital garden, and when either of us has free time she suggests a walk or a cup of tea in Lymington. I wish I could shake off this awful mood. Frank is at a loss and Cordelia has adopted a "jolly hockey sticks" approach which is tiresome.

September 15th 1942

Joan has started coming to see me almost every day. I had pretended to everyone that I had a heavy cold and that I was going to stay put for a bit and not do any gardening, but she didn't believe me. She could see how hard I was struggling. Yesterday something happened which would normally make me feel so embarrassed and ashamed. Joan made a very simple statement about how she could really imagine how terrible I must be feeling not knowing about whether he was dead or alive, and before I could stop myself I had completely broken down and wept. But she didn't tell me to pull myself together or look on the bright side or clumsily hug me to her bosom. She simply sat on the floor beside me, stroked my hand and soothed me. It was such a relief to feel so completely understood. Last night I slept right through the night for the very first time in months and I woke this morning feeling a fraction lighter.

September 20th 1942

At last I feel I have surfaced from out of the depths. These past few weeks have been a wearisome time, but today I feel slightly different. Nothing has changed, but something has shifted inside me. It was something Joan said about solitude as opposed to loneliness. She said that although she is very close to Millie and loves sharing their house, she also values the time she spends on her own, reading, walking, sitting or just watching the plants grow. I think I have always been rather afraid of being lonely, afraid of feeling deserted; just as I felt when Freddy went away, and then George, and then of course when John went off to school – and even now, with him off doing his duty in this awful war. It is as if I always need to be with someone and when they are no longer there I am so frightened that I won't be able to manage on my own. Other people seem to find a belief in God is helpful, but I have never had any sense of some higher power looking down on me, and even if there is one it simply isn't the same as having a human being nearby. Although, when I think about it, I quite enjoy being on my own, staring at the waves or watching the dunlins and curlews at low tide. It is only sometimes when I am indoors and instead of feeling secure with four walls around me I have a tremendous feeling of isolation. I suppose that is why I keep so busy, but it is exhausting. Perhaps the reason I am so drawn to Joan's friendship is that she seems so content within herself. She isn't lonely even when she is alone. She is happy to be with herself.

October 14th 1942

I had never thought that I could have such a close friendship again after Dorothy died. I think I am beginning to understand that getting closer to people means that you get to know them through and through; warts and all, as the saying goes. I was worried that Millie would mind that Joan had been spending so much time with me while I have been down in the depths but she said "Of course not. Our friendship works so well because we allow each other to be free."

CHAPTER 38

The queue of one thousand men and all their permitted baggage snaked in untidy loops along the dock front. John strained to see the *Conte Verde*, an Italian liner now allegedly taken over by the International Red Cross, that they had been told would transport them all to Japan. He wondered how many of them would have to share a cabin. The docks were still looking as bombed out as they were when he had last been here, when he had watched Bea's ship chug away from him into the darkness. All he could see now were two ships tied up by the quayside; a small, aged merchant ship dwarfed by an enormous freighter. Neither looked as if they were going anywhere.

They had left Changi that August morning after weeks of rumours and false starts about who was going and what they would be allowed to take with them. For John, the prospect of a change of scenery, even if only to another prison, was a welcome relief, especially since he was not going to be separated from his friends. Once more, Bill Ellerton had ensured that the officers and men of the Lancashires would not be separated. All of them looked forward to travelling away from the clammy heat of Singapore to a cooler climate and perhaps better food. There was a general sense of euphoria as if they were being set free, leaving the remaining troops imprisoned in Changi. They'd been allowed to send one brief postcard home in July – "Dear Min, Unwounded, well, happy. Being treated well. Love John." – and he felt confident that by now Min would have heard that he was unharmed. He wished he could have sent a few lines to Bea as well; but perhaps, once he reached Japan.

He had spent several evenings packing up books, paper, and other useful items he had picked up during Freedom Week a few months earlier. He was conscious that his two kit bags were far larger than many others, but had justified it by claiming that they were full of medical supplies. He felt as excited, as if he was packing to go away on a longed for holiday. A week before, they had all been marched to Artillery Square just outside the camp and there they had lined up to undergo a medical inspection, ordered by the Japs, who were fearful of any contagious diseases being carried to their homeland. The inspection consisted of a jab in the ear, which was harmless, and the indignity of having to drop one's pants, bend over and have a glass rod poked up the rectum to obtain a sample. No distinction was made between ranks in this public display of bare bottoms.

Now they had been joined on the quayside by a number of prisoners who had been shipped over from camps on Java and Sumatra as well as Sir Shenton Thomas, the governor of Singapore. For several hours, the queue inched slowly forwards and eventually John could see what was happening. The freighter appeared to be operating as a vast fumigation machine. For once, the Japs had everything well organised. In groups of fifty men at a time, they were ordered to dump their belongings beside the gangway to be sprayed liberally with liquid disinfectant, and then they were told to walk up the narrow gangplank. A guard with a megaphone issued instructions. On the count of "One", they stripped off all their clothing and shoved it into a labelled string bag. On

202

"Two", they jumped into a large steaming trough of hot water and disinfectant and washed themselves for a whole two minutes (their first hot bath in over seven months). On "Three", they were ordered out of the bath and under a cold shower and then had a couple more minutes to stand around and dry off. On the count of "Four", they were ordered to squat on the floor, still naked, where they received a cup of tea which was served to a tune played on a gramophone, and finally on "Five", they had to scramble to retrieve their bags of clothes and shoes which had also been fumigated, get dressed and then proceed back down the gangway into the hot sun. It was hard to maintain a straight face during this procedure and the whole pantomime was over in a few minutes, amidst much hilarity. Feeling fresher and more cheerful than he had for a while, he rejoined the snake-like queue and waited for the arrival of the cruise ship.

It was a very long wait. John pulled a book out of his haversack and attempted to read. Ellerton and Castle passed the time chatting to some of the men who had been in POW camps in Sumatra and as the queue began to slowly move they fell into step behind John.

'Find out anything interesting?' asked John over his shoulder.

'They've had a pretty rough time of it actually,' said Peter Castle. 'They've all lost a tremendous amount of weight and many of them have been quite badly treated. I think we need to consider ourselves quite lucky, even though conditions at Changi have been getting worse.'

'I can't believe they've had a worse time than us,' said King, turning around to face them as the line ground to a halt once more.

'Well just take a look, King, you can see how thin they are even from here,' said John.

'Any news about the war?' asked Holly.

'No more than we've already heard on the wireless,' said Ellerton,

'Wireless? What wireless?' said King. 'Do you mean to say that all this time you've had a wireless? Where did you get it? Why wasn't I told?'

'I'm sorry King, but I had to keep the number of people who knew about it to an absolute minimum. Anyway, it's academic now. It had to be dismantled. Poor old Lester was awfully cut up about having to leave it behind.'

'Not Lester! I might have guessed he'd be involved. I suppose he stole that as well did he?' said King, furious.

'No, actually he made it from scratch,' replied Ellerton

King paused and looked at Ellerton to see if he was telling the truth.

'I can't believe that you didn't tell me about it. Did you really imagine I'd go blabbing to all and sundry about something as important as that? For Christ's sake, give me some credit. I thought we were chums, Ellerton.' King looked deflated, as if all his hot air had been squeezed out. His face puckered and he turned away from them to blow his nose noisily on a piece of ragged handkerchief. He looked like a small child. The line began to move again and John shuffled forwards, listening with irritation to King muttering in front of him. Behind him, Castle and Ellerton seemed to have lowered their voices, but he caught something about civilian evacuation ships being bombed and he turned round sharply.

'What have you heard, Ellerton? Did anyone say which ships?'

204

'I'm sorry Garrett, they couldn't give me any details, but there were scores of ships that left in the last few days. There is no point in getting in a stew about it.'

John felt a sick pain in his stomach. He tried to hide his agitation. It had never crossed his mind that the Japs would bomb ships that had already left Singapore. For these past months, he'd had such a clear picture of Bea making her way back safely to England to be reunited with her family and managing to get word to Min that he was all right. He'd coped in the same way he had when he was at boarding school; by simply thinking hard about his mother, he could sense her very close to him, smell her skin and feel the touch of her hand on his brow. Now he suddenly felt that both Bea and Min were terribly far away. The voyage to Japan which had started as a bit of an adventure now seemed as if it was dragging him further and further away from them. His mantra that "All will be well" seemed hollow. He wondered if he could find the men Ellerton had spoken to and ask them for more details, but just then his section of the queue began to board the small merchant ship tied up alongside the fumigation freighter, whose blackened stern read *Fukkai Maru*.

'Oh bloody hell; there is no way we're all going to get *fukking* marooned on that old junk. God give me strength!' muttered King who'd regained his composure.

'Maybe this is just a small tug that will take us round to the Naval Base and there we'll pick up the cruise ship,' said Ellerton.

As they clambered up the gangway, along the deck and down the iron stairway to the Number four hold, it became apparent that the *Fukkai Maru* was already packed with several hundred Australian prisoners who had been boarded the previous day. They were squashed together on two tiers of shelves that were about nine feet long by seven feet wide. There was enough space to sit upright but not stand. Any sense of stoicism disappeared in the pushing and shoving and squeezing to find a space, any space in which to squat with their kit. The first night seemed endless as John sat huddled with the others, hungry and anxious in the stifling heat of the hold.

Alan Rose and Sid Melton were some of the last to get on board. Due to a mix-up, he and Sid had become separated from the rest of his field regiment who were in a different hold. Sid was a least a head shorter than Alan and had less trouble trying to squash himself into the tiny space that was left.

'I can't believe how much kit those officers have got with them,' said Sid as he looked around. 'No wonder we're all so cramped. It's not blooming fair.'

'There's always one rule for them and another for the likes of us,' replied Alan. 'I don't see how we're going to get all the way to Japan in this. Let's pray the Americans don't take it into their heads to bomb us; that's assuming there are any of them out there.'

Somehow, Alan managed to find a space where he could sort of lie down with his head resting on his kit and his knees bent. There was nothing to do except wait. Two tedious days later, they set sail in a convoy of four ships. Although there was slightly more room on board once the Governor and four hundred others had been removed to travel on another vessel, mealtimes still took about three hours, as it necessitated the entire company to queue twice round the deck of the ship in order to receive their ration of the predictable rice stew. As they chugged away from Singapore, every man who could find a space clambered onto the deck to watch the familiar coastline slip by. Alan found himself next to Captain Henderson and Doc Garrett, who smiled at him in recognition.

'Rose, isn't it? How's the leg doing?'

'Oh it's pretty good now Sir. Had a bit of trouble with infection, but you did a great job for me. Thanks very much.'

'I can't say I'm sad to see the last of this,' said the Doc, pointing to the shore.

'I know what you mean, Sir. Look, can you see the law courts? That's where me and Sid were holed up right at the very end,' said Alan.

'Can you see Raffles Hotel, John?' interrupted Henderson, who was standing on the other side of the Doc, and who had so far ignored him.

'Yes, and there's the yacht club where I used to take Bea sailing,' replied Garrett. Alan noticed the Doc's smile had disappeared and he looked rather forlorn. He wondered whether he should say anything. He thought better of it, but then found himself thinking aloud.

'It's a strange feeling, isn't it, watching it all disappear? It's as if you've been reading a novel and you've got to the end of a chapter and have a rough idea about what might happen next, but now you've turned over and the next few pages are quite blank. You simply can't imagine how the story is going to end,' said Alan.

'That's a good way of describing it,' replied the Doc, looking at him. 'Usually I'm pretty optimistic about life, but right now I don't know what I feel. Part of me wants to flip through to the end of the book and see what happens, but there again, what if those blank pages you're describing actually are the end?'

'Oh for goodness sake you two, enough of the gloom and doom,' said Henderson. He gave the Doc a hearty slap on the back. Alan felt uncomfortable and looked back out to sea. A short while later, there was a muted cheer from those gathered on the port side as they passed the far eastern tip of Singapore Island and the small dots of white-roofed buildings that signified Changi Camp.

The first few days at sea were not quite as bad as Alan had anticipated. It was calm and at least there was some breeze to keep the temperature in the hold at a bearable level. At night-time he stared up at the sky, watching the twinkling stars, and tried to imagine what his mother and sister might be doing all the way round the other side of the world. Twice a day, they were fed a small portion of rice and barley stew, occasionally augmented with tiny morsels of meat. Most of the daylight hours were spent queuing. Alan queued for his food ration; he queued for his turn to stretch his legs on deck and breathe some fresh air; he queued at irregular intervals to use one of the filthy latrines or splash the rationed fresh water over his sweaty body. When he wasn't queuing, he played cards with Sid, dozed or endlessly speculated how long they would take to reach Japan. He missed being able to draw; it was the only activity that helped him relax, but he'd run out of paper weeks ago. The only items on board that were not in short supply were tea and cigarettes. Six days after they'd left Singapore they made a brief stop at Cap St Jacques, the seaport for Saigon, where they could buy bananas from the bum-boats that pulled up alongside.

But the next week was hell. Every day it rained and the swell and roll of the sea made walking on deck virtually impossible. Tarpaulins were battened over the holds which left them all sweating together in semi-darkness. Not that the tarpaulins prevented the rain from penetrating; within a couple of days, the stacks of rice became sodden and began to ferment and stink. Flies multiplied in the humidity and at night rats scurried around, eating whatever they could feast on, either dead or alive. As long as he remembered just to breathe through his mouth, Alan managed to avoid gagging on the smell of vomit from those who were seasick. From time to time, he noticed a strange tingling sensation in his fingers and toes and his calf muscles cramped with pain.

'Must be due to the lack of exercise,' he said to Sid, shaking his hands to try and get the circulation going while trying to keep his balance.

'More like lack of food, mate,' said Sid. 'You should get the MO to take a look at you.'

'No, I'll be fine. At least I'm not throwing up. Mind you, if this storm keeps up, I'm not sure it's going to matter much. I suppose you've noticed that there aren't any lifeboats?'

By the time they finally made it to Takao, the southernmost port on Formosa where they were told the ship would spend two days refuelling, Alan was very unwell. He felt washed out, his legs were swollen and he couldn't stand up without Sid's help; he sweated all the time, and when he tried to speak his words were slurred. He began to feel quite terrified that he had some awful paralysis that had started at his feet and had now worked itself up his body and into his brain. What would the Japs do with a prisoner who was totally paralysed? He didn't even dare to contemplate the answer. Sid called Doc Garrett to come and look at him. The Doc looked worn out, though he sounded cheerful enough.

'Rose! Look at me, Rose. Now tell me what the problem is.'

Alan looked up wearily and tried to explain. 'It's my legs, Doc. I can't feel my legs. I don't know what's the matter with me. Everything hurts.'

'I think you've probably got beriberi. It's the filthy white rice. There aren't enough vitamins in it. Now don't you worry, now that we've reached a port, I'm going to protest to the Jap doctors that we need better food. There are others going down with the same thing, along with stomach upsets and malaria. Ideally I'd like to get you a shot of thiamine, but failing that we'll just make sure you get the right food.'

Alan had never heard of beriberi, but it didn't sound as awful as progressive paralysis. He shifted to try and get comfortable, noticing how flabby his muscles seemed to have become.

The two days at Formosa turned into ten. Alan was just one of many who were too unwell to go ashore. Others were suffering with a variety of ailments, including skin diseases and the dreaded dysentery. Sid was among those who were classed as healthy enough to unload the cargo of bauxite which had taken up one of the holds and refill it with yet more rice. Alan watched him return on board each night, totally worn out. Like others, he'd been steadily losing weight on the voyage, and although they were now receiving three scanty meals a day, the task of reloading the ship took more than seven days. Doc Garrett's complaint about the lack of vitamins in the food had been ignored, but each evening either the Doc or Sid made sure that he had some bananas, biscuits and even some fresh meat and bread that they had bought from the local traders. The heat on deck was stifling. Down below, it was almost unbearable. However, bit by bit he could feel the sensation returning to his feet. By the time the boat was ready to set sail again in mid-September, although he felt incredibly weak, he could at least walk unaided; that was until he, like many others, was struck with enteritis.

After changing course several times and apparently sailing round in circles, they were informed that they were no longer headed for Japan but were instead being taken to Korea; not that anyone much cared when the next storm broke.

CHAPTER 39

Richard staggered across the hold and up the slippery ladder. The tarpaulin hatches had been on again for last three days and the unexpected blast of rain and sea air, combined with the rolling deck, made him heave. As he joined the straggled queue for one of the twelve latrines, he felt his guts cramping with pain once more. Not caring who he shoved out of the way, he forced himself to the front, squatted over the hole and felt the watery diarrhoea run out from him for the third time that morning. This felt far worse than the brief spell of sea-sickness he had suffered between Saigon and Formosa, in the previous storm. He prayed that this was a stomach upset from eating some of the rotten pork the Japs had brought on board at Formosa, rather than dysentery. Squatting there, watching an enormous wave break over the bows, he couldn't remember what the exact difference was, except that if it was dysentery he would probably die. That would be the worst indignity of them all. Dying from his wounds in the battle or being bayoneted to death at the Alexandra would at least be respectable, but to die in full view of everyone with his shorts around his ankles, squatting over a filthy Jap latrine, leaking bloody shit, would be the ultimate humiliation.

Exhausted, he crept back down the ladder into the hold; the air was thick and foul and made him feel nauseous. Taking his place on the top shelf next to King and Roger Lester, he shivered despite the heat.

'Are you all right?' asked Lester.

'I think so, only a spot of the runs. I'm sure it was that disgusting bit of green meat we saw them adding to the rice. The queues for the latrines are unbelievable, so it's not just me.'

'No, you're right, Doc Garrett's been busy on sick parade. Now you stay there and I'll fetch you some tea.' Lester hopped easily off the shelf and went up on deck.

'It can't be long before we reach Korea. We'll all be much better once we're on dry land, wherever it is we end up. Do you want a game of cards?' asked King, trying for once to be cheerful.

'No thanks, not right now. I think I need to try and snatch some sleep.' He couldn't face talking to anyone right now. He curled himself up and laid his head on his kitbag. Biting his bottom lip, he desperately tried not to cry. Why me, he thought, why does it always have to me? Why can't someone else be me for a bit and see what it's really like?

He remembered how relieved he'd been to leave Singapore which held nothing but distressing memories for him. Somehow he'd imagined that everything would get better once he could get away. It was the same when he'd left school and later when he left the bank; get away, make a fresh start, have another chance. He felt as if he was still waiting for his real life to begin.

Ever since he could remember, he had always been controlled by other people who told him what to do, what to think, and how to behave. He had obeyed, partly because he didn't believe he had any choice, but partly because he didn't really know what else he wanted. The only thing he knew for certain was that he didn't like being himself very much.

For the first calm leg between Singapore and Saigon, he'd

managed to remain in fairly good spirits. He'd listened patiently while John had related his anxieties about Bea, all over again. Secretly he wished that John would simply forget about her and leave her behind, and eventually he'd managed to distract him.

In the last few weeks at Changi, Richard had started to write poetry again, having discovered that the Padre was a fellow scribe. He was glad to find something to do, and someone who didn't think that writing poetry meant composing soppy verses for girls. He and Peter had spent several evenings discussing why they both felt so moved by the poets of the Great War. Richard particularly liked Sassoon and Owen, who wrote because they had to; it was the only way they could make sense of the chaos that surrounded them. Peter knew about the nightmares Richard still suffered from and suggested that writing about his own experiences in the war might help. Richard had shyly shown him some of his early efforts.

On the fourth day at sea, after being prompted by Peter, he had suggested a different way of passing the time.

'Look chaps, I know you might think this sounds like an odd idea,' he'd stammered, 'but the Padre and I thought it might be a bit of fun to see who can come up with the best poem about any aspect of the war so far?'

King snorted, 'That's easy. How about this for starters – there once was a boat called the Fukkai, whose crew were a shitload of slit-eyes.' They all laughed. 'I've just got to work out the next few lines but I challenge anyone to beat me.'

'Er, very good King, but it wasn't quite what I had in mind,' said Richard, afraid that the idea had been hijacked and that no one would take it seriously now.

'Lordy, it's a long time since I wrote a poem,' said Ellerton. 'I'm sure we must have done composition for school cert, but I'm damned if I can recall what it was all about.'

'We had to learn big chunks of Tennyson as a punishment at our school,' said Holly, 'put me off the stuff for life. It was all so dramatic or else totally obscure.'

'Well it's not compulsory, but I fancy having a go.' said Peter.

'Perhaps we could have a number of different categories,' said John, looking rather pleased with himself. 'How about sonnets for soldiers, rhymes about rice and odes to the odious enemy? Actually I'm a bit rusty on all the different forms. Maybe you could remind me, Richard.'

'Excellent, Garrett,' said Peter, 'Who shall we elect to judge it, or shall we have a democratic vote?'

Although some of them had settled down with scraps of paper and a couple of shared pencils, Richard hadn't had much time to get his thoughts together before they made the brief stop at Saigon. Once they'd set sail again, poetry was the last thing on his mind. As the storm had taken hold, the boat had begun to wallow and roll through the waves and his stomach churned. Unable to reach the deck, he'd thrown up, narrowly missing King and Lester, who happened to be the nearest to where he was crouched. For days it was the same. John insisted that he try and eat, but none of the meagre rice ration stayed down. His clothes stank and it was only with Lester's help that he could summon up the energy to struggle on deck to stand in the torrential rain and get clean. By the time they had anchored at Formosa, he was weak but ravenously hungry. At least the boat was no longer rocking, but no one seemed to know how long they would remain here. For those not involved in hard labour the food had got worse, and he had only regained his strength because of the efforts of Lester and the Padre, who managed to buy bananas and bread from local traders. Gradually his strength had returned and he'd idled away the time writing notes, listening to the sounds of cargo being loaded and unloaded, or up on deck watching other merchant ships entering or leaving the busy port.

Now here he was again for a second time in this hateful voyage, curled up feeling pathetic, his guts churning, wishing he could be somebody else. Would it never end?

Roger Lester lit a cigarette and watched Henderson, who had finally fallen asleep. He felt sorry for him. At least his diarrhoea seemed to have stopped and he had no fever, which meant the risk of him having dysentery was reduced. Roger was scared of dysentery since Terry Peterson and Joe Foster, two of the men he liked, had both died from it barely two months ago. He'd been shocked by Henderson's mental state when he'd rejoined them all in Changi after the massacre at the Alexandra, but since he'd practically glued himself to Doc Garrett ever since, this was the first time he'd had spent any time with him.

Poor old Henderson, thought Roger, he'd seemed to have recovered and got back to his former self and now he'd lost it all again. When they'd all boarded the *Fukkai Maru,* Roger hadn't minded where he sat as long as it wasn't next to Major King, especially after his outburst on the quay about the wireless. At least this time Ellerton had given him credit for it, but in the end he had no choice but scramble into the only space left next to Henderson, Doc Garrett, King, the Padre and the CO. He wished there was more room on board so that at least he could walk around and chat with some of the men in whose company he felt more at ease. More than at any other time since the surrender, he felt caged in. All that talk about poetry reminded him of how different he was from his fellow officers who seemed to be all "public school and privilege", while he was a working class lad who'd happened to do well enough at grammar school. Henderson and poetry; well that made sense, he supposed.

Throughout the last six weeks of this interminable voyage, Roger had felt hungry. He couldn't recall the last time he had felt full and satisfied. The idea that he had ever left a meal unfinished now seemed outrageous. The only relief from dreaming about food was when he could go up on deck and stare out across the sea towards the wide arc of the horizon. Feeling the motion of the boat, he could imagine that he was standing on his uncle's sailing boat and escaping to freedom. At least when they had stopped at Cap St Jacques and Formosa he'd been able to pretend he was free as he bartered for food and fruit. When Henderson and some of the others had become so ill, he'd been pleased to have a useful role once more.

The storm had died down overnight. Sliding off the shelf, he climbed the ladder up to the deck to get some tea. Through the grey morning light, he saw the outline of a harbour tucked under the shelter of some wooded hills that sloped steeply down to the water's edge. He hurried back down to the hold to tell the others.

'Here, take this, Henderson,' he said, handing him a cup. 'With a bit of luck, it will be the last one you have to have from this hell-ship and hopefully we'll soon have some decent food. You'll be well in no time at all.'

But for two more tedious days they remained trapped on the boat in Pusan harbour, staring longingly at the shore. They were subjected to a further "black rod" procedure and some of the sicker ones were taken to a local military hospital. Henderson refused to go with them, insisting that he was well, and Doc Garrett thought he'd be better off not being separated from friendly faces. Roger enviously watched the guards eating regular meals while they continued with the twice daily ration of rice and rancid pork pottage. A stream of officials came and went bearing clipboards and stood talking intently to one another, but the results of their deliberations were never communicated.

Eventually orders were given to disembark and despite Ellerton trying to keep the regiment together by rank, no one was willing to argue with soldiers who prodded them with bayonets into a disorganised huddle to wait on the quayside while their baggage was inspected all over again. Finally they were informed that the Lancashires and some of the Australians would be travelling by train to Keijo (formerly known as Seoul), the capital city of Korea. Other regiments were destined for Jinsen, another camp about twelve miles away.

Ellerton explained that since 1910, the Japanese had occupied the entire Korean peninsula and had changed all the town names. They treated the native Koreans as virtual slaves, and the inhabitants of Pusan had clearly been ordered to attend the victory parade of prisoners, aimed at showing them how magnificent the Japanese had been in defeating the arrogant British. The streets were crowded with silent onlookers; some spat at them. It was midday when they left for the three-kilometre walk to the railway station. Roger didn't look back to the *Fukkai Maru*, he was too relieved by the prospect of being on dry land and the fact that there might be better food on the train. Refusing to play the part of the defeated enemy, one of the lads started singing *There'll Always Be an England*, and others joined in until the Aussies shouted them down with a song of their own. Five hours later, having marched several times around the town in hot sun with only a thirty-minute rest, they arrived at the station. Roger took turns with the Padre to support Henderson, who could barely stand on his own.

Once on the train, things began to get better; at least he could sit down on the wooden benches. Several times throughout the journey they were given little cartons filled with good quality rice accompanied by small pieces of fish, sausage and some pickle. The next morning, having not slept much, Roger gazed out of the window as the train climbed through valleys of rugged hills and passed over tall bridges which spanned wide stony rivers. There were miles and miles of terraced paddy fields and orchards of fruit; food seemed to be growing all around him. He began to feel quite hopeful.

Finally, at noon, the train arrived at Keijo station to another silent crowd, including several journalists with flash cameras. After a much shorter march than the previous day, along a street bustling with trams and bicycles, they turned into a narrow side road lined with dilapidated slum houses. At the end of the road was gateway into a yard, about 60 yards long by 30 yards wide, surrounded by a high wire fence. In one corner stood a decrepit looking, four storey brick warehouse and in front of it were a few small freshly painted huts.

Roger eased his gear down onto the broken rubble of the yard. He wondered why they had stopped here. Then it dawned on him; this fly-blown, poxy dust heap in the midst of an evil-smelling slum area had been especially reserved for them as their new camp. How on earth would several hundred of them squeeze in here?

After another incredibly long wait in the courtyard, Colonel Noguchi, the squatty camp superintendant, climbed onto a box to give him extra authority and began to address them. His speech was slowly translated by an aide with a megaphone, but the gist of it was that each person must sign a statement promising to behave and that if there was any disorder or escape attempts, everyone in the camp would be severely punished. Roger was about to protest until Ellerton silenced him with a look. Feeling defeated once more, he signed and, sullenly picking up his kitbag, he followed the others up the wooden stairs of the warehouse and into a large empty low-ceilinged room divided by a plywood partition.

Changi now seemed like a distant pleasant memory.

CHAPTER 40

Ivyholme, Lymington

November 14th 1942

My dear, lovely, wonderful John

The great news has arrived at last that you are alive and now I no longer feel I am writing to a ghost. Even if you never receive any of my letters, I know I am writing to someone on the planet. This last nine and a half months of silence have tried and tested me sorely. However brave, bright and bubbly I may have been on the outside, my heart has been breaking within.

It was earlier this evening when a wire arrived from the under secretary of State for War. I was so frightened that it might be the very worst news, but I made myself carefully open the envelope and there it was. "Capt John Garrett, previously reported missing, is now officially reported a prisoner of war". It said that a letter would follow shortly with news about your actual whereabouts. Oh John, John, you won't know how many times I have yearned to hear this news.

November 17th 1942

I have been so swept up with people's love. You will never know what this means to me and your heart would be as deeply touched as mine if you were here now; to know, to hear, to feel all the warm hearts rejoicing with me. I could never have imagined it could have affected so many so deeply. Frank seems to have telephoned everyone in my address book, even people I have almost lost touch with. I have been wept over and kissed and hugged and congratulated by one and all. I feel quite overwhelmed. I shall never forget these last few days. I have received telegrams from all sorts of people and letters from well-wishers pour in each day. Mr Hodgson, the vicar, mentioned it in his sermon and it was the very day that all the church bells were allowed to ring for the first time in months and months. Even a reporter got hold of it for the local paper and is going to print a little piece about you. So there we are, both of us in the limelight. Joan and Millie took me out to lunch to celebrate and it was so lovely to be able to smile and laugh with them once more.

I suppose it is rather strange that I am so delighted to hear that you are a prisoner. Imprisonment isn't something one would normally be pleased about. But you are alive; that's what really counts. How I long to hear from you personally, but at last I can see your face again, lit by torchlight and telling me "All will be well".

Your ever delighted Mother

Ivyholme, Lymington

December 15th 1942

Dear John

At last I have discovered where you are, although I ashamed to say, I had no idea where Korea was until I looked on my world map. I hadn't even considered that you might be moved. It seems that there were so many of you captured in Singapore that different regiments have been shipped all over the place. It must have been a long voyage all the way to Korea, but I can imagine how delighted you must have been to be back at sea. I hope you had a cabin to yourself; I know how much you like your privacy. The Red Cross say that I can write directly to you at the camp you are in, although they have warned us that it may still take more than six months to reach you. But at least I have an address and can visualise you better now. I have told everyone, so perhaps you will get letters from all sorts of people who miss you.

It is exactly three years now since you left the flat in Southfields. I am sure it has been a good experience for you, though it has been a sore test for me. I do so hope that you will not have outgrown me when you eventually return.

Best wishes and love from Min.

PART 4

CHAPTER 41

He was never alone. There was no corner where he could escape for a few minutes of solitude. There was always noise; the strident morning bugle call; the shout to collect food bowls; the clatter of boots as working parties descended the stairs; the incessant murmur of daily gossip; the shriek of train whistles as they pulled out of the station, tantalisingly close on the other side of the perimeter fence; the raucous laughter and bad language of men on the other side of the plywood partition. Even at night-time, there was the tramp of sentries' boots and the snores, farts and dreamy mutterings that emanated from the bundles of blanketed forms that lay in two neat rows like a platter of sausage rolls.

Initially the relief of no longer being crammed into the stuffy, heaving hold of the *Fukkai Maru* distracted John from the reality of how cramped their new living space was. Despite sleeping top to toe, the gap between the bulk of Charles King on his left and the sprawled figure of Peter Castle on his right was barely the width of a postcard. It was as if all forty-eight of them that inhabited this fifty-square foot section of the first floor of the warehouse were sharing one vast bed; if a thin straw mattress could be called a bed.

The day had started as always, with the bugle call. Even though there had been a further issue of blankets, he'd slept badly and could feel the beginnings of a sore throat. In the half light, his breath hovered in the freezing air; the meagre stoves would not be lit until after breakfast. Struggling into as many layers of clothes as he could before Nishiyama, the adjutant, arrived, he and his fellow officers had stood to some semblance of attention at the foot of their mats waiting for roll call; *ichi, nee, san, shee, go, roku, shichi, hachi, kyuu, juu ichi, juu nee, juu san* and so on. John's number was *juu nee*, eleven. The numbers had been assigned when they had first all stood on the parade ground and were subjected to Noguchi's welcome speech. It was pure chance that he had been standing next to Charles King and therefore rotten luck that he now had to sleep next to him. King snored all night and grumbled all day, but there was little John could do. Bill Ellerton and Holly were opposite him, with their backs to the window. Lester and Henderson were numbers thirteen and fourteen respectively and their bed spaces were on the other side of the Padre's.

Breakfast as usual had been a thin soya bean stew with rice and some vegetables served up with a straw-coloured liquid that was supposed to be tea, but worked better as shaving water. But it was his visit to the latrines that had been the final straw. Not only did the washhouse have six inches of ice in the long sink, but the open sewer running under the latrine was frozen, blocked and stank. And this, according to the Red Cross, who had visited Keijo camp in December, was allegedly a show camp – a camp that the Japs were using as propaganda to prove to the western world and their own people, that they were treating all their prisoners humanely according to the Geneva Convention!

Frustrated, he trudged back up the stairs, rolled up his bedding, plumped himself down on his blanket-covered soap box and lent back against the wooden partition. Attached to this partition were two narrow shelves which ran the length of the room, and on which each man had to store his clothes, food utensils and personal possessions. John's allotted space had a collection of novels, notebooks, sundry medicaments, a torch and several tobacco tins filled with odds and ends. He pulled the small rickety table – bought locally for six yen – towards him and opened his notebook. Writing was usually the only activity that could help him calm down, but however hard he concentrated, he couldn't block out the drone of King's voice beginning his daily liturgy of complaints. Why couldn't he bloody well shut up for once? Would it be too much to ask to have one day when King was not bleating on about something or other as if he was the only person suffering?

On the far side of the room were three windows, which at this gloomy time of year offered little light. The one on the right had an uninspiring view of red or grey tiled roofs. Through the central window John watched a billow of white smoke belching from one of the morning trains which he could not yet see, concealed as it was behind the buildings of the cookhouse and the trunks of the willow trees which lined the perimeter fence. He tensed himself for the piercing whistle as the train began to move out of the station. Exactly twenty seconds later, through the third window, he knew he would see the engine and the long line of carriages chugging slowly away; faces of free men and women looking out, travelling to somewhere of their own choosing.

And then he was with them on the train. First it would head north into China and then west into Russia. Skirting the inhospitable Mongolian mountain ranges, it would chug through days and nights across the Russian Steppes (if his

226

schoolboy geography map was correct). Then Poland, Germany (there was of course, no war) and finally across Belgium, into France and Calais. He strained his closed eyes to catch a glimpse across the calm sea of the smudge of white cliffs that meant home and Bea and Min and everything which was dear and precious to him. After a year in captivity, his heart ached with longing.

He opened his eyes and saw Richard squatting down in front of him. Richard had taken a long time to recover from the voyage on the *Fukkai Maru* both physically and emotionally. The fair hair that always flopped over his forehead was now cut short. For the first few weeks at Keijo camp, he'd had that same startled look as when he'd joined them all at Changi. As he gradually gained weight, he looked like a small animal waking up after a long hibernation, as the strength flowed back into his limbs. By the time John had persuaded him to write some sketches for the Christmas show, he was like a changed man.

'Are you all right John? For a moment there I thought you'd stopped breathing.'

'No I'm all right. I was on my way home on that train. Do you want to go outside for a smoke and a stomp? It'll be too bloody cold to stay out for long, but I could do with getting out of here for a while, if you know what I mean.' John nodded his head sideways to indicate King, who was now rearranging his clothes and attempting to dust his portion of the shelf behind them; he was still muttering to himself.

'Don't you have patients to see in the hospital?'

'No, the Aussie chap is on duty this morning until the evening sick parade, when I'll have to go and see how many more men have had their fingers half frozen off in the pointless activity of untying knots in rice-ropes.'

An icy blast smacked their faces as they emerged and walked briskly round to the rear of the cookhouse to find the only sheltered spot to light their cigarettes. John glanced at the other huddles of twos and threes who stood nearby, shielding the glowing tips from the gusting wind. Richard still spluttered on the first few puffs of his; he'd only taken up smoking since Christmas. Although there were plenty of other officers with whom both John and Richard could socialise, it was noticeable that almost no one had made the effort to cultivate friendships outside the small circles which had been established back in Changi. It was as if they all needed the security of familiar companions.

'You seem a bit down in the dumps. Has something happened?' asked Richard.

'No, nothing in particular, but like everyone else, sometimes it all gets too much. Today it was waking up and feeling the sodding cold as well as listening half the night to King's snores. By the time I got to the frozen latrines, I suddenly thought, I've had enough of this, I want to go home.'

'It's the not knowing, isn't it? I was saying just the same thing to Lester. Most prisoners are told how long their sentence is, but this goes on and on with random pieces of news about possible freedom that build you up and throw you down alternately. Perhaps we should plan another show. I really enjoyed writing those sketches.'

John smiled as he thought back to the Christmas show which had initially been the suggestion of Peter Castle. It started as an idea for a simple carol concert with the few bandsmen providing the music, but it had evolved into a witty

228

review, with a number of sketches and songs much along the same lines as the shows that had been held in Changi. Colonel Noguchi had not only cooperated by providing some material for costumes and props, but had wisely calculated that the Christmas show would be a perfect opportunity for further propaganda and had arranged for a civilian photographer to be in attendance all day. By the end of it all, John had been happy but quite tired, not from his role as stage manager, but from the sleepless nights he had spent beforehand caught up in a childish excitement. On Christmas day, he had made paper hats and crackers for the lunchtime meal and given homemade cards to his closest friends before roll call. He had tried to recreate the spirit of the previous Christmas when, despite the onset of war and the air raids, at least he had been with Bea.

Now, thinking of the card he had made for Bea made him recall that he had not written to anyone else that Christmas, not even Min. He felt a flush of shame for how badly he had neglected her throughout the time he had spent in Singapore, and now he hadn't heard from her in over a year. Grinding out his cigarette, he muttered, 'Look, I'm sorry Richard. I shouldn't have dragged you out here, I'm going to be rotten company today,' and strode back inside.

Richard pinched the end of his half-finished cigarette and put it back in his tin; he didn't really enjoy smoking, but it gave him a reason to step outside with some of the others and feel included. He watched John as he turned the corner, annoyed that he'd failed to cheer him up. He didn't think he could ever risk telling John how he felt about him; he believed he wouldn't have survived without him. He'd lain in the hospital room for four weeks after their arrival at Keijo camp, weak and hollow-eyed. Every day John spent a short time with him, sometimes reading to him or just talking. Gradually it had dawned on Richard that perhaps he could make a fresh start; he'd survived his injuries at Bukit Payang, had escaped the massacre at the Alexandra, and hadn't succumbed to dysentery on the *Fukkai Maru*. Why had he been spared when so many others had been left to rot in the jungle? Although he had no religious conviction, the only thing he began to feel sure about was that if he was meant to stay alive, from now on he would do what he wanted with his life, not what others expected of him.

They'd all had such a grand time preparing for the Christmas show. Not only did he have a sense of belonging, but more importantly, he'd found something he thought he could be good at; at least John and Peter had both been encouraging. Having written a couple of witty sketches and adapted three poems to be set to music, at last he had an idea about what he could do when this was all over. Not that he could expect any support from his parents. "Don't be ridiculous, you won't make a living from being a writer, my boy, you'll need to get a proper job", he heard his father say. Well, perhaps he'd show them. He didn't care. He already had the outline of a novel in his head, as well as a series of sonnets about the war.

He made a few desultory circuits of the parade ground – an area so small compared to the space in Changi that it only took him a couple of minutes. On his last lap he saw Lieutenant Uishihara, the interpreter, walking towards him. The poor man had been married to an American and lived in California before the war but had the misfortune to be on holiday in Japan when Pearl Harbour was bombed. He had been conscripted as he was boarding a ship waiting to take him back to his wife and children. He was a mild man who faintly resembled a bullfrog, but generally did his job and hid his dual allegiance. Richard saluted and asked if there was any news of letters from abroad. Uishihara shook his head. They had been allowed to send brief postcards home, first in November and then a couple of weeks ago, but the last he had heard from his own family was back in December '41, announcing the birth of his niece Vera, named by his sister after the "forces' sweetheart".

As he walked back up the steps of the warehouse, he could hear raised voices. King, very red in the face, was waving a notebook and yelling at John,

'I've had about enough of you, you sanctimonious little shit. What gives you the right to sit there smugly each day writing down what you think about us all?'

'And what gives you the right to read other people's private journals? We all made an agreement about the absolute need for this form of privacy,' shouted John, swiping the notebook out of King's clenched fist. Richard wasn't sure what to do and was grateful when Ellerton pushed his way between the two men.

'All right! All right! Calm down, both of you. Let's get this sorted once and for all. This feud has been going on for too long.'

King glared at him and turned to walk away.

'Come back here Charles, and that's an order! The rest of you leave us in peace and mind your own business.'

Richard gave Roger Lester a knowing glance and they both moved towards the window in attempt to demonstrate that they were out of earshot. Others busied themselves with tidying their shelves. After a couple of minutes, King pulled on his coat and followed Ellerton and John back downstairs to the exercise yard.

'King's had that coming to him for months,' said Roger. 'He could win a medal for being obnoxious.'

'It's a shame really, because underneath all that bluster, he's not really a bad bloke, and after all…'

'I know, I know, he saved your life back in Malaya,' Roger interrupted. 'But that doesn't stop him from being an arse. He and Garrett have had it in for each other since before the war even started. If anyone can sort them out, it'll be the CO.'

Outside, a train whistle screeched. It had started to snow. Richard watched the flurry of flakes hurtling towards him and shivered both with cold and delight. Their first snow fall had been on Christmas eve, and with the excitement of the show and the promise of real meat and even saki to drink for the evening meal, he'd almost been able to imagine himself back in "Merrie England".

'It's beautiful, isn't it?' He looked at Roger.

'Beautiful and bloody freezing. I feel sorry for the men having to work down at the quarry or on the farm. Poor sods take hours each evening just thawing out before it's time to sleep and start all over again. The Korean peasants aren't much better off. One of the lads said he's seen them freezing to death and their corpses just left by the side of the road. You'd think they'd make some sort of protest. I wish I could do something.'

'Oh really Lester, you and your ideas of liberation and freedom. What on earth can you do, stuck in here?'

'I don't know mate, but I'm working on it. The Japs can lock up my body but they can't lock up my mind.'

Alan Rose gingerly moved his leg to relieve the pressure on his shin bone. His leg wound when the axe slipped on the Caldecott working party had never really cleared up and from time to time the bone became so inflamed that he could barely walk. By now he was pretty familiar with the four walls of the hut that passed for the hospital. He'd spent his first two weeks in Keijo camp lying here, recovering from the beri-beri and enteritis he suffered on the ship. He'd lost so much weight, he'd been too weak to work, but once he recovered he'd was assigned to work alongside Sid at the quarry; that was until Sid's accident. Alan never wanted to go near that quarry again. It was only eight weeks since Sid had been crushed to death under a huge rock fall; the sight of his legs twitching and then motionless still gave him nightmares. How could they have come through so much together and have it end like this? There were others too, who had died from accidents and illness; even his old CO had succumbed to diphtheria and dysentery. After Sid's death, Alan had been transferred to work at the farm where the work was lighter but he felt weighed down with the blackest of depressions. Ironically, he was beginning to emerge from this dark place when his leg had given way and here he was once more on the sick list.

He looked up and saw Doc Garrett conducting the evening sick parade at the far end of the hut. A straggle of men, some clearly ill, others half-frozen mingled with a few of the usual shirkers. When the Doc had finished, he came over to Alan's mat, clutching a sheaf of papers. Alan thought he looked tired.

'Here, I managed to get you some more drawing paper.'

'That's very good of you Sir. I've got so many commissions

to draw portraits and caricatures, I could keep myself in fags for ages, but with no paper I'm stumped.'

Doc Garrett made no reply but plonked himself down on the crate that served as a seat.

'Doc, you look dead beat. I hope you're not going down with something are you?'

'No, I think I have a cold coming on but I've had one of those days. You know, when it all gets on top of you and something snaps?'

'You don't have to tell me Doc. Before Christmas, for me it wasn't just one of those days, it was a whole never ending string of them. I thought I was going to go under.'

'How did you manage not to?'

'Well, it'll probably sound daft, but it's a combination of praying a lot and of going into my head to take myself off for a walk. Shortly before you came in this evening, I was walking from Box Hill to Westcott. It was a warm summer evening and I could hear larks and blackbirds and even a cuckoo.'

'Well I'll be damned. I'm the same. I'm afraid I don't do the God bit, but my walks are usually across Dartmoor, or else I'm sailing on the Norfolk Broads with my old chum Jim. It's good to find a fellow mind-walker. Isn't it amazing what a bit of imagination can do to give one a sense of freedom?' John Garrett smiled and, with a conspiratorial wink, added, 'Anyway, I think you'll need at least another week to rest that leg before you're fit to rejoin the outside work parties.'

Alan smiled back and wondered, if things were different, whether they could become friends.

Garrett got up to leave but sat back down again. 'By the way, Colonel Ellerton was having a word with me and Major King today about setting up a programme of lectures like we used to have in Changi. We've jointly been given the task of finding as many volunteers as we can. I suggested to King that you might be willing to do something about architecture.'

Alan felt flattered and surprised that, not being an officer, he had even been considered. 'Well I don't mind, Sir. I'm sure I could put something together if you are sure that it would be of enough interest.'

'Of course it would be. As a matter of fact, I wondered if you'd be willing to give me a bit of individual tuition. You see I've had this idea about designing the house that my girl and I will live in once we're married. I'll probably become a GP and have a practice somewhere near the South Coast, so it will need a surgery and enough rooms for a troop of children. But I also need to design a small annexe which could accommodate my mother so that she can live nearby but still have her own privacy. When this is all over, I'm not going to leave her on her own again.'

CHAPTER 42

Ivyholme, Lymington

January 3rd 1943

Dear John

I have now received my first copy of *Prisoners of War* which is sent to the next of kin every month. It had a short piece about Korea which mentioned the climate and the life out there. I gather the winters are very different from what you have been used to in Singapore. I hope you have enough warm clothes. The Red Cross have told me that you are allowed to write letters but that they may take many months to reach us. Every day I watch for the postman. I try to imagine how you are passing the time. I wonder if you still have medical duties and whether you have access to any books or drawing materials. I would love to send you something but I don't know what is allowed.

It is a freezing cold day here, with heavy grey clouds and a chill that eats into my joints. Goodness, I feel old. Even my hair is getting flecked with grey. What will I look like when you return home?

I am sitting listening to Schumann's piano concerto played by Solomon and conducted by Adrian Boult. On the wall beside me is a beautiful watercolour that Miss Conway has painted of you from that photograph taken back in '38. The likeness is extraordinary. I talk to you every morning and sometimes I can almost hear your reply. It's a good thing no one can hear me chatting to you at odd intervals during the day, or they would have me put in the madhouse. I think perhaps I was heading that way last summer, but I am as right as rain now.

Best wishes, you ever loving mother

February 10th 1943

Now that everyone knows he is alive and safe, I am expected to return to my cheerful bubbly self. But it is one thing to know that he is alive and quite another to struggle with sending messages to him which he may never receive. Until I can read in his own words that he is well and is not suffering, I won't be able to relax. Every time I think I am coping, I feel as if I am walking calmly along a seashore, when a wave unexpectedly hits me, and the shock and coldness of the water takes me so by surprise, I fear I'll be sucked under by the advancing tide.

March 10th 1943

We have a sergeant-major billeted with us now. He is not a bad sort, but not nearly as charming as Duncan, from whom I have heard not a word since he left. This one, called Reginald, goes out early and comes home late and has little to say about anything, though he did mutter to Frank that it might all be over by Christmas, since the Russians are doing so well. But that doesn't mean that the Japanese will give up, does it?

The Red Cross have asked us to type our letters so

that they can be censored more easily. Fortunately I was able to put a new ribbon in my old Corona, and Frank was kind enough to oil it and make the letters that used to stick work more smoothly. But it is so hard to know what to write as I can't say anything that might be crossed out and daily trivia seems silly since he may not read any letter for nine months or more.

March 28th 1943

All day it has rained. An endless drizzle. Everything is sodden. I can feel myself sinking again. I have been quite tetchy with Cordelia, but she is such a trial. We have such different opinions about everything. Frank is no help. I wish that Joan and Millie were living here with me instead. We always have such interesting discussions about all manner of things. Since I was so down in the dumps last year and they were so kind, I have felt much closer to them, although our friendship still feels quite new. I do so miss Dorothy, but I think perhaps I am learning how to let people in rather than putting on a brave smile all the time and pretending that I am all right.

I have been thinking more about friendships and how they evolve from being superficial to something more solid. When you meet someone, assuming that you like each other initially, you begin by sharing bits and pieces about your present and past life. Then, over time, you develop a shared history of experiences you have had together – places and people you have met – that you can talk and laugh about.

Of course, this is one of the many, many things I miss

about not having John to talk to. How we used to spend hours reminiscing together. I so loved those evenings in the flat when he didn't go out with his friends and we would settle down in front of the fire after supper, and one of us would start, "Do you remember when…?" And then we were off; each recreating the picture of a time we had spent together, perhaps on holiday, perhaps a childhood memory. It was as if with each thread of memory, together, we were weaving the story of our life. But now the threads have started to unravel, the cloth is falling into holes, and when I try and patch them with our old photographs, I fail, since he no longer holds the other end.

April 12th 1943

Just a few brave daffodils are poking up their heads in the garden and I felt very brave today. I went up to London for the day with Joan and Millie. I hadn't been there for nearly three years. After what Cousin Martin had told me about the devastation, I really wasn't sure I wanted to go, but they persuaded me. In some ways, little had changed; people still bustled along the pavements, buses still wove their way along Oxford Street and pigeons still strutted around Trafalgar Square. But then there were huge gaps where buildings had vanished, leaving piles of rubble which were already growing weeds. Of course all the windows are taped and piles of sandbags guard the important buildings. It did bring it all home again, especially as Lymington has had no damage at all. I don't think I want to go there again. I will never forget the sight of Waterloo station, black as night; a seething mass of people struggling to get somewhere.

Ivyholme, Lymington

May 29th 1943

Dear John

Happy Birthday! I was very excited to see the latest issue of the *Prisoners of War* magazine which has a short account of your camp in it. It actually mentioned that there were three doctors there! I felt as if I was reading about you in person. I can't believe that today you are thirty. Really grown up!! I hope you are able to celebrate or at least have enough to occupy yourself with. I think your friend James will be quite impressed with all your experiences. I haven't heard from him for a while. We all get rather lazy about writing to each other these days unless there is something special to say. I wish you had been with me when I heard the news that our old favourite, Rachmaninov, had died. There was a tribute concert on the wireless last night; the evocative second piano concerto as well as the symphonic dances. You would have loved it. I wonder if you hear any music out there.

Here we just go rolling along within these four walls. I suppose we have all got used to each other, but one never knows from one day to the next. I am sorry I can't give you any more details apart from daily trivia, but we are told that we must be careful of what we write.

Your ever loving Min

CHAPTER 43

Alan thrust his fork into the drainage ditch and trapped the snake's head between the tines. 'Gotcha! Quick, grab him Bert, before he gets away!'

Bert seized its thrashing tail and within a minute had skinned and chopped it into sections to take back with them to the camp; fried up in a dab of margarine it would make a nourishing addition to the monotonous watery rice and turnip stew. Turkey-neck, the Korean guard hadn't noticed; he was mopping his brow and fanning himself as he surveyed the other workers, who were weeding between the rows of sprouting carrots and potato tops. Soon they would all stop for a tiffin snack of rice balls and bread and try and cool off in the shade of the willow trees that bordered the garden. Alan and Bert wrapped the snake chunks in sacking to be concealed later under their hats, when they would be routinely searched on their return to the camp. The Japs, being that much shorter, never thought to look under this rather obvious hiding place.

Alan had been involved with the vegetable garden project from the start, having been asked by Colonel Ellerton to draw up a design that Colonel Noguchi could approve of. The plot was two miles away through the slum houses on the outskirts of the town. Each morning, twenty officers, lead by Major King, and some of the men who were on lighter duties, were marched there from the camp. Back in the spring, once his leg had recovered, he had helped to prepare the ground using manure collected from the local farm. They had bought and planted vegetable seeds and now they had onions, carrots, melons and salad to supplement their dwindling rations. There were even plans for chickens and piglets. Their first Red Cross parcels of food, books and clothing had arrived in early February. Everyone knew they had arrived, since the boxes, clearly marked, were stacked up in the storeroom, and many hungry hours were spent speculating on their content. But for ten whole days the Japs denied that the parcels even existed.

When Alan, Bert, Fred and "Chaser" Charlie had finally opened their box, they were amazed. There was chocolate, margarine, biscuits, tins of cured meat, raspberry jam, thick condensed milk, boiled sweets, meat paste, fruit puddings and even proper soap. Once all the goodies were divvied up, Fred ate his entire ration straight away and was then quite ill since his stomach was so unused to the rich food; Bert on the other hand eked out his ration day by day, while "Chaser" Charlie lived up to his name, bartering and trading the choicest items, driving the prices up and up for the next few weeks. Alan had forced himself to be a saver and had rationed himself to one treat a day; a spoonful of jam with the evening rice meal; a dollop of condensed milk in his tea or on his bread roll. He had made his share last a good while and for the past couple of months there had been one small parcel every ten days to be divided between four men; that is, when the Japs didn't pilfer the contents for themselves. But now their supplies were dwindling and no one knew when more might arrive.

Feeling pleasantly full after his meal of fried snake, Alan settled down to do some drawing. He had a birthday card commission to finish for Chalky Harris as well as the sketches he had promised Colonel Ellerton to illustrate the war diary

242

he and Doc Garrett were writing. Now that his talent was well known – many of the lads wanted their portraits drawn so they could show their families what they looked like with whiskers or home-made hats – he had enough to keep him occupied most evenings. The men had to supply their own paper and Alan usually managed to buy crayons or ink.

He looked at the almost finished card; it depicted a caricature of "Turkey-neck", marching out of the camp on his way home; behind him was a row of buck-toothed, cross-eyed Jap guards waving him a tearful goodbye. Alan was just adding a ghastly shade of ochre to the Jap faces when a grey-gloved hand reached over his shoulder and snatched the drawing away. It was Major Goto, the camp deputy. He was a fat little man whose slanting eyes bulged when he was angry. Goto stood absolutely still and scrutinised the drawing, his mouth twitching and his eyes protruding more than ever. Alan felt the blood drain from his face together with a lurch in his stomach. He could be put in the cage for a couple of days for this and in the June heat, it would be unbearable.

'*Issho ni kite,*' snapped Goto and turned on his heel.

'Dear God, please let me get away with it this time.' Alan muttered a silent prayer, grabbing his coat – if they put him in the cage the nights would be cold – and quickly followed Goto to the camp office, where Uishihara sat with Lieutenant Tirada, one of the nastier guards. All three of them gazed at the drawing, jabbered together in Japanese and sucked their teeth. Eventually Goto mounted the box that Noguchi used when addressing the prisoners to give him added height, spat out a question and indicated to Uishihara to translate.

"Why have you insulted the Japanese Army with this disrespectful drawing?"

Alan wiped the sweat from his brow with his sleeve. He didn't want to drop Chalky in the shit, but he didn't want to anger Goto further by saying the wrong thing. He looked helplessly at Uishihara who gave him the slightest of winks while shouting,

'Apologise at once. Show him your shame. Tell him you realise you have made a grave error and that it will never happen again.'

Goto began to yell at him in Japanese while his face became redder and his fat neck bulged over his collar. Snatching up a bamboo fencing sword which was lying on the desk, he smashed it down on Alan's head. It sounded like a pistol shot. Surprisingly it did not hurt. Alan allowed his knees to buckle, let out a groan of agony and, with a surreptitious check at the look of satisfaction on Major Goto's face, reckoned he was performing correctly. From his position on the floor, he bowed his head and pleaded his apology which Uishihara translated. There was a brief silence. Then Goto smiled at him, tore up the drawing and ordered him to return to his quarters. Uishihara followed him out across the parade ground and in a quiet voice said,

'I am sorry Roko-ban, but these ignorant little soldiers have no sense of humour. If I bring you paper and pens, will you do something for me?' He pulled out a photograph of a young child. 'Will you draw for me a picture of my daughter?'

For the next few weeks, Alan was very careful; his belongings were searched regularly and all his drawings had to receive Goto's stamp of approval. He remained on garden duty but as the summer temperatures soared, his enthusiasm for drawing began to wane. Every day there were fresh rumours and the facts they could piece together from the uncensored portions of the newspaper (printed in English) made nothing clearer; "Someone has said Jerry has surrendered in North Africa." "I heard that the Allies are in Sicily, which means we're bound to be home by Christmas". Alan didn't know what to believe. Despite a fresh delivery of food parcels, when Bert, Fred and Charlie were randomly selected as part of a group of one hundred and forty prisoners to be moved from Keijo camp to work in the mines in Japan, he could feel himself slipping into that old dark place. With Sid dead and these three gone, he had now lost all his closest friends.

Then, one morning in August, they were told that a huge consignment of letters from home had arrived. If only he could read some words of hope from his mum and his sister, Betty; know that they were safe and that they had received the postcard he'd written in November. Another long week passed before the Japs decided to distribute them. Assembled on the exercise ground, they waited in the hot sun; it seemed to take forever. It was agony to hear nearly everyone else's name read out except his. All around him, men clutched close-written pages, savouring each line, smiling, reading parts out loud, clapping each other on the back. Alan had never felt more alone.

A few evenings later, Doc Garrett fell into step beside him as he wandered slowly around the perimeter fence. He liked the Doc and had enjoyed all the discussions they'd had about architecture, but right now he wanted to be left alone.

'How's things?' asked Garrett, offering him a smoke.

'All right, Doc,' muttered Alan, 'Thanks.' He accepted the cigarette out of habit and politeness.

'From the looks of you, you aren't all right at all. Is that because you had no mail? You must feel gutted. I know I would have done.'

They walked on. If the Doc had merely joined him to discuss house designs, he could have coped with that, but hearing the genuine sympathy in Garrett's voice was too much; it all tumbled out.

'You're right, Doc. I'd really hoped for a letter and I don't know how much more of this I can take. I am heartily sick of this place and half the people in it, and now they've taken all my pals away. I'm sick of our joyless, jabbering custodians with their petty killjoy approach to everything, their face slapping, their empty promises and their pilfering of our Red Cross supplies. I'm sick of the eternal rumours about how the rest of the war is going, of having my hopes raised and then dashed umpteen times a week. And I'm sick of the stinking latrines, the dusty, draughty, crowded, humanity-reeking squad rooms full of vile language and endlessly repeated obscene stories and threadbare jokes.' He took a drag on the cigarette and tossed it away.

'Go on,' said Garrett

'Okay. There's plenty more! I am sick of burning my fingers every mealtime on the stupid aluminium bowls and of having to eat watery stew with a fork. I am tired of disciplining myself against smoking my ciggy ration too quickly or eating everything in my parcel all at once. I'm fed up with feeling unwashed and putting on the same lousy old clothes every day; of the fleas in the straw matting; of having the same old tattered novels to read, especially ones where a delicious English meal is described in detail. I am sick of everything and worst of all I don't think I can stand the prospect of being here for another freezing winter.'

Neither man said anything for a while as they completed another half circuit. Alan felt a balloon had suddenly deflated.

Blowing his nose, he noticed Captain Henderson approaching them and was relieved when the Doc waved him away.

'I'm sorry. I shouldn't have said all that. I don't know where it came from.'

'Don't be. I was just thinking that I couldn't have put it better myself.'

By now the sun had set and the pale rose sky was streaked with wisps of charcoal. Other twos and threes walking in the opposite direction passed them but no one interrupted. Soon the guards would chivvy them all inside for roll call.

'I know you don't believe in God,' said Alan, staring hard at the ground, 'but when I was in that really dark place before, I remember telling you that I'd found a way through it by prayer. But right now, what's worrying me most is that I'm finding my faith is being sorely challenged just when I need it the most.'

'Well you probably need to talk to the Padre about that, I don't think I can be much help,' said Garrett. 'But to be frank, I'm not sure what I believe. I've been pondering it all recently. I have always thought that it sheds no light on the mysteries of our existence to repackage them in another mystery which we then call "God". The world – the universe, is certainly hard to understand, although a knowledge of science helps a bit, but to wrap all of life's secrets into another enigma called "God", which we then agree not to question, seems to me not to advance things much.'

'But how do you make sense of it all? I don't just mean this war and us being stuck here or all those poor sods who died for nothing. How do you make sense of why we are here on earth?'

'Well, I'm not sure that I do. It seems such a vast concept that I try not to understand the why of it all, but instead I aim to focus on the how of living day by day. But I think what you're talking about is a need most of us have for comfort in times of distress. Isn't it like a child who doesn't really understand what is happening, but can stay calm because the grown-ups seem to know what they are doing?'

'You think humans just invented God to make themselves feel better? No, I can't go along with that. I mean, look at all the religions worldwide, look at the evidence. There are many more people in the world who believe in a god of some sort than there are atheists.' said Alan, 'Even if you're not a Christian, surely you'll agree that a superior power must have created it all in the first place.'

They were the last ones circling the fence and could hear the shrill cry of Lieutenant Tirada urging them to return inside. Alan reluctantly turned towards the staircase that separated his dingy ground-floor billet from the officer's airy quarters on the next floor. As one of the ranks, he was not allowed to set foot into the officer's space unless he was on official business. When he'd been instructing Garrett in the rudiments of architecture they'd sat in a corner of his squad room or found a place outside.

'Well, I agree that is a bit of a thorny problem,' replied Garrett, 'what was there before the universe? But why don't we talk about it all some more? It ties in with a book I have just started reading about philosophy and literature. I'll lend it to you when I've finished it if you like.'

Alan smiled. 'Thanks. I'd appreciate that. You've done me a power of good.'

John bounded up the stairs, eager to get back to reading the book he had left face-down on his table. Now that more books were available, he had made up his mind that, provided he could, he would block out the noises around him, ignore the hungry grumble of his stomach and put up with his captor's pettiness. He would use this period of incarceration as a sort of enforced sabbatical. He was keen to study and grapple with the issues he'd been discussing with Rose and he was gradually feeling more confident of sharing his ideas with Bill Ellerton and Peter Castle. But roll call was about to start and afterwards there wasn't enough light to read the small print. Richard tried to persuade him into a game of cards that he, King and Holly had started and when he refused, he guessed from the look on his face that he'd resented John dismissing him when he'd been talking with Alan Rose.

Over the past few months, he and King had worked out how to tolerate each other, but he still disliked the man. John had initially been mortified when Ellerton had pulled them both outside after the fight over his private journal and had berated them equally for being idiots. What he thought of as his special relationship with Bill had evaporated in a couple of minutes. He had struggled not to show how hurt he felt and was even more confused when Bill continued to treat him as a close friend, as if nothing had happened. Ellerton had been clever, though, insisting that they must collaborate on the lecture programme. Now that King had men to direct and order about, which the garden project provided, he was much happier. Unlike John, he didn't care what people thought of him as long as they did what they were told. King's problem had always been boredom and a lack of self direction. It was strange how some men could provide leadership for others but were quite incapable of motivating themselves.

As he watched them play cards, he realised what it was about King that had so infuriated him; King envied him.

Before the war, he'd envied John because he had a girlfriend and a busy social life. Since they'd been prisoners, not only did he envy John's role as a doctor, which gave him status and gratitude, but he also envied his close relationship with Ellerton. Of course, King, as a major, believed he was superior to John, who was a mere captain, and King clearly hated to feel inferior to anyone. No wonder he'd attacked or belittled John at every opportunity. Suddenly John was back at Ivyholme, standing in the kitchen, listening to one of his father's jealous, sarcastic attacks towards his mother after she and John had returned from a pleasant afternoon walk along the river. He remembered Min shaking with emotion while she attempted to appear unruffled and how later he'd seen her brushing away her tears. Even thinking about his father filled him with fury. Then he thought about his own envy; of the boys at school who came from wealthy families, or at medical school, when fellow students recounted tales of jolly weekends in the country and intimate family gatherings.

Later, listening to the noises of sleep around him as he suffered from his usual insomnia, he thought about the letters he'd received from home; two from Min, posted the previous December, and one from Uncle Frank. Nothing from Bea. Of course it was possible that they still didn't know he was alive. They simply hoped and wrote. The effect of seeing Min's familiar writing – the up-stroke of certain letters, her quaint turns of phrase, her graphic descriptions of Ivyholme, the longing behind each word – had pleased and upset him in equal measure. How could she feel so close and yet so far away? He could still see her clearly, could almost hear her voice each time he re-read the letters. But for some obscure reason, he couldn't visualise Bea's face anymore, despite picturing her bustling around in her nurse's uniform, or sitting beside him on a picnic rug somewhere on the South Downs, or even snuggling down beside him in bed. He could no longer see her eyes or her smile or her nose, sprinkled with freckles in the sun. When they were next allowed to write a letter he would ask Min to contact her at her parents' address.

Through the open window, the last train whistled loudly as it pulled away. Climbing on board, he rocked himself to sleep, following the tracks over miles and miles towards home.

CHAPTER 44

June 5th 1943

Dearest John, my darling boy

It has come at last! This is indeed a Red Letter Day! Your postcard written in January this year says that you have sent me two previously and I can't bear the thought that weeks, perhaps months ago, I could have heard from you. But not to worry, finally I have something written in your own lovely handwriting. It seems that you have lost weight on what you call the Oriental diet. I suppose that means rice. I do hope you are given meat or fish as well. Perhaps the Red Cross will be able to send parcels. I have heard that prisoners in Europe are receiving them. The newsletter said that Korea had cold winters and I am glad to hear you were warm enough. I might have guessed that if there was an opportunity for some acting or stage managing you'd leap at it, though I can't quite imagine what your Christmas show was all about.

You say you haven't heard from me since before the whole thing went up in December '41. My poor love. I have been quite selfish thinking only of myself, floundering in the dark for all these months, without even considering that you have been equally helpless not knowing if I am all right; indeed, as I imagined, you still have not received any of the letters I have written since I heard you were alive. I can't begin to tell you how relieved I am to know that you are well and happy and that you are with your friends and have enough to pass the time. You say you would like me to send you poetry anthologies and books about philosophy. Oh my goodness, I am not sure that I will be allowed to, but I will do my best and get straight onto it first thing tomorrow. Oh my love, my love. All is indeed well!

Min

July 2ⁿᵈ 1943

My life feels like a switchback; one minute up and the next down. Since we are now only allowed to type on one side of the paper in our letters to them, it is fortunate that I can practice breaking this dreadful news to him here in my journal first.

When the letter from her parents first arrived this morning I couldn't understand how they knew my address, until of course I read the letter heading – Ivy Cottage, Holmes Road, Lyme Regis. Even though I had never met his girlfriend, Beatrice, I felt as if I'd known her quite well from everything he had said about her. It was so sad to hear that she was dead. Her poor parents have been waiting to hear what had happened to her for over a year, although they had feared the worst. It was so considerate of them to write and tell me. They seemed to know all about John, though not of course what had happened to him, but they felt he should be told.

Apparently the ship on which she was being evacuated was bombed not long after they left Singapore. She was shipwrecked and rescued but then the rescue ship was bombed as well. Margaret, the nurse she was with, survived and was captured, and it is only recently that she had been able to get word to her parents about what happened.

Beatrice sounds like she must have been a very courageous woman, because right up until the end, she had apparently been struggling to save the lives of others who were drowning before she was finally overcome with exhaustion and swept away. Perhaps I would have liked her after all.

But what should I do now? How can I write and tell him this, knowing how upset he will be? In any case, none of my letters have thus far reached him. Perhaps I should wait until he returns and break it to him then, whenever in the distant future that will be? But I couldn't bear for him to be holding out hope for her.

With the word restriction, I will have to phrase this news very carefully. Oh Lord, when will all this terrible loss come to an end?

August 8th 1943

At last I received his first two postcards, though they don't really tell me anymore than I already know. How I long for a proper letter. We are still not allowed to send books or parcels, but I am told that the Red Cross are sending these. He must be desperate for something to read.

Sept 6th 1943

Now we are only allowed to write letters of 25 words, and post once a month. Thank goodness I was able to tell him the terrible news of Beatrice before the restriction came in.

What on earth can I say in such a short space? I will have to try and be awfully creative. I suppose I could try several haikus and see if the censor allows them.

Ivyholme, Lymington

September 10th 1943

Only twenty-five words allowed: censors demand brevity. Love you, miss you, have become one word – longing. I remember your promise – "All will be well".

CHAPTER 45

Roger picked the last ripe tomato and sniffed his fingers in an attempt to preserve the tangy aroma of the leaves; a contrast to the usual smell of stale sweat and dirt. The sun was low in the sky and soon they would be herded back into line for the short march back to camp. Not a day went by when he didn't regret seizing the opportunity to escape which he'd been offered during "Freedom Week", when they'd been billeted away from Changi on the Caldecott estate. It had been a mistake to tell Colonel Ellerton and so nowadays he kept his plans to himself. When the right opportunity arose, he would go alone. The only problem was that having been in Keijo camp for over a year, he still didn't have a realistic plan. Not that he'd wasted his time, he kept telling himself: it was all to do with preparation. He still kept up his habit of hoarding bits and pieces which others discarded as rubbish, just in case; he had started a daily PE regime for both officers and men, not from any altruistic reasons, but as a cover for maintaining his own level of fitness. He'd attended Japanese language classes offered by their captors, knowing that not only would it be vital once he'd got over the wire, but also to curry favour with Goto and Noguchi. All this took time and there was always plenty of that.

Like Major King, he too had been grateful for the officer's garden project that started in the spring. All through the freezing winter, despite the tough working party jobs which the troops had to endure, he had envied the fact that they had something to do all day as well as being able to leave the camp. How many opportunities for escape had he missed as a consequence? He still found it slightly bizarre that strict rank and discipline was maintained, despite the fact they were all prisoners. Every day, marching the mile or so to and from the vegetable plot, he memorised every detail of the surrounding area and the possible routes to freedom. Though, the previous night, his ideas about who was free and who was in prison had been challenged. Shortly before midnight there had been a noisy commotion when an angry mob of nearly a hundred Koreans had attempted to break into the camp, shouting that the POWs had more food than they did. He had stood with Henderson at the window and watched the guards beating them back with bamboo sticks, kicking anyone who fell, back into the disorganised rabble. Perhaps freedom came at a very high price.

He had contemplated all the possible routes of escape once he had got clear of the camp; he could hide on board a train and head for Russia, or perhaps make it to the port and stow away on a ship. But without help from anyone else, he would still have a problem with getting identity papers, clothes, food, and worst of all, the twice-daily roll call. Sometimes it all seemed impossible and from the rumours about the progress of the war they could even be released by Christmas, so perhaps the risk simply wasn't worth it. However, the mob of Koreans had given him something to think about while he'd been gardening. If they could organise themselves into a large enough force to contemplate trying to break into the camp, they could be much more effective if they had help from the prisoners within. Surely there would be enough of them to overpower all the guards, especially at night-time. With a mass escape, they'd all have a chance, and if enough Koreans could see their potential, then perhaps they could throw the Japanese out of their country for ever.

Back in the camp, he loped up the stairs with the small handful of tomatoes he'd managed to pinch still hidden under his cap. Henderson, Doc Garrett and Colonel Ellerton looked up from their books and all laughed as he made a quick flick of his head, caught the tomatoes in his cap and held it out towards them.

'With the complements of the gardeners! Apologies because they probably now smell of my sweaty bonce and not as lovely as they did when I picked them.'

'Thanks a lot Lester, are you sure you can spare them?' asked Henderson.

'A perfect end to a happy day,' added the Doc, as he bit into the skin and slowly sucked out the juices.

'I'll second that, John,' said Ellerton as he smelt his, and took a tiny bite. 'Thanks for bringing us these, Lester.'

'It's only a few tomatoes,' said Roger, feeling slightly embarrassed as he sat down on his rolled-up bedding. 'It'll take a good deal more than that to make me happy. To be frank, I don't understand how you three can say you're happy when you're cooped up in here all day. At least I've been gardening in the fresh air.'

'Ah well, we've been gardening too,' said Garrett. 'We've been raking over the ground of our minds, digging for ideas, planting new seeds and weeding out all the tired beliefs that aren't adding any value. That's our version of gardening and it makes us feel quite contented.'

'Contented, occupied, it passes the time. But I can't believe you're really happy. Surely happiness is about feeling overjoyed, or excited or having achieved something worthwhile or being in love.' Roger couldn't imagine how he could feel content spending an entire day reading. On the days when it rained and there were no trips to the garden, the time always dragged.

'Well clearly different things make different people feel happy, but are you talking about a transient emotional state or a more enduring state of mind?' asked Garrett.

'Or you could ask, is happiness just a string of pleasurable events or is it something deeper?' added Richard.

'I think I could be happy for a pretty long time if I had my freedom and a full belly,' said Roger.

'Yes, but that's half the trouble with you,' said Ellerton with a smile. 'For the last eighteen months you have been unhappy because you've been longing for escape. You spend all day thinking about it, don't you? Just supposing you did escape and by some miracle you managed to get back to England, what then? What sort of happiness would you be searching for then – money, power, status, the perfect woman?'

'All of those, I imagine. What is so wrong with that?' Roger blushed, shocked to realise that Ellerton seemed able to know what he was thinking.

'Well surely that means you'll always be pursuing happiness as something outside of you, like a carrot on a stick, always dangling in front of you, and if you're lucky you'll be able to grab an occasional bite, before it swings away from you again,' said Richard.

'Yes, but at least I've got something I'm aiming for. I don't understand anyone can be happy without a goal. Perhaps since you've been reading all the books one of you can enlighten me,' Roger wished he'd never started all this. He felt stupid, as if there was something really quite simple that he was unable to grasp.

'No, of course there is nothing wrong with having goals and achieving them, but perhaps that is only part of the story,' said Garrett. 'I suppose what I'm saying is that we can choose to be unhappy right now because we're hungry and don't have our freedom, or we can choose to be happy because we are alive, safe, with good friends, have books to read and even tomatoes to eat.'

'So it's all about choice. But if I choose to be happy with my life in this stinking camp, that just feels as if I'm giving in to the Japs.'

'Well I don't know about that. Look at Noguchi, Goto and Tirada; they have their freedom and enough to eat but they never look happy.' said Richard.

'So how am I meant to achieve this state of happy acceptance? Am I meant to pray or meditate or sit and smile each day? How do you three manage to do it?' Roger was aware of the edge to his voice but couldn't hide it.

'I think the ingredients of happiness changes over the course of life,' said Ellerton. 'For the young, it probably is all about achieving goals and having exciting activities to pursue, but when you get older, I wonder if happiness comes more from having a sort of inner strength and an ability to feel connected both to yourself and to the world. I think it's being able to develop certain qualities such as curiosity and optimism and so forth, as well as having some sense of meaning or purpose.'

'For me right now, the art of happiness depends upon developing a consuming enthusiasm for the many small things in life that are interesting and a sublime indifference to those that are irritating,' said Garrett.

Just then, King strode into the room. They all looked up at him and fell silent. Roger saw Doc Garrett and Richard exchange a meaningful smile.

'What?' demanded King, 'What have you all been gossiping about?'

Ellerton scrambled to his feet and held out the last remaining tomato. 'We have been contemplating the happiness of a perfectly ripe tomato and we saved this one for you.'

King looked around at their smiling faces, still unsure if he was the butt of a joke. He took the tomato, wiped it on his shirt and swallowed it in one gulp.

'Very nice I'm sure, but grub's ready in the cook house. Just for a change they're feeding us rice.'

As the hours of daylight got shorter and the temperatures began to fall, a biting Siberian wind blew through every window crack and open door. No heating stoves would be permitted until the end of November and the thought of another freezing winter depressed them all, especially now they were receiving less food. Conversation focused on when another Red Cross parcel might arrive and whether the more optimistic news from outside could really be trusted. Italy, it seemed had now declared war on Germany; the Russians had apparently recaptured Kiev, the Allies were holding out in the Solomon Islands and the British had bombed Berlin. Surely the end must come next year. The Japs were clearly worried about air raids and had even ordered slit trenches to be dug in the camp and in the streets.

Roger felt hungrier than ever. When he heard that there had been a foiled escape from the POW camp at Jinsen, fourteen miles away, and that the culprits were all in jail, he thought again about how he could organise an uprising. He still believed that if the Koreans could be convinced that they had British support, they would be motivated to attack the camp once again. Perhaps if he could design some propaganda leaflets which the men on working parties, who had a reasonably good relationship with their guards, could distribute, they might have a chance. But he couldn't organise all this on his own. The time had come to speak to Colonel Ellerton.

'It's not a bad idea Lester,' said Ellerton. 'I'll support you on two conditions. Firstly, there is no sense in doing anything until the spring. Even if we were successful, the freezing weather would be a major handicap. Secondly, if you act without my authority and something goes wrong, you are on your own. I think the timing will be crucial and there is no point in taking an unnecessary risk if the end of the war is in sight. So in the meantime, I don't think it would be wise to discuss this with anyone. Am I clear?'

At first Roger was amazed that Ellerton was for once taking him seriously, but then he wondered if he wasn't being fobbed off. He could see Ellerton's point about the winter, but felt frustrated that he couldn't even talk about it with anyone else. But no one could stop him from making plans in his head or even drawing up a draft leaflet.

It was true. John did feel happy most of the time, except perhaps when the pangs of hunger got the better of him. But even on the days when he felt grumpy or annoyed, he knew he could reach inside himself and find that sense of contentment again. He was pleased with the way his studies were going and enjoyed the chats he had regularly with Bill and Alan Rose about developing some philosophy for living.

And he'd started drawing again. Once again, he'd enjoyed stage-managing the Christmas show (much bawdier than the last one) with Richard providing further material and Roger helping out with set design. He'd even found a way of not noticing what he ate, so that when he swallowed the bowls of rice and cabbage stew, or the bran mash of unpeeled potatoes, or the salt and lard-spread ersatz bread, in his mind he was far away, striding across the South Downs, or rowing up the Boldre River with Min. Following the second official Red Cross visit back in November, there had been another batch of food parcels delivered just before Christmas. It had been months since the previous ones and they had all learnt how to make the luxury foods such as jam or bully beef last a bit longer.

Finally, the almost daily snowfalls of February faded to a faint white sprinkle. News from outside was encouraging; the Russians had liberated Leningrad, the Allies were bombing the heart out of Germany and spring was in the air once more. At the end of March there was another delivery of letters. This time almost everybody had something; Alan was jubilant when he received a whole bundle. Bill had heard that his wife was safely settled back in England and John had another five from Min. He settled down on his box, dug out his last square of chocolate with which to celebrate and sorted the letters into the order in which they'd been written. The first three were typed, covered a side of paper and had been written over the summer of '43, but the last two were only a few lines long; clearly there was some new rule about word restriction. But at last here was proof that she knew he was alive. How on earth had she coped with nine months of not knowing? He felt so proud of her with all the voluntary work she was doing and chuckled when he read some of her descriptions of Aunt Cordelia and the WI.

He turned to the third letter, but as he began to read, the lines of type seemed to blur together. He blinked, rubbed his eyes, and held the letter towards the dim light of the window. He only seemed to be able to make out odd phrases; "I am so sorry… ought to know at once… not wait… until home… no easy way to tell… bad news… Beatrice. Her parents wrote… drowned…"

Still clutching the letter, he closed his eyes. He felt sick, as if a strong band was wrapped around his belly, squeezing his guts so tightly that he could barely breathe. What about their house, which he'd just finished designing? What about that lovely big garden and Bea pegging out the washing while their three children played on the lawn? What about their island dreams? Even though the room was full of chatter, it was as if he was at the far end of a long corridor. His cheeks felt wet. He saw Bea struggling to keep her face above the water and then being dragged under, over and over again. How could it be, since he had kept her alive for all these months? He'd spoken to her, reminisced with her, made plans with her each night when he couldn't sleep. What was the last thing he said to her? If only she had known he was there on the quayside as she boarded the ship. Gently he began to rock. He needed Min. He wanted to curl up, have her stroke his face and tell him that it would all be better in the morning.

He opened his eyes and gazed around the room. Nothing had changed. Everything had changed.

'What is it, John? Not your mother, is it?' Bill was sitting quietly on the floor opposite him.

John shook his head and held the letter out to him. If he

didn't say the words, perhaps he could make it untrue. Bill read the letter several times.

'Oh dear John. I am so sorry. She was such a terrific girl.'

John numbed his way through the next few weeks. The monotonous daily routine provided stability; roll call, breakfast, working parties clumping down the stairs, morning tea, lunch, working parties clumping back up the stairs, supper, sick parade, roll call, lights out. To those who only knew him as the Doc, he appeared the same as ever; cheerful, sympathetic to their physical ills, able to share a joke. But his friends watched him when the mask dropped and he disappeared into a lonely place inside himself.

What he couldn't work out was where she was now. If only he had some form of religion, he could imagine her in heaven, perhaps reunited with her brother. He remembered poor old Kelly and the conversation they'd all had about dying and going to heaven and wished he could have Peter Castle's certainty about these things. Perhaps if he tried to pray, as Alan had suggested, then a belief in God would follow. Some days, he yearned for some privacy so he could bawl his eyes out without interruption. Other times, he hated being alone. He began to wonder whether he was missing the actual woman whom he had not seen for over two years or the idealised vision he had created in order to cope with her absence and his incarceration.

Gradually, he made himself alter his view of the future. He tore up his house designs and instead imagined himself back with Min and their beloved Ivyholme. Each day his mind-walks grew longer. And as the bare branches of the willows and poplars disappeared under a canopy of green, he began to feel calmer.

CHAPTER 46

Ivyholme, Lymington

October 15th 1953

Remember those holidays? Dartmoor, Norfolk; bracken-scented picnics, wind in the sails, campfires, sausages, birdsong and laughter. Wasn't it fun? Come home soon.

Love, Min

November 4th 1943

I haven't felt up to writing in my journal since my silly accident, and certainly I can't write all about it in only twenty-five words to John. It was probably all my fault really, because my bicycle back light wasn't working properly, but Jack will have none of it; he takes full responsibility. It was rather a dark, drizzly evening when I was cycling home from South Baddersley church after the meeting about the bring and buy sale. His car came up behind me quite fast. Of course, my mistake was to look over my shoulder, because splat! I was suddenly in the ditch with my leg twisted under me. There was a dreadful crunch of metal as the car ran over my bicycle. I am only so grateful that he didn't run over me. Anyway, the car screeched to a halt and Jack got out and shouted, "Are you all right?" but I was so winded and shocked that I couldn't answer at first. Then I heard him saying, "Oh my God, what have I done?"

I was just able to squeak, "I'm down here, in the ditch." But he must have run back to his car for a torch because he didn't hear me. Next thing I was dazzled by the light of it and heard him saying "Oh thank goodness! You are alive." When he tried to help me stand, the pain was frightful and I couldn't put any weight on my foot at all. So he had scooped me into his arms as if I was a small child and placed me in the front of his car. A real knight in shining armour. He was so apologetic and drove me straight to the hospital, where fortunately they told me I had not broken anything but had a severe sprain. Now it is all bandaged up and I must not walk on it at all for several weeks. I must make a sorry sight, hobbling around the house on a pair of crutches like some poor soldier. Jack is such a gentleman, he has been to visit me two or three times since then, and today (I have no idea how he knew it was my birthday), he brought me a little cake and some chocolate. Oh, it tasted so good.

Of course, the down-side of being unable to walk is that I must put up with Cordelia's cooking and fussing, both of which taste frightful. She is desperately curious about Jack, whom she calls my new admirer. He is a nice man but to call him an admirer is quite ridiculous. He works as some kind of engineer attached to the military involved in building two airfields, one just near Baddersley, and the other at Needs Oar Point. I have no idea what we need an airfield down here for, but he tells me it is a military secret and that he can say no more. He is billeted in Lymington and his home is in Norfolk. He has a wife who is a teacher but they have no children. He is a keen birdwatcher and knows the Norfolk Broads really well. I know that John would like him.

December 5th 1943

What a strange, lovely day. It was one of those clear frosty mornings and I was hobbling with my stick down the drive to watch for geese on the river when Jack pulled up in his car. He leapt out, opened the passenger door and said he was going to take me for a drive in the New Forest. I was so surprised, I didn't even think to go back to fetch my coat or purse. I just eased myself in and we swept off across the toll bridge. I thought of John and his little car dashing around Singapore. Each time he has visited, he has always asked if I have heard any more news. He is so thoughtful. I hope that John will meet him one day.

It was so lovely to drive through the trees and see the bright winter sun sparkling on the frosty ground. I was surprised to see the number of military vehicles out and about, considering it was a Sunday, but Jack passed no comment. I felt so comfortable being with him that for some reason I began to tell him a little about George and the sorry tale of my marriage. He was very kind and listened attentively. Then I asked him about his wife and he laughed and said, "Imagine someone twice the size of Cordelia and three times as talkative!"

It seems they got married only about fifteen years ago, after his mother, who had been an invalid had died. He had always taken care of her, and although she had been a possessive, difficult woman, whom he had loved as a son loves a mother, when she died it was more of a release than a loss.

We stopped for some lunch at Brockenhurst and we just talked about everything under the sun. He loves music and since he has spent so much of the last few years away from his home, building airfields and other military structures, he has developed a love of reading. He likes all the classics; Dickens, Austen, Scott. If only I had married Jack instead of George. How different my life would have been, though of course I would never have had John, so perhaps it was for the best. I felt quite sad when he said it was time for us to return, but he told me quite genuinely that he had not enjoyed a day out as much in years.

December 28th 1943

Good news! At last the long wait is over. It has arrived; the first proper letter from John. It has got here remarkably quickly, written only in September. I can't wait to show it to Jack when he returns from his Christmas leave. This is quite the best Christmas present. At least I know that he has received ten letters of mine, as well as from other friends. How clever I was to remember to number them all. He seems to think that he won't be a prisoner for much longer and, with the good companions he has, he is not suffering. I have read the letter so many times I know it by heart.

February 24th 1944

There seems to be something going on. The area is filling up with American soldiers and the amount of army traffic trundling along towards the pier is on the increase. Jack has been working very long hours, but when I ask, he just smiles and says, "Mum's the word".

April 3ʳᵈ 1944

I had an unsettling conversation with Jack today. We were talking about what life will be like when all this is over. I told him that I imagined John would come home and take up a GP practice somewhere near here and how we would hopefully pick up again where we left off. Of course, I acknowledged that one day he would marry, but that I knew he would want me close by for help and advice. He looked at me very seriously and said, "Florence, do you not think that birds are more beautiful when you see them flying free than when they are in a cage. Please don't be tempted to keep your son in a cage like my mother did with me." Well, I'm afraid I lost my temper with him and told him he was being quite ridiculous. Much later when he had left, I had this dreadful feeling that perhaps he was right. But if John doesn't come back to me, what will I do with myself?

May 29ᵗʰ 1944

Another birthday! John and I are going to be so old when he finally comes home, we will both have grey hair! But I have high hopes that I will not have to wait much longer. There is so much happening down here. I think they must be planning a big offensive, but no one seems to know when. There are troops everywhere. Many of the roads through the New Forest have been widened and there is a constant noise of tanks and lorries rumbling along the roads. One can't go anywhere without being challenged by a sentry. Near the pier there are so many little boats moored together that they almost stretch across the entire width of the river. It looks like a small armada. Jack still tells me nothing, except that he is involved with building something he calls a mulberry, which is a code name I mustn't breathe to a soul. It is all rather exciting.

June 2nd 1944

I am on that awful switchback yet again. I feel so downhearted. I suppose I knew it was inevitable, but I have simply not wanted to think about it. Jack has told me that the project he has been involved with for all these months will shortly be coming to an end and he will most probably be returning home to Norfolk at the end of the week. How could I have been so foolish to think that he might have stayed down here indefinitely? I knew he would return to his wife, but in the back of mind I suppose I was hoping... Too many romantic notions. He was very kind when he told me. He said that I had made an enormous difference to his stay down in Lymington and that without my company it would have been a very grey time. But he told me that it is only by letting go that we can create a space for something else to come into our lives. It reminded me of what Dorothy had told me once; the trick of being a Scorpio is learning to let go. I suppose I have always been frightened that nothing would ever come to fill my empty space.

June 9th 1944

They are calling it the D-Day landings. Apparently more than 4,000 ships and several thousand smaller craft have crossed the channel to France, carrying hundreds and hundreds of troops as part of a major offensive to end the war. This has been planned for months and of course Jack was part of it all. I feel very proud to have known him. But all my excitement over the invasion of France is tempered by the fact that now he has gone. I feel sad, but for once I believe it is a sadness that I can bear. He has given me a lovely gift; a book called *The English Landscape in picture, prose and poetry*. It has so many passages from poets and writers whom we both enjoyed. He explained that he had seen it in a second-hand bookshop and what had drawn him to buying it for me was not only the title and contents, but the single wild flowers that someone has pressed between some of the pages; bluebell, celandine, daisy. Perhaps they are someone else's treasured memories of days out, such as we have had during these past few months of our friendship.

CHAPTER 47

With an irritable sigh, Richard re-read what he had written and once again scrubbed out half a dozen lines; the poem he'd been struggling with simply wasn't working. Across the room, Ellerton had a book propped up on the table in front of him but had nodded off in the stuffy heat. Holly, taking his usual post-lunch nap, lay stretched out on his mat, snoring softly. Roger was busy writing out a list of some sort in block capitals, and as Richard leaned towards him, he curved his arm around the paper like a schoolboy preventing anyone from peeking at his work. John was most probably busy in the hospital; another poor chap had been brought back that morning having been injured on a warehouse job. Richard had struggled to reach out to John in those first few weeks after the news about Bea's death. He'd felt annoyed and hurt that John had turned to Bill Ellerton and the Padre for comfort. It was only in the past few days, when they had all celebrated the incredible news of the Normandy beach landings, that John had seemed to have returned to his old self; the chance of being home soon excited them all.

He stared out of the window at the willow trees, grey-green against the pale blue sky. It was strange, after all the time they'd spent in such close confinement, that although they knew almost everything there was to know about each other, some still had secrets. Or at least, Richard assumed that since he still had a secret, others would too. Once you have lived a lie for so long, how do you then come clean? If others find you haven't been truthful about something so important, how can they believe that there is anything about you they can trust? He felt ashamed that he had joined in all their frank discussions about sex and had even made up some stories about girls that he had wild nights of passion with before the war. They had laughed and he had enjoyed the warmth of it. Fantasies about women were discussed almost as often as fantasies about food, though by an unspoken agreement, no one ever mentioned the soft moans and jerking hands that occurred under the blankets after dark.

'So, Mr Shakespeare, how is the love sonnet going?'

Richard jumped, startled by Roger's question. He felt an urge to cover up his writing in the same way Roger had done, although Roger had now put away whatever he'd been busy with.

'How do you know it's about love?' Richard blushed.

'That's all you do write about, isn't it?' said Roger grinning at him. 'Your unrequited love for a certain medical man?'

Richard couldn't hide the panic in his face. 'What on earth do you mean. Roger?' he asked in a lowered voice, checking to see if anyone was listening. Thank goodness Charles King was out with the other officer gardeners.

'Do you seriously believe that no one knows?'

'Knows what?'

'That you prefer men and that you're in love with John Garrett.'

'For Christ's sake, keep your voice down,' Richard hissed, quickly closing the notebook in which he'd been writing. 'I don't see how anyone could know. I have never told a soul. I mean…' It was too late. There was no going back now. He felt a mixture of indignation and relief.

'You didn't have to tell anyone, we've always known.'

'Since when?'

'Well I knew back in Singapore, when I saw you with a rather beautiful young man in one of the bars, and I suppose the others just worked it out for themselves. It wasn't that hard.'

'But John doesn't know and Charles definitely doesn't. He'd never speak to me again if he did.'

'You could be right about King, he can be incredibly dense at times, but you can't say the same for Garrett. But the thing is, Richard, no one is that bothered as long as you keep your hands to yourself, if you know what I mean.'

Richard felt stunned. Had he been that transparent? If they'd all always known, what on earth had they made of his boastful tales?

'Christ, Roger, what shall I do now?'

'Why do you need to do anything? Just carry on as before, I don't think there's any need for some great confession.' Roger stretched and got to his feet. 'Anyway, must go. Things to do, people to talk to. Don't worry.' He bent down, ruffled Richard's hair and made for the door.

It was as if all the breath had been pulled out of him. He suddenly felt naked and exposed. He couldn't believe that everyone had always known. If Roger knew he had feelings for John, then surely John must be aware of it too? He had even dreamed that, now with Bea gone, perhaps John would want to develop something stronger than mere comradeship with him. What an idiot he'd been. John was no more likely to become a queer than Richard was to become a straight man. He glanced surreptitiously at Ellerton. Was it his imagination or had Ellerton just returned his glance with a friendly wink?

275

He needed to get out of the room and get some fresh air, even if it was baking hot outside. He leapt up, tucked his notebook under his towel on the shelf and dashed outside.

As John headed back upstairs, he bumped into Richard, who gave him such a hurried greeting as he pushed past that John wondered if something awful had happened. Entering the room, he saw nothing untoward. The room, as always, looked like a large bric-a-brac shop; its walls and ceiling beams hung with the coats and towels of those who resided nearest the gangway, which itself was bordered on both sides by a continuous row of boots, shoes, and slippers. The shelves that lined the walls were crammed with piles of folded clothes, stacks of books, and odd assortments of boxes and tin bowls. The usual groups had already drifted into the afternoon bridge fours, Holly was rolling up his nap bedding and Bill was reading.

'I've just been practically knocked down by Richard tearing down the stairs. Do you know what's up with him?' he asked Bill.

'He's found out from Roger that we've known all along that he bats for the other side, as it were,' laughed Bill.

Instinctively, John looked round for King. Bill followed his glance.

'No, he still doesn't know. Let's keep it that way, shall we? I think poor Richard is feeling a little embarrassed. I'm sure he'll get over it. How is the poor lad they brought back from the warehouse job?'

'Oh he'll be fine. Cuts and bruises and shock mostly. What's that you're reading?'

'Peter passed it on to me. You can have it afterwards. It's called *The Art of Living* by a chap I've never heard of – André

Maurois. It's a whole series of essays discussing all topics we've been battling with, such as the art of happiness, the art of working, thinking and so on. I've nearly finished a chapter entitled 'The Art of Family Life'; most interesting.'

John sat down cross-legged on the floor in front of him and watched Bill as he continued reading. He thought about the difference between Richard's rather annoying crush on him and his own feelings of admiration for Bill. Despite the fact that he was only about fifteen years his senior, John always imagined him as older. He was wise, steady and thoughtful, and rarely lost his temper without very good reason; everything that John's father was not. But it wasn't a father-son relationship they had, nor was it the same as his friendship with his med school chum, Jim. This felt more mature, equal and enduring than anything John had experienced before. His support since the news of Bea's death had been unwavering. Over the last year, they had spent time most days, just the two of them, trying to work out what they wanted from their lives; what was important, how they should live, how, after being imprisoned for so long, they would try to make the most of their freedom.

Recently they had invented two watch-words which would begin to define their philosophy; "Explore" and "Experience". Exploring, they decided, would encompass any activity which was aimed at gaining understanding of the world, including history, geography, science, arts, religion, and psychology. Through the process of exploration, over time, a sort of mental map could be developed which would explain how everything fitted together. It was a bit like those ideas of theosophy that he had learned from Dorothy and shared with Bea.

"Curiosity!" Bill had exclaimed. "You have to have curiosity and perhaps a sense of wonder to have any sense of direction. Without it, life would just be a string of meaningless events leading to stagnation and our old friend boredom."

Experiencing, on the other hand, would be a less intellectual activity involving all the senses, such as really noticing the shape of a cloud, the taste of an apple, the sensation of floating on a wave, the pain of grief or the yearnings of love, or even activities such as flying in a plane, riding a horse or going to a football match. It was about being aware of what was happening moment by moment, as well as looking for novelty and trying things out for the first time in order to have the experience.

Bill stopped reading and looked across at John.

'So tell me what I ought to know about the art of family life?' said John, plucking the book from Bill's hands and flipping through the pages. 'I don't know anything about that, or rather, I know an awful lot about whatever the opposite is.'

'Well I think you'll discover that what Maurois says resonates with your own experience.' Bill took the book back and opened it. 'Here, in this passage, he describes how in our youth we can feel suffocated by our families and long to escape, but when we're grown up and find ourselves either in danger or surrounded by strangers, often all we yearn for is to return to the security of the family which we remember as loving and forgiving. Isn't that how you feel about your mother?'

Before John could reply, they were interrupted by King and the other gardeners trooping back into the room, hot, sweaty and noisy. Some grabbed towels and headed for the washroom, others flopped down onto their bedding rolls and continued chatting. King plonked himself next to Holly and started to tell him about how many carrots he'd dug. The moment was lost.

There was a pounding of feet up the stairs. Tirada and Uishihara strode into the room.

'Roll call on parade ground. You all must come. We are rolling the call, immediate, now!'

'What is this all about?' asked Ellerton.

'No questions. No talking. You all come now.'

'Oh for Christ's sake! What now? I haven't even had time for a wash.' said King.

Muttering to each other, they all filed downstairs and onto the exercise ground where John noticed Alan Rose already standing in line with the men from his squad room. Richard and Roger, who'd been outside, took their places beside Peter. Others shuffled into line, their towels draped over their arms. They stood to attention and recited their numbers; those in sick bay were accounted for. Colonel Noguchi and the remaining guards marched into the quarters. This must be yet another search, but it was most unusual for it to be held this late in the afternoon. John wondered what had triggered it; their diaries were regularly collected for censorship, but so far had always been returned.

The sun was still warm. There wasn't a breath of wind. All around him, and most especially from King, he could smell the stale sweat of unwashed bodies. He needed a pee. There was no chance of that. Time to go into his head for a walk to keep himself distracted; perhaps the coastal path from St Just to Sennen Cove.

They must have stood there for nearly hour before Noguchi, Goto and the guards emerged, clutching a sheaf of papers. They seemed to be coming straight towards him. He felt his heart beating and searched his mind for what they could have found. But they stopped in front of Roger Lester. Goto glared up at his face and slapped him hard on both cheeks with such force that Roger stumbled. Two guards pushed him to the ground, kicked him a few times and then dragged him towards Noguchi's office. It was all over so fast.

'You all will return to your quarters,' said Noguchi.

John, relieved he no longer had to ignore the pressure in his bladder, dashed to the latrine and then joined the others upstairs. The mess was unbelievable; the shelves had been cleared, their possessions strewn everywhere; tables were upended and their bedding rolls cluttered the gangway.

'What on earth can Roger have done?' John asked Richard.

'I've no idea, but I did see him writing something earlier today that he didn't want me catching sight of.'

'I was dreading this,' said Bill gloomily. 'I thought he'd got over all that need to start a revolution and escape.'

Wearily, they tried to re-establish some sort of order and began to stow their belongings back on the shelves. The room echoed with cries of exasperation as over forty men tried to locate their personal possessions, especially diaries and small mementos, and several arguments broke out as to what belonged to whom. John felt a sense of dread in the pit of his stomach.

After the evening rice and turnip stew had been consumed amidst endless speculation about what had happened, Bill was summoned to Noguchi's office. Most of the officers drifted down to exercise ground in the hope of being able to be the first to hear the news. John completed his evening sick parade in record time and joined Richard, Holly and Peter, who were standing as near as they dared to Noguchi's office. They must have each smoked at least three cigarettes before they were driven back indoors by the sentry.

Bill returned much later, looking grey-faced and totally exhausted. As he entered the room, all chatter abruptly ceased. Everyone looked at him.

'All I can tell you for now,' he announced, 'is that Lieutenant Lester has been arrested for planning an escape and attempting to corrupt some of the local Koreans. He has been taken to jail in another part of the town. Let that be a lesson to any of you who have entertained any ideas that you might try and get away from here before the war is officially over.'

There was a brief shocked silence and the chatter started up again, much louder than before. Bill went to his seat and sat down. John and the others gathered around him.

'Are you going to tell us what happened?' asked Holly.

'The fool, the bloody fool,' said Bill, thumping his fist down on the rickety table. 'I told him he wasn't to put the plan into action without my approval.'

'Do you mean you knew he had an escape plan?' asked King.

'It was something he mentioned more than six months ago. I told him he'd have to wait until the spring and then he'd need my full cooperation before he did anything. I had hoped that he'd given up on the idea and settled down, but not Roger – he always had to be doing something. Christ, what a mess. I don't know what'll happen to him now.'

'But what was the plan?' asked Richard. 'I saw him writing stuff but I had no idea it was part of an escape.'

'He was only planning to incite the local Koreans to riot,

promising that if they attacked the camp from the outside, we would join them and get rid of the guards. What they found in their search was a whole sheaf of flyers he'd written, and some sharpened implements he must have been nicking from the garden.'

'But how the bloody hell did they know where to look?' asked King.

'Well, it seems Uishihara had overheard him trying to persuade some of the men on the job down at the docks to take the leaflets and distribute them to the local workers.'

John felt a moment of panic as he tried to recall which working party Alan had been assigned to.

'Blinky blimey!' said Holly. 'Have any of the other men been arrested?'

'I think some were questioned, but since they had been heard to turn down Roger's request, they were let go with a beating.'

'Bill, tell us what happened in Noguchi's office,' said John.

'Well by the time I got there Roger had suffered a pretty good going over. His lip was bleeding and he had the beginnings of a black eye. He didn't look at me once – not until Noguchi asked me if I knew anything of Roger's plan. Then Roger looked straight at me, his eyes seemed to be pleading, and he gave me a slight shake of his head as if to say, "Tell them you knew nothing." When I took a deep breath and told them that I was as shocked as they were, Roger smiled with relief. I feel so bad about it now, because of course I did know and I had warned Roger that if he went ahead on his own that I wouldn't stand by him, but I never dreamed it would come to this. If I'd admitted I knew anything, every single one of us would have been punished, our food would be cut back and we could say goodbye to any food parcels or letters from home. I think because I've always had a reasonably good relationship with Noguchi he really wanted to believe me. The next thing, Roger was frog-marched out and I was dismissed.' Bill's voice trailed off.

'I think I'll go and say some prayers for the poor boy,' said Peter, getting up and looking across to the space where Roger should by now be rolling out his bedding mat.

'And I thought Uishihara was on our side. I'll never trust that bastard ever again,' muttered Holly.

CHAPTER 48

July 10ᵗʰ 1944

I have now received two more letters. Such a delicious treat! When I open them, I feel like a child tearing off the wrappings of a longed for present and for several hours after I have read them, my heart flutters and I can't stop smiling. He sounds so well and is having the read of his life, with a love of poetry substituting for music. I am so excited by his plans for us to have a little holiday together as soon as he returns, though of course I don't have enough money to splash out and buy him another Austin Seven as he has requested. I went through all our holiday photographs again last night and thought about where we could go. It is a relief to know that he is still receiving my letters, even if they say nothing at all, and that he knows the news about Dorothy and Beatrice.

Frank and Cordelia have gone to stay with friends in Hereford for a couple of weeks. They are thinking of moving to somewhere near there once the war is over. It is delightful to have the house entirely to myself. Joan came to tea and said that the New Forest is eerily quiet now that all the troops are in France and beyond.

We talked about the future and the plans John has for our little holiday. I told her what Jack had said about letting him go and how hard it is to contemplate my life without him living nearby. Because I have had to part with him for all these long years of war, not knowing what fate might befall him, it seems so unfair that he may return only to leave me once more. But she said I should think of it differently. It isn't about letting him go and never seeing him again; it is rather like gardening. You plant seeds and nurture them to grow into strong healthy plants. But the gardener's task is to let them grow in the direction they want, while she sits back and enjoys their beauty.

For the first time, she told me about her own failed marriage. Her husband was a weak man who demanded that she spend all her time with him. He was like a parasite, so busy needing her to love him above all else in her life, that he had nothing left to offer her in return. It was if he had a greedy emptiness that could never be filled. John's father was rather like that I suppose, though I have never thought of him as a weak man; he was too violent. But I can understand the message behind Joan's words well enough.

September 5th 1944

The last few days have been glorious; warm sun, fields of stubble after harvest, late blackberries and birdsong. With all the events going on in Europe, it really does seem as if we must be nearing the end of this awfulness.

At long last I have begun to sort through Dorothy's books and make space for them. I have started reading Blavatsky's *Key to Theosophy*. It is actually beginning to make sense; she would be very proud of me.

CHAPTER 49

At last Roger thought he could detect the faint glimmer of dawn through the thin strip of window just below the ceiling. There was perhaps only an hour or so to wait before the daily clang of doors, the shouts of the guards and the clatter of rice bowls that would herald another day of nothing; a another day of trying to be deaf to the cries of torture.

It had been Roger's turn to sleep nearest the piss bucket and since it was nearly full, the stench was disgusting. He was desperate for a cigarette and the mere thought of one set off a coughing fit. His bones ached; with the lack of food, he'd been losing weight steadily since he'd been here and his hip bone burned against the hard floor. He longed to roll over onto his back but that would mean disturbing Chin Ho, on one side, whose knobbly spine was squashed against Roger's chest, and Kyung, who was asleep behind him, wedged against the wall. Chin Ho, whose official Japanese name was Fusao, had been in this stinking cell for almost nine months now. He was the only one of the other eight Korean occupants who could speak a smattering of English, having lived abroad for a short while when he was a boy. The others were all about Roger's age and hadn't known anything other than life under Japanese occupation. They had been brought up to speak Japanese and had official Japanese names, but each of them also knew their secret Korean name and spoke enough Hangul to communicate when there was no risk of being overheard. The crime that had landed Chin Ho in prison was attacking the Japanese official who had forced both his sisters into sexual slavery.

Roger didn't know how long he had been in Seodaemun Prison. He guessed that it must be autumn by the shortening days and increasingly cold nights. When he had first been shoved through the door, his head shaved, his face bloodied and bruised, he couldn't believe that this overcrowded cell was anything but a temporary arrangement. His fellow cellmates looked at him curiously but had merely shuffled themselves along the wall to create a space for him by day, and later showed him how to curl himself around them like sardines in a tin for the night. Since he was a good foot taller than most of them, he always woke with an excruciating crick in his neck. At least he'd been spared the "coffins", unlike Kyung who'd spent days locked in an upright box, only six inches wide at the base, in between being dragged out and flogged until he confessed to anything they wanted him to admit to.

In the first few weeks, Roger had heard each man's story, translated slowly by Chin Ho. They had affectionately called Roger "Doju", which meant "escapee", after he had explained why he was here. He'd told them about what had happened to him during the war in Singapore and of his life in the Changi and Keijo prison camps. He'd entertained them with the stories of camp life, such as the time when Private Walton had stolen what he'd thought to be a large supply of ghee from the store room and had sold it off in small portions to most of the inmates, only to discover once they'd all had violent diarrhoea that it was in fact boot polish. He'd even tried to explain about the Christmas show, with its silly sketches and songs. Prison camp life and this hellhole couldn't be more different.

But that had all been in the first few weeks when he'd still felt a bit of a hero for not landing Bill Ellerton in any trouble. Roger had assumed that after a short punishment he would be allowed to return to the camp. He'd tried to imagine how impressed his parents would be when he told them about building the wireless, his sorties from Changi camp to smuggle in extra food rations, his escape plans, and about how he had taken the suffering of the Koreans as seriously as his mother had taken her fight for women's votes. At last his father would look at him with pride and affection.

But now he no longer felt like the brave hero. He missed his friends; Henderson's silly poetry, the ever cheerful Holly, grumpy old King and the sight of Doc Garrett sitting day after day at his table, wrestling with the meaning of life. Despite being squashed in the cell with eight others, he felt very alone. They weren't the same eight; two had been taken away and replaced by two more, who had spent weeks in the torture cells and who had stories to tell and be told. But lying here on the cold floor he'd had enough. He was tired, he wanted to go home, be reunited with his family, laugh with his sisters, taste his mother's apple crumble...

'No! Don't think about food; at least not until your belly has been lined with rice gruel,' he told himself severely.

'But I can't stop myself, I'm so hungry,' he argued back. 'Even watery rice would be better than nothing.'

'So while you're waiting for breakfast, take yourself off somewhere. Think about that sailing trip on the Broads that Uncle Harry took you on. Do you remember the glorious smell of freshness that first morning at Bell Hill when you walked together among the pine trees, cracking the thin ice that had formed overnight on the puddles? And what about how the steam rose from the heather as the sun came up and how tiny birds darted between the reed beds and the brown stems of bracken? Come on, think!'

'All I can smell is this reeking piss bucket right by my head.'

'Come on Roger, you have to try harder. Your mind is free to go wherever it wants to. You know you have a choice. Are you going to let these little yellow bastards take your mind and your imagination away along with everything else?'

'But it's so hard.'

'Of course it's hard, that's why you have to keep practising. You have to stay connected with everything that is good, that makes sense, that keeps you human and sane and free.'

'All right,' he conceded, 'I'll go back to the lists.'

He had thought up the list exercise just a few days previously. He'd started the list with half a dozen headings to begin with; girls, music, nice smells and so on. The next step would be to choose a category at random and select about ten examples to fit each one. He'd already decided on the ten best girls he'd been with to fit the first category. Now he had to choose his ten favourite pieces of jazz music; then to think of ten good smells to counteract the smell of piss and shit and sweat. Other categories could include treasured objects from each room of his childhood home, or the ten best unforgettable landscape views, or even occupations he could take up when he got home. Perhaps when he'd finished he could invent some people he could weave into a story involving an item from each category. The possibilities were endless and, provided he could keep his weaker self at bay, he could survive until they let him go.

He was aware that these conversations between his feeble

self and a strong other self seemed to be happening almost daily. He wondered if it meant he was going mad, and yet mostly, when he was able to give himself a good talking to, he felt better and he could cope for a bit longer until Chin Ho might feel like teaching him some more Japanese, or they were let out for a brief spell for what was called exercise.

Weeks passed. It grew colder. Now there was never any glimmer of dawn in the thin strip of sky; it was still dark outside when they were given their wet rice breakfast. Roger shivered and tried to move closer to Hansuke, the latest arrival. He had replaced Chin Ho, who had been taken away quite suddenly the previous week. Hansuke was barely a teenager and he didn't know his Korean name; every night he cried in his sleep. Now no one in the cell spoke English and Roger's grasp of Japanese was still limited. He had no idea which month it was; perhaps Christmas had come and gone. He tried to recall the show he'd been part of the previous year, but felt himself shivering again. He wriggled his bony hips closer to try and steal some of Hansuke's warmth. Every time he moved he coughed and each time he coughed it left him breathless and drained. He felt hot and sweat dripped from his forehead. The night felt as if it would last forever. He tried to gauge the time, but relying on the emptiness of his stomach or the fullness of his bladder had become increasingly unreliable.

He'd exhausted the lists; his memory didn't seem to be as good as it used to be. Now his main distraction was to pay a daily visit to the boatyard he'd invented, which was situated on the Norfolk coast. As the owner, he had to know the tide timetable, monitor which boats came and went, conduct running repairs, splice ropes and cope with the frequent North Sea storms. It kept him quite busy, in between the long arguments he had with his two selves.

"Stay connected. Don't let go!" was the mantra he urged himself to repeat whenever he felt himself slipping into the dark.

He shivered, he sweated, he coughed. He dreamt that a giant wall of water rolled towards the boatyard and broke all the boats into matchwood. He was running, running, leaping from one side of a dyke to the other as the water licked his heels. He ran so hard his chest felt as if it would burst. He woke up. The room was filled with grey light and Hansuke was shaking him. He struggled to sit up and was seized with another coughing fit. Bright red blood spattered the front of his dirty tunic.

CHAPTER 50

Ivyholme, Lymington

January 4th 1945

Dearest John, "From the depths I called –
    your words warm like summer sun –
    my petals unfold".
Hope you appreciate attempt at haiku.
All love, Min.

January 9th 1945

The start of yet another year apart. But from the way the war seems to be going, I am sure that we will be reunited soon. It simply can't go on forever. I always seem to be waiting for something or someone. In fact, my whole life has been one long wait; always looking into the future, frustrated with the now. Waiting to be old enough to be allowed to stay up as late as Frank; waiting for the school holidays, or for spring to arrive after a cold winter, or for the sun to set or for a dark, lonely night to be over; waiting to find a husband; for John to be born, for the husband to stop hurting me, and once again waiting for the school holidays and for John to come home. And now I am still waiting for him to return. I am heartily sick of it all; always looking forward. Let me just be, living in the present, without all this agitating about the future.

January 28th 1945

I feel almost ashamed of what I wrote about being fed up with waiting. I have just read the most appalling account of the liberation of Auschwitz concentration camp by the Russians. There have been thousands and thousands of innocent people waiting endlessly for food or freedom or death. How can human beings treat their fellow man this way? I have no right to complain about anything. Thank goodness John has not been held in such despicable conditions.

February 15th 1945

I went for a muddy walk today along the riverbank with Joan and Millie. We all had stout shoes on and were determined not to turn back, and besides, we had the most illuminating conversation. They were asking me what I wanted from my life. Without really thinking, I gave them the same answer as I gave Mrs Whittaker's lady's maid nearly three years ago; that all I wanted was for my son to return. And Millie said, "And then what? Surely you are not going to live your entire life through your son. What about your own life?"

Well, I was quite taken aback by the starkness of her question, but it made me begin to share some of my thoughts with them. I explained that I had never thought about what the purpose of my life was, apart from what I was brought up to believe; that a woman's role is to marry and have children. Being born into a class where women only worked as teachers or secretaries or nurses, if they were unfortunate enough not to marry, the question of what I wanted for myself was never raised. No one ever mentioned what we were supposed to do when the children grew up. Mothers, it is assumed, turn automatically into grandmothers and so that was what I was waiting for.

So I turned the question back onto them and asked how they had found purpose in their lives. Millie said that for her it was not about always aiming to get somewhere in life; it was more about embracing each day with a sense of wonder about what might evolve. She practices meditation and finds that it helps her feel more alive. Joan said that being creative in some form or other was important for her, be it through gardening or writing or even making dinner. What wonderful philosophies they both seem to have.

CHAPTER 51

There had been a light fall of snow during the night and a pale sun was struggling to break through the murky sky. Breath-steam rose in clouds from the muffled squads as the sentries yelled and stamped their feet, trying to get their charges into some sort of order before the working parties set off for their various tasks for the day. Already the barter market was open and the usual wheeler-dealers dodged from group to group, ensuring that the prices of certain goods would be established before the different squads were separated for the day's work.

'Here, Rosebud, I'll give you my portion of burnt rice, plus that odd right sock I found yesterday, as well as pages 125-249 of *Hangman's Holiday*, for your scarf and two Eagles.'

Although Alan's mouth watered at the thought of an extra helping of the tasty bits of overcooked rice that were scraped from the sides of the cooking cauldrons, the rest of the deal wasn't much use to him. He'd already read the novel and there were other lads more desperate for smokes with whom he could make a better bargain.

'No thanks, Alec, try someone else.' Alan pulled his scarf a little tighter and wrapped his arms around himself to try and warm up. He hated all this hanging around in the freezing mornings and, despite wearing a couple of pairs of trousers over his pyjama bottoms and a thick coat, now that he'd lost a bit more weight, the cold seemed to seep into his bones. He felt a stab of annoyance towards the officers who would be able to stay indoors all day if they chose. Many of the men were quite disgruntled about how well the officers had fared during these years of captivity; there was the incident over the bully beef rations, when the officers were initially given more tins between them than the workers; the bizarre arrangement that many of the officers still had batmen to do their washing for them; and of course more recently, the fact that increasing numbers of troops were being shipped out of the camp to work in the coal mines of Japan while the officers continued their leisurely existence reading their books and playing cards all day.

As he stomped off to the farm for another back-breaking day, his stomach churned with the resentment he suddenly felt for John Garrett and Bill Ellerton, who were probably right now warming their hands on the stove while they continued the discussion about whatever it was the three of them had started last evening. No amount of imagining himself striding along the beach at Titchfield Haven on a bright winter's day could help him shake off his simmering fury towards them. At lunchtime, he sullenly took his frozen rice ball and crust of bread but kept himself apart from the other lads who were, as usual, talking about food, sex and the latest rumours about the end of the war.

He wasn't sure where he belonged anymore. He wasn't an officer, but the range of topics he'd explored with his new officer friends was far more interesting than the tedious badinage he reluctantly engaged in with the chaps on working parties or in his squad room. There were some lads he quite liked, though no one could replace Sid, and there were plenty who joined him for the regular communion services that Padre Castle held on the parade ground. But none of them could really discuss with him why they took part or how they kept their faith in God when the dark days of depression enveloped them, as it did everyone from time to time. It was thanks to that first conversation he'd had with the Doc almost eighteen months ago, when he'd felt the need to defend his Christian beliefs against John's scepticism, that had got him really thinking about what he believed in. Since then, he felt as if he had been on a long journey of discovery. He felt a bond of friendship with John and Bill that he hadn't experienced before. Feeling what he now realised was envy was really quite uncomfortable.

As he reached into his coat pocket for the small square of chocolate he'd been saving, he was aware that the noonday sun was actually quite warm. The grey blanket of snow-cloud had rolled away and the sky was now a bright blue. He let the piece of chocolate gently rest on his tongue so that he could savour the intensity of the flavour as it slowly dissolved, and when he stood up to return to work he noticed that his bad mood had dissolved as well.

Of course, that was what they'd been talking about last night. They had been discussing how children, especially boys, are brought up not to show any emotion and to be ashamed of any unwarranted outbursts. Each them had admitted that at times during the Malayan campaign they'd wanted to "cry like a baby" over the loss of a fellow soldier, or been anxious that they might "lose their bottle" in the face of enemy fire. Although they'd agreed that sometimes it was necessary to squash one's feelings in order to get on with the business in hand, perhaps the rigorous suppression of all emotion was unhelpful. John had said that, from his recent experiences, he now wondered if in fact emotional suppression was the cause of a number of psychological problems he'd seen amongst the troops.

John had gone on to say that he'd been playing with the idea that one way of understanding both pleasant and unpleasant feelings was to view them like clouds that would eventually pass over. On the days we feel quite contented with our lives, it's as if the blue sky is dotted with just a few cotton-wool clouds. But then if something upsetting happens, and perhaps we experience sadness or anxiety or feel a bit depressed, it's as if the sky has become overcast or there is a never ending grey drizzle that deadens everything. Or again, at the times when we feel rather overwrought, it is equivalent to huge storm clouds with thunder and flashes of lightning which can be alarming or even cause damage.

Bill had said, "Well that's a very pretty image, but I don't understand how it helps when I'm feeling annoyed or irritable to pretend I'm a thundercloud."

"Hang on, I haven't finished," replied John. "I know it probably sounds a bit simplistic, but I wonder if the trick is not to rail against our moods or try and suppress them but instead just pay attention to what sort of clouds they are, such as anger, hurt, loss and so on, and know, that given time and attention the clouds will pass over and the mood will subside."

"So what you are suggesting,' Alan had said, "is that when it's pouring outside or blowing a gale, rather than close the curtains and pretend it isn't happening, we should wait patiently for it to stop before going outside to fix the hole in the roof."

"Exactly," John had replied. "And I suppose sometimes we have no choice and we have to go out, get wet, be buffeted by the wind and deal with the emotion immediately, but otherwise it's better to stand back a bit, even settle down with a good book until the storm clouds have passed, and then see if anything needs attention afterwards."

What a shame that he'd completely forgotten this discussion when he'd felt so furious with them both this morning. But that's how it is with new ideas, he thought. It takes time and practice for them to become properly embedded.

The remainder of the afternoon passed surprisingly quickly and as he marched back to the camp he noticed how lovely the snow looked in the late afternoon light and how, although his back ached, he could feel some strength returning to his muscles. After supper, he joined John and Bill for their evening circuits of the parade ground and told them how he'd felt.

'I suppose my first difficulty was realising that my fury about you chaps all cosy indoors while I was out freezing my whatsits off was in fact a nasty cloud call envy, and my fury or envy whichever it was, felt very un-Christian of me.'

'Come now, anyone in their right mind would have felt envious of us officers on a day like today,' said Bill. 'But you've hit on the nub of the problem, Alan. I've been thinking a bit more about it and I suppose it isn't so much the emotion that's hard to bear, but what we tell ourselves about it. You felt ashamed of having what you believed was an un-Christian response and that thought probably made you feel even worse. Today, I was recalling my horror in the last few hours of the battle when I imagined the men would think I was a weak if I showed how demoralised I felt about the inevitable surrender. I kept telling myself to be a man and stop being such a sissy. But I suppose John is right – once you can accept the so-called bad feeling as perfectly reasonable, albeit unpleasant, then you can let it go and have it blow over like a particularly stormy cloud.'

The three of them completed another circuit in thoughtful silence.

'That all makes sense once the mood has passed,' said Alan, 'but I find it jolly difficult at times to maintain that perspective when I'm right in the middle of it. It's as if I can't believe that the drizzle will ever stop.'

'I know what you mean, I do as well,' John laughed. 'I think it's going to take a lot of practice. But perhaps sometimes we simply have to let the weather get on with it, even if it does seem to go on and on, while we batten down the hatches, watch it from a safe place and escape into our minds for an imaginary walk, recall a pleasant memory or do something that will keep us occupied until it passes.'

'Look out,' said Alan. 'Here's Uishihara and Tirada and I don't like the look on Tirada's ugly face.' The two officers were ambling towards them. Tirada was smirking. The three of them stood still and waited.

'Oh Lordy. I'm sorry Alan. I think I know what this is about. There was nothing I could do,' said Bill, putting his hand on Alan's shoulder.

'Don't tell me I'm in the next batch to be shipped out to the bloody coal mines?' asked Alan, aware of how exhausted he suddenly felt. Bill nodded.

John looked miserable and offered Alan a cigarette. 'Alan, you have to think of this as a temporary break in our conversation which will be continued as soon as this infuriating charade is over and we are all back home.'

'Well it's certainly going to give me a chance to practice the art of letting my feelings pass like clouds. Let's hope I'm not in for endless weeks of rain and darkness, eh?' said Alan, trying to force a smile. As he walked ahead of the others towards Uishihara and Tirada, he wiped his eyes with the back of his hand. Just when I think I can hang on a bit longer, life deals me another blow, he thought bitterly.

That night, as he lay huddled in his blankets trying to sleep, all he could think about was the impending separation from these good friends and even this godforsaken place which had become so familiar. He felt hugely anxious that letters from home would never reach him if he was now moving to Japan; those letters from his Mum and from Betty which, after frustrating months of waiting, had kept him from falling over the edge and restored his faith in God. Letters and Red Cross parcels had become the only events that divided up the year. How long till I can realistically hope for the next batch of letters? Will they keep our letters sitting in the office for eight unbearable weeks like they did last time? How long since I last received a food parcel? How long can I make this tin of condensed milk last?

As he waited for daybreak, he could feel the steady trickle of tears rolling down his cheeks.

Two days later, Richard stood with Bill and John and watched the squad of fifty men, including Alan Rose, march away towards the station. Over the past few months, Keijo camp had been slowly emptying, to the extent that half of the remaining officers had been moved upstairs to a vacated squad room, leaving everyone twice as much floor and shelf space. Noguchi had informed them that by the time the war ended the camp would only contain officers and a few regulars, deemed unfit for labour, who would cook and do the chores. As Richard watched the men leaving, his thoughts turned to Roger Lester. In the last six months since Lester had been hauled off to Seodaemun Prison, nearly every day Richard had felt guilty for not preventing him from carrying out his harebrained propaganda plan. Despite Ellerton's best efforts, there had been no word about how long he would stay in jail and Uishihara had intimated that, with what he'd heard about the place, they'd be lucky to ever see him again. If only he had paid more attention to what Lester had been writing and less preoccupied with the revelation that everyone knew he was a queer. He hoped that Roger would remember what he'd said all those months ago about the Japs being able to lock up his body, but that they couldn't touch his mind. Richard missed him; missed his cheerful face with the ever-present cigarette dangling between his lips; missed his humour and his inexhaustible powers of invention. He tried to imagine how he would be coping, shut in a cell on his own or perhaps being confined in a small space with a few others who wouldn't even speak English, with no books and possibly no warm clothes to protect him from the freezing nights. Feeling guilty about the warmth of his own clothes, he gave an involuntary shudder.

Following John and Bill back up the stairs, he was relieved that it wasn't him being moved; there were definite advantages to being an officer and now that he'd overcome his initial boredom and settled into his writing, he felt quite lucky to be able to spend these chilly January days indoors. He could see that the others felt quite despondent that Alan Rose had been shipped off to Japan, and although he'd never got to know the man, he recalled how jealous he used to be when John had become friendly with him. How refreshing it was to have let all that go. Poor old Lester had actually done him a favour. Once he'd recovered from his embarrassment, he'd realised how stupid it would have been to ruin a perfectly good friendship by blurting out his infatuation. He'd muttered something to John about being a bit of a duffer since they been in the camp and John had smiled and shrugged. By getting rid of the ridiculous fantasy of him and John together, he'd been able to let the reality of their friendship grow and mature in the same way that he believed his writing had matured.

'You're going to miss Alan Rose, aren't you?' he said to John as he slumped back down onto his soapbox. Richard sat down on the bed roll nearby.

'Yes, he was a good man. We had some fascinating talks about practically everything under the sun. It's annoying that he's gone now because he'd been helping Bill and me with our own version of what we're calling the Art of Life. We've been trying to come up with a sort formula or creed to live by that will give our lives some kind of meaning once we get out of here.'

Richard felt a pang of the old envy and had to bite his lip to stop himself from making a silly, sarcastic remark. Instead he asked John to tell him what they'd all discussed, saying that perhaps he might be able to have some input about the importance of literature. As John began to explain, Richard could see how the ideas they'd come up with made pretty good sense. He liked the idea of a lifetime of exploring both what was on the inside and on the outside of himself; although he wasn't too sure he wanted to repeat any of the experiences he'd had when he felt so near to dying.

'So does being creative fit anywhere into your philosophy? You see, for me, learning that I could write and express myself reasonably eloquently has been one of the most important things that's kept me going since we've been cooped up in here.'

'Yes, of course. I think we assumed that creativity would

probably be included under the headings, "Explore" and "Experience". But tell me what it means for you,' replied John.

'Well, I suppose it can mean a range of things for different people. On one level, I think it's about being able to express myself or having the imagination to create something new or being able to look at ordinary things in a different way, like that poem I read to you last week using my holey socks as a metaphor. But on another level, don't you think that creativity has to be about adding something to the world that didn't exist before?'

Bill Ellerton was standing by the window, gazing vacantly towards the railway station. 'Hey Bill, come over here and listen to what Richard's got to say about something we've forgotten to include in our philosophy,' called John.

Ellerton came over and plumped down on the bedding roll next to Richard. In other parts of the room, their fellow officers had settled down to their daily routines of reading, playing cards or chess; life had become easier for everyone since Charles King had moved to the officer's new quarters upstairs. Holly had elected to go with him, leaving only Peter Castle from their original small group. Although Richard still spent time with King, he was relieved that the tension between him and John was now dissipated.

'You're right, Richard,' continued John. 'But what if creativity is more than that, more than writing or painting or sculpting or composing? What if we used the term like a broad brushstroke to include everyday activities such as gardening or cooking or even, dare I say it, sewing? You could almost use it to describe everything we do, since every day is new and different.'

'Well, I wouldn't know anything about gardening or cooking, but I can't imagine our gardener or cook believing that the work they do for my family is exactly creative,' said Richard with a grin. 'No, I think being creative must have something to do with the expression of one's inner spirit and being able to use one's imagination.'

'Perhaps,' mused Bill. 'Creativity is more an attitude towards life; a sort of camera lens through which we view the world in both a playful but also a purposeful way. Don't you think that perhaps a creative person is constantly looking for new ideas and new areas of interest? They like to find new problems to challenge them and then unravel new solutions. I don't mean on the scale of Copernicus, Beethoven or Shakespeare, but simply the everyday ingenuity of ordinary people. Even your cook and gardener have to make do, mend things and adapt to circumstances.'

'That's it!' said John, with excitement. 'Now we have three watchwords. To explore is what we do *in* the world. To experience is what we take *from* the world, and to create not only describes what we can *give back* to the world, but also encompasses the whole attitude we should have towards life. Aren't we brilliant?'

Richard looked at John's delighted smile and felt a rush of love for him; not the blind adoration he'd been consumed by for the best part of four years, but something cleaner, less fettered. For most of the day, they meandered through fields of ideas, exploring the importance of art and literature and music. Richard felt contented and at ease.

It was late in the afternoon, when the light had begun to fade, that they were interrupted by Peter Castle rushing into the room.

'John, Bill, come quickly. Roger's back but he's in a really bad way.'

Richard followed the others without worrying that Peter hadn't actually included him. He wondered what "in a bad way" would actually mean. The four of them crowded through the door of the hospital hut and looked round for Roger's curly head and big smile. Initially all he could see was one other lad propped up on his pillow, rather startled by the sudden arrival of the Doc, the CO and the Padre. Then, on a cot in the far corner, he saw a huddle of blankets. Peter led them over to where Roger lay. His shaved head had just a few wisps of stubble, his mouth and lips were covered with sores, his skin looked grey and his brow shook with beads of sweat. As if he could sense them all standing around him, he slowly opened his eyes, managed a weak smile and croaked, 'Nice to be home.'

CHAPTER 52

It was the blood that had done it. A prisoner coughing up blood most likely had TB and, not wishing to put themselves at risk, the guards at Seodaemun had wasted no time requesting that Roger be bundled back to Keijo camp.

'I hope he looks worse than he actually is,' John whispered to Bill, as the four of them stood around Roger's cot. 'But if it is TB, there won't be much we can do.' To Roger, in what he was aware was an unnecessarily loud voice, as if he had lost his hearing as well as every other ounce of his dignity, he said, 'It's good to have you back. We'll soon have you well again. All you need is some decent food and some proper care.'

As if to prove what he needed, Roger began to cough and struggled to sit upright. Richard quickly supported his shoulders and John grabbed some gauze to wipe the pink frothy sputum that trailed from his mouth. Once the fit of coughing had subsided, Roger collapsed back on the pillow and closed his eyes.

'Sorry' he muttered.

While Bill and Peter went to find Colonel Noguchi to see if they could persuade him to order some medicine, John, with Richard's help, gently pulled off Roger's ragged clothes, washed him and eased him into clean ones. The contrast between the boisterous, muscular, curly-haired officer he had known just a few months ago and this sickly old man with sallow skin stretched taut over the skeletal ridges of his ribs was shocking. That night they took turns to sit with him while he slept fitfully between coughing bouts that left him limp and worn out. Though none of them verbalised it, it seemed to John as if they all felt guilty for the ordeal that Roger had clearly suffered.

But after a week of saying very little, waking only to be fed watery rice stew or take sips of water, Roger did appear to recover some strength. His temperature fell and some of the grey pallor disappeared. He wanted to know what had been happening in the camp while he'd been away and even attempted to smile while John sat beside him, trying to cheer him up with witty stories about the Christmas show and about how the Japs were reacting to the increasingly encouraging news from Europe. But when John read him a couple of the brief twenty-five word letters which had arrived from his family and saw tears trickling down Roger's face, he began to get a sense of how totally isolated Roger had been.

'Do you want to talk about it?' he asked gently.

'It was all such a waste. I did it so that they'd be proud of me,' said Roger, brushing his eyes with his hands and gesturing towards the letters. 'And now it's too late.'

'What do you mean it's too late?' asked John, wondering if Roger had some premonition or had overheard something.

'My parents would never understand what I've been through but even if they did, in their eyes I still wouldn't be good enough. That much I worked out while I was in that hellhole.' He began to cry again.

John could identify with the bitterness in Roger's tone. He stroked his thin arm and said, 'Tell me.'

After a while, Roger's tears stopped and he asked John to prop him up a little. In between coughing and lapsing into exhausted silence, over the next hour, Roger described the beatings he'd received, the cries of mere boys thrown into the cell after being tortured, the nagging hunger and the endless days and nights surrounded by the smell of piss and shit. John listened, making no attempt to conceal his horror. He couldn't conceive how anyone could survive such an experience and felt ashamed of the jolly tales of his own prison life he'd just described. He mumbled an apology.

'No, don't apologise. It was knowing that you would all carry on here in the same way that kept me going, helped me feel connected with you,' Roger rasped. 'I discovered that if I could keep everything joined up like a daisy chain then I wouldn't fall off the edge.'

'Actually, we were all really worried about how you would cope,' said Richard, who had slipped in quietly and now sat on the other side of the cot. 'We knew how you always liked to be doing something and couldn't imagine how you'd survive if you were confined.'

Roger told them about how the voice in his head kept telling him to stay connected with everything and everyone and had made him return to the lists every time he lost hope.

'Stay connected. Don't let go,' he muttered, as he sank back to sleep.

John caught Richard's eye and smiled at him. He had changed so much over the past few months; he no longer seemed like a devoted dog padding around after him, endlessly trying to please and flinching if John's tone ever had an edge of irritation. He seemed happier within himself and relaxed in John's company. Together they left Roger to rest and made their way back upstairs where Bill was playing chess with Peter. John gave them a brief summary of what Roger had described.

'He thinks he's let everyone down and it seems that all he ever wanted was to know that his parents would be proud of him.'

'Christ, he should be bloody proud of everything he did,' protested Bill. 'He may have been a bit headstrong at times, but without him we wouldn't have had the radio or those extra supplies in Changi.'

'And it was his care and cheerfulness that kept me alive on the ship and his plain talking last year that helped me see sense,' said Richard, looking at John and blushing slightly. 'I wish I'd kept a better eye on him once we got here and could have stopped him from getting into trouble.'

'But for Roger it seems being proud of his own actions wasn't enough; it was his parents pride in him that he needed. It's hard to be proud of yourself if your parents are endlessly critical,' said John, fiddling with one of the captured chess pieces. 'Do you suppose that most parents want to be proud of their offspring's achievements in order to make up for their own perceived failings, or is it so that their friends will envy them for having such accomplished children?'

'Well, mine certainly fall into the latter category.' said Richard with a short laugh. 'With them, it's all about appearance. They'll only be proud of me if I live my life the way they think I should. It doesn't matter what I might want. Though, come to think of it, even as a child I could never win. Whenever I was pleased because I had achieved something, my father would tell me not to become big-headed, or wag his finger at me, saying, "Pride comes before a fall". Pride is one of the seven deadly sins. Isn't that right, Peter?'

'Oh yes, pride has always been deemed the very deadliest of sins. But personally I think the word was badly translated and what they should have said was arrogance – the need to feel superior to others – comes before a fall. I believe that taking pride in what one has done is about appreciating oneself and having value, and it should generally be encouraged. But going back to Roger, I think it's a shame he can't feel proud of what he tried to do, both for us and for the Koreans,' said Peter.

They all lapsed into thoughtful silence, broken only by the shrieking whistle of a train.

Listening to Richard made John think about his own childhood. His father had always been totally indifferent to him and yet Min had been proud of almost everything he'd ever done. The inevitable result was that he'd been bitterly ashamed of his father for being a useless drunk, a coward and a bully who couldn't provide for his family, and yet filled with pride for how his mother had managed to cope and was still bravely coping through this long separation. Perhaps pride worked best when it was equal and it flowed both ways. He stood up and stretched. 'I think I'll go and see if I can help Roger feel better about himself.'

But over the next few weeks, as the trees outside the camp once more began to cover themselves in shades of green, Roger slowly seemed to fade. Each day, when John listened through his stethoscope, he could hear his lungs becoming more clogged with mucous and watched his breathing became more laboured. Gradually his skin began to turn a sickly yellow. This wasn't TB. Roger was probably dying of lung cancer. Even if there was any medicine, it would be useless, though eventually John managed to persuade Noguchi to authorise a few ampoules of morphine. The first injection calmed Roger's breathing and as he slipped in and out of sleep he kept muttering about a boatyard and needing someone to take it over.

A few evenings later, after another injection, John once more sat one side of him with Peter on the other. He listened as Roger's gurgling breaths slowed, seemed to stop and then started up again. John wondered what it would be like to die like this. What would he want? Who might he want to have beside him? Would he fight or would he be ready to let go?

When Roger's breathing finally stopped, it was not like any death John had witnessed before. There wasn't the drama of the battlefield where he'd had to make snap decisions and turn his back on some poor lad, leaving him to die alone. Nor was it like the deaths he'd dealt with back at St Thomas' where all he'd had to do was to certify the body and leave the rest to the nurses. With Roger, it was if he could actually see all the energy draining out of him like a wave that finally dissipates all its energy as it crashes onto the shore. As he listened to Peter praying, as he had done when Kelly had died, which felt like a lifetime ago, John mused that although he still didn't believe in the conventional idea of God, perhaps there was something about the soul that made sense. But then thinking about waves brought the ghastly image of Bea drowning back into his mind. She didn't have a peaceful death. Her soul didn't slip quietly out of her body, and even if it did where was it now? His eyes brimmed as he looked back at Roger's empty face. His thoughts rushed to Min. What would he do if anything happened to her before he returned home? Now that her letters to him were only twenty-five words long, it was impossible to know how she really was. She sounded cheerful, but what if she was concealing something serious about her own health from him?

He felt a hand on his arm and Peter's voice pressed through the flurry of his panic. 'John, it's all right. I know it's alarming, but I really believe that we just have to trust that when death comes we'll know how to handle it. Just takes some deep breaths for now and concentrate on being alive.'

Roger was buried in the same place as Alan's friend, Sid, and the others who had died at Keijo camp; it was on a pleasant hillside under pine trees beside a rocky gorge, about half an hour's march away from the camp, the town and the shrieking trains.

By now it was April. There was blossom on some of the trees which they could see on their way to the officer's garden, though there were far fewer men to dig and weed, since so many had been transferred elsewhere. The daily roll call, the dismal food, the petty rules and rages of some of the guards were at the same time both tedious and comfortingly predictable. One evening, when John and Richard could finally bring themselves to sort through Roger's few possessions and Bill began to compose a personal letter to be sent to his parents, John recalled what Roger had said about how staying connected had helped him through his ordeal.

'Hey, I think Roger hit on something which could underpin our whole philosophy. There is no point in exploring the world to gain better understanding, or being open to a whole variety of experiences, or expressing oneself creatively, unless you can connect it all together somehow.'

'Actually, I think you could be right,' said Bill, looking up from what he'd been writing. 'We have to be able to make good connections, both on the inside via our thoughts, memories and so on, as well as on the outside to other people through language, images and ideas, otherwise we would all be working in isolation. And the richness of our lives depends on the quality of those connections. Well done, Roger. That's something else he could have been proud of.'

'Yes, it is about the quality of those connections, isn't it?' said John. 'I think we've all been pretty fortunate that, in spite of being crowded together in here for three years, we've got along pretty well and respected each other's needs for solitude and time on our own, haven't we?'

'Well, I think those of us in our little corner of this room haven't done so badly, but John, I think you may be ignoring some of the conflicts and animosity that have infected other areas. You could hardly describe your relationship with King as being exactly positive,' said Bill.

'Ouch,' replied John, feeling the sting of Bill's remark. 'Fair enough; I suppose there will always be exceptions.'

'Perhaps we could explain it like this,' said Richard. He grabbed a scrap of paper and a blunt pencil and for a while drew an assortment of triangles, squares and circles, scribbling each of them out and starting again. 'Here, I think this might do.' He drew three large overlapping circles. Beside one of them he wrote the word Explore, beside the second, he wrote Experience and by the third, the word Create. 'Now here in the very centre, where all three concepts overlap, we could write the word Connect. Do you think that represents what we are trying to say?'

John looked at Richard's drawing in silence. He felt a rush of excitement. This was incredible. They had actually devised something which seemed really important. His "All Will Be Well" mantra had been an enormous help in times of anxiety, but this new credo, "Explore, Experience, Create and Connect" reached something much deeper.

He looked across at Bill and Richard and, with a huge grin, said, 'Well, that's the purpose of life sorted out. What's next?'

CHAPTER 53

May 1ˢᵗ 1945

What news indeed! Hitler is reported to be dead. Does that mean the war in Europe is over or will some other evil man take his place? I simply don't know what to think. I can't believe that the end is very nearly here. More and more news has filtered through about the German atrocities towards the Jews and others. I felt physically sick when I heard Richard Dimbleby's broadcast about when the Americans entered the concentration camp at Belsen. It is too awful to take it all in.

Sadly, there is no news of the Far East. I have now had 6 letters and 5 postcards from John and I am so pleased that he is receiving mine. He seems to have taken the news of Beatrice's death with his usual stoicism. I did love the phrase in his last letter, which I received in January: "Health and contentment continue in the mind's garden with many ideas in bloom and enough books (and friends) to dig with!"

I think he will be delighted to hear that my own mind is beginning to bloom, since I have begun reading Dorothy's books and had such absorbing discussions with Joan and Millie.

Ivyholme, Lymington

May 8ᵗʰ 1945.

VE day, my joy restrained, champagne stayed unopened.

Sadly waved a little flag. Can't wait till I can hold you. Come back soon – longing, longing.

May 9th 1945

Oh my goodness, what a day it was yesterday. I don't think I've ever seen anything like it. On Sunday, Mrs Timberlake from the WI asked if I would be able to bake one of my special cakes filled with carrot marmalade for the celebration in Lymington planned for VE day on Tuesday. Well, I had plenty of jars of marmalade but had run out of dried eggs, so on Monday I cycled into Lym and the High Street was busy with everyone and anyone tying gaily coloured bunting between the lampposts and the shop fronts. I pedalled home and got cooking and she collected the cake from me first thing on Tuesday. The celebrations were lovely. There was a parade with the British Legion Boys' Band, as well as the Home Guard and some of the nurses from the hospital. Everyone cheered and shouted, although of course there was a little part of me that still felt quite downhearted. It seemed as if they had all forgotten that the war is still going on in the Far East and that not everyone is free.

In the evening, Joan and Millie joined me on the quayside, where there was an enormous bonfire. So strange to see one after all these years, where flames have always meant something was being destroyed. Apparently there was dancing in the streets well into the early hours, but I was tucked up in bed well before then.

What next, I wonder?

CHAPTER 54

Although it was past midnight when Alan was woken by the boom of the explosions, he felt as if he'd only just drifted off to sleep. Yet another bombing raid; now they were happening most nights. Sometimes, when the camp sirens went off, they were all marched to an underground shelter, but that seemed to depend on which set of guards were on duty. These days, Alan was too shattered to care. The ten-hour shift in the mine, shovelling coal onto the conveyer belt and then the half-mile march back to the camp seemed to be getting much harder. These days, his legs felt quite weak.

He had been in this prison camp, attached to a mine, for the past seven months since he'd arrived earlier in the year; it was one of many on Kyushu Island in Japan. Working in the mine had been every bit as awful as he'd imagined when Bill had broken the news to him. Being tall, he had what felt like a permanent crick in his neck from stooping, and although they were rotated between working on the surface and going underground, those endless days in dimly lit passages choked with black dust seemed to come round all too often. There were frequent roof falls and someone got injured almost every week. The only thing that made it bearable was that he'd been reunited with some of the lads from his old regiment, who'd been held in Jinsen. They all worked for ten days of shifts, followed by a rest day, and had the luxury of a large communal hot bath every night to soak off the coal dust.

Initially, the camp itself wasn't too bad. At least the supply of Red Cross parcels from Canada, USA and Australia was more frequent than it ever had been in Keijo, which was just as well, as the food supplied by their captors was dire. But best of all was that he'd received some letters from home, albeit a year old, and there was even a photo of his mum with his baby niece. He prayed that they knew he was still safe, though now it seemed to be a toss-up as to whether it was more dangerous working down the mine or being back in camp and caught by a stray bomb. Even on rest day, he wasn't able to continue his portrait drawing to earn extra rations or cigarettes – not that he had the energy – since they had no access to paper or pens. The only encouraging news they had gathered over the past few weeks was that the war in Europe was over and that the Americans must have recaptured somewhere in the Pacific to be able to mount the ever-increasing air raids. The downside was that every time the US planes struck a major target in Japan, the amount of face slapping and beatings they all received from the guards increased.

He lay in the darkness, straining to hear any further explosions. No; only the coughs and snores of his fellows. Good, at least he wouldn't have to get up, though it was curious how his toes felt like pins and needles and his calf muscles ached. Perhaps he'd pulled a muscle or something. He slept fitfully, but the following morning he found that he could hardly stand up without Joe's help. Of course, now he remembered, he'd felt like this on the bloody *Fukkai Maru* and it had been the first signs of beriberi. Joe helped him stagger to the sickbay, a corner of the main accommodation, where the Jap doctor merely glanced at him and pointed towards a mat. Several days later, the paralysis had crept all the way up his legs. He felt like a baby from the waist down and wondered how he'd ever recover from it this time, without the extra food that Sid and Doc Garrett had given him on the voyage to Korea. He missed them both; Sid for his wicked sense of humour, and John for his optimism and thirst for ideas.

Dear God, why are you doing all this to me? he thought. How many times in these last three years had his faith been challenged? Surely he'd done nothing that sinful to be tested like this? Desperate to find some answers he turned to the only book he'd been able to bring with him; the now tattered Bible he'd rescued from the courthouse in Singapore in the final battle. Although some of the pages of Revelation were missing, purloined by Curly to roll into cigarettes, he spent the next few days re-reading big chunks of the Old Testament, including the Book of Job and some of his favourite psalms. He still couldn't feel his legs, but in his heart he began to feel better. Of course he hadn't sinned. All of life was a test, and after all, if he wasn't lying here immobilised he'd be back at the coal face. As he mulled this over, he could hear John's persistent voice in his head, arguing that the world was quite complicated enough without bringing God into it – and again, how humans had merely invented a superior being to establish social control and allay their fears about death. No, he decided, he could accept John's philosophy for living up to a point, but for him faith and friendship would be his maxim. That evening, Tommy Butler was killed in another roof fall.

Over the next few weeks, as the food supplies to the camp worsened, others began to develop the same symptoms as Alan. Some even became night blind, which meant they could no longer work down the feebly lit mine. It wasn't until the supply of labour became critical that anything was done about it. When the Jap doctor insisted that those affected could be cured by eating snake livers, able-bodied prisoners were dispatched in small parties to capture snakes from the local countryside and a large snake pit was dug just outside the sickbay in which to house them. Every morning, the hospital sergeant would descend into the pit, wearing high boots, and select a few of the writhing inmates, kill them by cracking them like a whip and skin them, still wriggling. Steamed snake, snake soup, fried snake – none of it tasted of anything, but it did make a small improvement in Alan's legs.

One afternoon, balanced on some crutches, he stood propped up at the door of the sickbay. It had been raining for hours, just like the monsoon rains of Singapore. Out of the corner of his eye, he noticed the large metal grating which covered the snake pit begin to rise and roll towards the fence; it was being borne on a mass of twisting snakes that had been flooded out of their pit.

'Quick,' he shouted over his shoulder and pointed with one of his crutches. 'There goes our dinner.'

Anyone who could walk made a grab for those snakes that had already slithered off into the castor oil plants, while others bailed out the overflowing pit with a bucket.

'Blooming heck, Alan, come and take a look at this,' said Curly, squatting by the edge of the pit. 'It's enough to give you nightmares.'

Alan hobbled over to him, peered in and shuddered at what he saw. Some of the snakes at the bottom of the pit, unable to escape, seemed to have drowned. But many more were engaged in trying to eat each other, like one long chain. Although most of the snakes were recaptured, the meals became almost inedible; soon they were eating millet seed stews flavoured with the meat of dog, cat and even the poor horse who'd collapsed one day while pulling the cesspit cart.

In the first week of August, the raids started to occur both night and day. There was a constant din of machine guns and cannons. Alan and Curly stood by the door to the sickbay and watched hundreds of large silver planes thundering overhead. Two of them were hit, broke into pieces and twirled down to the ground, their wings fluttering like leaves, a mile or so apart.

'Blimey O'Reilly, this must be the end, surely,' said Curly, deftly rolling a handful of pine needles into Revelation, Chapter 13 – the supply of tobacco had dried up weeks ago.

'Well I should jolly well hope so, but the trouble with these Japs is that they think they have to fight on until the bitter end. They'll never surrender. It's simply not in their vocabulary. Look at the contempt they showed us when we gave in after Singapore. But if it carries on like this, we'll either get bombed to pieces by the US planes, die of starvation when the supply of horse dries up or get blown away in a typhoon like the one we had the other night,' said Alan, as he went to lie down again and rest his aching legs.

On August 9th, they woke to a beautiful clear day. It was a rest day and no one had gone to the mine.

'Hey, lads! Come and see this,' shouted Reggie, rushing in from the washroom. Within minutes, a small crowd had gathered outside, craning their necks towards the horizon. In the direction of Nagasaki, they could see an enormous pillar of cloud, brown at the base, amber in its centre and white at the top, stretching forever into the sky.

'That's one hell of a big fire. I've never seen smoke like that before,' said Curly. 'Oh jeepers-creepers, look at it now!'

From out of the top of the pillar emerged a giant white

mushroom of cloud that billowed and hung there like some kind of grotesque flower or monster's head.

'That ain't no ordinary fire. I reckon that could be some kind of special bomb,' said Jimmy.

John stood slightly apart from the others, taking nervous drags on his cigarette, as he waited for the remaining gardeners to assemble. He still felt groggy from his lack of sleep. It looked like it was going to be another scorching day and he hoped that the breeze in the officer's garden would keep him relatively cool. He had taken to joining the gardening party once he'd discovered that the gardeners got slightly more food than those who stayed in camp. Having never taken much interest in gardening, he had begun to see the satisfaction that he might have one day from a garden of his own, planting seeds and watching them grow into mature plants. The only drawback to the work party was the twenty-minute march to the garden, flanked by sentries, through the ugly, tattered streets, which painfully reminded him of his prisoner status, which he could almost forget when he stayed indoors either reading or talking with his friends.

He watched Charles King saunter from group to group, chatting and laughing. His whole appearance was quite different from the rounded-bellied major John had fallen out with a couple of years ago. Now, his ruddy cheeks sagged, his hair had thinned and the combination of no alcohol, poor food and regular exercise had trimmed his waistline. But he looked extremely well and, according to Richard, who still enjoyed his company, he had mellowed. John still didn't trust him, though he had felt slightly sorry for him when he'd heard that King's father had been killed in an air raid. Now he'd have no parents to welcome him home.

That is, if any of them were going to make it home, after what Bill had blurted out the previous evening. Apparently Noguchi had coldly informed him that since all Japanese soldiers had been ordered by the Emperor to die at their posts, rather than surrender to either the Russians or the Americans, steps would be taken to ensure that all POW officers would be shot first.

There had been no time for them to discuss the awful implication of this before lights out and after that there was little possibility of sleep. He'd felt sick and overwhelmed with a panic he'd never experienced during the fighting. To have come this far; to have survived numerous battles, followed by a nightmare voyage to this godforsaken country; to endure three long years of imprisonment and be robbed and starved, insulted and taunted and to have it all end now, with a summary execution. Until the early hours, he had lain on his mat, struggling with worry and rage, trying desperately to visualise himself walking up the front drive at Ivyholme and being hugged by Min on the doorstep, as if the more intensely he imagined it, the more he could force it to happen.

At breakfast time, Bill had muttered, "Look, it's probably only the threat of a coward. If the Russians get anywhere near Keijo, we'll have a plan of some sort."

John hadn't felt at all reassured and, unwilling to show Bill how rattled he felt, he decided that for once he needed to spend as much time as he could outside the wire.

'Morning, Garrett. Gracing us with your company today?' said King, wandering over to where John stood. 'I'm hoping that the milk-man will have some firm news today.' The "milk-man" was an eighteen-year-old Korean who slipped a newspaper through the garden fence when the guards were distracted in exchange for Red Cross Parcel food. The paper (now only available in Japanese) was then surreptiously translated by a young lieutenant who'd been transferred from Jinsen earlier in the year.

'Yes, I thought I'd have a change,' said John. 'And besides, Noguchi and Goto are so jittery at the moment, it's best to keep out of their way.'

'Bloody right! They should be quaking in their boots now that the Russians have advanced into Korea, and only yesterday the lad muttered some rumour about two huge bombs that had been dropped over Japan and killed thousands, though there was nothing in the paper about it, so it might be another stupid rumour. But you shouldn't worry. I bet it won't be long before it's all over. You mark my words.'

'Yes, but I bet you don't know what that might mean for us,' John snapped in a sudden rush of annoyance. King looked puzzled and John found himself torn between wanting to wipe the arrogant smile off his face and desperate to have someone else with whom to share the awful news. In a lowered voice, he briefly outlined what Bill had told him, taking care to emphasise that it had been told to him and him alone.

'Look, we'd probably better not make too much of a thing about it for the sake of morale,' he added, worried now that Bill would be annoyed with him for saying anything at all.

'Bloody Norah!' said King. 'That bloody man never bloody tells me anything. Well I don't care what he's said to you about keeping it quiet, I think we need as many brains as possible to work on an escape plan PDQ. Come on, there's Mortimer and Williams, let's talk about it with them while we're digging up the veg.'

By the time they reached the garden, everyone was buzzing

with the news. John felt even more worried; not only had King not reacted as he'd expected, but now everyone knew and Bill would probably be furious. Few felt much like gardening and King had to urge them all to act normally and not draw attention from the guards, especially when the milkman was due. Shortly after they had all stopped for the midday meal, the Korean lad arrived. Thrusting the newspaper through the fence with a beaming grin, he shouted, 'Japan has surrendered. You go home now!' and he left, running back towards the town. No one knew what to do. The guards shouted at them to keep working and so the last couple of hours were passed with some pretence at gardening and a huge amount of chatter.

But the afternoon march back to camp was like nothing John could have imagined. The guards were totally confused, as no one had apparently told them the news, and they struggled to keep their prisoners marching in an orderly line through the streets, now thronged with jubilant Koreans yelling and embracing. Children smiled and danced and clapped their hands and old women stood waving with tears streaming down their cheeks as they all passed. And as they approached the camp gates, a tram approached, now triumphantly bearing the Korean rather than the Japanese flag.

Back at camp they were greeted by Bill, Richard and the others who'd stayed behind, who confirmed that the news was indeed true: after the atom bombs, the Emperor had little choice but to give in. Noguchi and his cronies were in the office, frantically burning papers and records.

John dared to believe that perhaps once more he'd been spared. 'All is well. It bloody is well,' he chanted as he ran up the stairs.

For two days, John roamed around the camp, joining in the numerous discussions about what would happen next. He could smoke where he liked, he didn't have to salute the sentries and he could go to bed whenever he chose. On the very first day, the Korean guards walked out and on the next, an American lieutenant arrived to issue instructions about the POW supply planes that would shortly be arriving to drop food. But to John's frustration, not only was there no information about how long they would have to wait before they would be shipped home, but they were also bluntly informed that until the surrender agreement had actually been signed, they were all to remain within the compound.

A week later, the drone of two huge silver B29s circling the camp had everyone rush out on the parade ground and stare up at them in wonderment. There was a brief panic when the planes appeared to be flying away, as if they hadn't seen the large yellow and black P.W. painted on the square, but shortly they reappeared from the east with their trap doors open, so close to the ground that when the thirty-two canisters were dropped on a small area outside of the camp, few of the parachutes had time to open. Shirts, trousers, boots, tins of pork and beans, ham, peaches, cocoa, tomato juice, condensed milk, chocolate, packets of cereal, chewing gum, tobacco, Raleigh cigarettes, packets and packets of matches, medical supplies, newspapers and magazines. All that could be heard while the boxes were unpacked were cheers, whistles and shouts of 'Hey, look at this!' Some of the damaged tins were taken immediately to the cookhouse to be used for a sumptuous evening stew; the rest were stacked into the storeroom and placed under guard from the greedy or unscrupulous. John noticed how easy he found it, with all this delightful manna from heaven, to conveniently ignore the fact that a Korean woman and her child had been killed by one of the falling canisters.

In the first week of September, exactly six years after Chamberlain had announced that Britain was at war with Germany, the camp gates were thrown open and in drove a tank, three army lorries and a large American staff car. Out of the car jumped a burly company commander who, having checked who was in charge, strode towards Bill Ellerton, saluted him and said, 'Say Colonel, who d'ya want shot?'

They were all free men, and although they still wouldn't be departing for a few more days, they could leave the camp and explore the local town and countryside if they wished.

John and Richard clambered aboard one of the lorries that took a group of them down to the river. While some of their fellow officers roamed the nearby streets, searching for saki and entertainment, John and Richard found a couple of skiffs and rowed upstream for some way to land on a small beach. The light yellow sands stretched away for miles beside the placid blue river, fringed by a long line of poplars. In the distance they could see blue-green hills dotted with jagged white rocks and trees.

'Shall we?' asked John, pointing to the water.

'Oh I really think we should,' said Richard with a grin. Pulling off their clothes they rushed into the water and within a few strides they had both swum out into the main current. Treading water, John watched with incredulity how the muscles of his arms and legs seemed to know how to keep him afloat; how the beads of water glistened on his skin; how good it was to be completely naked, and how if he stretched out flat on the surface, he could flow with the current and feel completely free. They raced each other up back and forth across the river, swimming front crawl and back crawl. They splashed and dived under the water and then, swimming back to the spot where they had left their clothes, stood waist high, rubbing their arms and legs as if to wash off the grime of three years' incarceration.

'Come on, let's climb up that hill and see if we can get a better view,' said Richard, pulling on his clothes. Like two excited school boys on a day out, they set out.

'Goodness, I'd forgotten what it's like to exert myself,' said John, pausing to catch his breath. 'Shows what a lazy life I've got used to.'

At the top, they turned to look back over the estuary. The view was utterly beautiful. Away from them, to the north, a flat plain stretched towards the distant mountains, bisected by the river which meandered through sandbanks, bordered by patchwork plots of rich green. Swallows darted about the hillside and a magpie flew out of the fir trees behind them. All they could hear was the ticking of crickets and an occasional bird call. There were no other sounds. There were no other human beings. There were no guards, no sentries, no uniforms, no barbed wire, no houses or people or squalor, no raucous bugle, no shrieking trains.

'We're free!' they shouted to each other, and danced around madly on the grass.

CHAPTER 55

Ivyholme, Lymington

August 15th 1945

Dearest John. My precious boy

It is finished! They have surrendered. I have laughed and cried and cheered. To think that at long last I may be seeing you again, and perhaps have you here for Christmas or even before! I cannot realise it yet. A long nightmare is turning slowly into a kind of vague lovely dream. The thought that I can send you a proper letter after three stark years of censored words makes me almost feel tongue-tied.

Perhaps we shall not know each other and will have to start all over again like two shy people on their first encounter. Right now I could overflow onto so many pages, but I think for now I am too full for words to say more. All I want is to feel, to hear, to touch, to smell down the back of the neck etc, etc… Come home now.

September 3rd 1945

And today of course is the day it all started, so long ago. What a journey we have all taken. I sat outside for most of the afternoon, since it was warm and sunny. I recall what the garden looked like when I first returned here; all bedraggled and uncared for, much as I felt myself. These past years it too has changed. First I had to get rid of the weeds, and decide which flowerbeds and plants I would keep. Then Frank got our own vegetables growing; all those straight rows of lettuces, onions and carrots. Finally, this year I have been able to pay attention to the roses, enjoy the hydrangeas and rub my fingers through the lemon balm.

September 29th 1945

Today's letter says that he arrived in Manila over a week ago, and so by now he may have already started out on his long voyage home. He sounds so excited. I think, perhaps, that I won't be making many more entries in this journal. Soon I shall speak to him in person and have no need for this outlet, although it has been a godsend over these past years.

From what he writes, he clearly believes that he has somehow grown up all over again. He talks of having developed a new philosophy for life, but I shall have to wait until he sees me, so that he can explain it properly. How I long to simply talk and talk for days and days, with no interruptions from anyone. I am so relieved that Frank and Cordelia have now moved away to Hereford and I can get the house all ready for him on my own. Of course they will want to visit and see him for themselves, but all in good time.

I think I have probably grown up a little bit myself. I'm not sure what the future will bring, but I truly feel more open to a variety of possibilities.

CHAPTER 56

John took another swig of beer, looked down at his empty plate and patted his full belly; never had roast turkey with all the trimmings tasted so good. This was the third time it had been on the menu since they'd arrived in Manila. In the weeks of waiting for evacuation, he had felt a mixture of euphoria and impatience. Hearing that those in Keijo camp weren't a priority had irritated him, and it wasn't until they had arrived to join thousands of others in Manila that he realised why they'd been made to wait for so long.

Seated next to him, Richard and Charles King were having an animated conversation about the merits of the Gracie Fields concert of the previous evening, and opposite, Bill and Peter Castle were chatting with an American padre who'd recently arrived from Burma. With the din going on all around, John could hardly hear what they were saying. The canteen was packed with American, Australian and British troops. A sea of newly issued khaki jackets hung awkwardly from skeletal shoulders; a variety of caps balanced on wispy hair which framed wizened faces; shiny black boots, loosely fastened, protected raw, blistered feet.

Initially, when John had first seen the condition of the majority of other POWs he'd felt embarrassed, almost ashamed; clearly what he had thought was hunger, all the time he'd been in Keijo, was nothing compared to what others had endured. He felt like a fraud relating anything about his own experience to men who had suffered so much.

After the first few days listening to their horrific tales, he now tried to avoid talking with anyone whom he imagined might resent him for getting off so lightly. He yearned for the safety and quiet of Ivyholme and yet he feared that, in a few weeks' time, as they all returned to their separate lives, he might lose the solid bonds of friendship, which had kept him nourished for the past three years, forever. As if to check that it was still there, he felt for Min's letter in his top pocket; it was the first uncensored letter of more than twenty-five words, which he had received just two days before. It was consoling, seeing her writing, knowing that she was well and waiting as urgently for him as he was for her. He could so clearly see himself sitting beside her in the little back room, the French windows ajar, the late afternoon sun slanting across the lawn, and the pair of them talking and talking and laughing and hugging each other.

After lunch, torn between joining Richard and the others and wanting some time alone, he wandered down to the harbour where small craft and fishing junks wove in all directions, dwarfed by cruisers, destroyers, transport ships and one enormous aircraft carrier. Every gangplank seemed to flow with men; some newly arrived, others on their way home. He thought about the kindness that he and his companions had received on their ship from Korea to Manila; a full medical inspection, hot showers, new clothes, sweets, cigarettes, beer, three good meals a day, sleeping between sheets and delightful comfort bags, donated by the Red Cross ladies, which contained shaving gear, a comb, hair oil, soap and shampoo. Some men had been quite ill at first from attempting to eat meals too large for their shrunken stomachs and had taken several days to adjust. During the voyage, with

333

access to the latest papers, John had started slowly catching up with uncensored news from the rest of the world. It was a lot to take in. Even now, perched on a pile of crates and watching the bustle around him, freedom still felt quite overwhelming.

Two days later, queuing with his kitbag to walk up the gangplank of the aircraft carrier *HMS Implacable*, he caught sight of a familiar freckled face just ahead of him.

'Alan, Alan Rose, is that you?' he shouted and waved. Alan turned, causing those behind him to bump into one another and beamed back at him before he was jostled forwards.

'Goodness, John, it is so good to see you,' said Alan, giving him a hug, as soon as John had staggered on board and they could move out of the muddle of people trying to locate the berth deck. 'Is Bill with you?'

'Oh yes, we're all here somewhere. But how have you been, are you all right? You look as if you have lost a lot of weight.'

'I could have done with you. It was that blessed beriberi again, but I'm pretty much on the mend now.'

Much later in the evening, once they had both got themselves settled into their respective quarters, avoiding the overcrowded bar, they met at the top of the steps that lead to the enormous flight deck. Once John had updated him on the news from Keijo, including a graphic account of the sour look on Noguchi's face when the Americans arrived, Alan told his own story. John listened quietly as he described the perils of working in the coal mine, the arbitrary brutality of the guards, the helpless weeks, unable to walk despite eating the prescribed snakes liver, and how his mate Curly and seven others had died of poisoning after drinking contaminated local beer just days after their camp was liberated. His account of how his evacuation train had travelled through the desolate wasteland that was once Nagasaki, where everything looked like pulverised dust, and how, on the hills on either side of the valley, only a few skeleton-like trees remained, was quite disconcerting. Once again, John felt the comfort of freedom being tarnished with a reality he'd rather not know about. He was shocked by Alan's story, but also aware how thankful he was that they were both safe and now reunited; this was a friend he did not want to lose touch with again.

John looked across the flight deck towards the sea, glad for a moment of the darkness. 'I know it sounds a bit lame, but I've been feeling awfully guilty about how relatively easy I have found this term of imprisonment. When I listen to what you've been through since you got sent to Japan and hear the grim tales of what most of the chaps have suffered, I wonder what part I actually played in it all.'

'Actually John, I know what you mean. Somehow, I've been able to accept that men I knew from before the war got killed in the fighting, but I simply can't come to terms with the fact that good mates like Sid and Curly died in the camps. They didn't deserve it.'

'It was Roger's death that did it for me. It was as if everyone who I'd had to leave behind, to die of their wounds in Malaya, and all those poor sods who died of dysentery in Changi, not to mention my girlfriend, all came back to haunt me. And I wasn't injured; I actually enjoyed the battles. I haven't been sick, except once, and I wasn't beaten at all. Instead of feeling grateful, I feel as if I've failed them all somehow. I can't imagine how I would have coped if it had been any worse for me.' Fumbling for a cigarette, he was aware that he had never put these thoughts into words before and felt profoundly relieved that Alan understood.

'But John, of course you would have coped. You found a way of escaping, which you would have used regardless of where you'd have ended up. I'm sure that you've had your ups and downs like the rest of us, and times when you've probably had to contend with depression and boredom, but your real skill was to detach yourself and use your imagination and memory to transport you to somewhere quite different. Not many chaps can do that, you know, and when I was going through my blackest times, it was your optimism and philosophy for survival that kept me going.'

For a long while, neither spoke. Occasionally, John could hear the strains of music from a distant radio or the call of one fisherman to another. It was as if, for now at least, no more needed to be said.

'And anyway,' said Alan, breaking the silence, 'it wasn't our fault that we ended up in a show camp. I just praise God that I did and that now I'm going home.' He paused and turned towards John. 'By the way, how is your relationship with God these days?'

'No change there, I'm afraid,' said John with a rueful smile. 'But let me update you on the additions we have made to our great philosophy of life.'

Alan approved of Richard's diagram. 'Ah, connection, of course, that was the missing part, wasn't it? If you ask any of the chaps on board who've been to hell and back over these past years, I reckon they'd all say the same. It was staying connected with each other and with the memories of those at home that kept them alive.'

John gazed up into the vast black sky, peppered with a zillion stars, and tried to imagine Bea and all those who had not survived looking back down and forgiving him. He felt very small.

Nineteen days later, *HMS Implacable* reached Vancouver, having stopped briefly at Hawaii on the way. There had been two thousand officers and troops on board; three officers shared each cabin and the troops were accommodated in the upper hangar, which had been cleared of aircraft and replaced with tight rows of canvas pipe cots. The meals had been lavish; John had to remind himself to eat slowly and savour each mouthful, after so many months of training himself not to notice the taste of anything.

Aware of how little time they had left together, Bill made sure that they all shared the same train carriage for the trip across Canada. They never exhausted the conversation of what they would each do in those first days and weeks back home. Bill wanted to take his wife dancing and have tea every weekend at Fortnum's. Pater Castle's mission, he told them, was to find himself a wife and settle down in a country parish; church fêtes, weddings and baptisms seemed terribly attractive after the number of funeral rites he had conducted.

'What about you, Richard?' asked John, noticing that he'd been silent for a while.

'Well, my father has written to say there is a place for me at the bank, but he did add, only if I wanted it, which shows he has mellowed somewhat. I really want to make a go of being a writer, but I am going to have to find something to do to pay my rent until I become a world-famous author. However, I don't think that living at home with my parents will be compatible with the lifestyle or the company I am likely to keep,' he said with a mischievous smile.

Throughout the long train journey across Canada, first through the Rockies and then across the wide open plains of Alberta and Saskatchewan, John sat facing east. He couldn't bear to sit looking back to where he had come from; it had to be forwards, urging the train onwards towards his future. Back in Keijo, he had always imagined that when he returned home, he would visit Bea's parents and tell them about their daughter's last few months of happiness with him, but now he was aware of his reluctance. Since that first night on the steps to the flight deck, gazing up at the stars, he knew he must leave her behind. He was no longer the same cocky but under-confident man who had wooed and won her, only to lose her again. He felt as if he had travelled as far as anyone in his imagination and that, having passed through numerous phases of belief, doubt, disillusion and discovery, he had now grown up. With his three circles of meaning and purpose he felt equipped to start his new life.

On the last day of October, the white pinnacles of the Needles, which John had imagined for so long, at last came into view. As they passed slowly up Southampton Water towards the docks, he could barely contain himself as he strained to make out familiar landmarks.

Weighed down by baggage and the scramble to disembark, it was hard to find a free hand to return the shakes and grasps of the hands stretched out to him. All around were cries of 'See you soon!', 'Don't leave it too long!', 'Mine's a pint!' and then he was suddenly away from them all, in a railway carriage heading towards Lymington. How strange to be the only person in uniform; the war over here had ended more than five months ago. He couldn't help but smile as he gazed fondly at the yellowing leaves of English trees, the tawny heath of the New Forest, and then best of all the sight of the Boldre River.

He could have caught a taxi at the station, but that would have been too quick. He didn't want to rush the moment he had been dreaming of. Leaving his heaviest luggage behind to be collected another time, he set off down Waterloo Road and turned into Bridge Street. It was dusk. The air smelt of autumn. Small gusts of chilly wind caught at his lapels as he drew closer to the toll bridge. A couple of swans rooting around the reed bed looked up, startled by his footsteps. Across the ripples of dark water, he could just make out a faint glimmer of light from the landing window of Ivyholme. A plume of smoke rose from the chimney. As he drew nearer, he felt his heart banging in his chest and his throat tightening. The gravel crunched under his boots as he walked up the drive. He took a deep breath and knocked at the door.

ACKNOWLEDGEMENTS

The Mind's Garden is based on the true story of my father and grandmother's experiences of the Second World War as revealed by their letters to each other and in my father's journal. I have transcribed both the letters and his journal and they are now housed in the Imperial War Museum. I am very grateful to Alan Toze, one of the men with whom my father was imprisoned. Before he died, I was able to have many conversations with him about his own journal and his recollections of their time together in captivity.

Most of the characters in the novel are based on real people whose names I have changed. I am grateful for Lt Col Elrington's account of the Loyal Regiment which was printed in *The Lancashire Lad* regimental magazine.

I would like to thank Rod Suddaby of the Imperial War Museum for his enthusiastic support.

I am also very thankful for the feedback and support that I received from Dick Price, Patrick Gale, Louise Dean, Helen Overell, Maureen Jivani and others.

The sculpture on the cover is called Mind's Garden and is a WW2 war memorial created by Jo Fafard. Images in the panels are open to interpretation and it is the artist's intention that the viewer become the creator of the work by imagining what the images represent.